THE MANOR HOUSE
OF DE VILLERAI

broadview editions
series editor: L.W. Conolly

MADAME LEPROHON.

From a photograph taken not long before her death. Kindly furnished by her husband, the late Dr. Leprohon.

Rosanna Eleanor, daughter of Francis Mullins, Esquire, was born in Montreal, November 9th, 1832, and educated at the Convent of the Congregation de Notre Dame. When only fourteen years of age, she commenced to write in prose and verse under the initials "R. E. M," for Lovell's *Literary Garland*, and continued her contributions to that well-known magazine as long as it remained in existence. Subsequently she wrote for the Boston *Pilot*, the Montreal *Daily News*, the *Canadian Illustrated News*, *Le Pionnier de Sherbrooke*, the *Journal of Education*, the *Saturday Reader*, the *Hearthstone*, and various other periodicals. Among her novels, some of which appeared in book form, were "Ida Beresford," "Florence Fitzhardinge," "Eva Huntingdon," "Clarence Fitzclarence," "Eveleen O'Donnell," "The Manor House of De Villerai," "Antoinette de Miracourt," "Armand Durand," "Ada Dunmore," and "Lillian's Peril." She married, in 1851, Dr. J. L. Leprohon, afterwards Spanish Consul at Montreal, and was the mother of several children. She died in Montreal, September 20th, 1879, and is buried in Côte des Neiges cemetery there ; her husband, who died later, being also buried there. After her death, her poetical productions were published in book form, with an introduction by Mr. John Reade, in which that accomplished writer pays a fitting tribute both to her literary genius and to her virtues as a woman. "Her literary life," he says, "constituted but one phase in a life nobly, yet unostentatiously, consecrated to the duties of home, of society, of charity, and of religion. Mrs. Leprohon was much more than either a poet or a novelist—she was also, in the highest sense, a woman, a lady."

202

Portrait of Rosanna Mullins Leprohon, from Henry J. Morgan, ed., *Types of Canadian Women and of Women Who Are or Have Been Connected with Canada*, Vol. 1 (Toronto: William Briggs, 1903), 202.

THE MANOR HOUSE OF DE VILLERAI, A TALE OF CANADA UNDER THE FRENCH DOMINION

Rosanna Mullins Leprohon

edited by Andrea Cabajsky

broadview editions

© 2015 Andrea Cabajsky

All rights reserved. The use of any part of this publication reproduced, transmitted in any form or by any means, electronic, mechanical, photocopying, recording, or otherwise, or stored in a retrieval system, without prior written consent of the publisher—or in the case of photocopying, a licence from Access Copyright (Canadian Copyright Licensing Agency), One Yonge Street, Suite 1900, Toronto, Ontario M5E 1E5—is an infringement of the copyright law.

Library and Archives Canada Cataloguing in Publication

Leprohon, Mrs. (Rosanna Eleanor), 1829-1879, author
   The manor house of De Villerai : a tale of Canada under the French dominion / Rosanna Mullins Leprohon ; edited by Andrea Cabajsky.

(Broadview editions)
Includes bibliographical references.
ISBN 978-1-55481-130-4 (pbk.)

   I. Cabajsky, Andrea, 1971-, editor II. Title. III. Series: Broadview editions

PS8423.E6M3 2014   C813'.3   C2014-905289-8

Broadview Editions
The Broadview Editions series represents the ever-changing canon of literature in English by bringing together texts long regarded as classics with valuable lesser-known works.

Advisory editor for this volume: Michel Pharand

Broadview Press is an independent, international publishing house, incorporated in 1985.

We welcome comments and suggestions regarding any aspect of our publications—please feel free to contact us at the addresses below or at broadview@broadviewpress.com.

North America
PO Box 1243, Peterborough, Ontario K9J 7H5, Canada
555 Riverwalk Parkway, Tonawanda, NY 14150, USA
Tel: (705) 743-8990; Fax: (705) 743-8353
email: customerservice@broadviewpress.com

UK, Europe, Central Asia, Middle East, Africa, India, and Southeast Asia
Eurospan Group, 3 Henrietta St., London WC2E 8LU, United Kingdom
Tel: 44 (0) 1767 604972; Fax: 44 (0) 1767 601640
email: eurospan@turpin-distribution.com

Australia and New Zealand
NewSouth Books
c/o TL Distribution, 15-23 Helles Ave., Moorebank, NSW 2170, Australia
Tel: (02) 8778 9999; Fax: (02) 8778 9944
email: orders@tldistribution.com.au

www.broadviewpress.com

Broadview Press acknowledges the financial support of the Government of Canada through the Canada Book Fund for our publishing activities.

Typesetting and assembly: True to Type Inc., Claremont, Canada.

PRINTED IN CANADA

Contents

Acknowledgements • 7
Introduction • 9
Rosanna Mullins Leprohon: A Brief Chronology • 33
A Note on the Text • 37

*The Manor House of De Villerai,
A Tale of Canada Under the French Dominion* • 43

Appendix A: Contemporary Reception of Leprohon's Works • 209
  1. From Susanna Moodie, "Editor's Table," *Victoria Magazine* (June 1848) • 209
  2. From George P. Ure, "Prospectus of *The Family Herald*," *The Family Herald* (16 November 1859) • 209
  3. From George P. Ure, "Our First Number," *The Family Herald* (16 November 1859) • 210
  4. From Henry J. Morgan, "Mrs. Leprohon," *Sketches of Celebrated Canadians* (1862) • 211
  5. From Edmond Lareau, *Histoire de la littérature canadienne* (1874) • 212
  6. From Anon., "The Late Mrs. Leprohon," *Canadian Illustrated News* (4 October 1879) • 213

Appendix B: Commentary on Canadian Literature and Nationality in the Confederation Period • 216
  1. From Thomas D'Arcy McGee, "The Mental Outfit of the New Dominion," *Gazette* (Montreal) (5 November 1867) • 216
  2. From John T. Lesperance, "The Literary Standing of the Dominion," *Canadian Illustrated News* (24 February 1877) • 224
  3. From Edmond Lareau, *Histoire de la littérature canadienne* (1874) • 229

Appendix C: Literary Precedents • 232
  1. From Samuel Richardson, "Preface by the Editor," *Pamela; or, Virtue Rewarded* (1740) • 232
  2. From Sir Walter Scott, "A Postscript, Which Should Have Been a Preface," Chapter XXIV of *Waverley; or, 'Tis Sixty Years Since* (1814) • 233
  3. From John Richardson, "Introductory," Chapter 1 of *Wacousta; or, The Prophecy: A Tale of the Canadas* (1832) • 235

Appendix D: Historical Sources • 239
1. From Colonel Malcolm Fraser, *Extract from a Manuscript Journal, Relating to the Siege of Quebec in 1759* (1759; rpt. 1866) • 239
2. From William Smith, "Preface," *History of Canada; From Its Discovery to the Peace of 1763* ([1815] 1826) • 245
3. From William Smith, ["The Battle of Fort Ticonderoga,"] *History of Canada; From Its Discovery to the Peace of 1763* ([1815] 1826) • 246
4. From François-Xavier Garneau, "Preliminary Discourse," *History of Canada, From the Time of Its Discovery Till the Union Year (1840-1)*, Volume 1 (1845; tr. 1860) • 247
5. From François-Xavier Garneau, ["The Fall of Quebec,"] *History of Canada*, Volume 2 (1846; tr. 1860) • 251

Appendix E: Historical Documents • 253
1. From General James Wolfe, "Major-General Wolfe to the Earl of Holdernesse. On Board the Sutherland, at Anchor off Cape Rouge, September 9, 1759" ([1759] 1838) • 253
2. Article IV, Treaty of Paris (1763) • 257
3. From John George Lambton, First Earl of Durham, *Report on the Affairs of British North America, from the Earl of Durham, Her Majesty's High Commissioner* (1839) • 257
4. From *Parliamentary Debates on the Subject of the Confederation of the British North American Provinces* (1865) • 262
   a. Hon. George-Étienne Cartier, Attorney General East (Montreal East) • 262
   b. Hon. Thomas D'Arcy McGee, Minister of Agriculture (Montreal West) • 265
   c. Hon. L. Letellier de St. Just (Grandville) • 267
   d. Hon. H.G. Joly (Lotbinière) • 268
   e. Mr. C.B. de Niverville (Three Rivers) • 270

Appendix F: Contemporary Maps and Illustrations • 272
1. From Reuben Gold Thwaites, "Eastern North America (1740)," *France in America, 1497-1763* (1905) • 272
2. John Henry Walker, "Engraving. Winter Attack on Fort William Henry, 1757" • 274
3. Anon., "A View of the Taking of Quebec September 13th 1759" • 276

Select Bibliography • 279

Acknowledgements

This publication was supported by a Standard Research Grant from the Université de Moncton's Faculty of Graduate Studies and Research (FESR), course release for research provided by the FESR, as well as through funds provided by the Social Sciences and Humanities Research Council of Canada (SSHRC) Aid to Small Universities Grant. I am grateful to the Department of English, to the Faculty of Arts and Social Sciences, and to my colleagues at the Université de Moncton. For his generosity and openness to discussing all matters Leprohon, I would like to thank Thomas Hodd. The librarians at the Bibliothèque Champlain's interlibrary loan service were particularly efficient and helpful. Special thanks go to my research assistants, Sarah McIntyre and Soraya Gallant, both of whom read aloud the serialized version of *The Manor House of De Villerai*, including punctuation, and proofread it against the typescript. Sarah McIntyre was also indispensable in the initial stages of transcription and thus deserves particular acknowledgement for her dedication and professionalism.

I am grateful to the McCord Museum for their permission to use the images "Winter Attack on Fort William Henry" and "View of the Capture of Quebec." I am also grateful to the editorial team at Broadview Press, especially Marjorie Mather, Leonard Conolly, and Michel Pharand, for their help at various stages in the preparation and publication of this book.

Last, but certainly not least, I would like to thank my husband, our two daughters, and my parents for their continuing encouragement and support of my research. Himself a native of Montreal, my husband tolerated a great many excursions to various parts of the city (most often, it seems, in the dead of winter) in my desire to get a feel for the landscape in which Leprohon was raised. As always, he deserves special thanks for his patience, support, and good humour.

Introduction

Rosanna Mullins Leprohon: A Brief Biography

Rosanna Eleanor Mullins Leprohon was born Rosanna Ellen Mullins (she later changed her middle name to Eleanor)[1] in Montreal on 12 January 1829. She died in that city 50 years later on 20 September 1879. The second of five children, Rosanna Mullins was the daughter of Rosanna Connolly (alternatively spelled Conelly in official documentation). Her father, Francis Mullins, emigrated from Cork, Ireland, sometime after 1819 and flourished in Montreal as a store-keeper, ship chandler and, later, in real estate and importing. He also sat on Montreal City Council from 1858 to 1860. The granddaughter on her mother's side of schoolmaster Michael Connolly, Rosanna Mullins was raised in a household that valued education for all its children. As Henri Deneau notes, "[i]t is worthy of remark" that, in all Rosanna Mullins Leprohon's novels, "either the heroines were favored with the same home training [as she herself had received] or else the failing is sorely deplored" (6n1). By the age of 11, Leprohon had enrolled in the internationally respected Convent of the Congregation, where she was encouraged in her creative writing by her mentors, the Reverend Sister of the Nativity (née Catherine Caggar, born in Armagh, Ireland) and the Reverend Mother Sainte Madeleine. At the age of 17, Leprohon published her first poem in *The Literary Garland* (Montreal, 1838-51), thereby launching a prolific writing career. Between 1846 and 1851, she published at least a dozen poems, one short story, and five serialized novels. On 17 June 1851, Rosanna Mullins married Jean-Baptiste-Lucian (Jean-Lukin) Leprohon, a physician. Her marriage, together with the collapse of *The Literary Garland* in December that year, caused an apparent interruption in her writing activities and ended what is often described as the first phase of her career.

In 1859, Leprohon embarked on the second phase of her writing career with two works of fiction: "Eveleen O'Donnell," published in serial instalments in *The Pilot* [Boston]; and *The Manor House of De Villerai*,[2] published serially in the Montreal-

---

1 See Deneau 3n4.
2 In capitalizing "De" in the title of *The Manor House of De Villerai*, I have taken my cue from the original serialization published in *The Family Herald*, which capitalizes "De" in all instances.

based *The Family Herald* between 16 November 1859 and 8 February 1860. By this time, Leprohon had been married eight years, had given birth to six children (one of whom had died in infancy), had become active in charitable work in Montreal (like the characters Blanche De Villerai and Miss De St. Omer in *The Manor House*), and had otherwise become proficient in managing a busy household (as the wife of a prominent physician) and a prolific writer in her own right. Her husband was well-respected—"one of the *doyens* of the profession" (577; original italics) as Henry J. Morgan describes him in his handbook of Canadian biography, *The Canadian Men and Women of the Time* (1898). Prior to his marriage to Rosanna Mullins, Jean-Lukin Leprohon had founded the short-lived medical journal, *La Lancette canadienne* (Montreal, 1847; *The Canadian Lancet*). Over the course of his marriage, in turn, he became Professor of Hygiene in the medical faculty at Bishop's College in Lennoxville, Quebec, co-founded the Women's Hospital of Montreal (1870), became Vice-President of the College of Physicians and Surgeons, served as an alderman for Saint-Antoine Ward (1858-61; see *Ville de Montréal*), was appointed Vice-Consul for Spain at Montreal (1871), and published a report on smallpox in Canada (1874). It is worth noting the Leprohons' shared interests in women's health and public hygiene. Apart from its obvious privileging of women-centred themes, *The Manor House* anticipates Jean-Lukin Leprohon's report on smallpox in the attention it accords that disease in relation to urban poverty and hygiene, both of which comprise the backdrop to the subplot that surrounds the heroine, Blanche De Villerai.

In 1879, Rosanna Mullins Leprohon died of heart failure. Although her health was known to have been fragile throughout the 1870s, her death seems nonetheless to have caught her peers by surprise. The author of an anonymous obituary published in *Canadian Illustrated News* (October 1879) describes her death as "untimely," despite the "feeble health" she had suffered over the course of "the past decade or so" (see Anon, "The Late" 211). Insisting that Leprohon's "name" would "live in Canadian history" owing to the author's contributions "to our literary annals" (211), the anonymous author echoes the bulk of Confederation-period commentary, including that of John Reade, the presumed editor of the posthumous *The Poetical Works of Mrs. Leprohon* (1881), and the biographer, Henry J. Morgan ("Leprohon, Mrs." 409), who measured Leprohon's legacy in terms of Romantic nationalism, underscoring her treatment of Canadian history, culture, and nationality. Seventy years later, in the conclusion to his Master's thesis on "The Life and Works of Mrs. Leprohon" (1948), Deneau describes her legacy in similar terms of cultural nationalism: "Mrs. Leprohon deserves a lasting place in our Canadian Literature because ... [s]he has the signal honour of being the ONLY Canadian writer of her time whose set purpose was to effect better understanding between the two races living under the same rule" (129). Deneau's conclusion, that Leprohon was the "only" Canadian writer of her time to deploy literature in the service of intercultural rapprochement, does not hold true today given the attention that critics have paid to other novelists in this context, such as Philippe Aubert de Gaspé (*Les Anciens Canadiens* [1863]) and William Kirby (*The Golden Dog* [1877]). Nevertheless, Leprohon's status as a pioneering writer in the Confederation period remains a matter of critical consensus. Recognition of Leprohon's contributions to the national literature and to cultural self-understanding persisted after her death, especially in Quebec, where at least five reprints of Joseph-Édouard Lefebvre de Bellefeuille's French translation, *Le manoir de Villerai*, appeared between 1884 and 1925.[1] Owing to the unavailability of *The Manor House of De Villerai* in English, John R. Sorfleet transcribed it and published it as a special issue of the *Journal of Canadian Fiction* (1985), a century-and-a-half following its first appearance in the *Herald*. The remainder of this introduction will locate *The Manor House* in pertinent historical, material, and critical contexts, concluding with a reflection on its dual reception histories in Quebec and English Canada.

Historical Background

Sitting at the cusp of a flowering of literary activity, the 1850s were a time of profound change in Canada. In 1859, the year that *The Manor House of De Villerai* first appeared, "Canada" referred to the union of Upper and Lower Canada (today's Ontario and Quebec), which were separate from the Maritime colonies of New Brunswick, Nova Scotia, and Prince Edward Island—although that was about to change. Canadian Confederation (1867) was less than a decade away. Debates about Canada's national character, political structure, cultural constituency, emergent national literature, and reading practices were fre-

---

1 Deneau notes reprints for the years 1884, 1892, 1901, 1910, and 1925, all published by Beauchemin (93n3).

quently waged in the pages of newspapers and literary magazines in the years bracketing Confederation. Noteworthy examples in this context include the well-known speech, "The Mental Outfit of the New Dominion," delivered by Thomas D'Arcy McGee (1825-68), a Father of Canadian Confederation, in Montreal on 4 November 1867 and published in the Montreal *Gazette* the following day. McGee's speech famously defines "active conscientiousness in our choice of books and periodicals" as one of the civic responsibilities of constituents in the newly-founded nation.[1] In the 1850s, the city of Montreal, where Leprohon lived nearly all of her life, was a vital and dynamic urban centre and the site of remarkable changes in print culture. Printers and publishers, such as the famous Lovell and Desbarats dynasties, worked actively to promote literary culture in both English and French, translating popular works, including Leprohon's own novels, often within a year of their first appearance in English. The popular demand for cheap newspapers and magazines had grown exponentially over the course of the nineteenth century, driven in part by a revolution in the printing of advertisements and illustrations. This revolution proved to have important roots in Montreal where, a decade following the appearance of *The Manor House*, William Augustus Leggo, Jr., (1830-1915) pioneered the photomechanical processes that enabled local newspapers, such as the *Canadian Illustrated News* (1869-83) and *L'Opinion publique* (1870-83)—both of which published Leprohon's poems and fiction—to offer stunning new visual imagery.

The Manor House of De Villerai was thus published during a period of significant political and material change and a foundational time for intercultural relations among Francophone and Anglophone Quebeckers and Irish-Catholic immigrants. In 1859, the "Black Rock," also known as the Commemorative Stone, was completed in Montreal, marking the site where the remains of Irish immigrants had been uncovered during the construction of the Victoria Bridge. The immigrants had been refugees of the famine in Ireland who perished in Quebec as a result of the typhus epidemic of 1847-48. At this time, tensions within the French-Canadian community itself, notably between conservatives and liberals, also came to a head, centring in part on debates about acceptable reading practices and the preservation of communal values in the face of easy access to foreign books and periodicals. For example, between the 1840s and the

---

1 For relevant extracts from McGee's "The Mental Outfit," see Appendix B1, p. 216 of this Broadview edition.

1870s, the liberal *Institut canadien de Montréal* provided its members with debating rooms and a library whose contents comprised books that had been banned by the Catholic Church, including works by Alexandre Dumas (1802-70) and Eugène Sue (1804-57). Among the *Institut*'s members were the future Prime Minister of Canada, Wilfrid Laurier (1841-1919), and French novelist Victor Hugo (1802-85). The famous "Guibord case" (1869-74), in which the Bishop of Montreal, Monsignor Ignace Bourget (1799-1885), refused ecclesiastical burial to a recently deceased printer named Joseph Guibord (1809-69), a founding member of the *Institut*, bears witness to the tremendous stakes involved in the circulation of print materials and ideas. Given Montreal's fraught ideological climate, it is important to understand *The Manor House*'s narrative commentary on various issues, from reading practices and social propriety to cultural customs and Catholicism, as forms of intervention into contemporary debates about cultural self-preservation, a crucial topic for a French-Catholic minority surrounded by a predominantly larger Anglophone and Protestant population in the rest of Canada.[1]

The narrative of *The Manor House of De Villerai* contains clear signs that Leprohon was acutely aware of her multiple audiences and tried to strike a balance between potentially conflicting perspectives, at once Francophone and Anglophone, and Catholic and Protestant. Nevertheless, literary critics are slightly divided in their assessments of the place that religion holds in the larger historical lesson her novel imparts. Carole Gerson regards Leprohon as a kind of mediator, promoting Christian conduct while also "carefully avoiding specific references to church or religion, advo-

---

1 According to the *Census of the Canadas. 1860-61* (1863), the total population of Montreal in 1860-61 was 90,323 with 43,509 of "French origin" (see Canada 4) and 21,668 of English, Welsh, Scottish, and Irish origin combined (4). By contrast to Montreal, the city of Toronto, which was comparatively smaller in size, had a proportionately larger population of British descendants. For example, Toronto's total population was 44,821, with a mere 435 of "French origin" (48) and 22,514 of English, Welsh, Scottish, and Irish origin combined (48). With respect to religion, 65,896 residents of Montreal identified with the "Church of Rome" (84) and 21,941 with the "Church of England," the "Ecclesiastical Church of Scotland," the "Free Church of Scotland," "United," and other Protestant denominations (84). In Toronto, by contrast, 12,315 identified with the "Church of Rome" and 28,993 with the "Church of England" and other Protestant denominations (128). It is worth keeping in mind that the census does not differentiate between French- and English-speaking Catholics.

cating general Christian principles which would meet the approval of Catholic and Protestant alike" (Gerson, "Three Writers" 220). By contrast to Gerson, John R. Sorfleet emphasizes Leprohon's favourable treatment of Catholicism, with particular reference to *The Manor House*, which, he writes, treats "the Catholic faith as one bastion" of French-Canadian "'survivance'" (8). The "connection between religion" and French-Canadian identity is thus central to the novel's treatment of "historical conflict and Conquest" (Sorfleet 8). Readers should be prepared to carefully assess Leprohon's multi-faceted treatment of Christianity and Catholicism. Not only is the Christian theme linked to characterization and nationality, it also figures in the intricate reasoning the narrator provides to help bring about the eventual resolution to both interpersonal and political conflicts, thus playing a subtle though significant role in justifying the close of the novel. Whether or not readers will agree with Sorfleet's conclusion—that "the key to the future" at the novel's close relies implicitly on "English assent to the preservation of [French-Canadian] laws, language and religion" (8)—those same readers should nonetheless attend closely to passages that variously suggest the mutual implication of religion, history, and nationality to themes of gender, identity, and intercultural rapprochement.

The Manor House of De Villerai registers the cultural, social, and material crises of both the 1850s and the 1750s, that is, of its contemporary milieu and of the historical context it seeks to revive. In the 1750s, periods of sustained warfare as a result of the Seven Years' War (1756-63), along with processes of urbanisation, had carried with them unprecedented problems with urban poverty, hygiene, and disease. These modern, urban problems make their way into *The Manor House of De Villerai* whose main theme, history, unfolds against a backdrop that expands to include the poor and the disenfranchised, including widows and children. The real-historical smallpox epidemics of the late 1750s make their way into the novel, playing a formative role in the main plot involving the heroine, Blanche De Villerai. In *The Manor House*, a nameless mother is left a widow, and rendered destitute, when her husband, a member of the French-Canadian militia, dies in battle. The French-Canadian militia, in turn, is deployed to provide emergency relief for starving urban populations in Montreal and Quebec City owing to real-historical shortages of basic material supplies.[1] By the end of the novel, the step-brothers and

---

[1] Although Leprohon does not elaborate on the reasons behind the shortage of material supplies, historians have suggested that its roots lie in

step-sisters of Rose Lauzon are on the brink of starvation, fighting over a blackened crust of bread. With the fall of New France, the French army leaves the colony to return to France. Leaving with it are some members of the French-Canadian elite fleeing a society in flux. On the one hand, numerous men of marrying age had perished in battle. On the other, numerous romantic courtships between French-Canadian women and French soldiers required resolving as the latter left the colony for France. The future, it will be seen, remains decidedly uncertain, and the allegorical implications of the novel's close are complex.

The Manor House of De Villerai is inspired by two key moments in Canada's political and cultural history: pivotal battles in the Seven Years' War that eventually resulted in the fall of New France (1759-60); and the publication of the historian François-Xavier Garneau's *Histoire du Canada depuis sa découverte jusqu'à nos jours* (1845-48; tr. *History of Canada, from the Time of Its Discovery Till the Union Year (1840-1)*). An appreciation of *The Manor House* requires some knowledge of both these historical periods and their political and cultural repercussions. In 1763, residents of the Province of Quebec experienced the transfer of power from France to Britain. During the Seven Years' War itself, however, the idea of Britain's victory was rarely secure. The French had enjoyed important military successes under the command of General Louis-Joseph de Montcalm (1712-59). Leprohon weaves a number of these battles into her plot, including the Battle of Fort William Henry and the pivotal Battle of Fort Ticonderoga (known in French as Fort Carillon), where the British suffered a decisive loss. The unexpected victory by the British at the Battle of the Plains of Abraham (September 1759), together with France's failure to send reinforcements to Quebec in 1760, ultimately sealed the fate of New France. After the Battle of Montreal (April 1760), the French capitulated. Quebec was subjected to military rule until the period following the ratification of the Treaty of Paris (1763), which set the terms of France's transfer of its colonial possessions to Britain.

---

part in inflation to fund the Seven Years' War, as well as in extensive fraud committed by the Intendant of New France, François Bigot (1703-78). According to J.F. Bosher and J.C. Dubé, "[w]hile Bigot and dozens of officials and officers in Canada were making private fortunes, the Canadian populace was suffering from inflated prices, food shortages, and occasional severe famines. A serious economic crisis developed in which prices rose by 1759 to perhaps eight times their pre-war level, and in the same year goods in Canada were estimated to cost about seven times more than in France" (n. pag.).

After the post-Conquest period, popular responses to French Canada's membership in the British Empire changed in relation to political events and legislation. Significant in this context is the Constitutional Act of 1791, which divided the Province of Quebec into two jurisdictions, Upper and Lower Canada, while creating a legislative assembly and retaining French civil law— and with it the seigneurial system that had been guaranteed by the Quebec Act of 1774. Nevertheless, social and political unrest persisted and, in 1837, violent uprisings took place in Lower Canada, spearheaded by the *Patriote* party and their figurehead, the politician and orator, Louis-Joseph Papineau (1786-1871). The following year, 1838, John George Lambton, First Earl of Durham, was summoned by the Prime Minister of Britain to travel to Canada, where he was charged with the task of investigating the causes of uprisings that had taken place, not only in Lower Canada, but also in neighbouring Upper Canada (today's Ontario). With a reputation for liberal-mindedness, Durham was welcomed to French Canada by an enthusiastic populace grateful that its complaints about misgovernment would finally be heard. By the summer of 1839, however, French-Canadians' impressions of Durham had soured considerably. In July, Durham published his *Report on the Affairs of British North America*, which blamed French-Canada's semi-feudal seigneurial system for hindering Canada's economic development, while defining French-Canadians themselves as a people "without history or literature" (45). The Durham Report, as it is commonly known, exerted a decisive influence on British legislators and resulted in the Union of Upper and Lower Canada (1840-41), which rendered the French-Canadians a numerical minority in relation to the English-Canadians. The Union was followed a little over a decade later by the abolition of the seigneurial system (1854). Having married into a prominent French-Canadian family, Leprohon would have been acutely aware of French-Canadian responses to the Durham Report. As a member of Montreal's Anglo-Irish community, she would also have been aware of the sociohistorical and cultural factors underpinning sustained tensions between the two linguistic groups—Anglophone and Francophone—that, in the 1850s and 1860s, were being called upon to form the political and symbolic basis of Canadian Confederation.

A decade-and-a-half prior to the appearance of *The Manor House of De Villerai*, François-Xavier Garneau published his three-volume *Histoire du Canada*, whose resounding success lay partly in its implicit response to Durham, together with its portrayal of the French-Canadians in ways that radically departed from the dominant version of history to which they had become accustomed. Instead of seeing them as a conquered people, and, by extension, as history's "losers," Garneau encouraged the French-Canadians to see themselves as resilient, surviving and even thriving when threatened with near-extinction. Garneau's *Histoire* became phenomenally popular. It resulted in French Canada's first cultural renaissance, known as the "School of the 1860s," a wave of unprecedented literary and cultural activity that spanned the 1860s to the 1880s. In English Canada, it resulted in a number of imitators, such as John Mercier McMullen, whose *History of Canada from its First Discovery to the Present Time* (1855) aimed to do for the English-Canadians what Garneau's history had done for their French-Canadian counterparts—that is, to inspire a passion for history and an ensuing wave of cultural activity. Garneau's *Histoire* became extremely influential. In addition to the first edition, published in three volumes in the 1840s, a revised edition was published in 1852 and an English translation (by Andrew Bell) in 1860. As Sorfleet has observed, *The Manor House of De Villerai* was among the earliest Canadian novels to give fictional voice to Garneau's revisionary, sympathetic account of the Fall of New France (5). Indeed, Leprohon quotes explicitly from Garneau, particularly in the novel's historical chapters that recount the Battles of Fort William Henry, Carillon, and the Plains of Abraham. As one of the first Canadian novels to give fictional voice to Garneau's revisionist point of view, *The Manor House* anticipates a great deal of postmodern historical fiction, both in its revisionary discursive aims and in its rejection of historiography written from the perspective of history's victors.

The Manor House of De Villerai, A Tale of Canada Under the French Dominion

The Manor House of De Villerai is the first of three novels by Leprohon to feature a French-Canadian setting, forming what critics often refer to as a trilogy with *Antoinette de Mirecourt* (1864) and *Armand Durand* (1868), set in post-Conquest and nineteenth-century Quebec, respectively. As the purveyor of a number of literary historical "firsts," *The Manor House of De Villerai* represents a significant milestone in Canada's early literary history: it is the first historical novel, in either English or French, to portray the fall of New France from the French-Canadian point-of-view. In doing so, it legitimates both the fall and the French-Canadian perspective as suitable for novelistic representation. Within the context of English-Canadian literary history, Leprohon's novel represents, as Sorfleet rightly observes, the first English-language novel "to feature exclusively French protagonists and to be set in the colony of New France" (5). Finally, owing to the popularity of its French translation, *The Manor House* represents one of only two English-Canadian novels in the nineteenth century to have been accepted into the canon of Quebec literature.[1] As a pioneering novel, *The Manor House* adapts, to its purposes, key features of nineteenth-century historical fiction—notably, the fictional treatments of national characters, gender, and history standardized by Sir Walter Scott (1771-1832), the Scottish poet and novelist traditionally viewed as the originator of the historical novel. As the remainder of this section demonstrates, in the adjustments it makes to the standard features of historical fiction, *The Manor House of De Villerai* works to defend the viability of traditional characteristics of French-Canadian nationality, while simultaneously establishing the domestic sphere as a relevant constituent of sociopolitical life.

The Long Shadow of Sir Walter Scott

As a bilingual Montrealer, an Irish Catholic, a woman, and a member, through marriage, of a prominent French-Canadian family, Leprohon straddled key linguistic, gender, and cultural boundaries in her milieu. Such a straddling of boundaries proved indispensable to Leprohon, who was uniquely placed to deploy French-Canadian history, folklore, and local colour to develop plot, characterization, and setting in *The Manor House of De Villerai*. As innovative as her novel may be, it is also worth keeping in mind that Leprohon's treatment of folklore and local colour presents clear parallels with those of Sir Walter Scott, whose representation of the Scottish Highlanders in *Waverley; 'Tis Sixty Years Since* (1814) standardized the historical novel's treatment of the customs and manners of a traditional society on the verge of obsolescence. In *Waverley*, Scott also furnished his metropolitan English readers with their ideas about Scottish manners, in particular their "celticized" ideas of the semi-feudal Highlanders as

---

1 The other novel is Kirby's *The Golden Dog*, translated into French by Pamphile Le May (1837-1918) as *Le Chien d'or* (1884).

they existed "sixty years since," during the tumultuous wave of Jacobite uprisings (1745-46) that resulted, in part, in the abolition (1746) of the Scottish clan chiefs' traditional rights of jurisdiction. "There is no European nation which, within the course of half a century, or little more, has undergone so complete a change as this kingdom of Scotland," the narrator declares in *Waverley*'s famous "Postface which should have been a Preface" (492).[1] Scott's narrator locates political unrest in a superseded past while defining reconciliation—between the Highlanders, the Lowlanders, and the English, between Jacobites and Hanoverians[2]—as the prerequisite for modernization, civility, and commercial success. Central to readers' understanding of the narrative's treatment of history in *Waverley* is their understanding of the mutual interdependence of intercultural reconciliation and modernization.

By linking intercultural reconciliation to modernization, Scott provided nineteenth-century Canadian novelists with a usable model with which to portray French-English relations at the roots of the emergent Canadian nationality. It has become a critical commonplace to credit Leprohon, as do J.D. Logan and Donald G. French, with "creating" the "nativistic ... romance" (92) in her novels of Quebec: "Her characters, properties, and settings are largely Canadian, and she evidently set out consciously to create a nativistic literature by writing romances which should definitively portray life and manners in the society of the Old French *Régime*" (93). Logan and French's evaluation of Leprohon's role in conveying French-Canadian manners to English-Canadian readers relies implicitly on criteria supplied by Scott. In *Waverley*, Scott established local colour and traditional manners as dynamic vehicles for reviving the spirit of a lost past for the benefit of readers in the present. Readers should not be surprised, in this context, to come across Leprohon's long Chapter VII, which effectively interrupts the main narrative in order to retell French-Canadian legends. Partly narrated by a *voyageur* (that is, a French-Canadian boatman) named Baptiste Dufauld, this chapter serves to introduce readers to such well-known legends as that of the *loup-garou* (were-wolf) and such customs as the storytelling circle. Throughout this chapter, Lep-

---

1 For a relevant extract from Scott's *Waverley*, see Appendix C2, p. 233.
2 Jacobites: followers of Jacobitism, the political movement devoted to reinstating the Roman-Catholic Stuart dynasty to the British throne; Hanoverians: adherents of the House of Hanover, the German royal dynasty that occupied the throne of Britain from 1714 to 1901.

rohon shifts narrative perspectives in order to align readers' points-of-view with a folkloric and customary past. Whether she does so in order to lament a dying connection to the past, or to introduce English-Canadian readers to living French-Canadian customs, depends largely on how readers view the close of the novel.

In his introduction to the Penguin edition of *Waverley* (1972 ed.), editor Andrew Hook observes that, with Scott's popular success, the genre of the novel gained "a new authority and prestige," becoming "the dominant literary form of the nineteenth and twentieth centuries" (10). With Scott's success, Hook continues, the novel gained something "even more important perhaps," that is, "a new masculinity" (10). The insertion of history, a respected discipline, into the novel (a form lamented by many male commentators as the domain of women writers) proved key to the perceived rehabilitation and remasculinization of the novel form in the nineteenth century. As a woman writer, Leprohon would have been aware of such a male gendering of historical fiction. In this context, both setting and characterization in *The Manor House of De Villerai* acquire a dual significance, not only for their potential to "Canadianize" the historical novel while revising dominant historiography, but also for their potential to lay claim to the historical novel as the legitimate domain of women writers. With its titular manor house and the variously unmarried or widowed women who reside in it, namely Blanche De Villerai and her companions, Madame Dumont and, later, Miss De St. Omer, *The Manor House of De Villerai* shifts the historical novel's standard setting from the battlefield and the patrilineal manor house to a domestic sphere whose female inhabitants debate the social value of love-based marriage and the boundaries of filial duty. Far from suggesting irreconcilable differences between the domestic sphere and the male-dominated battlefield, these female protagonists represent important meditations on the kinds of femininity that can survive in the siege-culture of New France during the Seven Years' War. It is noteworthy that, in Blanche De Villerai, Leprohon creates a militant nationalist, as the opening paragraphs make clear when they describe Blanche's response to Gustave, a soldier in the real-historical Royal Roussillon regiment, who has returned to Canada from France in order to "draw [his] sword in [Canada's] defence" against the British (50). The narrator goes to some lengths to describe and even evaluate the meaning of Blanche's response to Gustave, who is eager to defend Canada: "Here a quiet and answering flush suffused the cheek of his betrothed, and flashing eyes gave even surer proof that the noble sentiment had awoke responsible echoes in her own womanly but frank, firm, intrepid nature. There is patriotism out of the sterne sex. Men may dare, but women do endure. Men may falter, women never flinch" (50). A memorable narrative intervention, this passage illuminates and defends Blanche's patriotism, while revealing, paradoxically, her adherence to the social codes of conduct that limit its expression.

At the time that *The Manor House* was published, only a handful of novels with historical themes had appeared in Canada in either English or French. These include Julia Catherine Beckwith Hart's *St. Ursula's Convent, or, The Nun of Canada* (1824), John Richardson's *Wacousta; or, The Prophecy, A Tale of the Canadas* (1832), Philippe Aubert de Gaspé, Jr.'s, *L'Influence d'un livre* (1837; tr. *The Influence of a Book*); Joseph Doutre's *Les fiancés de 1812* (1844; "The fiancés of 1812"); Douglas Huyghue's *Argimou* (serial 1842, book 1847); and Georges Boucher de Boucherville's *Une de perdue, deux de trouvées* (serial 1849-51, book 1874; "One lost, two found"). *The Manor House* is thus best understood in terms of the innovations it confers on a genre that was relatively young in the Canadian context. Readers may wish to keep three factors in mind as they consider the novel's treatment of history: first, the material factor, that is, the impact that serialization versus publication in book form may have had on the novel's plot and themes; second, the formal factor, namely the debates about history versus fiction that were waged in Quebec throughout the nineteenth century, particularly in the latter half; and third, the thematic factor, that is, the structural relationship between the novel's interconnected historical and courtship themes. In considering these factors, readers may also wish to think about the weight they assign to the novel's didacticism and defence of love-based marriage in relation to history and the Seven Years' War.

Serial Novels in the Confederation Period

Of the nearly dozen novels that Leprohon published in her lifetime, all but two—*Antoinette* and *Armand Durand*—first appeared as serializations in contemporary periodicals. In this context, *The Manor House of De Villerai* occupies an unusual position: according to an editorial note published in the first instalment of *The Family Herald*, Leprohon had intended to publish her novel in book form until she was invited by a mutual friend to submit it to the *Herald's* editor, George P. Ure (see Appendix A3, p. 210). According to the Prospectus (see Appendix A2, p. 209), *The Family Herald* was a "weekly journal, devoted to Literature, Art, Science, Horticulture, Agriculture and General Intelligence, free from political or other party bias." It aimed to "furnish ... acceptable reading" (210) for "family circles of all classes in Canada" (210). While its family orientation would have suited Leprohon's tastes, its stated didactic and moral objectives would have suited her purposes: "With political journals in our midst characterized by great ability and commendable enterprise—with denominational papers of the highest respectability,—we are nevertheless destitute of that species of journalism which aims at the cultivation of the taste, the diffusion of information, and the encouragement of innocent amusement, on ground common to people of all shades of political and christian opinion" (210). *The Family Herald*, the Prospectus concludes, "is intended to supply the omission" (210). It is impossible to know the extent to which Leprohon may have adjusted elements of the plot or characterization after she agreed to publish her novel in the *Herald*. Indeed, *The Manor House* seems to have been nearly ready for submission to a publisher, for Ure himself suggests in his editorial note that it was "about completed for publication as a volume" (211). Ure goes so far as to apologize to his intended readership for *The Manor House*'s opening chapters, which "may seem devoid of that dramatic interest, which they would doubtless have possessed had it been designed for the columns of a periodical" (210-211). He nevertheless promises his readers that "the power of the author is strikingly manifested" in later chapters, "as the persons and incidents of the tale are developed" (211).

Serial novels, intended for the mass reading public, were often heavy-handed in distributing moral themes and in upholding didacticism. In Canada, as elsewhere in North America and Europe in the nineteenth century, many members of the literate classes were mistrustful of serializations, concerned that the kind of light reading that common periodicals frequently published risked corrupting the values of emergent readers. As Richard D. Altick observes, in England in the years 1850-1900, "[m]ore people were reading than ever before; but in the opinion of most commentators, they were reading the wrong things, for the wrong reasons, and in the wrong way" (268). In the English-Canadian context, Gerson has highlighted the literary historical significance of Leprohon's "decidedly conservative position" in treating literature as a didactic medium. In response to the widespread unease about reading "bad books," Leprohon's novels, Gerson argues, can be viewed "on one level [as] fictionalized conduct manuals" (Gerson, "Three" 236). In French Canada, in the meantime, literary commentators in the latter half of the nineteenth century were arguably as distraught as their Anglophone counterparts about a trend that Altick describes as "the apparent decline of serious purpose in reading" (368). Nevertheless, around the middle of the century, when Leprohon published *The Manor House*, serializations had not yet become as widespread as they would within a few decades. As a result, by 1874, the literary historian Edmond Lareau could confidently declare, in his *Histoire de la littérature canadienne*, that French-Canadian literature had managed to remain free of such undesirable scenes as "intrigues of the boudoir" and the "improbable" "accumulation of feelings" (274) that had weakened the moral fabric of foreign literatures (see Appendix B3, p. 229). Although Lareau is arguably overstating the case, given that early French-Canadian literature bears evidence of foreign influence, it is significant that, within a short decade after Lareau, literary commentators in Quebec were unable to ignore the widespread popular taste for light reading that had resulted from the proliferation of serializations in periodicals and the popular press. For example, by 1885, the literary commentator, Joseph Desrosiers, would name serializations as the first of three offenders responsible for diminishing the quality of local literature: "Serialized fiction, police novels, sensation dramas, these are what I see encouraged all around me" (160).[1]

Such novels as *The Manor House*, therefore, bear the textual evidence of writers' attempts to provide suitable reading for family audiences. Passages in Leprohon's novel that, for instance, condemn the reading of books by French writers such as Eugène Sue (1804-57) and Honoré de Balzac (1799-1850), bear the weight of contemporary debates about reading "good books" that took place in English and French Canada alike, while also registering the specific reaction to foreign serial novelists in Quebec that would grow in intensity in the last half of the nineteenth century. Arguably as much as serializations, historical novels were caught up in debates surrounding suitable reading practices. Although Leprohon was writing for an Anglophone audience, she

---

[1] "Le feuilleton, le roman judiciaire, le drame à sensation, voilà ce que je vois encouragé au milieu de nous."

arguably never lost sight of her potential Francophone readership. In writing *The Manor House of De Villerai*, she would thus have been aware of the similarities and differences between the two communities in their respective responses to the historical novel. For instance, Gerson notes that, "by calling for a Walter Scott for Canada, [English-Canadian] cultural leaders acknowledged and sought to exploit the political power of popular fiction" (*A Purer* 70). In French Canada, by contrast, the features that had rendered historical fiction socially acceptable in the mid- to late-nineteenth century were less popular and more political. As Yves Dostaler observes, in reviving the spirit of the past, the historical novel helped to intensify the patriotism of a minority culture constantly fighting to safeguard its survival ("la sauvegarde de ... sa survivance"; 121). The historical novel also responded to French-Canadians' concerns about achieving moral honesty in fiction ("[le] souci d'honnêteté morale"; 122).

While the question of moral honesty preoccupied conservative commentators in English Canada, who praised historical fiction's capacity to edify and instruct, the question of moral honesty preoccupied French-Canadian commentators to the extent that they evaluated a novel's "honesty" in part by its unfalsified treatment of history. In *Histoire de la littérature canadienne*, for instance, Lareau emphasizes the social value of "honest novels" (275), whose features include history and legends, and whose exemplar is the historical novel, the only literary form "called upon to live in Canada" (see Appendix B3, p. 229). While Lareau was an obvious defender of the historical novel based on the idea of its "honesty," historical fiction's detractors voiced their concerns about that same genre based, paradoxically, on the same notion of "honesty." As Dostaler notes, conservative commentators complained of the historical novel's "anti-social" potential ("anti-sociale"; Dostaler 122). Such commentators include Desrosiers ("Le roman"), who insisted that Walter Scott's novels represented a "deformation of history" ("déformation de l'histoire"; Desrosiers 211) to French-Canadian Catholics, given Scott's perceived Anglo-Saxon and Protestant biases. Although they postdate the publication of *The Manor House*, Desrosiers' comments are worth keeping in mind in terms of *The Manor House*'s treatment of history. Readers will notice that Leprohon effectively segregates history from fiction, relegating the Battles of Ticonderoga and the Plains of Abraham to separate "historical" chapters (XIII and XXI), while also paraphrasing liberally from at least two of her three primary sources, Garneau, Smith, and

Colonel Malcolm Fraser (1733-1815).[1] While the narrative's refusal to blend history smoothly with fiction may be symptomatic of *The Manor House*'s "unintegrated" historical and fictional structures (Sorfleet 10), it may also represent an expedient response to contemporary debates about moral honesty in the fictional treatment of history. At the very least, *The Manor House*'s "unintegrated" historicism, to borrow Sorfleet's term, serves to underscore the narrative's strict adherence to historical sources.

History versus Fiction

An acquisitive form of literature, the historical novel is famous for its ability to soak up features from other literary genres and to adapt them to its purposes. Hence, it is not surprising to find features of sentimental fiction embedded within many nineteenth-century historical novels, including *The Manor House*, whose sentimental narrative is sufficiently developed that it warrants treatment on its own terms. Indeed, the novel's sentimentalism has prompted Gerson to identify the English novelist, Samuel Richardson (1689-1761), as a potential influence on Leprohon. Comparing *The Manor House of De Villerai* to Richardson's *Pamela* (1740) and *Antoinette de Mirecourt* to his *Clarissa* (1748), Gerson observes that Leprohon's novels portray a "virtu[ous]" heroine "in distress," along with the triumph of "virtue rewarded" (*A Purer* 139).[2] The sentimental novel has been traditionally preoccupied with characters' mutual regard for one another. Its characteristic features are perceptible in *The Manor House*'s opening scene, which introduces readers to Blanche as she stands gazing out the window awaiting the arrival of Gustave, to whom she was betrothed in infancy by her parents, now deceased. From this point onwards, much of the plot revolves around crises of perspective: characters regard one another in the two senses of the term, to look at and to assess; as the plot progresses, so too do Blanche's changing assessments of Gustave as an appropriate husband for her; in the end, characters' changing regard for one another (in particular, their changing perceptions of Rose from a fortune-seeker to a worthy bride) literally bring about the novel's climax and resolution. Indeed, of all the characters, Rose Lauzon most clearly resembles the traditional hero-

---

1 For relevant extracts from Leprohon's historical sources, see Appendix D.
2 For a relevant extract from Richardson's *Pamela*, see Appendix C1, p. 232.

ines of novels of sensibility, with her propensity to express sympathetic distress at the sorrows of her friends and benefactors, or to blush perceptibly while enduring, however silently, her own private hardships. As a victim of communal gossip, Rose functions as a barometer of social morality. In learning to refine her natural goodness in response to public criticism, Rose manages to convince readers that she is worthy of Gustave's love and, by extension, of the leap in class-standing that her marriage to Gustave entails.

Like female authors in the United States and Britain, including Louisa May Alcott (1832-88) and Jane Austen (1775-1817), respectively, Leprohon deals with issues of social class and politics that were often deemed to fall outside the bounds of appropriate subject matter for women. To read *The Manor House* thus involves reading it with a subtle eye, attuned to the intricate ways in which the trope of sensibility works to challenge dominant perceptions about class, gender, and the social roles of women in such politically fractured and culturally fragile societies as New France on the verge of conquest. As an embodiment of sentimentalism, Rose presents a valuable counterpoint to Blanche, who is more rational than she is emotional. Together, Rose and Blanche play a central role in the narrative's advocacy of love-based marriage. Sorfleet draws attention to Leprohon's complex treatment of love-based marriage, first, by praising Leprohon's willingness to intervene in early feminist debates, pointing out that the American Margaret Fuller's *Woman in the Nineteenth Century* (1845) had been published "around the same time" (10) as *The Manor House*. Second, however, Sorfleet complains that Leprohon does not go far enough in redefining gender roles: while her "comparative liberalism shows the influence of middle-class ideas on her portrayal of [French-Canadian] society," her treatment of gender, especially in relation to women's social roles, remains only "somewhat revolutionary" (10), limited ultimately by her overriding social conservatism. Readers should keep this apparent paradox between feminism and class conservatism in mind when they reach the novel's close, especially when responding to such passages as those that contain the narrator's concluding words of praise for Rose, who "never forgot ... that she was the humble peasant girl, whom [Gustave's] generous love had raised to so proud a destiny" (208). Does the novel's message about class mobility rely for its effectiveness on the stability of traditional gender roles? While posing such a question about gender and class in relation to Gustave and Rose, however, readers should also keep in mind that the narrative does not treat all female characters identically. That is, the novel's treatment of Rose stands out differently, in the end, from its treatment of Blanche. At the end of the novel, Blanche holds a highly-charged position as the symbolic representative of the depopulated landed class and of a French Canada on the verge of absorption by the British Empire. It is thus significant that she rejects the idea that she must marry in order to be happy, choosing instead a life of celibacy. In a memorable passage, Blanche explains her decision to remain in Quebec to Gustave, who has asked that she participate in the exodus to France: "I will remain in Canada, my home, my birth-place, and even though I will henceforth be under a foreign rule, I am a woman and can easily bow my neck to it" (192). Given *The Manor House of DeVillerai*'s simultaneously revisionary and conservative impulses—Leprohon challenges some aspects of accepted gender roles while rarely displacing the larger moral structure in place—Blanche's response to Gustave is two-pronged. Gerson has read it as the narrative's reinforcement, with "no conscious irony," of the conduct lesson that "submission ... is a woman's lot" ("Three Writers" 236). Carrie MacMillan and Lorraine McMullen, in turn, have read it as provocatively "down to earth [for Blanche] simply prefers not to marry" (34). Sorfleet, in turn, has focused on a different exchange between Blanche and Gustave, albeit one that falls within the same passage, in which Blanche defends her decision not to marry while admonishing Gustave in the following terms: "I hope, Gustave, you do not share the vulgar error, that an unmarried woman must necessarily be unhappy" (192). Responding to Blanche's admonishment of Gustave, Sorfleet praises it as a "significant ... expression of feminism in fiction ... [which] probably found much agreement among [Leprohon's] middle-class women readers" (10). While furnishing recent critics with a source of debate, these and other passages, resonant with female patriotism, appear also to have exerted some influence on Leprohon's contemporaries. It is worth noting that Blanche acts as an important precursor to another memorable protagonist, Blanche d'Haberville, the heroine of Philippe Aubert de Gaspé's *Les Anciens Canadiens*, who defends her refusal to marry her Scottish suitor, together with her decision to remain celibate, as the only effective patriotic acts available to her after the conquest of Quebec by the British.

The allegory of intercultural reconciliation, whereby novelistic narratives charge heterosexual courtship plots with the symbolic power to resolve cultural conflicts, has remained a standard feature of historical fiction since the appearance of *Waverley*. Because readers and critics alike have often seen Leprohon's *Antoinette de Mirecourt* as a kind of sequel to *The Manor House of De Villerai*, it is necessary to point out that the two novels treat the allegory of intercultural reconciliation remarkably differently from one another. George Woodcock has suggested that *Antoinette* represents an exemplary instance of Northrop Frye's concept of the "garrison mentality," whereby, in Woodcock's terms, "patterns of intercultural conflict" (14) not only rest at the core of the plot, but they also make possible the novel's symbolic resolution between the French-Canadians and the British. Differently put, the marriage of the title character, Antoinette, with the Englishman, Colonel Evelyn, exemplifies "the process of reconciliation which [Leprohon] believed must be attained between the French in Canada and the English intruders" (Woodcock 16). Despite his Frygian analysis of *Antoinette*'s allegorical marriage plot, Woodcock admits he is concerned that critics have applied Frye's concept of the "garrison mentality" too widely to Canadian literature (16).[1] Certainly, readers of *The Manor House* will notice that the concept is of limited relevance here, for Anglophone characters are conspicuously—even remarkably—absent throughout. The final lines uttered by the haughty Pauline De Nevers to the ridiculous Count De Noraye—that it is little wonder that "such a powerful race of heroes" as the British "should have defeated such puny adversaries as you Gallic gentlemen" (200)—are emblematic of the narrative's larger assertions, however comically rendered, of irreconcilable differences in character, constitution, and mentality between the French-Canadians and the Continental French, rather than between the French-Canadians and the British "intruders," as Woodcock describes them.

The notion of intercultural reconciliation, however, retains its relevance to *The Manor House of De Villerai* through the narrative

---

1 In his "Conclusion to a *Literary History of Canada*" (1965), Frye famously likens intercultural, political, and sectarian relations in Canada to a "garrison," while defining the latter in the following terms: "A garrison is a closely knit and beleaguered society" (226). He adds that it is "eas[y] to multiply garrisons, and when that happens, something anti-cultural comes into Canadian life, a dominating herd-mind in which nothing original can grow" (226). It is worth noting that Frye goes on to investigate some "positive effects on [Canadian] intellectual life" that have resulted from the "more creative side of the garrison mentality" (226).

perspective that aligns English-Canadian readers with the French-Canadian point of view. Readers familiar with Leprohon's poetry, such as the frequently anthologized poem, "Canada in Winter," will recognize the patriotic passages that run throughout *The Manor House*, mounting a sustained defence of Canada against unjustifiable prejudices or seemingly ridiculous snobbery. A case in point involves De Noraye, who, readers learn, "had landed in Canada under the impression that he was arriving on the very outskirts of human civilization" (56), while growing to believe that "the climate of Siberia was mild when compared with that of Canada" (60). Associated with Voltaire's severe assessment of Canada's worthless "acres of snow,"[1] De Noraye serves as a scapegoat for the narrative to question France's commitment to New France during the Seven Years' War. By rendering De Noraye an object of ridicule, the narrator works to unify the two perspectives, French- and English-Canadian, in their mockery of the French. By contrast to such early Canadian writers as John Richardson, whose *Wacousta* (see Appendix C3, p. 235) repeatedly addresses a readership presumed to be British, Leprohon addresses a uniquely Canadian audience. By interpolating her readers in passages that variously defend the local landscape and customs, Leprohon calls into being a Canadian readership that is both the subject of, and the audience for, *The Manor House*'s revisionary historiography.

Reception in Quebec and English Canada

Despite the contemporary success of its author, *The Manor House of De Villerai* suffered the same fate as many novels published in nineteenth-century magazines: having never been published in book form, it was easily overlooked. Nevertheless, literary commentators frequently referred to it as one of Leprohon's most important works of fiction.[2] Over time, Leprohon has enjoyed a more vibrant reception in Quebec than she has in English Canada. Major factors behind her relative popularity in Quebec include her acceptance into the Quebec literary canon, thanks to

---

1 François-Marie Arouet, pseud. Voltaire (1694-1778), prolific writer and philosopher, whose reference to Canada's "few acres of snow" ("quelques arpents de neige") in Chapter 23 of *Candide* (1759) is metonymous of his larger negative assessment of Canada's lack of economic and strategic value to France.
2 See, for example, the extracts from Morgan and "Anon." in Appendix A and Lesperance in Appendix B.

the rapid translation into French of four of her novels—*Ida Beresford*, *The Manor House*, *Antoinette*, and *Armand Durand*—and her participation in the wave of literary activity that followed the publication of Garneau's *Histoire du Canada*. An important, albeit underappreciated, secondary factor behind Leprohon's relative neglect in English Canada involves the material circumstances surrounding the preservation of *The Family Herald*. As Deneau observes, "the early collapse of [the *Herald*] and the all but total disappearance of its few issues barred all readers of the succeeding generation from a first hand [sic] appreciation of [Leprohon's] work" (72). According to Deneau, the material disappearance of the *Herald*, and with it the effective withdrawal from circulation of instalments of *The Manor House*, help to explain "why the enthusiasm with which [the novel] was first received soon subsided into nearly utter oblivion" (71). The near oblivion of *The Manor House of De Villerai* may help twenty-first-century readers better understand why Leprohon's novel was not reissued in English until Sorfleet edited and published it as a special issue of the *Journal of Canadian Fiction* in 1985. Other factors worth considering include Leprohon's apparent preference, as Gerson observes, for "[Montreal-based] publishers and presumably [for] local distribution" ("Three Writers" 197), along with the fact that Leprohon effectively published her most memorable novels a generation too soon to benefit "from the wave of English-Canadian interest in Quebec" (Gerson, "Three Writers" 197) that followed Confederation and the publication of influential texts such as James MacPherson Le Moine's *Maple Leaves* (1863-1906) and the American historian Francis Parkman's multi-volume *France and England in North America* (1865-92).

It is arguably impossible, however, to investigate the reasons behind the relative neglect of *The Manor House of De Villerai* without taking into account the critical tendency throughout the twentieth century to favour works of literary realism over works of romance. In *The Madwoman in the Attic*, Sandra Gilbert and Susan Gubar famously observe that women writers in the eighteenth and nineteenth centuries, from Jane Austen to Emily Dickinson, "all dealt with central female experiences from a specifically female perspective" (72). Nevertheless, "th[e] distinctively feminine aspect of their art has been generally ignored by critics" and has even seemed "'odd' in relation to the predominantly male literary history" (72). Gilbert and Gubar's observation is appropriate in this context. The corpus of criticism on Leprohon is marked by a recurrent complaint about the author's tendency to indulge in sentimental romance at the expense of sociohistorical realism. A case in point involves Elaine Kalman Naves, who commends the "sophisticated themes" of Leprohon's novels while lamenting their "stilted, melodramatic and conventional" narratives (36). Naves's terms echo those of John Stockdale, who describes *Antoinette de Mirecourt*, for instance, as a "romantic, stilted novel" (n.p.) in his entry on Leprohon in the *Dictionary of Canadian Biography*. It is worth noting Gerson's explicit response to Stockdale's complaint: "Romantic and stilted as Leprohon's work may appear to modern readers, it met the wholehearted approval of her contemporaries" ("Three Writers" 212). Gerson recalls Susanna Moodie, who declared in her short-lived *Victoria Magazine* (1848-49) that Leprohon, then an emergent writer, promised to "become the pride and ornament of a great and rising country" (Gerson, "Three Writers" 212).[1] The formal bias that shaped the terms of Leprohon's reception in the twentieth century has arguably resulted in a limited critical understanding of the formal work that romance conventions perform in Leprohon's oeuvre. As the first publication in book form of *The Manor House of De Villerai*, this Broadview edition aims to encourage a revival of interest in Leprohon's neglected novel, while also participating in a larger recovery and renewed understanding of works of literary romance and domestic fiction written by women in the nineteenth century. A critically informed, formally nuanced, and historically aware investigation of the aesthetic, material, and ideological factors that inform *The Manor House*'s characteristic combination of realism and romance, of historicism and sentimentalism, is overdue.

In Canada, recent trends in revisionary criticism, notably influenced by feminism and cultural materialism, have brought back into the public gaze works by lesser-known nineteenth-century writers, especially women. (See, for example, Tecumseh Press's "Nineteenth-Century Contexts" series and its related "Women Writers" series, or, indeed, Broadview's own "Broadview Editions" series.) Over the last few decades, critical interest in the fiction and poetry of Rosanna Mullins Leprohon has risen noticeably, as a result of influential feminist and materialist scholarship. This body of criticism includes scholarship by Mary Jane Edwards (1972, 1990), Carl F. Klinck (1973), Elizabeth Brady (1975), Gerson (1983; 1989; 2010), Kathleen O'Donnell (1985),

---

[1] For Moodie's editorial from the *Victoria Magazine*, see Appendix A1, p. 209.

Carrie MacMillan, Lorraine McMullen, and Elizabeth Waterston (1993), Michelle Gadpaille (1995), Misao Dean (1998), Pilar Cuder-Dominguez (1998), Glenn Wilmott (2001), and Andrea Cabajsky (2013). Three of Leprohon's short stories, "Alice Sydenham's First Ball" (1849), "My Visit to Fairview Villa" (1870), and "Clive Weston's Wedding Anniversary" (1872) have been regularly collected in anthologies of Canadian short stories over the last forty years (1973, 1976, 1978, 1993, 2000), while Leprohon's two other novels that deal with Quebec, *Antoinette de Mirecourt* and *Armand Durand*, have been recently reissued by McClelland & Stewart (2000 and 2010) and Tecumseh Press (1994), respectively. An earlier edition of *Antoinette De Mirecourt* was also published by Carleton University Press (1989). This Broadview edition thus inscribes itself into the growing corpus of early Canadian literature, of writing by nineteenth-century women, and of nineteenth-century historical fiction. It represents the first publication in book form of Rosanna Mullins Leprohon's neglected first novel of Quebec, *The Manor House of De Villerai*.

Rosanna Mullins Leprohon: A Brief Chronology

[As a young writer who had already published a number of poems, short stories, and serialized novels, and having recently married into a prominent French-Canadian family, Rosanna Mullins Leprohon was well-situated to write *The Manor House of De Villerai*. Unfortunately, relatively little is known about the life of the woman who wrote three of the most important nineteenth-century English-Canadian novels about Quebec, *The Manor House of De Villerai* (1859-60), *Antoinette de Mirecourt* (1864), and *Armand Durand* (1868). There exists no substantial body of correspondence, no surviving private journal, and no definitive Leprohon biography. We owe the few details of her life to original archival research conducted by Adrian Deneau (Brother André) for his unpublished Master's thesis (1948). An anonymous reference to a collected edition of her *oeuvre*, which Leprohon was purportedly preparing at the time of her death, remains unsubstantiated (see Anon, "The Late," in Appendix A6, p. 213). Deneau's single most important accomplishment is arguably his correction of an error surrounding Leprohon's date of birth. Although many of her peers and descendants believed that she was born in 1832 (obituaries in both *Canadian Illustrated News* and its sister paper, *L'Opinion publique*, note her birth year as 1832), Deneau unearthed Leprohon's birth certificate to prove that she had actually been born three years earlier, in 1829 (see Deneau 3).]

1829 Born in Montreal on 12 January to Francis Mullins (b. Cork, Ireland) and Rosanna Connelly (alt. Conelly, b. Montreal).
1839 Begins studies at the Convent of the Congregation of Notre Dame.
1846 Publishes first poem in *The Literary Garland* (Montreal).
1847 Publishes first novel, *The Stepmother*, serially in *The Literary Garland* between February and June.
1848 Publishes second novel, *Ida Beresford; or, The Child of Fashion*, in *The Literary Garland* between January and September.
1849 Publishes first short story, "Alice Sydenham's First Ball," in *The Literary Garland* in January; publishes third novel,

Florence; or, Wit and Wisdom, in the *Garland* from February to December.

1850 Publishes fourth novel, *Eva Huntingdon*, in *The Literary Garland* between January and December.

1851 Publishes fifth novel, *Clarence Fitz-Clarence; Passages from the Life of an Egoist*, in *The Literary Garland* between January and May; marries Jean-Baptiste-Lucain (Jean-Lukin) Leprohon (b. 7 April 1822) on 17 June; the *Garland* ceases publication in December.

1852 Gives birth to son, Lucien, who dies within the year.

1853 Gives birth to daughter, Gabrielle.

1855 Gives birth to son, Rodolphe; the Leprohon family moves from Saint-Charles-sur-Richelieu to Montreal.

1856 Gives birth to son, Claude.

1857 Gives birth to daughter, Geraldine.

1859 Publishes the long short story, "Eveleen O'Donnell," in *The Pilot* [Boston] between January and February; publishes *The Manor House of De Villerai, A Tale of Canada Under the French Dominion* in the inaugural issue of *The Family Herald*, from November 1859 to February 1860; Leprohon's nephew-by-marriage, Josef-Édouard Lefèbvre de Bellefeuille, translates *Ida Beresford* into French, under the title *Ida Beresford, ou la Jeune Fille du grand monde*, and publishes it serially in *L'Ordre* between September 1859 and February 1860; Leprohon gives birth to son, Édouard.

1860 At the invitation of City officials, Leprohon translates a cantata by Édouard Sempé into English to be performed during the Prince of Wales's visit to Montreal; de Bellefeuille translates *The Manor House of De Villerai* into French, under the title *Le manoir de Villerai, roman historique sous la domination française*, and publishes it serially in *L'Ordre* between November 1860 and April 1861; de Bellefeuille's translation of *The Manor House* is published as a book by de Plinguet of Montreal, making it the first novel by Leprohon to be published in book form; George Ure, editor of *The Family Herald*, dies; *The Family Herald* ceases publication as a result.

1862 Henry J. Morgan publishes an entry on "Mrs. Leprohon" in *Sketches of Celebrated Canadians*; Leprohon gives birth to son, Joseph Arthur Lukin, who dies in infancy.

1863 Gives birth to daughter, Gertrude Ida.

1864 Publishes *Antoinette de Mirecourt; or, Secret Marrying and*

Secret Sorrowing, in book form with Lovell; E.H. Dewart publishes a half-dozen Leprohon poems in *Selections from Canadian Poets* (Toronto).

1865 Joseph-Auguste Genand, editor of *L'Ordre*, translates *Antoinette de Mirecourt* into French and publishes it serially in *L'Ordre*; Montreal publisher, Beauchemin & Valois, publishes *Antoinette* in book form in French; Leprohon gives birth to daughter, Marie Antoinette Selby, who dies within the year.

1866 The *Pionnier de Sherbrooke* publishes the French version of *Antoinette* in serial instalments between October 1866 and October 1867; Borthwick publishes selected poems by Leprohon in *The Harp of Canaan*.

1867 Henry J. Morgan publishes an entry on "Leprohon, Mrs. Rosanna Eleanor" in *Bibliotheca canadensis*; the *Pionnier de Sherbrooke* publishes the French translation of *The Manor House of De Villerai* in serial instalments between October 1867 and August 1868; Leprohon gives birth to daughter, Eleanore Florina, who dies within the year; Canadian Confederation declared on 1 July.

1868 Publishes *Armand Durand; or, A Promise Fulfilled*, serially, in *The Daily News*, as well as in book form with the Montreal publisher, Lovell; gives birth to daughter, Marie Florence.

1869 Publishes *Ada Dunmore; or, A Memorable Christmas Eve: An Autobiography* in the inaugural issue of the *Canadian Illustrated News* between December 1869 and February 1870; Genand translates *Armand Durand* into French; Genand's translation, *Armand Durand, ou la Promesse accomplie*, is published in book form by J.B. Rolland (Montreal) and is published serially by the *Pionnier de Sherbrooke* between June 1869 and May 1870.

1870 Publishes "My Visit to Fairview Villa" in the *Canadian Illustrated News* in May; gives birth to son, Jean de Niverville.

1872 Publishes a short novel, *The Dead Witness; or, Lillian's Peril*, in *The Hearthstone* from August to October, 1872; publishes a short story, "Clive Weston's Wedding Anniversary," in the inaugural issue of the *Canadian Monthly and National Review*, between July and August; gives birth to daughter, Maude, who dies within the year.

1873 Auguste Bechard translates *Ada Dunmore* into French as *Ada Dunmore, ou Une veille de Noël remarquable. Autobi-*

ographie, and publishes it serially in the *Pionnier de Sherbrooke* between April and November.

1874 Publishes "Who Stole the Diamonds?" in two parts in the *Canadian Illustrated News* in January; publishes a memorial poem for her former mentor, the Reverend Sister of the Nativity, upon the latter's death; the Leprohon family moves to 237 Saint-Antoine St., Montreal; the *Union des Cantons de l'Est* publishes the French translation of *Armand Durand* in serial instalments between December 1874 (beginning with the Christmas issue) and July 1875.

1877 Publishes "A School-Girl Friendship" in the *Canadian Illustrated News* between August and September.

1879 Dies of heart failure in Montreal on 20 September.

1881 The Montreal publisher, Lovell, issues *The Poetical Works of Mrs. Leprohon (Miss R.E. Mullins)*, presumably edited by John Reade; the Montreal publisher, J.B. Rolland & fils, reissues the French edition of *Antoinette de Mirecourt*.

1884 The Montreal publisher, Beauchemin & Valois, reissues *Le manoir de Villerai*. This version will be reissued at least five times between 1884 and 1925.

1886 The periodical *Nouvelles soirées canadiennes* publishes the French version of *Antoinette* in serial instalments.

1892 The Montreal publisher, C.O. Beauchemin & fils, reissues the French version of *Armand Durand* in book form.

1922 The Montreal-based newspaper, *La Presse*, reissues the French version of *Armand Durand* in serial instalments from July 1922 to January 1923.

1925 The publisher Beauchemin (Montreal) publishes a fifth (seemingly last) French edition of *Le manoir de Villerai*.

1985 John R. Sorfleet edits and publishes *The Manor House of De Villerai* as a special issue of the *Journal of Canadian Fiction*.

A Note on the Text

Leprohon had been planning a book publication of *The Manor House of De Villerai* when she was invited by a mutual friend of *The Family Herald*'s editor, George P. Ure, to submit it to his new weekly magazine. *The Manor House* was featured on the first two pages of nearly every issue, from the inaugural issue of 16 November 1859 to the final instalment of 8 February 1860. The only exception to this pattern of publication is the Christmas issue of 28 December 1859, where *The Manor House* appears on the third and fourth pages, having been supplanted by "The Belle of the Season: A Christmas Story" by "Mrs. E.L. Cushing," appearing on pages one and two, followed by "Tom Singleton; or, How My Aunt Dorothy Left Her Money," by "Mrs. Moodie," appearing on pages two and three.[1] It should be noted that *The Family Herald* erroneously identifies two separate chapters of *The Manor House* as Chapter XVII. I have corrected the numbering within the body of the novel by continuing the sequence, thus identifying the second "Chapter XVII" as Chapter XVIII. I acknowledge my corrections to numbering within the body of the text in brief explanatory footnotes that fall at the beginning of each relevant chapter.

Each instalment of *The Manor House* was preceded by a poem that appeared in the same column, immediately above it. Many of the poets are anonymous; however, others are identified as Miss Strickland, Alexander Laing, J. Heiton, and Robert Gilfillan.[2] The 13 instalments appeared in *The Family Herald* as follows:

1. Chapters I, II, III: 16 Nov 1859, pp. 1-2; poem: Anonymous, "The Advancing Light"
2. Chapters III (continued), IV: 23 Nov 1859, pp. 1-2; poem: Miss Strickland, "Sweet Lavender"
3. Chapters IV (continued), V, VI: 30 Nov 1859, pp. 1-2; poem: S.E., "Woman's Love"

---

1 Eliza Lanesford Foster (Cushing), American-born Canadian writer and editor (1794-1886); Susanna Strickland (Moodie), English-born Canadian novelist and short-fiction writer (1803-85).

2 Agnes Strickland (1796-1874), sister to Susanna Moodie; Alexander Laing (1787-1857), the Scottish poet and editor; John Heiton (b. 1777), author of *The Laird of Darnick Tower* (1858); and Robert Gilfillan (1798-1850), Scottish poet and songwriter.

4. Chapters VI (continued), VII: 7 Dec 1859, pp. 1-2; poem: Alexander Laing, "The Invitation"
5. Chapters VIII, IX, X: 14 Dec 1859, pp. 1-2; poem: Anonymous, "Coming Winter"
6. Chapters XI, XII: 21 Dec 1859, pp. 1-2; poem: Anonymous, "The Love That Meets Return"
7. Chapters XIII, XIV: 28 Dec 1859, pp. 3-4; poem: Anonymous, "Make Home Bright and Pleasant"
8. Chapters XV, XVI: 4 Jan 1860, pp. 1-2; poem: Alexander Laing, "The Trysting Tree"
9. Chapters XVII, XVIII: 11 Jan 1860, pp. 1-2; poem: Anonymous, "As Slow our Ship"
10. Chapters XIX, XX: 18 Jan 1860, pp. 1-2; poem: Alexander Laing, "The Young MacLean"
11. Chapters XXI, XXII: 25 Jan 1860, pp. 1-2; poem: J. Heiton, "A Darnick Lay: Lillian"
12. Chapters XXIII, XXIV: 1 Feb 1860, pp. 1-2; poem: J. Heiton, "A Darnick Lay: Woman's Love"
13. Chapters XXIV (continued), XXV, Conclusion: 8 Feb 1860, pp. 1-2; poem: Robert Gilfillan, "Oh! This Were A Bright World."

Because the serialization of *The Manor House of De Villerai* is the only known version published in the author's lifetime, it must serve as the copy text for this edition. Typical of its kind, the serialization contains a variety of errors and anomalies that reflect the time constraints under which the author, type-setters, and printers laboured. Such anomalies include variant spellings of "Manor House," "Manor-house," "manor-house," and "manor house," as well as a mixture of French and English terminology, where "Mr." and "M." (the abbreviation for "Monsieur"), as well as "Mrs." and "Mme." (short for "Madame"), are used interchangeably for the same sets of characters.

It is impossible to know whether such errors have their origins in imprecise authorial handwriting, problems in the compositor's room, or elsewhere. Consequently, I have adopted a conservative editorial policy when addressing these textual issues. I have silently regularized the use of italics for French words (except naturalized words like "belle" and "beau," which remain consistently unitalicized in the copy text). I have resolved blatant anomalies, such as the variant spellings of "manor house." I have resisted the temptation, however, to modernize syntax and punctuation, and have only standardized spelling where the use of multiple variants demanded consistency. I have added or subtracted punctuation only in instances where my failing to do so could cause confusion. Similarly, I have only modernized place-names where necessary to avoid confusion. Other specific changes include occasional reconstructions of passages that are damaged in the original copy (infrequent tears or stains that obscure wording). I have reconstructed these passages by appealing to both John Robert Sorfleet's edition of *The Manor House*, published in the *Journal of Canadian Fiction*, and the French-language translation, *Le manoir de Villerai* (1860). When I have reconstructed words that are missing in the copy text owing to a tear or an obstruction, I have alerted readers in footnotes. I have also corrected the spelling of the historical General Bourlamaque's surname, spelled "Bourlamarque" throughout the copy text. While this is a potential misspelling, it may also suggest that Leprohon was reading *Le Canada sous la domination française* (1855) by Louis Dussieux, which similarly misspells the surname. Unless stated otherwise, I have resolved these issues silently in the main narrative.

I have retained the copy text's practice of consistently capitalizing "De" in surnames, such as De Villerai, De Montarville, De Rochon, and so on. I have also retained unusual punctuation where it is used consistently throughout, such as commas within parentheses, as well as commas preceding and following em-dashes, colons used in place of semi-colons, Monsieur and M., or Madame and Mme., used interchangeably, as well as the mix of British and American orthography (e.g. "favour" and "favorite"). Original authorial notes in the body of the novel and the appendices are so noted in footnotes. I have retained the copy text's spelling of the word "christian" with a lower-case "c" where it appears in adjectival form. It is worth noting that, in this respect, I differ from Sorfleet, who capitalizes "Christian" in the *JCF* edition. Finally, where it occurs in the original text, I have retained the word "Indian" in reference to Canada's Aboriginal peoples.

Footnotes to the present text of *The Manor House of De Villerai* clarify historical, geographical, religious, and literary references, while also defining those terms of vocabulary that may be unfamiliar to modern readers. In the preparation of these notes, I have found the following sources particularly useful: the Bible (King James Version); the *Oxford English Dictionary Online*, Oxford UP, December 2013 (http://www.oed.com); *Le Grand Robert and Collins*, HarperCollins, December 2013 (http://www.rc2009.bvdep.com); the *Dictionary of Canadian Biography*, University of Toronto/Université Laval, December 2013 (http://www.biographi.ca); the *Encyclopaedia Britannica Online*, Encyclopaedia Britannica, December 2013 (http://www.britannica.com); the *Cambridge Guide to Literature in English*, 3rd ed., ed. Dominic Head, Cambridge UP, 2006; *The Columbia Encyclopedia*, Columbia UP, December 2013 (http://search.credoreference.com); and the *Encyclopédie Larousse en ligne*, Société éditions Larousse, December 2013 (www.larousse.fr).

After significant initial success, *The Family Herald* came to a premature end when Ure died unexpectedly in August 1860. *The Manor House* was published again, over a century later, as a special issue of the *Journal of Canadian Fiction* edited by Sorfleet. Although it was popular in Quebec, having been reissued seven times in French translation, either serially or in book form, between 1861 and 1925, *The Manor House* has become all but inaccessible in English. Today, copies of Sorfleet's special issue are difficult to obtain, for the *Journal of Canadian Fiction* has ceased publication. This Broadview edition thus represents the first publication in book form of *The Manor House of De Villerai*.

Paper versions of the serialization of *The Manor House of De Villerai* have been extremely difficult to obtain since at least the early to mid-twentieth century. In his unpublished Master's thesis, André Deneau (1948) suggests that issues of *The Family Herald* "all but ... disappear[ed]" after its demise in 1860. Following an exhaustive attempt to locate a hard copy of the *Herald* in Canadian and American libraries (67), as well as in public libraries in Montreal, Quebec City, and Ottawa (68), Deneau finally obtained a copy belonging to Leprohon's grandson, "the Lt.-Cl. Georges Edouard [*sic*] Leprohon, ... [who] had at least some numbers of the extinct magazine" (68). In the end, the copy belonging to Leprohon's grandson was incomplete. As Deneau explains, "the whole novel was there except for the instalments in three missing numbers" (68). Unfortunately, Deneau does not indicate what happened to the hard copy he consulted, which seems to have disappeared. A different copy was, in turn, discovered a generation later, this time with all instalments intact. In his autobiography, Carl F. Klinck (1991) refers to the unexpected discovery of "an old and rare copy of *The Family Herald*" in "about 1964" at "the office of the *Montreal Star*" (161). As a result of this discovery, Klinck tried to procure a contract with McClelland and Stewart to reprint *The Manor House* as part of the New Canadian Library series (160-61). He was unsuccessful. Leprohon's novel remained unpublished until the appearance of Sorfleet's *JCF* edition two decades following the rediscovery of the rare copy to which Klinck refers. This rare copy of the *Herald* seems, moreover, to have gone missing. Despite my best efforts, I have been unsuccessful in locating a paper copy of the serialization of *The Manor House of De Villerai*. I have thus prepared this edition from microfilm.

THE MANOR HOUSE OF DE VILLERAI, A TALE OF CANADA UNDER THE FRENCH DOMINION

First Instalment of *The Manor House of De Villerai*, *The Family Herald*, 16 November 1859.

CHAPTER I.

The scene, gentle reader, of this essentially Canadian tale, is chiefly laid on the banks of that beautiful river, so remarkable for the quiet gentle loveliness of its shores and that wondrous fertility which at one time obtained for it the name of "the granary of Canada"—the Richelieu or Chambly. The abundance which justified that appellation no longer exists, but its waters are as clear, the verdure of the fields and trees that clothe its banks as bright as ever. The period, however, at which our story opens, was not exactly the one best calculated to display to advantage the natural beauties of which we speak, for it was on a dark wintry afternoon towards the end of December, 1756.

It was the first snow-storm of the season and that magic change wrought within the few hours that the snow had been falling so softly, lightly and yet so busily, was indeed wonderful. A carpet of dazzling whiteness had kindly covered the black unsightly fields and highway, long since denuded of Summer's emerald mantle, whilst the trees were gently bending beneath the feathery burden that clothed their naked branches in such graceful yet fantastic drapery.

In the farm-yards, the humble sheds and out-buildings were transformed into towers and fortifications flanked by mounds of snowy whiteness. The overturned cart—the gate, its rough bars changed to swansdown—even the farm-well with its long threatening arm stretching aloft, had all assumed an unwonted, yet pleasing and picturesque appearance. Standing out—a dark though prominent feature in that still white landscape—was the manor house De Villerai. A plain old-fashioned building of rough stone without the slightest pretensions to architectural beauty, (little thought of in those days,) there was yet an air of solid strength, of substantial comfort about its rude exterior that fully compensated for its deficiency in point of symmetry and elegance. The narrow paned windows, sunk deep in the solid masonry of the walls, were defended by heavy iron shutters, and the doors were secured in like manner,—a prudent measure of defence in those wild days when, in a lonely mansion, the lately deposed Indian lords of the soil might at any unexpected moment venture on terrible reprisals for the wrongs they had themselves endured.

Like most of the country houses of that epoch belonging to the gentry, the hall consisted of a large square room comfortably fitted up with sofas and easy chairs, and answering the purpose of a modern sitting-room. A large double stove stood in the centre of the apartment, and the light that streamed through its loose joints and "cracks" gave, if not as much light or brightness, at least treble as much heat as a grate fire could have done.

Reclining in a comfortable easy chair, within the full influence of the intense heat which the radiant mass of metal emitted, (as a friend of ours sometimes observes, "*stoves were stoves* in those days and were made for use and durability,") was an elderly lady of quiet gentle demeanour. As she sat slowly rocking herself to and fro, she had insensibly suffered her knitting, that infallible resource of elderly ladies, to fall on her lap, and with an earnest thoughtful look she continued watching the figure of a young girl, who stood motionless as a statue in the *embrasure* of one of the deep windows.

The young girl in question was Blanche De Villerai, the orphan *seigneuresse*[1] of the fief of De Villerai given by the French government to one of her direct ancestors for useful deeds of arms done in its cause. If Fortune had been generous in endowing her with wealth, she had been equally lavish of her other gifts, and a figure of striking elegance and grace, combined with the most delicately chiselled features, told that Miss De Villerai in addition to her title of heiress, possessed that equally coveted one of beauty. Some indeed might have thought the features too calm, too expressionless in their chiselled perfection—others might have hinted that the large dark eyes emitted at times too proud and flashing a light, but even the most critical or captious could not but have acknowledged that she was a very lovely being. Whether it was that the chill loneliness but loveliness of the snowy scene without, on which she was then gazing, influenced her mood at the moment, or that her own secret thoughts were not as joyous as those of girlhood usually are, there was a shade of sadness resting on that fair young face that seemed to increase instead of diminishing its beauty. At length, however, her reverie was interrupted by her companion suddenly exclaiming:

"Blanche, dear, what are you doing? For the last three quarters of an hour,"—here she glanced as if for corroboration at the tall old-fashioned clock that solemnly ticked in a corner of the

---

1 "In Canada, the holder of a seigneury; one of the landed gentry" (*OED*).

apartment,—"you have stood silent and immoveable at that window. Ah! I know well what you must be thinking of."

A sudden flush mounted to the girl's temples and with her face still turned to the window, she quickly rejoined:

"'Tis not difficult to divine, dear Aunt.—Dear Aunt, I am thinking of Gustave De Montarville."

"Spoken as you always speak, Blanche, frankly and fearlessly. Yes, what other subject could occupy a young girl's thoughts on the eve of meeting with her betrothed after an absence of several years:—But, do you remember him well, *petite*? You were a mere child when he sailed for France six years ago."

"Yes, dear Aunt, I remember him as he was then, but doubtless he must have changed since."

"Yes, as greatly as you have done yourself my dear. Who would recognize in the *stately* young lady before me, the pale little shy girl in convent costume, who bade such a careless constrained farewell to her boy *fiancé* in this very room. You did not seem to care much for him then, Blanche."

"Oh! I liked him well enough, though not near as much as I liked my kind teacher, Sister St. Mary and some of my young schoolmates but then, we saw so little of each other."

"True, true, and you were always such a distant, impracticable little girl. 'Tis to be hoped, your feelings towards him, will soon acquire a somewhat friendlier character."

"I do not know, Aunt. That depends entirely on himself;" and as she spoke, the earnestness of her look and tone deepened.

"Now, child!" rejoined the Aunt somewhat piqued. "If you do not like him, you have no alternative but to learn to like him. He was the husband chosen for you by your good, kind father, when you were, I may say, in your cradle—he was the husband chosen for you by your dear, good mother, who, when confiding you to my care on her death-bed, solemnly enjoined me to see that that sacred engagement should be fulfilled. Of course, in such a matter, no well-brought up or discreet young lady dreams of having a will of her own. Her parents select. That is their duty—hers obedience."

Blanche De Villerai did not immediately reply, but an involuntary contraction of her dark pencilled brows betokened as plainly as words could have done, that she did not unreservedly assent to Madame Dumont's sweeping doctrine of complete filial submission. A pause succeeded and then the elder lady softly resumed:

"But are you certain *petite*, that he will come to-day? The weather has turned out unusually stormy, and that and the roads being very heavy, for 'tis drifting terribly, may oblige him to defer his visit."

Her beautiful lips compressed, promptly the niece with heightened colour rejoined:—"He wrote to me, Aunt, that he would be here to-day—and, consequently, he *ought* to be here to-day."

"Mercy on us, Blanche!" exclaimed the elder lady, taking off her spectacles and nervously replacing them again, "you are excessively proud. You know our good Curate has indirectly hinted, on more than one occasion, that it was a great pity a *demoiselle* so sensible, religious and amiable as yourself, should ever suffer the failing if not sin of Pride to acquire any empire over her."

"Well, dear Aunt," was the half smiling, half careless reply. "Being as yourself and Mr. Lapointe kindly say, sensible, devout and amiable, if I had not some fault I should be perfect, and we all know that perfection does not belong to mortals."

The old clock here loudly chimed forth the hour of four, and a deeper shade stole over Blanche De Villerai's brow as she turned completely towards the window and rested her cheek against it. The scene outside was growing stormier, more desolate, colder and drearier every hour. In many places, brushwood fence and knoll had well-nigh disappeared beneath the heavy drifts; or like small black, scattered specks amidst an ocean of whiteness and whirling, spray like flakes shewed their tops. The long five-barred gate was elevated into the dignity of a marble wall of tolerable height and width, to which the low fir trees at either side, now thoroughly enveloped in snow, served as bastions. Darker grew the gathering twilight, but softly, busily as before, fell the noiseless snow.

"Blanche, dear," exclaimed at length Mrs. Dumont. "Come away from that lonely window and seat yourself beside me. Gustave is either storm-stayed in some cottage by the road, or else in his comfortable quarters at Montreal. Read from the excellent book, which that good man, Mr. Lapointe, lent us yesterday, a chapter or two aloud. It must interest, instruct and doubtless solace us both, my dear."

Passively the girl obeyed, but if the Aunt derived as little satisfaction or edification from the lecture as did the niece, it was indeed time woefully misspent. Suddenly Blanche abruptly stopped. Her quick ear had detected the tinkle of distant sleigh bells; but, fearing disappointment, she almost immediately resumed her reading. Nearer, however, and more cheerily came the bells, ringing out clearly on the keen wintry air, and now there was no longer room for doubt or uncertainty, for they stopped before the porch. Hurriedly Blanche rose, then resumed her seat, and finally as the heavy iron rapper fearlessly asked admittance, she yielded to a natural feeling of girlish embarrassment, and made her escape from the room.

A moment after, the outer door opened, and a tall manly figure, enwrapped in a shaggy bear-skin coat, and covered from head to foot with glittering particles of fast dissolving snow and icicles entered.

Friendly and affectionate was the meeting between Mrs. Dumont and Gustave De Montarville, and then the newcomer, apologizing, hastily proceeded to divest himself of his outer coat.

"We should have received you, perhaps, elsewhere, Gustave," exclaimed his hostess, "but, here, in this very room in which you parted from your affianced wife,—in which you sat with us so often in old times, do I wish you to meet her again. In a moment Blanche will be here," she continued, replying to the eager questioning glances the young man cast around. "But, if you are impatient, excuse me for a second and I will go for her."

We hope our readers will not precipitately set down our hero as a coxcomb, if we inform them that his first act when he found himself alone, was to spring to his feet and approach a mirror ornamenting the mantelpiece before him. The reflection it rendered back might have satisfied the most fastidious. His tall but slight and elegant figure bore the stamp of energy and activity and showed that he was one who could fearlessly confront difficulties and determinedly surmount them.[1] His hair clustered in thick dark curls around a well-formed head, whilst his features were as faultless as even those of Blanche herself. Splendid teeth and bright dark eyes completed the *tout ensemble* of a countenance which more than one Parisian beauty had found all but irresistible.

"How will she like me and how will I like her," he whispered to himself as he brushed away the white dissolving flakes still nestled in his dark hair. "Terribly awkward interview upon my word. How I wish it were over, but, courage, I must go through it."

---

1 A tear in the original copy text renders the full sentence illegible. After having consulted the French-language translation, *Le manoir de Villerai*, together with Sorfleet's *JCF* edition, I have adopted Sorfleet's resolution: "His tall but slight and elegant figure bore the stamp of energy and activity [and showed that] he was one who could fearlessly [confront] difficulties and determinedly surmount them" (Sorfleet 17).

Barely had he reseated himself when the door opened, and Mrs. Dumont, accompanied by her niece, entered the apartment.

If Gustave were embarrassed, his lady-love certainly was not; for, beyond a certain shy dignity in giving her hand, which he found inexpressibly fascinating, there was no token of the schoolgirl's constraint; and so, soon after their entrance, he found himself conversing with an ease and self-possession which seemed impossible to him a few moments previous. Many and various were the topics touched upon. His ill-fortune which had chained him to a bed of sickness at the very time that his regiment, the Royal Roussillon, with others, had left France for Canada, under the personal command of the gallant Marquis of Montcalm[1]—the brilliant success which had crowned them in the taking of Forts George, Frontenac and Oswego; and his own bitter regrets at having missed such golden opportunities of winning the military fame and glory so dear to every soldier's heart. Then he reverted to his mode of life on the continent, his college successes and defeats, and—topic most absorbing of all—the then disturbed state of Canada, swayed and divided between the dread of England's fast encroaching power and her confidence in the mighty aid of France; confidence which the sequel so little justified. Gustave possessed, in a remarkable degree, that ardent generous love of native land which suits so well the young and brave; and, in answer to some remark which Mrs. Dumont had made, rejoined with heightened colour.—"Yes, dear friend, even if no fair bride had wooed me to Canada, I would yet have hurried back to her forests and snows to draw my sword in her defence." Here a quiet and answering flush suffused the cheek of his betrothed, and flashing eyes gave even surer proof that the noble sentiment had awoke responsible echoes in her own womanly but frank, firm, intrepid nature. There is patriotism out of the sterne sex. Men may dare, but women do endure. Men may falter, women never flinch. Their affections, loves, hatred, die only with themselves. Their patience never tires, their hopes never flag, their courage never fails them in the hour of need. Fire and water cannot stay their settled purposes, especially where affection stimulates.

The evening sped quickly over, and Mrs. Dumont remembering the severity of the weather and impracticable condition of the

---

[1] Louis-Joseph de Montcalm, Marquis de Montcalm (1712-59), commander of the French forces in North America during the Seven Years' War (1756-63), who died at the Battle of the Plains of Abraham on 13 September 1759.

roads, offered hospitality to their young visitor for the night, which was instantly and frankly accepted.

CHAPTER II.

The following morning Lieutenant De Montarville descended early to the sitting-room, and as he had hoped and expected, found Blanche there alone. She frankly gave him her hand, but when he raised it to his lips with a courtly grace and gallantry which had more than once been admired in the gilded *salons* of Paris, accompanying the act with some words of delicate flattery, she calmly replied; "you are not at Versailles,[1] nor in the Faubourg St. Germain[2] now, Mr. De Montarville. We Canadians, are more rugged than the polished people from whom we have sprung, and care little for flattery. Another thing," she quickly but naively added, seeing he was about interrupting her, "'tis quite unnecessary that, because we two are engaged, we should be always acting an overstrained, artificial part towards each other. I will dispense with daily flattery and whispered compliments, whilst you will be equally generous and allow me all the latitude I am willing to extend to yourself." Young De Montarville, somewhat disconcerted by this unexpected 'plain speaking,' merely bowed, rejoining; "As *Mademoiselle* wishes," and then walked towards the window, feeling half tempted to order his *carriole*[3] and brave the mountains of snow-drifts before him, which he inwardly vowed less cold and frigid than his beautiful *fiancée*.

Whatever Gustave's first impulses may have been, he certainly did not act upon them for that day, and yet another saw him a willing guest at the manor house. Blanche De Villerai was too gifted a being to be lightly won or lightly left, and even in her coldest moods extorted the warmest involuntary admiration from her suitor. No great proficient in music, either vocal or instrumental, her chief attraction lay in the resources of her own richly stored mind, and as Gustave listened to her brilliant yet easy conversation, he sometimes wondered how the young girl, in the tenor of her short life, could have acquired such stores of varied information.

---

1 The Palace of Versailles, where the French court was situated from the reign of King Louis XIV in 1682 to the French Revolution in 1789.
2 An aristocratic district of Paris in the seventeenth and eighteenth centuries.
3 "A small open carriage with a seat for a single person" (*OED*).

It was the third day after his arrival at De Villerai, and whilst he and Blanche were warmly discussing some interesting topic, Mrs. Dumont suddenly exclaimed,—

"Do tell me, Gustave, have you not seen your cousin, Mrs. De Choiseul, since your arrival in Canada?"

The young man coloured, and, in a tone of considerable embarrassment, replied in the negative, adding that he "had come direct from Montreal, and that the roads were really so impracticable—"

"'Tis only six miles from here," interrupted Miss De Villerai, with a slight smile, "and I fear that Mrs. De Choiseul may blame us for detaining you."

"There is no fear of that," he rejoined, "but *beau temps* or *mauvais temps*,[1] he would certainly start that afternoon."

The conversation had not yet regained the easy flow which Mrs. Dumont's inopportune question had checked, when that lady's confidential *suivante*,[2] Fauchette, entered the apartment, announcing that "little Rose Lauzon wished to speak for a moment with *Mademoiselle*." "Let her come in," replied Blanche, whilst Gustave, inwardly chafing at this fresh interruption, threw himself into a chair at some distance, and took up a book, indolently wondering what sort of a being the little Canadian *paysanne*[3] would prove to be.

Rose Lauzon entered, and the young officer's glance had no sooner fallen on her than he started and barely repressed in time the expression of admiration that rose to his lips. His amazement was excusable, for the young girl that stood before him, in her dark skirt of home-spun cloth and calico *mantelet*, was as beautiful a being as his affectionate and eagle eye had ever yet rested upon. Rose Lauzon was neither as tall nor as fair as Miss De Villerai, but the clear transparent skin, through which the brightest roses glowed, and the exquisite proportions of her slight, delicate and fine, though small figure, left no superiority in point of attraction to the young *Seigneuresse*. She possessed the daintily shaped hand and foot which are common to her country women, even among the lower orders, and her dark, full affectionate eyes and heavy lashes, harmonized well with her raven hair, so plainly but neatly put back beneath the little stuff hood she wore—a perfect "beauty unadorned" and then "adorned the most." In art,

---

1 No matter the weather.
2 Attendant.
3 "A countrywoman; a peasant woman" (*OED*).

in nature as in dress, simplicity is beauty—taste adaptability to person, circumstance, arrangement! Overdoing is deformity. It were well if Misses and Mammas remembered this more. The pockets of papas would not be taxed, their tempers suffer less and "Caudle lectures"[1] not so often needed and therefore not so inefficacious.

"Oh! what a pity," thought De Montarville, "that so matchless a form should enshrine the undeveloped intelligence of a poor peasant girl," and already he inwardly shrank from seeing the spell her beauty cast over him, dissolved by the accents of the somewhat coarse *patois*[2] in which the good *habitants*[3] of De Villerai expressed their homely thoughts and frank opinions. He was delightfully disappointed, however, as the young girl replied, in a low musical voice, in excellent French, to some remark Miss De Villerai made to her.

She had come to say that Madame Messier, the good curate's widowed sister, who resided with him, taking care of his simple establishment, was confined to her bed by a severe cold and wished to know if Miss De Villerai would superintend Rose in the decoration of the church for the Christmas midnight mass.

Blanche instantly expressed her willingness to do so, and at the same moment put some money into the messenger's hand to purchase some articles necessary for the object in question.

Young De Montarville quickly rose and requesting permission to contribute his share towards so good a cause, placed a gold piece in the girl's palm. Surprised, startled, she raised her bewitching eyes to his face, but instantly bent them again to the ground, whilst a tide of rich crimson suffused her cheek. Was it the eager admiration involuntarily expressed in his face, or a shadow of destiny that swept over her at that moment, discomposing, disconcerting her, till she could only falter a timid word of thanks, and steal from the room?

---

1 "Mrs. Caudle's Curtain Lectures": a comic series of "curtain lectures" (that is, "reproof[s] given by a wife to her husband in bed" [*OED*]) featuring the middle-class Mrs. Margaret Caudle scolding her husband on various subjects, from spending habits to socializing. Written by Douglas Jerrold (1803-57) and first serialized in *Punch Magazine* in 1845.
2 "A ... regional dialect; a variety of language specific to a particular area, nationality, etc., which is considered to differ from the standard or orthodox version" (*OED*).
3 "A native of Canada (also of Louisiana) of French descent; one of the race of original French colonists, chiefly small farmers or yeomen" (*OED*).

"Does not our village beauty, as she is styled, well deserve her title?" asked Blanche.

"Unquestionably, but she appears quite a superior person altogether. Her language and accents are almost as irreproachable as that wondrous pretty face of hers."

"Yes, and there is a degree of refinement about her rarely met with in one of her station, but I can partly explain the reason. When quite a child she was brought into the house to be a sort of companion or playmate for myself, and shared with me the instructions of Miss Rocrai, my governess. When I entered the convent at the age of twelve, Aunt Dumont also sent her there for three years, a favour Mr. Lapointe, our kind priest, himself solicited in her behalf, for Rose is a great favorite with him. At the expiration of that time, she returned home possessed of an education infinitely above her position in life."

"And do you think her the happier for that, Mademoiselle?" inquired De Montarville.

"I fear not," was the thoughtful reply. "Some years ago, her mother, a most gentle and amiable woman, died. The father married again, and his second choice was one calculated to make him daily deplore the loss of the first. Poor little Rose! Hers, I fear, is but a very sad life. I would willingly take her into the house, but she either shrinks from occupying a station, which after all would be merely that of a dependant, (for I could not conveniently make a companion of her now,) or else she remains, out of filial love, with her poor father, whose stay and comfort she is."

Mrs. Dumont here entered with a note which she wished to send to Mrs. De Choiseul.

"I will expect you back, next week Gustave," she said. "We will have a few friends to spend the holydays[1] with us, and you must be foremost on the list. You may bring that young Frenchman belonging to your regiment, that you spoke to us so often about. Even if he is foppish and conceited, he is a perfect stranger in Canada, and besides was kind to yourself in France,—two powerful claims on our hospitality."

De Montarville expressed his thanks, shook hands with Mrs. Dumont and his betrothed, the latter smilingly but firmly forbidding all further display of sentiment, and set out for the residence of his cousin, Mrs. De Choiseul.

---

[1] Days "consecrated or set apart for religious observance, usually in commemoration of some sacred person or event; a religious festival" (*OED*).

"Well, Blanche, how do you like your future husband?" interrogated Mrs. Dumont a few moments after Gustave had taken his departure.

"Sufficiently well from what I have lately seen of him."

"*Tant mieux!*[1] It renders it less difficult to give a definite reply to a question I think it my duty to have settled as soon as possible,—that of the time when your nuptials may probably take place. The sooner the happier for both parties, I think. You know you are nearly eighteen."

"I will never marry him, dear Aunt, till I have learned to love him," was the quiet but determined reply.

"What do you mean, Blanche, in saying that you do not love him? Is he not your affianced husband?"

"Love him, Aunt Dumont," and the fair speaker's lips slightly curled, "why, I scarcely know him yet."

"Well, well," rejoined the elder lady, nervously polishing her spectacles, her usual resource when vexed or troubled;—"a young girl so carefully brought up as yourself, so well instructed in her duties, to talk in such a manner. 'Tis absurd, reprehensible in the highest degree, positively shocking!"

An irrepressible smile stole over her young companion's features at this somewhat singular accusation, but Mrs. Dumont too much engrossed by her subject to perceive it, energetically continued;

"Yes, in my young days, a parent or an aunt presented a gentleman to a young lady, saying, 'here my child is the husband that has been chosen for you,' and the *demoiselle*, if she were discreet and modest, perhaps barely raising her eyes to his face, murmured, ''tis well, I accept him,' and it was *une affaire finie*."[2]

Despite her efforts, a slight laugh broke from Blanche, and she rejoined with a smile;

"Ah! we have terribly degenerated, dear Aunt, since then. Still, methinks, if in the one furtive glance you permitted yourself to steal at my much lamented uncle, the late Mr. Dumont, had you found him either repulsive or disagreeable, you might have hesitated a moment before ratifying the contract."

Mrs. Dumont partly disarmed, smiled in spite of herself, but still as she rose to busy herself about some household duty, she exclaimed; "That would have made no difference, *petite*; I was too well brought up to have a will or a wish of my own."

---

1 "All the better" or "So much the better."
2 "A done deal."

"Do I love him, will I love him?" softly murmured the young *seigneuresse* when she found herself alone. The answer came not; and leaning her head on her hand, she was soon lost in thought.

CHAPTER III.

Some short time after De Montarville's first visit to the manor house, a cheerful party were assembled within its hospitable walls. M. De Choiseul, *Seigneur* of the neighbouring parish, and his amiable light-hearted young wife,—Viscount Gaston De Noraye, Captain in the Roussillon regiment, a young French exquisite of the first water, who had landed in Canada under the impression that he was arriving on the very outskirts of human civilization, a delusion he still persisted in cherishing, notwithstanding the continued proofs he daily received to the contrary,— Miss De Morny, an admired *belle* from Montreal, a graceful though fragile looking girl, with the pale golden hair and deep blue eyes so rarely met with then in the colony. She was very quiet, not to say inanimate, and only awoke to something like interest when the foppish young Frenchman, with his studied smiles and hissing voice addressed her. Others there were too, dark-eyed merry girls, smiling courteous cavaliers, but as these enter not in any manner with the details of our story, they need not be specified.

Playing the part of hostess with rare grace and affability, yet retaining even the somewhat proud reserve which formed one of the most salient points in her character, Blanche De Villerai without desiring it, filled more than one young ardent heart with admiration for herself and envy of De Montarville. The latter seemed both proud and happy in his lot. Ever foremost in every excursion of pleasure, ever imparting the spirit of cheerfulness to their circle by his frank bright smiles and ringing laugh, he was the very life of the party. If anything like a shadow did at times cross his brow, it was when the young Viscount with his listless languid air, commented on the shocking climate, on the incomprehensible customs of the strange land to which he had come. Generally, these passages at arms, of which they had several every day, ended with a laugh or smile on both sides, but an event occurred a little later which threatened for a moment to prove more serious in its results.

Gustave was returning to the manor house in the early twilight of a December afternoon, when at the entrance gate of a lane leading to the back of the mansion, he came suddenly upon the Count De Noraye, who was leaning against it, as if to prevent the egress of a young girl in whom notwithstanding the ample dimensions of the cloak and hood in which she was enveloped, De Montarville instantly recognized the village beauty, Rose Lauzon.

"But, I tell you, *ma belle*," mockingly exclaimed the Count, "you shall not pass in such an unreasonable hurry. Tell me at least your name and residence, and then I'll not only allow you to pass, but may also carry that little basket of yours to your destination."

The girl looked inexpressibly distressed and embarrassed, and in her agitation appeared ten times lovelier than ever.

"Please, sir," she faltered, "allow me to pass. I have no time to lose."

"But I have, pretty one, and in proof of that will keep you here, till you give me your name and place of abode. No, not so fast," he added catching her little hand as she strove to push back the gate. "Now, you are my prisoner and I shall detain you as such till you become more submissive."

Unaccustomed to such questionable marks of gallantry, Rose, after a desperate effort to withdraw her imprisoned hand, burst into tears when De Montarville as every true hero should do, stepped in at the right moment to her assistance. "You will oblige me, Count De Noraye, by letting that young girl pass," he stiffly, indeed angrily exclaimed.

"And, why, my dear Sir, should I do so, till I feel so inclined?" rejoined the other with the most serene though provoking composure.

"Simply, because Miss De Villerai will not easily overlook any annoyance you may cause to a young girl she specially favours and protects."

Yielding to the only threat that could have had the slightest influence over him, for De Noraye though vain and frivolous was brave as a lion, he murmured some words of apology to Rose and instantly drew back to allow her to pass. She quickly did so but not till De Montarville's gaze had again noted her wondrous beauty, so much enhanced by the deep flush of agitation mantling on her cheek.

"Surely, that exquisite fairy-like creature is not a common *paysanne*," enquired the young Viscount, following her receding figure with intently admiring gaze.

"What! is it possible you can admire her, Count?" replied De Montarville sarcastically. "Why, she is merely a Canadian peasant, and—" "Oh! *mon cher*, she is a *houri*,[1] an angel, a goddess!" interrupted the young Frenchman enthusiastically. "She reminds me of those graceful Andalusian peasants we sometimes see represented on the stage in Paris."

"In friendship, I tell you, Viscount," was the low and somewhat stern reply, "that our Canadian peasant girls and those you may have seen in the theatres in France, are somewhat different. Listen, then to a friend's advice, and trouble Rose Lauzon no more." There was a degree of quiet menace in his tones which at other times would certainly have provoked an immediate cartel[2] from his thoughtless companion, but at the present moment he merely said; "pshaw! man, you are simply jealous. I wonder how the beautiful Miss De Villerai would like the wonderful degree of interest you take in her pretty *protégée*. Let us go back to our friends, however, for if we remain much longer here, we shall certainly end by a quarrel and its unavoidable accompaniment 'satisfaction.'"[3] De Montarville accepted the tendered olive branch and they returned to the manor house, conversing amicably together.

Why was it that Gustave was so thoughtful, so silent all that evening? Why did he listen to Miss De Morny's sweet strains, despite his ardent love of music, with such apathetic indifference, an indifference from which the bright smile of his beautiful betrothed at times failed to arouse him? Perhaps he could not have answered satisfactorily, even himself.

It was Christmas Eve. The weather was intensely cold but the bright sun that shone down on the dazzling snow, causing its particles to glitter and flash like diamonds, fully compensated for the keen breath of the wintry atmosphere. The guests of the manor house were wiling the time in whatever way they individually found most pleasant, enjoying to the full, the delightful freedom from restraint, the total *laissez-aller*,[4] so peculiarly the characteristics of life in our country homes.

Mrs. Du Choiseul and several others had gone out sleighing, whilst in the sitting-room, Miss De Morny and Count De Noraye were trying their skill at a bagatelle[5] board, the lady more bent

---

1 "A nymph of the Muslim Paradise. Hence applied allusively to a voluptuously beautiful woman" (*OED*).
2 A challenge, likely to a duel.
3 Meaning a duel.
4 "Absence of restraint; unconstrained ease and freedom" (*OED*).
5 "A game played on a table having a semi-circular end at which are nine holes. The balls used are struck from the opposite end of the board with

perhaps on displaying to advantage her graceful figure and pretty hands, than interested in the success of the game itself—her companion evidently animated by the same laudable ambition. The only other occupant of the apartment was De Montarville, who heedless of his companions, stood listlessly looking forth from the window.

(To be continued.)

[No. 2—Vol. I]   [MONTREAL, WEDNESDAY, NOVEMBER 23, 1859]

CHAPTER III—*Continued.*

Suddenly the door opened, and the young hostess, wrapped up in rich furs, entered the room.

"Where are you going, dear Blanche?" languidly enquired Miss De Morny, turning from the bagatelle board with a wearied look.

"To our little church, to aid in decorating it for the Midnight Mass."[1]

"May I accompany you," interrogated De Montarville, eagerly advancing.

"And I? and I?" chimed in the Count and his companion.

"I suppose there is no use in saying nay," replied Blanche smiling, "but if I recollect aright, Count, you declared this morning at breakfast, that none but bears and such other animals equally well protected by nature against the cold, should venture forth in such weather as this."

"Ah! but where Miss De Villerai leads, we cannot but follow, no matter what may be the dangers or privations that lie in the path," replied the Count, with his most graceful bow. Blanche, without noticing this latter speech, her invariable mode of receiving De Noraye's compliments, told Miss De Morny she would wait till she was dressed, if the latter were really serious in her wish of accompanying her. Of course Miss De Morny replied in the affirmative, and after a half-hour's tedious waiting, her com-

---

a cue. The name is sometimes applied to a modified form of billiards known also as *semi-billiards*" (*OED*).

1 A liturgical tradition in the Catholic Church that occurs on Christmas Eve.

panions saw her return to them, looking very elegant and very charming, in her dark winter dress.

They were soon *en route*, Count De Noraye solacing himself by assuring *la belle Montréalaise*, as he occasionally called Miss De Morny that "the climate of Siberia was mild when compared with that of Canada, and that he wondered the parent government had never chosen the latter colony as a place of punishment for their convicts, supposing that motives of mercy alone had prevented them." They soon arrived at the pretty little church, already decorated with evergreens and festoons, producing a simple but charming effect. Close to one of the small side altars, a niche of fir branches had been formed, and thither Miss De Villerai, after a short but solemn prayer before the chief altar, directed her steps. A careful and skilful work-woman had apparently already preceded her, for the little alcove was charmingly decked out with gauze-flowers and gay-coloured ribbons, whilst reposing on its little couch of straw, lay an exquisite waxen representation of the infant Saviour. Here many a pious-hearted mother in the village had often brought her little ones, and whilst their young eyes dwelt with admiring awe on the *crêche de Noël* (Christmas Crib) in whispers, told them of the wondrous birth of the mighty love—and still more wondrous works of the Babe of Bethlehem, whose image lay before them.

Some little touches however remained to be given to the work of decoration, and whilst Blanche busied herself about them, De Montarville endeavouring to make himself as useful as his limited knowledge of such matters permitted, Count De Noraye and his fair companion amused themselves by examining and laughing at the extraordinary specimens of sculpture in wood which the little Church presented. It must be acknowledged these latter were not a little grotesque in their way. Round-eyed cherubims with puffy distended cheeks—Saints with scowling and implacable features, strangely at variance with the meek sanctity of their characters and calling, all betokening that however great the zeal, and fervent the piety of the Sculptor may have been, his skill was certainly at fault. Blanche De Villerai, however, was one of those who justly think that nothing can excuse irreverence in a place of worship; and, after enduring for some few moments the continued whisperings and suppressed laughter of the two critics, she abruptly turned towards the Count and in a low tone said:

"M. De Noraye will please remember he is in a Church—not a theatre."

"*Ciel!*[1] what a bigot!" whispered De Noraye a moment after in Miss De Morny's ear, to which proposition the latter lady conveyed her ungracious assent by silently but smilingly nodding in the most unequivocal manner. A check was given to the somewhat unpleasant state of feeling beginning to creep over the little party by the entrance of the pretty village girl, Rose Lauzon, bearing in her hand a bunch of geraniums and other humble household flowers, for the manor house could not boast of a conservatory. Timidly, yet gracefully she came on, never even glancing at any member of the high-born group, in the centre of which she now found herself; but with a skill and quickness plainly indicating that the previous decoration of the alcove, was chiefly due to her, proceeded to mingle her floral tributes with the dark green boughs of the evergreens. Once, while in the act of reaching forward, the flower she held in her delicate little hand, fell to the ground. Quick as thought De Montarville sprang forward to lift it, and as he presented it to the young damsel, with the same graceful courtesy which he would have displayed towards Miss De Villerai herself, their eyes for the first time fully met. Rose! gentle pretty Rose! ah gaze not too often into those dark earnest eyes, but turn from the eager admiration expressed in those glances, for what couldst thou and the high-born De Montarville—bewitching the wealthy lover of the *seigneuresse* of De Villerai—ever have in common?

On leaving the church, De Noraye, who still smarted under the uncompromising reproof he had just received from Blanche, and who besides piqued himself on being *tant soit peu philosophe*,[2] exclaimed in a mocking tone, disguised under an apparent desire for information:

"Pray, Miss De Villerai, will you inform us what is the object intended by placing that wax doll in so conspicuous a position? Is it to encourage a love of the fine arts in the vulgar or simply to provide them with harmless diversion?"

"Neither the one nor the other, Count—Methinks you must have entirely forgotten the lessons which, as a Catholic, you doubtless received in childhood, or you would not fail to remember that the image you speak of, is only one of those simple symbols which often bring home to childhood—aye, and to the heart of maturer age as well—more plainly than hours of other

---

1 "Good heavens!"
2 "Even (remotely)" or "ever so slightly a philosopher."

instruction could do—the great truth of the son of God descending from Heaven—taking upon himself our feeble guilty natures—and undergoing unspeakable sufferings for our sake."

Silenced if not convinced, De Noraye made no reply, whilst De Montarville notwithstanding his evident pre-occupation, could not help inwardly admiring the christian[1] courage and consistency of the young girl at his side.

But on Midnight Mass we will not dwell, though painters might have loved to linger on that solemn, strange and motley scene. The feeble sheen of tapers struggling bravely with midnight, darkness—an indistinct and doubtful light solemnly permeating the obscure corners and recesses of the little temple, and forming fine effects of light and shade—the centre altar illumined with brighter lights, yet dimly shewing through clouds of incense—like vapours hovering round it,—emblematic of the homage then swelling up from countless hearts to Him of Galilee, who at that same midnight hour some eighteen centuries before, was born in a stable to teach humility to fallen man—through suffering and forgiveness for him,—and shew unfathomable love by offering Himself up as a willing sacrifice on the accursed blood-stained Cross for his and our redemption.

The impressive ceremony over, the congregation quickly dispersed and the scene outside, soon became as joyous and animated as the one within the temple had been solemn and touching. It was one of those glorious moonlight nights peculiar to northern winters. As if in rivalry of their Queen,—the Lady moon,—myriads of stars twinkled and flashed in the clear blue sky, whilst in one part of the heavens, the Aurora Borealis showed its quivering sheets of phosphorescence, or magnificent and vivid streams of light, from one part of the firmament to the other. The attendance was fully as large as a Sunday at morning service, and the whole front of the space before the church, was filled with *carrioles* and *traineaux*[2] of all imaginable kinds and colours. The horses, coated over with stiff hoar frost, and neighing and champing, were sending up clouds of vapour from their nostrils, whilst their masters were mutually shaking hands or exchanging harmless jests or pleasantries with that imperturbable good-humour which seems the birthright of, so natural is it to, Canadian peas-

---

1 "Of persons and their qualities or actions ... marked by genuine piety" (*OED*).
2 "A sledge, a sleigh; in northern Europe formerly esp. one drawn by one or more horses over snow or ice" (*OED*).

ants. And all this, under the open midnight sky with the thermometer ranging at some 25 degrees below zero, exasperated the chilled and shivering Count De Noraye beyond measure, who, with a contemptuous shrug of the shoulders, murmured,—"What a singular people! Who can comprehend them?" What, perhaps, he comprehended better, was the delicious collation, or *réveillon de Noël*,[1] awaiting them on their return home, and so after imbibing a few glasses of the choice Burgundy which the cellarage of the manor house afforded, he patronizingly declared that the custom was not so bad after all, especially as it came but once a year.

The morning following that of Christmas, De Montarville proposed at the breakfast table that they should get up a snow-shoeing party, the hard crust which had, by reason of a slight intervening thaw, formed on the roads and fields, rendering the occasion most favorable for participating in that healthy and invigorating exercise. De Noraye as usual smiled and sneered, but Gustave who knew that the only effectual means of influencing or silencing him, was to pique his self love, carelessly explained.

"Oh! I would advise Count De Noraye not to join us, for simple and silly as snow-shoeing may appear to the uninitiated, it sometimes proves both difficult and fatiguing though no-ways dangerous to one unused to it."

"Difficult! *mon cher*," echoed the Count. "It really requires some stretch of imagination to believe so. Why?—the whole mystery lies in turning in one's toes, assuming an ungainly, rollicking, awkward gait, and wearing a coarse white blanket coat, and singular livery. But I shall judge again for myself to-day, if you can organize a party."

"Oh! he will have no difficulty in that," exclaimed a chorus of youthful voices. "We will all join." A short time after beheld our excursionists assembled in front of the mansion, the gentlemen kneeling as *preux chevaliers*,[2] in such cases, should do, at the feet of fair *demoiselles*, fitting, and warping, and tying the thongs of the snow-shoes around their daintily moccasined feet and ancles. Some members of the party wore the *milas*, or leggings of white flannel, edged with scarlet cloth or fringe, which, under the circumstances, looked both comfortable and picturesque.

The morning was most beautiful,—large masses of white pearly clouds dotting the clear blue sky. A slight shower of rain

---

1 "Christmas Eve dinner." In Christian tradition, the primary meal of the Christmas season, usually eaten on Christmas Eve or Christmas Day.
2 "Gallant knights."

had fallen during the previous night, congealing as it fell, and no fabled genii of the Arabian nights had ever wrought more wonders with his magic wand than it had done. Every tree, branch and shrub was clothed in glittering matchless diamonds, from which the crimson sunlight reflected a thousand gorgeous hues. A fairy-like, enchanting spectacle, were the grim, lonely old woods extending far away behind the manor house.[1] Their long shadowy vistas, and lofty solemn arches, whose clustering boughs bent beneath their load of brilliants, were all relieved, and softened to the eye by the rich dark emerald hue of the evergreens. To those accustomed to such sights, the scene was grand in the extreme, and some of the company were viewing it with admiring gaze, when De Noraye languidly remarked, "Well now, we only want the blanket and tomahawk to be perfect. How refreshing thus faithfully to keep up the traditionary customs and Costumes of the aboriginal lords of the soil."

Whether the latter part of his speech was said in raillery, or earnest, no one cared to enquire, and the Count soon found that he had quite enough to do to keep up with his companions, and preserve his equilibrium. Most wretched amusement indeed, did it seem to him, and he could scarcely control his impatience at the enthusiastic expression of pleasure ever and anon uttered by some of his companions. Much did he wonder at the apparent ease with which the fairer members of the party maintained the brisk pace at which they had originally set out, and he could not help thinking that if they appeared a little less languidly graceful than the fair French *élégantes* whom he had once regarded as the most perfect type of woman, they looked infinitely more charming, handsome and happy. A light and bracing winter's day brings out Canadian *demoiselles*, of every lineage, in flocks; and then, in all their glory of attire, the exercise they are so fond of—smart walking, which the cold necessitates—displays their grace of gait—gives to the skin a pearly whiteness, and to the cheeks that brilliant soft and roseate hue, which, with the dark bright eyes and heavy lashes so common to the pure Canadian race, at once takes captive and subdues the "lords of the creation," by the fascinating and all-potent spell of pearless[2] womanly beauty. Well

---

1 The word "extending" is obscured in the copy text. Sorfleet wraps square brackets around it in his *JCF* edition (28). Because the French-language translation uses the word "s'étendaient" (45), I have retained "extending" here.
2 Most likely a typographical error for "peerless."

may they love and well enjoy a bright and bracing winter day. Then their easy elegance of gait—lively affability of manner and rosey and healthy look, is doubly charming—their beauty most triumphant—and then the streets of her fair cities bear hourly ample testimony to the simple truth of our description. A bright, cold, bracing winter day—just snow enough—the world abroad—the gladsome smiles and hearty whole-souled laughter, commingling with the sweet jingle—loved music—of countless merry sleigh-bells in cavalcades, is the common glory of the race. By anon, whilst skirting the edge of the wood, the distant muffled sound of the axe suddenly struck upon their ear, and after a moment's consultation, the party turned into a narrow beaten track and soon reached an open space where a couple of hardy *habitants* were at work, leveling the stately trees destined to serve the double humble purpose of barn building and fuel during the winter. One of the men had just applied his axe to a lofty elm that towered proudly above most of its forest compeers and our party stood silently grouped around awaiting its fall. Soon a sort of quivering seemed to run through the old tree, the foreshadowing of its impending doom; then majestically, resistlessly, it bent forward, lower and yet lower, till at length with a crash that reverberated in startling echoes through the woods, it came to the ground crushing all before it in its fall. After the lapse of a few moments, the band retraced their steps, challenging each other to a race in the open fields. Then they halted for a moment's breathing time, and the gentlemen wiled the interval by trying their skill in leaping. Count De Noraye who could never bear to remain a moment in what is familiarly called the "back-ground," advanced to prove his proficiency, and with a vigorous bound sprang forward, but unfortunately in alighting, one snow-shoe caught or crossed the other, and as a consequence was pitched downwards into a deep bank of snow with an impetus that drove him head and shoulders completely into it. The accident we need not say was greeted with bursts of laughter; and, for a moment so general and overwhelming was the hilarity that not one of the party could afford him the slightest assistance. Soon, however, De Montarville came to the rescue, and drew the Count from his snowy bed, but as he was still unable entirely to repress his mirth, he willingly forgave the curses deep and dire, which the gallant Frenchman showered on everything and everybody.

After another hour's pleasant walking, the party returned to the manor house in the highest spirits, and with what Gustave called "magnificent appetites." De Noraye dismissed his unfortunate share in the morning's expedition by vowing that "as it had been the first time he had participated in the senseless and barbarous amusement of snow-shoeing, it should also be the last," and he faithfully kept his word.

CHAPTER IV.

We must ask the indulgent reader now, to leave the pleasant manor house, and enter with us beneath the humble abode of Joseph Lauzon, the father of our pretty Rose. Lauzon was a thrifty, comfortable *habitant*, whose rough but substantial stone house, and neat white-washed out-buildings, all in perfect repair, told that he observed to the letter at least some of the golden rules of agriculturists. We do not pretend to say that his cattle emulated in any degree the prize animals now paraded at our agricultural exhibitions, or that the small scraggy sheep gave promise of turning at a later period into dainty, tender mutton, but they were at least cleanly kept and well attended to. The interior of the farm-house fully corresponded to its comfortable exterior. The most scrupulous cleanliness pervaded every detail from the strips of *catalogne* or home-made carpeting, covering the floor of the best room, to the delf cup-board which adorned its corner, every article of which glittered like a polished mirror. Through the half closed door of an apartment opening off the centre one, glimpses were caught of a high bed surrounded by draperies of spotless whiteness, whilst at the back of the house was the large roomy kitchen with its clean well scrubbed floor, containing no furniture, however, beyond a wooden "settle,"[1] table, a few low chairs, and the large double stove invariably to be met with in every farmer's house.

Seated beside the latter, enjoying the solace of his pipe, was an elderly man, whose features though sad and careworn, bore traces of having been once remarkably handsome. Opposite him, patiently endeavouring to soothe and amuse an irritable, overgrown baby of thirteen months was Rose Lauzon. The sadness that rested on the father's face was in part reflected on the daughter's, and after a long silence, the old man gravely remarked;

---

1 I.e., a wooden seat, or settee.

"yours is a sad life, *pauvre petite*. Oh! why, why, was I ever so foolish as to marry a second time."

Joseph Lauzon had daily repeated this for the last six years, but of course without any good resulting from it.

Rose sadly shook her head, saying:—"'tis useless, papa, regretting the past—it cannot be amended."

"But 'tis a comfort—a relief to me to do so," rejoined her father energetically. "What would become of me without that solace? What would become of me if I could not relieve my heart now and then, by telling you that your stepmother is one of the most ill-tempered, insufferable women living. What sort of a life does she lead us both? Do I dare speak almost in my own house unless she pleases, and then, why should you be obliged to be always nursing and amusing that troublesome imp—why, should you have to put up with her tyrannical scolding from morning till night? Yes, well may I ask:—why did I ever marry a second time?"

Here he sighed heavily—resuming his pipe, and thus went on smoking again as if determined to bid defiance to fate.

Meanwhile the restless little charge in his daughter's arms, tumbled, tossed and kicked, till both itself and its delicate nurse were well nigh exhausted.

"Why don't you slap it—pinch it!" suddenly questioned Lauzon, abruptly taking his pipe from his mouth, and knocking it fiercely against the stove, to shake out the superfluous ashes.

"It can't tell her.—Don't let yourself be worried by *it* also."

This time, Rose smiled, but instead of following a piece of advice, the christian morality of which appeared so questionable, she patted and petted the rebellious morsel of humanity in her arms, till at length in fair despite of itself, it fell asleep. "Thank heaven for that at least!" exclaimed the farmer, as Rose gently laid the infant down in its simple wooden cradle. "Like mother, like child! There is no mistaking to whom that baby belongs!" In his indignation the good man seemed to have almost lost sight of the fact that he was the lawful father of that same refractory youngster.

"But, tell me, Rose," he continued, "now that we can have a moment's quiet talk together,—they begin to whisper in the village that André Lebrun finds you the best and prettiest girl in it, and thinks of placing you mistress over his fine farm and new stone house. If true, what a great piece of good fortune that would be for you, *petite*."

It may seem strange, but, the daughter's delicate crimson lip slightly curled at this latter remark, and she hastily exclaimed. "I assure you, dear papa, I want neither André Lebrun, his farm, nor his fine house."

"Rose, dear, don't be childish. The prospect of such a piece of good fortune should fill you with delight."

"But, papa, surely you who have found marriage so fatal to your domestic peace, ought not to advise me to risk it."

"It was the second marriage, little one:—it was the second that brought me misery. In my first, I was happy as a king. Besides, that terrible stepmother of yours is determined to drive you from the house. What a satisfaction then to leave it for one of your own far finer than that of which she calls herself mistress."

Rose saw that arguing the point as to the advantages likely to accrue from her becoming Mrs. Lebrun was useless, and she therefore contented herself with rejoining, "How could I consent to leave you alone, poor papa? Who would console and cheer you:—who would listen to your griefs and troubles when I would be gone?"

"True, true," sighed her companion. "Old age they say is selfish, and I suppose it is true, for I do not think that I could make up my mind to part with you—still I have often regretted that you refused Charles Menard. He was such a good, well conducted lad and so very fond of you. True, the poor fellow was not rich, and you who are counted the prettiest girl in the whole parish, might naturally look for one of the wealthiest men in it."

"It is not because Charles was poor, dear father, that I refused him. Oh no, but because I did not love him well enough to marry him. I liked him, though, as a brother. Knowing him as I have done since I was a little girl,—I cannot express how sorry I felt the morning he asked me to be his wife and I had to say no."

"Yes, and now that he has joined the soldiers, I suppose we'll never see him again; but hush! here comes *la bonne femme*. What will she begin about now?"

As he spoke,—the door opened and the redoubtable Mrs. Lauzon entered. She was a stout, rather coarse looking woman, apparently about thirty, with bold black eyes and a complexion tanned by exposure, to a non-descript shade between brown and yellow. With a harshness of tone and manner fully justifying poor Lauzon's unceasing regrets over his second hymen,[1] she turned towards Rose, abruptly exclaiming, "What have you done with

---

1 Marriage.

poor little Jacques? Put him to bed of course. Oh! yes, anything to get rid of the trouble of nursing him. And you," she continued, turning sharply upon her husband. "How can you sit smoking and dozing there, when you know there is not a second stick of wood in the house? Do not tell me there is a pile just at the door:—you know well I want it carried inside next the hearth, and laid up." Thus scolding and jerking her things angrily about all the while, at length she passed into the inner apartment to divest herself of her outer clothing. The conviction that her husband and step-daughter had just been enjoying together the luxury of a quiet conversation of which she herself had probably formed the most engrossing topic, exasperated her tyrannical temper beyond all bounds: and in a few moments, she returned with a couple of books in her hand which she threw down on the table, violently exclaiming,

"What is this, *Miss* Rose? More of your nonsense and affected imitation of your betters. Have you no wool to spin—no knitting, washing, sewing, to occupy your dainty fingers, that you can thus find time to play the great lady, and amuse yourself with books indeed."

"It was Mr. *Le Curé*[1] who lent me those last Sunday," rejoined her step-daughter gently.

"Yes, just like the rest of them, he does his best to turn your silly head, though I have told him many a time that you were spoiled enough already. Why, don't you go up to the manor house, and sit with the fine ladies there, grimacing and courtesying. You are too grand for a poor house like this, and the sooner you leave it the better," she added *sotto voce*,[2] as she proceeded to drag a table to the centre of the room and make other noisy demonstrations of being busily employed.

Meanwhile what did Rose do or say during this uncalled for tirade? Nothing. An involuntary quiver of the delicate little lip that seemed formed but for smiles and sunshine, alone betrayed that she had heard it. Alas! experience had bitterly taught her that silent patience was her best, her only resource. The virago of the farm-house was still in full voice, when a tap at the door, followed by the raising of the latch, brought her harangue to a sudden close. "Ah! good evening, André Lebrun," she exclaimed in a friendly tone as a sturdy, rather good-looking young man, dressed

---

1 The parish priest.
2 In a low voice (Italian).

in a *surtout* or *capôt*[1] of the warm home-spun cloth of the country, confined around his waist by a scarlet sash, entered the apartment. There was a certain jaunty self-satisfied air about the newcomer that plainly indicated he was troubled with no misgivings regarding his own merits and importance, and so with easy composure he bade good evening to the elder members of the family, bestowing at the same time what he intended should be a killing bow and smile on Rose.

"Anything new, Mr. Lauzon?" he questioned, as he approached the stove and lit his pipe, which he had first filled from a sort of leathern pouch carried ready for all emergencies, in his breast.

"Nothing, André," replied the old farmer, his countenance brightening at the prospect of a little peace, for his better half was generally on her good behaviour when visitors were present.

A pretty brisk conversation was soon entered upon. Farm matters—the increasing scarcity of provisions—prospects and plans for the spring, were all discussed, each one occasionally giving an opinion with the exception of Rose, for whose benefit it was easy to see, one of the interlocutors was alone speaking. Cleverly as he thought, Lebrun contrived to introduce from time to time into the conversation, remarks tending indirectly to bring forward his wealth, his importance in the village, the flourishing condition of his worldly affairs, and at each diplomatic stroke thus hazarded, he cast a sidelong glance at the young girl who sat so quiet, her head intently bent over her knitting. Nothing of this was lost on the sharp-sighted hostess, who was quite a manoeuverer in her way; and, after a time, she discovered some very important message which her husband must convey to a neighbour's, before the lapse of another second.

"Can I go, *mamma*?" quickly asked Rose, starting up as she spoke.

"No indeed," was the sharp reply. "Remain where you are and finish your knitting." The nominal head of the family, submissively arose, and after donning his outside gear, departed on his mission, while its real chief betook herself to the adjoining apartment to attend to some domestic duties.

(To be continued.)

---

[1] A surcoat, or loose coat, sometimes made with a blanket.

CHAPTER IV—*Continued.*

Whilst Lauzon was drawing on his heavy overcoat, he was assisted as usual by his daughter; and, most admiringly, the young farmer followed every movement of that light graceful figure, thinking, as he marked how carefully, how tenderly, the loving little fingers tied the warm muffler around the old man's neck, what a pleasant thing it were to be so tended and cared for by such hands. Certainly, in some things, André Lebrun, evinced both discrimination and good taste.

As the door closed upon her father, Rose silently resumed her seat and her knitting. For a few minutes longer, Lebrun energetically puffed away at his pipe—then, suddenly laying it down, he approached his fair companion and seated himself beside her. The embarrassing silence which he vainly hoped the latter would break still continued; and, after a cough of desperation, he plunged into the matter with a boldness which many a braver man, in like circumstances, might have envied.

"Have you been thinking, *Mademoiselle*," he enquired, "of what I said to you the other evening coming home from Baptiste Préfontaine's husking-bee?"[1]

Provoking little Rose!—Without raising her eyes she coldly replied,—He "had said a great many things but she was not quite certain to what he alluded in particular."

"Well, I will tell you again, Miss. I said I was the owner of a handsome house and a fine farm, but that I still wanted an object more necessary to my happiness than either of them; and that was a—wife, *Mam'selle.*—You cannot but remember my saying that?"

"Yes, Mr. Lebrun, and I also remember telling you that there were plenty of pretty amiable girls in the village who would make good wives."

"So far so good," rejoined the young farmer, somewhat disconcerted by the coolness of the girl's manner, but still utterly unable to believe that she could in reality prove indifferent to the advances of the best match in De Villerai—the beau *par excellence* of the village. "So far so good, *Mam'selle* Rose,—and now I may as well clear up all further doubts on the matter by telling you that you are the very one I want."

---

[1] A gathering of farming families and neighbours to husk corn.

"I am sorry indeed, André Lebrun, that you have told me this,"—rejoined Rose, nervously twitching her knitting needles and feeling rather vexed with her suitor:—"I am indeed very sorry for you:—But, I can never be your wife."

"What! you will give me a downright determined *no*!" rejoined her companion, in his intense amazement starting from his chair. "You will refuse to become Mrs. Lebrun, with the finest farm—and the finest house in the parish?" He was also going to add—the finest husband but, fortunately, checked the words in time.

"Yes, I must refuse all those advantages, Mr. Lebrun," replied the young girl.

"Is that your final, your last word, Rose Lauzon?"

"Yes, my last," was the low toned but firm reply.

"Then, will you please tell me, *Mam'selle*," he exclaimed, his indignation entirely getting the better of his grief, "who do you want for a husband if André Lebrun, the richest man in De Villerai, a school commissioner, and a magistrate, besides, is not good enough for you. Perhaps, though," he added with a sarcasm which he intended should utterly annihilate his cold-hearted companion,—"*Mam'selle* Rose may prefer some of the fine gentlemen who are visiting at the manor house just now. I must not forget that she writes, draws, and is quite *la grande dame* in her appearance and manners—something quite above a humble *habitant* like myself."

Neither this irritating speech, nor the mocking tone with which it was uttered, produced the least effect upon its object. Calmly and softly she replied, "Why are you angry with me André Lebrun? If I refuse you, 'tis not that I have any disdain of yourself, or of the advantages you offer, but simply because I do not wish to marry."[1]

"But who would ever have dreamed of such a thing?" exclaimed the young man, considerably softened by her gentleness. "The whole village rings with stories of the miserable life you lead here: and I, of course, not unnaturally supposed that you would jump at so good a chance of leaving it."

---

1   A tear in the original copy text obscures the previous two sentences. After having consulted the French-language translation, *Le manoir de Villerai*, together with Sorfleet's *JCF* edition, I have adopted Sorfleet's resolution: "... produced [the least effect] upon its object. Calmly and [softly she replied,] "Why are you angry [with me, André Lebrun? If I refuse you, 'tis not that I have any disdain of yourself,] or of the advantages you offer, but simply because I do not wish to marry" (Sorfleet 35).

"Yes, André, but I would have to leave my father too, and my love for him overbalances, you must know, every annoyance I may have to endure as I am."

"*Mam'selle* Rose, you are an angel!" vehemently rejoined the young man, his eyes, despite his efforts, filling with tears.—"Yes, and I am determined not to give you up so easily. I will wait, and wait, and then, when *la belle mère* (stepmother), will have rendered this house unbearable to you, you will then know where to find another and a better one awaiting you."

Kindly—well-meant though it was in the fullness of his heart's best affection—Rose felt anything but grateful for the hope thus held out to her. However, as her persevering admirer here took up his hat to go, she made no reply, but responded to his somewhat moody "good night" with her usual gentleness of manner. Scarcely had he left the house when Mrs. Lauzon—her unprepossessing features disturbed with passion—burst into the room.

"What is this I hear!" she exclaimed, angrily stamping her foot on the ground. "*You* penniless, wretched, little Rose Lauzon—*you* have dared to refuse such a match as André Lebrun! Are you mad: or, has the little wits you may once have possessed been completely destroyed by those trashy books you are always reading when you get a chance? Do you think I am always going to keep you on hand in this house when there is a respectable chance for you to leave it? Answer me that, *malheureuse!*"[1]

Poor child!—no answer of hers could allay the storm of passion that had thus suddenly exploded over her devoted head; and so, in silence and despite herself, she sat dismayed and trembling—her lips convulsively pressed together to restrain the sobs that struggled in her breast.

"Yes," continued the tyrant, in her anger, perfectly regardless that she was betraying how closely she had been playing eavesdropper. "What a farce, you little doll-faced, useless creature—*you* to tell André Lebrun that you would never be his wife—that *you* could never leave your father. How dare you?"

"What is all this, wife?" enquired Lauzon, entering just in time to over-hear the concluding sentence.

This was the signal for a fresh outburst of wrath,—and Joseph, in order to shield his daughter from its violence, hastily exclaimed,—"Run, quick, Rose! and shut the stable door, which I stupidly left open. Some of the cattle may get out!"

---

1 Wretch.

Gratefully the poor girl seized the pretext of escape thus held out to her, and, in another moment, she was leaning against the outhouse door—its open state was merely a fiction of her poor father's imagination—unconscious, in her fevered, excited state of mind, that she was there exposed, without cloak or covering, to the frosty breath of a keen and biting wintry air. Still no shade of anger or passion passed over that beautiful young face as there, with beating heart, she stood—her hands tightly pressed together and her bosom swelling with suppressed emotion; but there was, instead, an agonized—almost despairing expression, infinitely more sad. At length her pale lips unclosed and her crushed and broken spirit, half unconscious, murmured to herself, "Oh! would not anything be better than the life I lead here! Why!—why should I not become the wife of André Lebrun? And, while yet she spoke, her gaze fell upon the graceful figure of a horseman advancing up the road, who passed some twenty feet or so from the spot where she was standing. That horseman was Gustave De Montarville. On recognizing Rose, which he did at the very first glance, he raised his hat and bowed with courteous deference. The young girl stood gazing after him till he was out of sight. Then slowly turning towards the house again, she shook her pretty head, and murmured as she went:—"Oh! no, never, come what will, never can I marry—never will I marry André Lebrun!"

CHAPTER V.

Quickly and pleasantly at the manor house the days passed over; but, at length the time came for its guests to take their departure. Lieutenant De Montarville saw with mingled feelings of regret and satisfaction the appointed period for joining his regiment draw nigh. Rejoicing in the prospect of that stirring, chivalrous life which his ardent temperament craved, and farther incited by hopes of the military fame—to be won in so sacred a cause as that of his country—there were hours when he almost accused time of lagging in its flight. Again in other moods, he could not, without deep regret remember, that he must so soon abandon the too happy life he was leading and the companionship of the gifted Blanche De Villerai. Did any recollection of a face and form as fair as even those of his betrothed ever flash across his mind? Did no remembrance of the faultless beauty and timid grace of the humble Rose, pretty, gifted Rose Lauzon, ever recur to his thoughts, lingering with, and clinging to them, despite all efforts to drive it away? It may have been so, but the young man shrank from confessing it even to his own distracted heart.

It was a cold snowy afternoon, blustering and stormy. And now the comfortable *carriole* stood in front of the manor house and De Montarville well wrapped in furs, was by the side of his betrothed in the room in which they were first introduced to the reader, both parties looking much more serious than was their wont. The momentary silence was broken by De Montarville, who exclaimed. "By storm and snow was I heralded in, and in storm and snow must I take my departure. But, do I flatter myself overmuch in supposing that my leaving, awakens a kindlier feeling in hearts I could mention than my arrival seemed to do?"

Blanche coloured deeply as she replied, "I will tell you that when next you return to see us."

"You are right, Blanche," was his quick rejoinder, and his eye kindled as he spoke—"I will then be worthier of you, for I will have drawn my maiden sword in a holy cause. Even though I return simple Lieutenant as I leave you, I will be nobler in my own eyes, and, also in yours, I feel assured." Blanche did not reply; but, after a moment, placed her small hand in his and softly said,

"You must go now, Gustave. And—may Heaven guard and protect you—farewell."

Quickly and ardently De Montarville kissed the little white hand he so reluctantly yielded up; and in another second, he was gone.

As the young girl had stood watching at the window for so long a time on the day of his arrival, so did she now, long after his departure, stand gazing forth from it again. Mrs. Dumont who had entered the apartment sometime after, made no comment on her niece's evident preoccupation for, in fact, it secretly pleased her, affording as it did a sort of guarantee that she would the sooner see the wish of her heart,—that wish whose fulfilment she looked on as the chief care of her life,—accomplished.

The regret which young De Montarville naturally experienced on parting from his betrothed was speedily forgotten in the bustle and military activity which he found pervading head-quarters on his arrival in Montreal.[1] Preparations were then making with the view of organizing an expedition for the taking of Fort William

---

1 Garneau's *History of Canada*. [Leprohon's note] [François-Xavier Garneau's three-volume *Histoire du Canada* (1845-48). See Introduction (pp. 16-17) and Appendices D4 and D5.]

Henry at the head of Lake George, or St. Sacrament, as it was also called. Notwithstanding the intense cold of the winter which was one of unusual severity—the thermometer ranging generally from 20° to 27°[1]—a body of 1500 men under the command of Rigaud De Vaudreuil,[2] and the Chevalier De Longueuil,[3] set out on their march on the 23rd of February. The amount of suffering and fatigue endured by this heroic band was only equalled by the resolute courage with which they bore their hardships. They crossed Lake Champlain and Lake George on foot, traversing a distance of sixty leagues on snow-shoes, and dragging their provisions with them in *traineaux*, whilst the snowy ground formed their couch at night—a canvass tent and a buffalo robe being their only protection against the biting cold of our northern winters. On the 18th of March they found themselves before Fort Henry. M. De Rigaud, seeing that the strength of the place would prevent its being taken by storm, was obliged to remain satisfied with destroying all the stores, mills and shipping—in fact everything outside the Fort itself. The attack commenced on the night of the 18th and was kept up till the 22nd under a brisk fire from the English troops, when the assailants, having done all the harm they possibly could, set out on their homeward march. Their return was marked by the same phenomenon experienced by Bonaparte's army in Egypt[4]—which, though occurring under different circumstances, was probably the result of causes almost similar. One third of the detachment were on the way affected by a species of Ophthalmia,[5] brought on as it was thought, by the dazzling whiteness of the snow, and their anxious, pitying companions were obliged to lead them by the hand the rest of the *route*. Happily for them, however, on their arrival in Montreal, they were promptly attended to, and at the end of two days, recovered that precious sight which not a few of them had thought lost for ever.

Eagerly, anxiously, the Colony awaited the succours which they had so urgently demanded from the parent country; but the

---

1 Fahrenheit.
2 Canadian-born Pierre de Rigaud de Vaudreuil de Cavagnial, Marquis de Vaudreuil (1698-1778), the last governor general of New France.
3 Paul-Joseph Le Moyne de Longueuil, Chevalier de Longueuil (1701-78), officer in the colonial regular troops.
4 Napoléon Bonaparte's campaign in Egypt and Syria (1798-1801).
5 "1. Inflammation of the eye; (in early use) *esp.* conjunctivitis; 2. Disordered mental perception" (*OED*).

latter, or rather her ministers, seemed more anxiously bent on furnishing money for supplying the shameless prodigality of the immoral court of Louis XV and his royal favorites, than on protecting their soldiers and colonists, so nobly struggling for independence in a distant land. Madame De Pampadour's sneering declaration that "Canada—a country of frozen deserts and trackless forests—had already cost far more than it was worth" was enough to induce a time-serving ministry to leave that Canada completely to its fate.[1]

After some further time lost in expectation of help from France, Gen. De Montcalm, the French Commander-in-chief, resolved on profiting by the departure of Lord Loudon, general of the American army, who had left New York with part of the English troops for Louisbourg, to renew his (Montcalm's) attack on Fort Henry. In furtherance of this object he concentrated during the following month of July, 7,600 men at Fort Carillon, which became at a later period the important Fortress of Ticonderoga.[2] On the 30th of the same month, the expedition set out under the personal command of General De Montcalm. Accompanying the latter, were the renowned Chevalier De Lévis,[3] created afterwards Marshal of France, his gallant aid-de-camp De Bougainville, equally dear to Science as to Fame from his later important maritime expeditions and discoveries, Colonel De Bourlamaque so universally popular with all classes of society during the campaign of 1758,[4] and Rigaud De Vaudreuil, brother of the Governor General, a man distinguished perhaps more for

---

1 Jeanne Antoinette Poisson, Marquise de Pompadour (Madame de Pompadour, 1721-64), Louis XV's chief mistress from 1745 to her death. The source of the quotation is actually Pompadour's contemporary, the French philosopher Voltaire (1694-1778), who, in *Candide* (1759), famously described Canada as "a few acres of snow" when dismissing its economic and strategic value to France.
2 Now visited by Tourists merely as an interesting ruin. [Leprohon's note] [The site of the important Battle of Carillon (or Battle of Ticonderoga) on 8 July 1758, Fort Ticonderoga has been a popular tourist destination since the early nineteenth century.]
3 François-Gaston de Lévis (Chevalier de Lévis, 1719-87), second-in-command to Montcalm; Louis-Antoine de Bougainville (Comte de Bougainville, 1729-1811), aide-de-camp to Montcalm, famed also for having been the first Frenchman to circumnavigate the globe (1766-69).
4 François-Charles de Bourlamaque (1716-64), to whom *The Family Herald* repeatedly refers as Bourlamarque, an error.

his goodness of heart and devotion to the cause for which he fought, than for brilliant military talents.

The result of that expedition is well known. On the 4th of August the French troops arrived before Fort Henry, and on the 9th it capitulated after a gallant resistance. The terms of surrender were, that the garrison should be allowed to march out with the honours of war, bringing with them arms, stores and ammunition, on condition, however, that they should not take up arms for eighteen months against the French troops or their allies, and that all the prisoners detained in the English colonies, whether French or Indian, should be sent back to Carillon.

The same lamentable occurrence which had distinguished the capitulation of Fort Oswego, tarnished the laurels of this later success. The Indian allies, deprived by the terms of capitulation of the pillage on which they had counted, attacked the English on their retreat, brutally murdering some, robbing others, and taking numbers prisoners. The chivalrous De Montcalm, when informed of these barbarities, exerted himself to the utmost to check them. He obliged his ferocious allies to surrender their prisoners, conducted them into Fort Henry; and, having supplied them with fresh clothing, sent them back to their own country under the protection of a powerful escort. Two hundred prisoners were brought to Montreal by the Indians, and the Marquis De Vaudreuil, having ransomed them at most exorbitant prices, sent them on, in like manner, to the States. Fort William Henry was razed to the ground, and the army re-embarked for Carillon. In all these events, the regiment to which De Montarville belonged—the Royal Roussillon,—took a most active part. Difficult as it was to distinguish himself for bravery where all were brave, the young Canadian was fortunate enough to attract the favourable notice of the gallant De Bougainville, who, perhaps found in his daring, reckless bravery, an answering echo to the ruling impulses of his own breast. With both fellow-officers and soldiers, Gustave was wonderfully popular. The light hearted, almost boyish gaiety of his temperament, a disposition as remarkable for kindliness as courage, and a generosity which placed his usually well filled purse at the disposition of almost any friend who solicited its aid, rendered him an universal favorite.

About this time an event occurred which brought most vividly to his recollection friends he had left in De Villerai. While sitting one evening, in the quarters he occupied at Carillon, a soldier entered to say that a dying man, a young Canadian volunteer, earnestly desired to see him. In a minute he had donned his shako[1] and was on his way with the messenger. Arrived at his destination, one glance at the pale, youthful face of the occupant of that couch of pain, assured him that the latter was utterly unknown to him. He, however, seated himself beside the sufferer; and, kindly taking his hand, enquired if he could be of any service to him. Eagerly the sick man scanned his face, and then, apparently encouraged by its expression of gentle compassion, feebly thanked him, and then added—"report says that *Monsieur* is not only acquainted with, but engaged to Miss De Villerai. Is it true?"

Greatly surprised at this question, De Montarville answered in the affirmative. "'Tis not to speak of her, *Monsieur*, that I have sent for you, but of one as dear to me as that lady is to you. At the manor house, have you ever heard there, or met with, a young girl, called Rose Lauzon?"

Gustave involuntarily started as he answered—"Yes."

"Well, when you return to De Villerai proud and happy, to win your bride, would it be asking too much of you to beg that you would seek out Rose Lauzon and tell her that Charles Menard died, thinking of her, and blessing her with his latest breath. Oh! M. De Montarville, I am but an ignorant humble peasant; but no gentleman ever loved with more sincerity and devotion, than I loved little Rose."

"And does she love you in return?"—questioned Gustave with an indefinably compassionate expression in his full dark eyes.

"Alas! No, *Monsieur*. Had she done so, I might now have been tranquilly working on my farm in De Villerai, for it was not glory, nor love for a soldier's life, that made me join the troops. But when I asked Rose to be my wife, and she said she never could,—kindly, gently though she did so, for she is an angel if ever there was one,—I got desperate, sold off the little I possessed, and, in short, I am here."

With increased kindness of manner De Montarville took the poor lad's hand in his own, exclaiming, "Courage! friend, you will yet get well." "Ah! no," faintly interrupted the other, "Dr. Lebert says this wound in my side is hopeless, and I do not wish it were otherwise. Rose would never be mine, and though I am no coward, I do not care for glory or war. What have I then to live for? Give her, kind Sir, that little packet. 'Tis not much—the few shillings of pay I have hoarded up—but tell her to pray for, and think of me sometimes."

---

1 "A military cap in the shape of a truncated cone, with a peak and either a plume or a ball or 'pom-pom'" (*OED*).

Tears glistened in the speaker's eyes who hastily put up his weak, trembling hand to wipe them away, but he need not have been ashamed of his own emotion, for De Montarville's eyes were brimming over when he took the packet, solemnly promising that it should be faithfully delivered as the dying soldier wished. "And, now, *Monsieur*," continued young Menard, "accept the grateful thanks of a dying man whose last hours you have lightened and cheered. I have kept you here too long."

"Not so, my poor friend," was the gentle reply. "If you will allow me, I will remain with you a little longer. Would you wish me to read for you?" and as he spoke he took up a small manual of prayers that lay on the coverlet.

"Thank you, *Monsieur*. Good Mr. Larue has already been here preparing me for my last long journey, but I would be most happy to hear some prayers read over again."

After reading for some time with a solemnity and depth of feeling, at which some of his gay companions would have wondered, others perhaps smiled, Gustave laid down the little volume, fearing to fatigue his listener, whose thoughts were evidently commencing to grow slightly incoherent. The object to which, ever and anon, his mind recurred was Rose Lauzon; and many an anecdote and little trait of character, he recounted to the earnest listener beside him—all tending to prove that it was not so much the young girl's beauty, as her sweet, womanly disposition and worth, that had won the love of that tender, faithful heart. Gradually, however, his voice became fainter—his steadfast eyes grew dim—the clammy chill of death was on his brow; and between twelve and one—that solemn hour, when the last great change comes over so many suffering mortals—he had quietly passed away into the long, deep sleep of never-ending eternity. Gustave, who had all the while tenderly, carefully watched over him, closed his eyes; and, after a short but solemn prayer beside that lifeless image of mortal clay; with serious, saddened thought and feelings sought his quarters. But he could not keep his heart at rest nor his mind from constantly recurring to the solemn, tender, touching scene—the sweet memories—and undying love of poor Charles Menard, and the lovely, but, alas! not happy young being who had inspired it.

CHAPTER VI.

General De Montcalm would willingly have followed up his late success at Fort Henry by an attack on Fort Edward; but, in the actual state of things, that was out of the question. Famine had been weighing for some time past with an iron hand on the hapless people, and its terrible grasp was daily closing more tightly upon them. The harvest of the preceding year had completely failed in many parts of the country. Owing to this circumstance and to the remissness of France in sending the provisions which had been so earnestly demanded, every article of food rose to an almost fabulous price. To remedy all this as far as possible, the militia were disbanded after the taking of Fort Henry, and allowed to return to their respective homes to assist in getting in the crops. The heavy rains, however, which had so perseveringly fallen during the season again blighted all hopes of relief, and the harvest proved a more complete failure than even the previous one had been. The situation of Canada, despite the success which had generally heretofore crowned her arms, was daily becoming more sad and discouraging. When winter arrived, the army was ordered into the interior, and owing to the extreme dearness of provisions and, the consequent clamours raised against the Government;—which latter were greatly increased by the shameless system of pillage and peculation carried on under the unprincipled Intendant Mr. Bigot,[1] it was late in the following year before De Montcalm could again take the field to watch the movements of the English troops. Sometime after the return of De Montarville and his regiment to Montreal, he obtained leave of absence and set out for De Villerai,—certain of obtaining, after the late successful campaign, a warm welcome from such ardent patriots as Miss De Villerai and her Aunt. In fact, he found himself secretly wishing *en route*, that he had received a sabre thrust or sword scratch to invest him with still higher claims on their sympathies,—"however," he smilingly added to himself, "I will yet have plenty of time and chances to receive both one and the other before the war is over."

His arrival proved as welcome as a ray of sunshine to the inhabitants of the manor house; for the contradictory rumours and statements propagated, or rather fabricated, each successive day, joined to the sufferings of the *habitants*, in consequence of

---

[1] François Bigot (1703-78), intendant of New France from 1748-60, whose tenure was notorious for widespread fraud and corruption.

the increasing scarcity of provisions, which was already beginning to make itself keenly felt throughout the country districts, had cast a gloom over those cheerful walls which they had perhaps never known before. Blanche received her lover with an eager friendliness, doubly flattering in one of her usually reserved character, and De Montarville kept continually asking himself, as much, perhaps, in secret accusation as self gratulation—"Ought he not to feel wonderfully happy and grateful in the love and preference of so noble a heart."

He had not forgotten his promise to Charles Menard; and, the second day after his arrival, he sought the sitting-room with the intention of asking Mrs. Dumont some directions regarding Rose's place of abode. To his surprise, the first object on which his eye rested, on entering the apartment, was Rose herself, who, needle in hand was kneeling beside Mrs. Dumont's easy chair, busily adjusting a new damask cover on its substantial cushion.

On hearing the door open, she looked up and recognized the intruder. A look of startled surprise rose to her face whilst her cheek and brow became crimson. How she hated herself at the moment for that unbidden evidence of emotion—how she blamed, contemned the agitation that caused her little fingers to tremble to such a degree as to render proceeding with her work next to impossible! Her confusion doubly increased when De Montarville approached her and entered on the commission with which poor Menard had entrusted him. With down-cast gaze she listened, never once raising her eyes to his face; but as he went on describing the young Menard's death and repeated the touching message sent her from that dying bed, tears trickled down her cheeks, and dropped like sparkling diamonds on the damask which her fingers still held.

What a fascinating study De Montarville found that sweet young face—how eagerly, how intently he followed each varying emotion that passed across it, unconscious all the while of the expression of deep earnest admiration that rested on his own.

(To be continued.)

CHAPTER VI—*Continued.*

Suddenly the door opened and Blanche De Villerai entered with a gay smile on her countenance; but the brightness of her smile was almost instantaneously checked. Was it that she had divined her lover's thoughts and feelings:—or, was it simply his earnest attitude as he stood there, leaning over Rose, and gazing down so intently into her tearful face that pained her? Certain it is, her countenance became more serious, and she quietly seated herself without bestowing a second look on either of her companions. De Montarville slightly disconcerted, soon came to a pause, and Rose, feeling that his tale was fully told, falteringly thanked him; and, respectfully bidding "Good Morning" to Miss De Villerai, left the room with her needle work. As she passed close to Blanche, the latter bent a quick, earnest glance upon her. There was no jealous anger, no disdain in that momentary gaze, but a questioning, searching expression which would have puzzled Rose strangely had she observed it. Despite all Miss De Villerai's efforts there was a slight shade of coldness in her manner towards De Montarville, who not only felt, but with the singular perversity of many people in similar circumstances, inwardly resented it. Quickly, however, he entered on the tale which he had just related to Rose; and, under the influence of the saddened feelings it begot, the shadow soon passed away from Blanche's brow. The transition from such a subject to the scenes of strife and danger through which he had lately passed was easy; and, for more than an hour, he poured into his companion's ear, tales and anecdotes to which his own matchless style of narrative imparted a peculiar charm.—And then gradually yet almost imperceptibly he came to subjects nearer to them both, hinting at, rather than openly speaking of the ties so holy and binding, which were yet to unite them together.

Very little girlish timidity, still less girlish emotion did Blanche De Villerai betray, as she listened in total silence to the burning words flowing from De Montarville's lips, and when at length he passionately prayed her to name even indefinitely the period within which the promises that bound them should be made irrevocable by the Church's blessing, she raised her beautiful eyes to his face and calmly enquired.

"Did he think that they already knew, much less loved each other enough for that. Enough, enough," she continued, gently raising her small hand as if to check the torrent of protestations ready to flow from his lips. "We are both young, Gustave, and can afford time to wait and sound the depths of our own hearts ere rashly entering on a step which may be regretted but can never be recalled."

De Montarville was pained, piqued, and with a constrained calmness which contrasted singularly enough with his late rapid earnestness, said,—

"But, do you not think, Blanche, that the wishes of our deceased parents, who so earnestly desired our union should be sacred to us?"

"Yes, to a limited extent. If, at the expiration of a period long enough to permit of our becoming thoroughly acquainted with each other, we find that a mutual affection influences and obliges us both, we shall then conform to the sacred wishes you speak of; but, if it should prove otherwise, we shall be free—virtually, unconditionally free."

"And, how long, Blanche, is this period of probation, you have just fixed on, to last?" he questioned, vainly endeavouring to conceal the annoyance and mortification, his countenance as well as his voice so plainly indicated.

"That depends on circumstances," she rejoined with a slight but indefinable smile:—"Perhaps till the war is over."

"It may be that Miss De Villerai calculates on the chances of my being killed in the course of the campaign, thus deciding in the shortest and most decisive manner the unwelcome question of our union," he replied, perversely taking her playful remark in a serious sense.

Again, Blanche smiled, as she rejoined, "If I did make any calculations, Gustave,—which, however, I most distinctly disavow,—they would more probably have been founded on the chances of your rapid promotion, and your soon becoming Major or Colonel of your own gallant regiment."

"True *Mademoiselle*," he replied with rigid gravity. "I must not forget how small a claim an humble subaltern like myself has to aspire to the hand of the *Seigneuresse* of De Villerai"; and, with the boyish petulance which occasionally developed itself in his character, he coldly bowed to his betrothed and left the room.

In another instant he was rapidly striding over the sparkling snow, murmuring to himself,—"Well! whatever now may happen, she will only have herself to blame. I honestly wished to press on our marriage whilst I could yet answer for my own heart and its affections;—but, she refused, determinedly refused, so, betide what will, the fault will. be hers." He might have spoken less hastily had he on his abrupt departure, seen Blanche lean her head on her clasped hands sighing.—"Yes, yes," she murmured, "I have acted for the best. Let him study well his still unsettled heart and prove himself, before ratifying that sacred vow which no man may break. Better for me to suffer a little now in self-love, nay,—even in affection, than be wounded deeply and unceasingly hereafter, as an unloved, perhaps neglected wife."

CHAPTER VII.

It was night, a cold wintry night, but in Joseph Lauzon's comfortable habitation, a more joyous spirit pervaded the atmosphere than that despotic female Autocrat, its mistress usually permitted to reign there. It was the anniversary of her marriage with the unhappy Joseph, that marriage which the latter so unceasingly and so bitterly regretted, and, notwithstanding the small amount of connubial bliss that either party had apparently found in the union, Mrs. Lauzon always persisted in celebrating its annual return with great pomp, betraying thereby a determined obtuseness of judgment, an heroic indifference to the fitness of things, which is often displayed by people in much more elevated stations in life.

Everything was going on most satisfactorily. The dancers were displaying an untiring vigor of limb, worthy of those illustrious religious jugglers, the leaping Dervishes,[1] whilst the orchestra, consisting of one asthmatic violin, was equally indefatigable. The ample supper had been done full justice to; the culinary powers of the hostess praised to an extent calculated to satisfy the most exacting vanity, and that worthy lady full of importance and smiles, for she could assume the latter with Protean[2] facility when she chose, moved about from place to place and from guest to

---

1 "A Muslim friar, who has taken vows of poverty and austere life. Of these there are various orders, some of whom are known from their fantastic practices as dancing or whirling, and as howling dervishes" (*OED*).

2 "Of or relating to Proteus, like that of Proteus. Hence in extended use: adopting or existing in various shapes, variable in form; variously manifested or expressed; changing, unpredictable" (*OED*).

guest, dispensing a pleasant word to each. One o'clock had just struck—the little group around the stove was every moment receiving accessions in the person of some deserter from the dancers. The little circle thus commencing to recruit its numbers so successfully, was enveloped—veiled from the outer world in a cloud of tobacco smoke, which surrounded, over-canopied, clung to them, like that most penetrating thing in nature, a Highland mist; but neither the pungent strength of the Canadian narcotic emulating in power its Virginian rival, nor the intense blazing heat the immense double stove emitted, seemed to trouble in the slightest degree the most delicate member of the company present; it was but the composite indoor atmosphere with which the native Canadian is familiar from infancy. Conspicuous amongst the little circle just mentioned was a tall man of Herculean strength and stature. His thick dark beard, rough and shaggy in the extreme, long straight black hair, a complexion darkened and tanned by exposure, to a hue rivalling in swarthiness that of the dusky aboriginal owners of the land, and a sort of half reckless, half savage character pervading his whole appearance, stamped him unmistakeably as one belonging to that famous class of men, the Canadian *voyageurs*.[1] Large circular gold rings decorated his ears, whilst his feet were encased in Indian moccasins, profusely adorned with gay coloured bead work. This worthy individual whose name was Baptiste Dufauld, excelled most of his contemporaries in three points. He was the most untiring smoker; the most imperturbable drinker—no amount of alcohol seemed capable of affecting him;—and the best story teller in the parish. His legends were as eccentric as they were grotesquely terrible, and the marvellous tales which he had heard amongst his companions whilst braving the cold winters of the North West, or sitting smoking around its campfires, were hoarded up in the capacious store-house of his memory, to be brought forth at every tale-telling emergency. When the party of which he formed so important a member, had wearied of discussing the chances and successes of the late campaign, and of what interested them quite as closely, the reigning famine pressing already heavily enough upon themselves, but crushing so mercilessly the inhabitants of the towns and large villages, Baptiste Dufauld was pressingly called on by several

---

[1] "In Canada, a man employed by the fur companies in carrying goods to and from the trading posts on the lakes and rivers; a Canadian boatman" (*OED*).

members of the group, to introduce a diversion in the night's amusements by relating one of his wonderful tales.

"Yes, yes, Père Baptiste," added one of the young beaux of the village. "And, pray let it be as marvellous and terrible as the two last ones you told us about the headless Indian warrior that hunts by night on the shores of Red River, or the fiery spectral dog that followed a *voyageur*'s canoe for a whole night."

Baptiste Dufauld never required much pressing, and after regarding the last speaker with a steady glance which might have been interpreted either as one of warning or assent, he laid down his pipe, and passing his hand through the broad scarlet sash that confined his stalwart frame, commenced,—first informing his attentive auditors, that the adventure he was about to relate, incredible as it might appear, had been told to him by an uncle of his own, an old *voyageur*, who had himself been the hero of it, and whose veracity had always been regarded as unimpeachable. Either finding it more impressive or dramatic, or else, anxious to confine himself more closely to the original narrative, Baptiste spoke in the first person, always premising, of course, that it was the hero himself who narrated.

"It was a beautiful evening in the month of May. We had just left the Ottawa and were entering the Riviere Des Prairies, on our way to Quebec, bringing with us several bark canoes laden with costly furs and various articles of Indian workmanship, which we had received from the hunters in exchange for our brandy, powder and shot. Being all of us tolerably fatigued with our long day's work, we resolved to light a pipe at the first house we passed, and then let ourselves drift down with the current. We soon perceived on the right bank a light shining through the small half-broken panes of a wretched little hut. Being the youngest of the party, I was deputed by the others to land and ask at the habitation in question, a burning brand for our pipes. I knocked pretty loudly at the door and receiving no reply, unceremoniously entered. Seated opposite each other at different sides of the hearth were an aged couple, a man and a woman, rigid, motionless as statues, and gazing fixedly on the embers of the dying fire. The feeble glare of the latter lighted up the bare whitewashed walls of this miserable habitation whose naked poverty struck painfully upon me, for it contained neither bed, table nor chair, literally nothing. I addressed the two strange personages before me with as much civility as a rough *voyageur* can command, but my politeness was apparently thrown away, for they deigned no reply—they did not even raise their eyes to look at me. I am neither timid nor superstitious by nature, I had besides already met with many strange adventures in the North, but, I will frankly confess there was something in the unnatural, awful immobility, of the two beings before me that almost froze the blood in my veins with terror. Had not the dread of encountering the mockery of my companions, who were impatiently waiting at the beach below, restrained me, I would have abandoned all farther thoughts of accomplishing my mission and fled at once from the house. With the courage of desperation, however, I rapidly, though tremblingly advanced to the chimney place—seized by the yet uncharred end, a lighted splint of wood, and darted from the accursed habitation as swiftly as my limbs could carry me. On arriving at the canoe, I sprang into it with the brand, which it had cost me so mighty an effort to obtain, and passed it to my companions, carefully abstaining from breathing a word of my adventure, which I knew would be received with incredulous shouts of laughter;—wonderful to relate however, the fire I had brought with me had no more power to burn than an icicle. "In God's name!" asked one of the men, who had been perseveringly applying it to his pipe for some minutes without the slightest success, "What does this mean! This fire does not burn."

I was just about relating to them the singular reception I had met with at the little cottage, when all at once the light gleaming from the window of that strange abode burst forth like an immense conflagration and then instantaneously disappeared, leaving us in darkness and awe-struck silence. At the same instant a wild harsh mewling or wailing broke upon our ears, and we perceived two enormous cats, their eyes glowing like coals, swimming towards us. In another moment they were clambering up the sides of the canoes, still uttering the same weird cries. Suddenly a happy idea struck me. "Throw them their light!" I shouted to the man who still held the burning brand. "In Heaven's name throw them the light!" He at once promptly obeyed and the two terrible animals discontinuing their hideous outcries, sprang upon it and fled back to the ill-omened hut in whose window the light soon again reappeared."

Here Baptiste abruptly ceased and resumed his pipe, thereby intimating that his tale was concluded. A short silence succeeded, but suddenly André Lebrun, who as the reader may remember, was our pretty Rose's lately discarded lover, somewhat flippantly exclaimed "A pretty good story, *Père* Baptiste, but rather difficult to believe. I, for one, must acknowledge that I do not credit it."

The old *Voyageur* took his pipe from his mouth, and quietly measuring the speaker with a look of profound contempt, replied, "Of course not, André Lebrun, how should you? The greatest adventures you have yet met with, are probably the killing of some unruly calf for market, or perhaps shooting some peccant crow whilst trespassing on your corn fields."

A suppressed titter followed this sharp rebuke; and the object of it, with a flaming countenance rivalling in depth of colour the celebrated brand which had played so conspicuous a part in the preceding tale, whispered his conviction to the young girl at his side, that "when Baptiste's uncle had seen the wonders just related, it was probably under the influence of deep draughts from the rum or brandy flask, without which no *voyageur* in those days ever travelled." Comments on the late tale were freely passed, some slyly hinting their incredulity, others gravely declaring that things more strange and terrible had often happened before, and would happen still, whilst a third party, prudently fearing to commit themselves, were satisfied with giving a silent shake of the head, which might mean either assent or dissent.

At length one of the "true believers," energetically exclaimed, "*diantre!*[1] Why, should it not be true? I, myself, could tell you a tale and a true one too, just as strange as that which Baptiste has related to us." "Were you the hero of it *monsieur* Michel?" demurely interrogated a dark haired damsel, whose mirthful curving lips, spoke of anything but implicit belief in such wonders. "No, Miss Marie, but I heard it from the son of the man who was, and I hope you'll acknowledge that is sufficient authority for a little damsel like yourself. Well, my tale is about a *Loup-garou*."[2] At this dreaded name, most of the listeners involuntarily began to look serious, for amongst the many strange fictions which the superstition of the Canadian peasants has created, that of the *loup-garou* is one of the most dreaded, and some years ago, was one of the most universally believed. To this day, in some of the out-of-the-way parishes below Quebec, the mention of the name at night, will cause many a cheek to turn pale.

"But, tell us, Mr. Michel," interrogated a quiet little girl of

---

1 "Obsolete French euphemism for diable (*devil*)" (*OED*).
2 Werewolf. In Quebec legend, one risks becoming a werewolf not as a result of a bite from another werewolf, but rather as a punishment for failing to take the sacraments of the Roman Catholic Church, such as failing to go to confession for seven consecutive years, or to take communion at Easter, or to attend mass on Christmas Eve.

fifteen, who was seated near the grey-haired personage she addressed, "what is really a *loup-garou*?" "A *loup-garou*, child, as every one here knows, is a man who has given himself up to all sorts of sin and vice for seven years, without ever turning even for a minute to God. At the end of that time the devil obtains power over him, and turns him into a hideous beast, doomed to wander in lonely places by night till he is fortunate enough to meet with some one who has courage to deliver him, which is done by wounding him sufficiently to draw blood. But to commence my tale. You have been in Montreal, my friends, many of you? Have you not?" Several heads nodded in the affirmative.

"Well, you know the wild, lonely road, leading up by the Côte des Neiges to St. Laurent.[1] Near to where you enter on it, at the base of the mountain, stood in 1706, a little house of most desolate and ruinous exterior. The doors and wooden shutters were always tightly closed, so that naturally the passers by supposed it completely abandoned. The neighbours remembered that this house had formerly been inhabited, though the last occupant had suddenly and most unaccountably disappeared. For several years past, however, no signs of life had been perceived, except at rare intervals during the night, when a pale, tremulous light might be seen gleaming through the chinks of the shutters. Of course this enchanted or accursed habitation was universally avoided. The country beau, on his way to spend the evening with his belle, if obliged to pass at all in its vicinity, described as wide a circle as possible, singing all the while at the top of his voice in order to keep up his courage. A few brave individuals had on different

---

1 This road, now beautified for a considerable extent from Montreal, by elegant buildings and handsome private residences, was at the period of our story, the resort of robbers and marauders, whose deeds of violence were matters of public and daily comment. Sometime in the early part of the last century, the French government with the intention of striking salutary terror into the hearts of these "gentlemen of the road," resolved on making a fearful example of one Belisle, who had been taken prisoner, after previously having distinguished himself by the daring and merciless cruelties of his crimes. He was accordingly condemned to be quartered or drawn asunder by four wild horses, one attached to each limb. The terrible sentence was literally fulfilled, and the criminal's mutilated remains interred beneath the place of execution. A tall wooden cross, painted red, was erected over the precise spot, but at a later period was removed, owing to its obstructing the road, some paces back, where it still stands, a sad monument of fearful crime and fearful punishment. [Leprohon's note]

occasions ventured close to it, but they never repeated the experiment, for the rattling of chains, plaintive cries and strange unaccountable noises that broke upon their startled ears, induced at once a rapid retreat. One day, however, a farmer from St. Laurent, a sober, god-fearing man, was passing by the mountain on a warm summer afternoon. The intense heat of the sun darting down on the dry, dusty road, determined him on resting awhile at the first habitation he should come to, which proved to be one in the neighbourhood of the haunted house. After asking an hour's hospitality from two men who were smoking and conversing together in a corner of the apartment, he seated himself at some little distance, but soon involuntarily became an interested auditor of their conversation. "Do you know, Xavier, said one, that it is not prudent for you to continue living so near that terrible house? I am sure you see and hear strange things sometimes."

"You may well say that," was the emphatic reply, "and of late, things are rapidly growing worse. Often at night, now, I hear the strangest noises, and last night, it was just midnight, and stiflingly hot, happening to put my head out of the window, for a breath of air, I saw not twenty feet from my own door, a sort of large black animal, such as I have never yet seen before, and, which I pray heaven, I may never see again."

"Ah, Xavier! in your place, I would leave here as quickly as possible."

"And so I will, I think. It may be some sort of unholy goblin which may yet work us harm." Here the traveller who had been listening with intense interest to all that had been said, hastily rose and approaching the two men, exclaimed, "excuse me, friends, but I have already heard there was something of that sort in the mountain. Is the house you speak of far from here?"

"About nine acres. 'Tis the third from this. The one between is of course uninhabited."

"I would like to visit it," said the stranger. "Can I?"

"To be sure, but you will likely do as many a brave spirit has done before you, come back quicker than you went."

"Perhaps so, but I'll try. The strange animal you saw was a large, black—"

"Yes, and looked something like a man on his feet and hands."

"Exactly! Thank you, Mr. Xavier, I know now what it is. 'Tis a *loup-garou*."

"Heavens! Is it possible?"rejoined the host.

"Yes, I have already seen two myself—and better than that,

delivered one of them which had been a *loup-garou* for more than ten years."

"*Oh! mon Dieu*! since you understand all that, would you try what you could do for the one we have just been talking about?"

"Willingly. That was my intention from the first." After a few more remarks, every thing was agreed upon, and Xavier and his companion volunteered to share the expedition. "As midnight is the only time in which anything can be done," said the stranger, "we may as well take a few hours' rest and then we will be fresh for starting." At half past eleven that night they were all ready, when the traveller asked for a knife—a strong and sharp one. It was given him. "Now, you can both follow me at a distance, but beware of making the slightest noise. Even a whisper might be fatal to us." The three men now set out, the stranger perfectly calm, his companions, nervous and agitated. It was a magnificent moonlight night, every tree, leaf and stone, stood out as plainly as in the light of day. Cautiously, silently the party proceeded till they were within about twenty feet of the haunted house, when Xavier and his friend suddenly halted, sturdily announcing their determination to go no farther. Their leader offered no opposition to their resolve, and drawing forth his long knife, passed his finger across the blade to assure himself that it was sharp and sure. Then he continued to advance with such precaution that his feet seemed scarcely to touch the earth. After a time he stopped, looked earnestly around. Nothing was to be seen or heard. Another few steps nearer, and then a most terrible out-burst of noise, like the revelry of demons, burst upon his startled hearing; wailings, blasphemies, shrieks, howlings, repeated by countless voices, some wildly imploring, others harshly terrible. For a second he wavered, turned pale, but by an effort he mastered his weakness, and in another moment stood in front of the house, the infernal orgies going on within, increasing all the while in violence. He leaned for support against a tree, and wiped away the cold perspiration bedewing his forehead. After a moment of terrible expectation, he heard a dull, stealthy step. Eagerly he looked around him and by the faint light of the moon then partly obscured behind a cloud, he perceived crouched at one end of the house a black unsightly form. Now was the time for action. With a murmured prayer to heaven, he sprang towards the terrible object and in another moment ran his knife into its side. A weird, unearthly shriek rang throughout the haunted house, and then all was silent, whilst a voice exclaimed, "Midnight! I'm saved!" The next moment a man threw himself into the arms of the intrepid stranger, murmuring, "ah! thanks, Paul! you have freed me!" It was indeed a friend of the traveller's boyhood,—a *loup-garou* for many years, whom his intrepid courage had just delivered. Nothing could induce the lately freed man to ever open his lips with regard to what had happened to him during his terrible captivity, but till the hour of his death he ever retained the warmest feeling of gratitude towards his deliverer."

When Michel had concluded his tale, the doubters if there were any, prudently kept their incredulity to themselves, one of the party merely asking what would have happened if the stranger had failed in his courageous attempt.

"Why, I suppose, the *loup-garou* would have torn him to pieces."

Here Mrs. Lauzon beginning to think the company were growing rather serious for so joyous an occasion, asked one of the young men for a song, in the well known chorus of which the chief part of the company most heartily, if not most musically joined. And now some reader, who, perchance feels interested in our pretty Rose, may ask, "where was she all the evening, that her name during the recital of its events, has never once been mentioned."

We must candidly confess that she was where Mrs. Lauzon (who was most singularly tenacious of her rights as sole mistress of the establishment) always wished her to be as much as possible—in the back ground,—distinguished only from the other young girls around her, by her own rare loveliness and her peculiar gentleness of look and voice. Still despite the latter precious quality, she was pretty generally stigmatized as proud, beyond her station, not only by the young men to whose somewhat broad compliments she listened with such apathetic coldness; but also by her young female companions, who found her a most uninterested listener to their feminine gossip and lengthy discussions regarding the merits and demerits of the village beaux. Poor child! She was indeed sadly out of her sphere amid such scenes—conversing on such themes, and when she laid down to rest that night, it was with an aching head and a weary heart.

(To be continued.)

CHAPTER VIII.

Life was proceeding peacefully enough at the manor house and yet there were times when an observant spectator might have divined that some elements of discord lurked beneath that seeming calm. Blanche, quiet and passionless, went about her ordinary avocations with unruffled tranquillity, but her betrothed was restless, preoccupied, at times almost irritable. Whether it was that his ardent spirit chafed against the perfect inaction, so wearisome to one of his impulsive nature, whether his pride rebelled against Miss De Villerai's somewhat cold reserve, or that some other secret feeling known only to his own heart, annoyed him, Gustave was certainly not as light-hearted and mirthful as on that dark December afternoon when we first introduced him to the reader. Such being his mood, it is not difficult to understand that notwithstanding his apparently enviable position, he saw the period fixed as the limit of his stay, draw near without any very lively feelings of regret. It wanted now but two days of that time, and one afternoon, Blanche being confined to her room by head-ache, he set out for a long walk, glad to exchange the somewhat monotonous conversation of Mrs. Dumont and the intensely heated atmosphere which that worthy lady loved, for solitude and the pure bracing air of the snowy plains without. He walked at a most rapid pace and just as he reached a narrow spot where the lonely country road was intersected by another, he came suddenly and unexpectedly upon Rose Lauzon. He immediately accosted her, with smiling, though deferential politeness, and continued to walk by her side, disregarding in the pleasure of watching her downcast eyes and flushing cheek, her perturbation and the unwillingness she most plainly evinced towards being so accompanied.

In the graceful courteous strain peculiarly his own, he spoke of her father—herself—then he alluded to his own approaching departure, recurred to the mournful fate of young Menard, in short touched on any and every topic that afforded him a pretext for prolonging the enjoyment of the moment. His satisfaction however was evidently unshared by his companion whose nervousness of manner was every moment increasing, till at length unable any longer to control her uneasiness, she timidly exclaimed,

"Pardon me, Sir, but though you are kind enough to overlook that I am but a poor country girl, I must not forget it. We must separate here," and she abruptly stopped, waiting for him to pass on. "Nay, Rose," he kindly rejoined in his softest tone. "This is pushing humility and fastidiousness beyond their utmost bounds. What possible harm or wrong am I doing?" "It is not right, Sir," she rejoined with a little more firmness than she had yet displayed, "that Mr. De Montarville, the rich and high-born *fiancé* of Miss DeVillerai, should walk and converse with an humble girl like myself, as if I were an equal."

"And, do you think, child, I look on you as an inferior?" he passionately rejoined, surprised for the moment out of his self-command. Noting, however, the startled anxious look his last impetuous exclamation had called to her countenance, he softly added,

"Our positions in life, gentle Rose, may be different, but surely human nature is the same in all classes, and we may exchange courtesy and sympathy with each other, without derogating in any manner from what is due to our respective situations in the social scale."

But the pure-minded village girl was no sophist, and she only rejoined with more earnestness than before. "I beg of you, Mr. De Montarville, let me pass! I do not perhaps understand all that you have just been saying to me, but I know it is not right for you to detain me thus. Pray—pray, leave me!" "Well, be it as you wish," he rejoined. "Not for worlds, gentle child, would I trouble or grieve you."

"Too late—too late!" murmured the girl in a voice of unspeakable distress, and, as she spoke, a handsome winter *carriole*, drawn by the smallest but sturdiest of Canadian ponies, approached them at a rapid pace.

It contained the Priest of the village, and as his glance fell on the two young people, he started in irrepressible amazement, but instantly recovering himself, he replied to De Montarville's respectful salutation, by a most frigid bow and casting an anxious severe glance towards Rose, rapidly went on his way.

"Oh! Mr. De Montarville!" passionately ejaculated the girl, whilst the tears gushed to her eyes, "See what you have done!— What will M. le Curé say or think of me?"

"Why, Rose, this is childish," hastily rejoined Gustave, infinitely grieved by her evident distress, but proportionately angry with the good Curate whom he looked on as the sole cause of it. "I will go to the Presbytery immediately and explain every thing, if you wish it; but I must say that if such a trifle possess the power of injuring you in the estimation of Mr. Lapointe, I am really amazed at the narrowness of his judgment."

"Oh! I do not want anything of you, but that you leave me immediately," was the agitated reply.

"So be it, Rose, but first assure me that you freely forgive the annoyance I have just caused you? In proof of that, shake hands and say good-bye, for I leave De Villerai to-morrow. If, like poor Menard, I fall in battle I know your kind heart will whisper to you to remember me, as you remember him in your prayers."

With tremulous agitation Rose placed her slender little hand in his, and yielding to the irresistible impulse of the moment, he pressed it passionately again and again to his lips. Before she had time to chide him, he was gone, dashing onward through the deep snow as if a kingdom depended on his swiftness. Suddenly he halted, exclaiming, "am I mad that I act thus! Why, why did I ever meet that angelic creature, or rather, why am I bound by such close ties of honour to another!"

CHAPTER IX.

That evening, Gustave De Montarville was pre-occupied beyond any degree that he had yet been, and his absent look throughout the long course of the evening, the deep crimson spot dyeing the clear olive of his cheek, told that some powerful emotion was at work within his breast. Mrs. Dumont perfectly convinced that his approaching separation from her fair niece was the true and only cause, was serenely compassionate, and hinted pretty unequivocally that she hoped the time would soon arrive when such painful separations should be at an end. Blanche, more incredulous or more penetrating, did not seem to share her relative's flattering conjectures, and more than one scrutinizing glance she stole towards her betrothed, as he stood looking from the window on the darkening landscape without, or sat silently studying the monotonous pattern of the carpet with downcast abstracted gaze.

The morning of departure dawned, clear, mild and bright, one of those days which make us love stern winter, those days when the tiny snow-birds hover around our dwellings for hours, when in our farm-yards the weary pent-up cattle are released from their tedious dark stables for a while, and stand turning their large patient eyes around them, bewildered by the white dazzling hue every where meeting their wondering gaze.

The two young people, Blanche and her betrothed, were alone in the sitting-room, and conducting themselves 'tis needless to say, with as much strict decorum as if that Princess of duennas,[1] Mrs. Dumont, were presiding in person over their interview; conjectures as to the results of the approaching campaign and the probable movements of the troops, forming, to borrow a somewhat mercantile phrase, the chief staple of their conversation. At length Mrs. Dumont entered and after a few unimportant remarks, turned to her niece exclaiming.

"Do not forget, Blanche, that you promised Gustave some time since, some of those handsome sketches you have made of the scenery in our neighbourhood. There was also a little watch-case in beads and chenille, was there not?"

Blanche replied by a monosyllabic yes, whilst De Montarville was of course profuse in protestations of gratitude.

"Go, my dear," continued the elder lady, "and put them up in a parcel. Some of the very sketches I speak of are lying about, mixed up with the music in the drawing-room—and, listen, Blanche," she continued, as the young girl rose to leave the room, "send some of the girls to tell Rose Lauzon I want to speak to her about some sewing this afternoon."

"Shall I tell Fanchette, Aunt, to go?"

"No, dear, she complains of feeling ill this morning. Let me see, which of them will I send. They have nearly all quarrelled on one account or another with that over-bearing Mrs. Lauzon."

She paused a moment and looked interrogatively towards her companions as if seeking from them some suggestion, when young De Montarville exclaimed, "If you will allow me, Mrs. Dumont, I shall be most happy to fulfil your message."

A flush, a very slight flush, rose to Blanche's cheek at this proposition but she made no remark, and as the unsuspicious Mrs. Dumont exclaimed, "Thank you, dear Gustave, you are always kind—always obliging,—" she quietly left the room.

Not quite at ease with his own conscience for thus seeking as it were temptation, De Montarville set out on his mission, but all self-reproach was soon stifled—forgotten, in the pleasurable anticipation of meeting again the young girl who unacknowledged to himself, occupied already so large a portion of his thoughts. A word of direction sufficed to indicate to him Rose's

---

[1] "The chief lady in waiting upon the queen of Spain.... Any elderly woman whose duty it is to watch over a young one; a chaperon" (*OED*).

place of residence, for he remembered having already seen her in the neighbourhood of her own home on one occasion that he had been taking a ride through the country. He wondered as he walked rapidly on for he had unconditionally refused Mrs. Dumont's proposition of waiting for a horse and sleigh, in what mood he should find the gentle village beauty. Would she evince pleasure, embarrassment, or annoyance on his arrival? He could scarcely decide. Indeed he would have been equally well prepared for any of the three, but he certainly was unprepared for anything like the circumstances under which he was in reality to meet her.

On rapping at the outer door of Lauzon's habitation and receiving no reply, he followed the universally established custom of the country, and entered without further ceremony. The first apartment was vacant but he was left in no doubt as to the inner one being occupied for his ear was instantly saluted by that most disagreeable sound in human nature, the loud shrill accents of an angry woman. At first an expression of simple annoyance and distaste passed across his face, but suddenly that look gave place to one of intense indignation, for a word or two of pleading gentleness uttered in Rose's soft voice, and instantly followed by a stream of vituperative abuse from her ill-matched companion, proved that Rose herself was the object of this outburst of feminine wrath.

"Don't dare to tell me that you can't love André Lebrun, or that you won't marry him!" continued the stepmother, her voice becoming shriller and shriller in its angry intensity. "What right have you to play off such airs and graces just as if you were a lady, you useless, puny, good-for-nothing creature? You should only be too grateful that a man of means like young Lebrun would look at you, instead of choosing some of the other healthy, strong girls in the Parish, who would be a help instead of a hindrance to him. I have already said plainly enough that I do not want to keep you an eternal fixture in my house, and if you persist in thus rejecting every chance that offers of honourably leaving it, I shall know how to make it uncomfortable enough for you, that I promise!"

Unable longer to control his anger, De Montarville flung back the door abruptly, and after measuring Mrs. Lauzon with a glance of scornful contempt, which that strong-minded woman could not but interpret aright, turned to her young companion who stood a few paces distant, tears glistening not only on her long dark lashes, but on her deeply, painfully flushed cheeks.

"Mrs. Dumont wants you up at the manor house, this afternoon, *Mademoiselle* Rose. Can you go?" he enquired, in a tone of respectful deference, which doubly irritated Mrs. Lauzon, contrasted as it was with the contemptuous look the young man had previously turned on herself.

"Can you go! *Mademoiselle* Rose! indeed!" she mockingly repeated. "How grand, how fine we are growing all at once! Why, you will soon be as great a lady as Miss De Villerai herself."

"Silence, woman!" thundered young De Montarville, who was almost as much irritated as the wrathful dame herself.

"This to me—in my own house!" she retorted, meeting his flashing eyes with dauntless courage. "And, who are *you*, my young *Monsieur*, that you should speak to Madame Lauzon in such a manner, beneath her own roof? A fledgling—a little Lieutenant—a raw recruit. You are not our *Seigneur* yet, thank goodness, nor never would be, if Miss De Villerai was of the same opinion as myself, young Sir."

De Montarville barely able to master his passion, made a step towards her, and there was something in the expression of his countenance that quelled in a measure the virago's wondrous volubility.

Daunted but not vanquished, she turned a malicious look on her step-daughter, sarcastically exclaiming. "Ah! Miss Rose, I have found out at last the secret of your rejection of all your humble lovers. When we have a fine town gentleman to fall back upon, we are not likely to look favorably upon poor ignorant *habitants*. But, have a care, *ma belle*, or that dainty doll-face of yours, may yet bring you more trouble than luck."

This was beyond endurance and ere the speaker had quite finished her tirade, she found her arms pinioned in the iron grasp of the young officer, who almost carried her towards the open doorway (through which he unceremoniously pushed her) with a rapidity and ease which indignation alone could have imparted to him, for Mrs. Lauzon was no sylph either in form or weight. Perhaps inspired by salutary awe, for if he had gone so far what might he not do next, or else thinking there was surer and more effectual revenge to be obtained than that of returning and renewing the contest, she snatched down a large shawl hanging on a nail close to the door sill, and wrapping it around her, darted off in the direction of the manor house to relate there her grievances.

De Montarville no sooner found himself alone with Rose, than turning to the trembling agitated girl who had sunk sobbing into a seat, he exclaimed in a tone, touching beyond measure in its deep, tender sympathy:

"Oh! my poor gentle child! what a fearful life is yours! Can you, will you bear it longer?"

Still too much agitated, she made no reply, whilst he inwardly remembered with a strange sinking of the heart, that her only means of escape was wedding one of the rude country boors that sought her hand. The thought was actually terrible to him, and after a moment's mighty inward combat, he suddenly threw his arms around her and drawing her towards him, passionately exclaimed:

"Rose, my peerless beautiful one, you are not made for such a destiny! Confide, trust in me, and my love will shield you now and forever from the sorrows and miseries of life!"

Startled beyond all bounds the girl sprang to her feet and pushed De Montarville from her, whilst her cheek and lips became ashy pale.

Catching her small hand in his, he continued with the same impassioned earnestness: "Yes, you shall listen to me and no one shall come between us. I will bring you with me to sunny France, anywhere, everywhere, so that you will only be mine. Speak, my beloved; shall it not be so?"

But Rose had now recovered her voice, if not her self-possession, and in a tone of mingled anguish and reproach, she faltered:

"What have I done, Mr. De Montarville, that you should outrage, insult me thus? Ah! I had not expected this from you!"

"Outrage—insult"—he wonderingly repeated; and then, as her meaning dawned suddenly upon him, he whispered, whilst his rich tones assumed a deeper tenderness, his dark eyes a softer light: "And think you, Rose, I could seek to injure, to bring sorrow or shame to one I love so well? Ah! no; you are too dear to me for that; and I ask you to become mine, only as my loved and honoured wife—wedded to me before God and man."

For a second the girl raised her large dark eyes and fixed them on his face, as if she would have read into his soul, but the open, noble expression of that manly countenance, told there was no deceit or mockery there; and then whilst her gaze drooped and the warm blood mantled tumultuously over her hitherto marble countenance, she murmured:

"Ah! you should not speak to one in my station thus. Are you not the affianced husband of the good and noble Miss De Villerai?"

"Don't talk of her Rose!" he impetuously, almost fiercely rejoined. "I did not seek her, or single her out as my wife. We were affianced to one another in our unconscious childhood, and must a whim of our parents lay the foundation of wretchedness for us during the course of our lives?"

"But you could not put such an affront on a virtuous highborn lady as to desert her for a wretched peasant girl like myself," was the low-toned reply.

"She does not care for me, Rose, she put off our marriage to an indefinite time when I was heart-free enough to wed her."

"But she never rejected you, Mr. De Montarville, and, till she does, your mutual engagement is as sacred as the plighted word of an honourable gentleman can make it."

"Oh! you will drive me wild, Rose, with your cruel, cold reasoning! You know not how I love, how I worship you! From the first hour my gaze rested on you in the manor house, you have filled my heart. I have striven manfully, desperately, to banish you from the place you had won, without any desire or effort of your own, but vainly Rose, it is destiny! You *must*, you *shall* be mine! I know too that you love me. Your lip would not quiver thus, your colour come and go so swiftly if you did not. Answer, is it not so?"

"I do indeed like you too well, generous, noble hearted Mr. De Montarville," softly rejoined the girl, "to permit you to thus rush into what would prove your ruin. Ah! this madness of a moment would be bitterly expiated by a life time of regret!"

"But, Rose, if you have no pity on me, have at least pity on yourself. What hope of peace or happiness can the future have in store for you, if you continue to dwell beneath the same roof with that accursed woman? And then the terrible alternative! You, with a form and mind which the loveliest might envy, to profane the gifts of God by wedding one of the wretched boors who aspire to your hand."

"Mr. De Montarville," was the distinct yet gentle reply, "I would rather wed one of them, greatly as my very soul might shrink from such a lot, than blight your future life by accepting the hand you deign to offer me. In wedding a lowly peasant like myself, I would at least feel assured of not entailing misery on him, and grief and bitterness on the noble high-minded young lady who has been my kindest friend and protector, she to whom I chiefly owe the little advantages you seem to set such store on." There was a firmness, a resolution, in the gentle voice and lovely face, softened as both were by such exquisite womanly tenderness, that convinced De Montarville, there was no hope for him, and he sadly, gloomily replied.

"You are determined then, Rose, on sealing my misery as well as your own?"

"Oh! no," she rejoined, tears gushing to her eyes, "your happiness and that of Miss De Villerai is dearer to me than aught else and in assuring it, I will best assure my own. Listen to me, Mr. De Montarville," and yielding to the generous enthusiasm that elevated her for the moment above every minor consideration, she laid her little hand on his, exclaiming, "I will tell you what you will do. You will wed the high-born young lady who doubtless loves you well, though maiden timidity may prevent her shewing it—you will make amends to her for the momentary faithlessness of to-day by increased love and devotion, and religion as well as the world's sanction will both smile on your union."

"And, you, Rose, what will you do?" he sadly asked.

"I will never marry," she rejoined, her voice sinking to a whisper, whilst the eloquent blood mantled over cheek and brow.

"Never?" he eagerly repeated.

"Never," was the now clear, firm rejoinder. "I promise in the most solemn manner, never to change my single state."

Had that exquisite delicacy, intuitive to some natures, whispered to that artless child of the country that the promise thus so solemnly uttered was the one best calculated to soothe De Montarville's agitated mind? Certain it is that a calmer expression stole over his features, and when at length she prayed him to return to Mrs. Dumont's and say that she would be with her that evening; he pressed her hand to his lips and hurriedly left the house.

Long the girl stood at the window watching his receding form, and there was a look of proud yet gentle triumph on her young brow as at length she turned from it, murmuring, "Oh! 'tis bliss—rapture enough, that he has loved me—asked me to be his wife! Chivalrous, noble hearted De Montarville, I have made the only return that love and generosity like thine deserved. I marry!—Oh, never! Even when he will be the happy husband of Miss De Villerai, perhaps dwelling in another land, the thought of this proud hour will be a talisman to support me under all the miseries and loneliness of my future life."

CHAPTER X.

Slowly, thoughtfully, Lieutenant De Montarville retraced his steps to the manor house, and even whilst resolving to obey Rose's injunctions to the letter, and atone to Miss De Villerai for his late faithlessness by increased devotion, his thoughts would obstinately wander back to the image of the young girl, who, he felt even now at the moment that he had resolved upon giving her up for ever, was dearer to his heart than she had ever yet been. Admiration for the nobleness of character she had displayed—deep compassion for the sad destiny in which her life had been cast—a secret feeling that told his own deep love was not unreturned, and lastly that solemn promise she had made, over which even whilst inwardly chiding himself for his selfishness, he rejoiced, occupied entirely heart and thoughts till his arrival at the manor house.

With a feeling of embarrassment, he vainly strove to shake off, he entered the sitting-room in which he found only Mrs. Dumont. It would not have aided in dispelling his mental trouble had he known that Madame Lauzon had just left the house, having previously recounted in glowing colours, and of course in the most one-sided manner, to Miss De Villerai and her aunt the late scene at the farm-house. At any other time, Blanche would have instantly laughed such a tale to scorn, but of late, the peculiar interest which her lover seemed to take in Rose had not escaped her, and though she listened to Mrs. Lauzon's tale in frigid silence, it nevertheless sank deep into her heart, awakening some very natural feelings of irritation against the volatile De Montarville. Unwilling to meet him in her then frame of mind, she pleaded a head-ache, and begging her aunt to excuse her to their guest, sought her own room where she paced the floor with a heightened colour and compressed lip which told, perhaps, more of offended womanly dignity than wounded affection. Mrs. Dumont thought not so, however, for as the door closed upon her niece she murmured to herself "head-ache indeed! heart-ache, rather, my poor darling! Ah, this is what comes of protracted marriages, put off according to the senseless caprice of young girls or foolish lovers!"

When De Montarville entered the apartment where the worthy lady sat, he could not have failed observing, had he not been so greatly preoccupied, her unusual coldness of manner. He did not do so however, and simply delivered Rose's message which was received in chilling silence. Suddenly, as if unable longer to control the thoughts surging within him, he exclaimed,—

"What a wretch that Lauzon woman is! How shamefully she tyrannizes over her poor step-daughter!"

Mrs. Dumont made no reply beyond a cold monosyllable, but Gustave unnoticing her reserve rapidly entered on a forcible narration of the scene he had just borne a part in at the cottage. Well was it for it him that he did so, for silence on the topic would certainly have confirmed in the most marked manner, Mrs. Lauzon's distorted relation. Gradually the overcast countenance of his hostess relaxed, and when at length he described the summary manner in which he had ejected the female despot from the very abode where she reigned with such undisputed and sovereign sway, his listener gave way to a hearty burst of merriment. "Blanche must hear this!" she exclaimed, leaving the room.

After a short time she returned accompanied by her niece, who looked paler than Gustave had ever yet seen her do, and that circumstance, coupled with the remorseful feelings which the representations of Rose had awakened in his breast, infused into his farewell, a gentleness, a tenderness in which his manner had of late been, perhaps, somewhat deficient. Still there was a shadow between them, a vague indescribable feeling which rarely exists in that halcyon period when Love, sanctioned and permitted, fills two happy young hearts.

The merry ring of the sleigh bells announcing De Montarville's departure had scarcely died on the silence reigning at the moment, in and around the manor house when Mrs. Dumont, as if following some secret train of thoughts, abruptly exclaimed.

"I do not blame him, Blanche, I blame her."

"Rose, do you mean, Aunt?" asked her companion with a quickness that seemed to tell her thoughts were also wandering in the same direction.

"Yes, just that shy, demure, deceitful little creature. We know well that young men will always smile on a pretty face when they meet one, but they should not receive in return the encouragement she appears to have given Gustave. Well, well, who would ever have believed it! Really, I have not patience to see her this afternoon—I should say perhaps too much. Go and dress yourself, Blanche; a drive will do your head-ache good, and I, meanwhile, will tell Fanchette that when *Mademoiselle* Rose, as Gustave so punctiliously styles her, comes this afternoon, she is to say we are too busy to receive her."

CHAPTER XI.

Still sustained by the high courage which the knowledge of De Montarville's love seemed to have infused into her breast, Rose listened in patient silence to the torrent of stormy wrath which her step-mother poured upon her after her return from Mrs. Dumont's, and then when that terrible tongue was at length wearied, and her own domestic tasks fulfilled, she dressed herself and set out for the manor house. On her way she had to pass the Presbytery and as she glanced towards its windows, she saw the good Priest looking forth, breviary in hand.

He beckoned her to enter, and for the first time poor Rose felt her courage somewhat fail her. She obeyed, however, instantly, and as he led the way to the little sitting-room, kept in such exquisite order by his widowed sister, she perceived even in that passing glance that the expression of his face was one of cold and pained disapprobation. He motioned her to be seated, but still standing himself, he abruptly exclaimed. "What is all this I hear, Rose, about you and young De Montarville? Your step-mother has been here to-day and related to me a story which has filled me with pity and surprise, not to use harsher terms."

"Surely, *Monsieur*, you do not believe all that she says of me?" inquired Rose with tearful eyes.

"In this case, I fear I must, at least in part," was the reply. "My own observation has, I grieve to say, tended to confirm it. Should a modest young girl who values that unsullied name which is her richest possession, stand talking for a half hour on a lonely country road with a gay and fashionable young gentleman, with whom she can have no excuse for conversation whatever? Ah! Rose, beware lest that fair face which a kind providence has given you,—that education which my urgent request obtained for you from Mrs. Dumont, prove not fatal gifts which vanity or passion may yet turn to your destruction."

This reproach from the benevolent curate, who, till now had never even looked coldly upon her, stung Rose to the quick, and involuntarily she raised her crimsoning brow, exclaiming, "But, Mr. Le Curé, what have I done to deserve so terrible a rebuke?"

"Listen to me, Rose, I obtained but one passing glance yesterday at De Montarville and yourself as you stood together in the early winter twilight, but in that glance, I read admiration, passion, in his face;—embarrassment, timidity in yours. Does this look well in the young girl who pushes her reserve with the young men of her own rank so far as to refuse to walk or converse a moment alone with one of them? One question I will put to you, and if you can reply to it in the negative, I will retract and apologize for my suspicions at once. Has Mr. De Montarville never yet addressed you in terms of love or admiration?"

No words could do justice to the vividness of the blush that suddenly overspread his companion's face, dyeing cheek and brow with scarlet, and knowing not how to exonerate herself without compromising De Montarville, she stood with bent head and down-cast gaze, looking as guilty as even Mrs. Lauzon could have wished her to do.

More gravely and coldly than he had yet spoken, Mr. Lapointe resumed,

"Rose, I am answered! Unfortunate child! has it come to this? Had not your own maidenly reserve; your gratitude to Miss De Villerai; power to preserve you from the snares into which vanity has led you. Have I watched over you from childhood, directing, exhorting, encouraging, and all to such little purpose?"

The stern voice which the good priest had assumed at the commencement of his address, involuntarily changed to one more consonant with the usual gentleness of his character, and when he concluded, his tones were faltering with emotion. Rose hesitated no longer. She knew that with him her secret would be sacred, and to remain under the disapprobation of the kind friend and protector of her youth, was more than she felt called upon to do. It was therefore with burning cheek, faltering voice, and many an embarrassed pause, that she recounted what had passed between herself and Gustave De Montarville.

Of course she did not weave into her narrative, the impassioned vows and protestations of the young lieutenant, but enough she told to prove that his honourable affection for herself, was only equalled in nobleness by her own generous abnegation, and grateful devotion to Miss De Villerai's happiness.

Proudly, approvingly, the worthy priest listened to her tale and when she had finished, he exclaimed, "you have acted well, my child, and God will bless you; still, I fear if you persist in keeping this secret from all but myself, the breath of blame will not leave you untouched. You were seen with him yesterday, alas! by more than myself, for André Lebrun, who was passing through the fields at some distance from the high-road, perceived you both and was here this morning early to tell me of it; then your step-mother gives a most exaggerated account of his visit to your abode to-day. The world is very prone to believe evil of others."

"It may believe what it likes," sighed the girl, "but I cannot, I must not set it right. Think you, *Monsieur*, that Miss De Villerai, who is so high spirited, would ever look at her lover again if she knew what had passed between us? Think you that M. De Montarville himself would not bitterly regret after a time, the fair, noble, young wife he had forfeited for the sake of a passing fancy? And, then, kind good Mrs. Dumont, her whole heart is wrapped up in the fulfilment of this marriage. Oh! no; my happiness is not to be put in the balance with theirs; and, no matter what I may have to suffer, the path of duty lies plainly before me. You have kindly promised me secrecy, *Monsieur* le Curé!"

"Yes, my child; and, if you insist, I shall keep my word; but, do you not think it would best ensure your happiness, Rose, and silence effectually at the same time all the unpleasant gossip which will be circulated about you if you were to wed some good respectable young man in your own rank in life?"

"But who would take me now, *Monsieur*, after all that has lately passed?" demurely enquired the young girl, casting down her bright eyes.

A humorous expression flashed across the priest's face, as if he somewhat doubted the extent of his young companion's apparent humility, acquainted too as he was with the circumstance of her having unqualifiedly rejected all the suitors who had hitherto presented themselves. Gravely, however, he rejoined:

"Not so, my daughter. This very morning, André Lebrun in informing me of your delinquency of yesterday, added in the same breath, that the only effectual means of guarding you against the insidious seductions of this gay young officer, would be to wed you to a worthy *habitant*, offering generously to come forward himself for the purpose, and requesting me to use my influence to obtain your consent."

As near an approach to a pout as her gentle nature would permit, curled Rose's little crimson lip, and she decisively exclaimed:

"Never, never, M. le Curé! Please tell André Lebrun that I will never marry him, nor," she mentally added "any one else!"

"Enough, my child—I will not press you. Heaven in its own good time will bring about all things for the best. 'Tis a weighty burden that your young life has embraced to-day. May you have strength to worthily bear it!"

With returning emotion the kind-hearted priest bade her

farewell, and saw her go forth on the world, with the secret which was to bring so many weary hours of sorrow and loneliness to her young heart.

On calling at the manor house, she found that the ladies were absent, but Fanchette told her to return the following afternoon, when she would probably find them at home.

It was with a presentiment of coming trouble that she timidly entered the ensuing day the sitting-room in which Mrs. Dumont and her niece were seated. The reception she met with fully justified her fears, and whilst the elder lady sternly exclaimed, "I have something to say to you, Rose Lauzon, which it grieves me to the heart to have to say," Blanche, who had ever previously greeted her with a kind look and smile, now stooped over her embroidery in affected unconsciousness of her presence.

"There are strange reports rife in the village, about you, and M. De Montarville." It was with an effort the old lady pronounced the latter name, as if it mortified her pride even to mention the fact.

A bright flush rose to Blanche's cheek, but it instantly receded, leaving her even paler than before; and looking earnestly into Rose's agitated countenance, she impetuously exclaimed:

"Speak, Rose! tell me that it is false! I know it is. You whom I have always treated almost as an equal—a sister—you have not plotted thus against my honour—my peace!"

Oh! how deeply this touching appeal affected the young girl, even to the inmost recesses of her being, and how hard that whilst she was sacrificing every hope, every feeling of her warm young life for Blanche De Villerai, that she must pass in her eyes for a worthless ingrate, an intriguing despicable hypocrite. Acutely did she feel the bitterness of the chalice, which she had, in her own noble forgetfulness of self, raised to her lips, and unable to frame a reply, she burst into a passionate flood of tears.

"Oh! I thought as much!" exclaimed Mrs. Dumont with an angry countenance. "Tears! tears, indeed! They are an excellent answer when one has not a better to give, but that cannot explain nor excuse your long twilight walk with Mr. De Montarville of which I was informed on good authority to-day, nor your touching interview with him yesterday in your mother's cottage."

"Have patience yet a moment, Aunt," interrupted Blanche, whilst her very lips became pale with emotion. "Speak out, fearlessly, Rose. Explain everything if you can. Tell us that 'tis not you who have striven to win my affianced lover from me, but that he has sought you out—followed your footsteps to whisper his vows to an unwilling ear. In a moment I can free him—restore him his liberty if he covets it."

This was what Rose dreaded, and clasping her hands, she sobbed forth, "Oh! Miss De Villerai, I have nothing to say. Question me no farther on the unhappy past."

"I told you so, my niece," exclaimed Mrs. Dumont triumphantly turning towards Blanche who had listened to this implied confession more in sorrow than in anger. "I told you so, but you would not believe me. Yes, 'tis just as I divined. This vain silly girl priding herself on her pretty face, has striven with unmaidenly eagerness to attract the admiration of a young gentleman belonging to a rank in life which should have utterly precluded such a thing, and who more than that, should have been sacred from the attacks of her vanity, being as she well knew the betrothed husband of the benefactress of her childhood. Go, unworthy girl, never to re-enter beneath this roof for whose hospitality you have made so base a return.—Go, but, beware lest that beauty which you perhaps now prize above all other things, prove no better than a curse to you!"

Sobbing passionately, Rose passed silently out and it needed all the strength she found in the recollection of the gratitude she owed both De Montarville and Blanche, to support her under this most bitter trial. Poor child! It was but the preliminary to many others, for her reception at the manor house soon became public through the officiousness of Fanchette, who had always felt secretly jealous of the affectionate preference the young *Seigneuresse* on all occasions displayed for the village beauty. That incident was enough to confirm every idle tale, and the petty shafts of malicious gossip—of poisoned calumny, of envious distraction were soon showered upon her defenceless head. The young girls shrank from her as if they feared moral contamination, the beaux of the village whose vanity her coldness had often before mortified, openly avoided her, whilst her home, that mockery of a sacred title, became more insufferably wretched than ever. It was indeed enough to make her regard the day on which she had first met Gustave De Montarville as the most unfortunate of her sunless life. But did she do so? No! fond childish dreamer! The remembrance of his love, seemed now the dearest portion of her past existence all the more precious from the misery it had entailed on her, and like some priceless gem in the depths of a dark mine, it lighted up the dreary gloom that at times filled her heart.

But two kind friends remained unchanged mid all those who had grown cold or indifferent. Her poor father, who without explanation or excuse from Rose, felt perfectly convinced that she was irreproachable, and the gentle parish priest, whose increased kindness to herself, drew forth many a biting remark on his perverse blindness and unconquerable obstinacy.

CHAPTER XII.

The winter proved long and tedious to Gustave De Montarville, and yet it was not that the good town of Montreal in which his regiment was stationed, was either dull or inhospitable. True, at that early period of our annals, nothing could surpass the complete isolation which the winter with its frozen rivers and lakes— its deep snow and trackless wilderness brought with it. Then there was no going over to Europe in December, none of our later wondrous facilities for travelling, and beyond the few Indian hunters and that equally hardy venturesome race, the Canadian *voyageurs,* none entered or left the colony during the six months that the Frost King reigned with undisputed sway. This very isolation, however, seemed but to give a greater and more lasting impulse to the social feelings of a pleasure-loving people, and balls, *soirées* and sleighing parties, following in endless succession, robbed the season of all dreariness.

The winter of which we speak, owing to the insecure state of the colony, threatened by a mighty enemy without and famine within, was far inferior in point of gaiety to other years when Canada was in a more peaceful and prosperous state, but still there were many, who from pride or choice, kept up the old spirit of pleasure and routine of dissipation.

Pre-eminent favorites in most of the gay saloons of the day, were the fascinating officers of the dashing Roussillon regiment, that to which De Montarville belonged, and of which he was considered one of the most irresistible cavaliers. Invited everywhere, compelled by the mingled raillery and solicitations of his companions to accept the invitations constantly showered upon him, a prouder heart even than that of Blanche De Villerai might have trembled at times for his allegiance. Without reason, however, for neither the sparkling *piquante* daughters of the wealthy citizens who so gracefully dispensed the hospitalities of their elegant homes, nor the stately *demoiselles* of the old *noblesse,* whose names, borne by elder branches of their families, were then ringing in the courts, the cabinets, the battle-fields of Europe, had power to estrange Gustave's heart from the little village of De Villerai and those it contained.

It was a grand reception night at the old Chateau, the temporary residence of the Marquis of Vaudreuil, and now the unpretending site of the Jacques Cartier Normal School.[1] This simple building, humble in its exterior, is yet rich in historical reminiscences to the student of Canadian history, and though boasting neither towers, dungeons nor fortifications, not even a murderous loop hole through which to point a cannon, it offers instead as magnificent a view from its eastern windows as the skill of the painter could imagine or portray. The isle of St. Helen's with its dark wooded dells, slumbers in summer beauty amid the bright sapphire waves of the St. Lawrence, whilst far to the east stretch plains of emerald verdure and distant mountains, which rise calm and solemn against the clear sky.[2] The *château* was built by Claude De Ramezay,[3] Governor of Montreal towards the beginning of the sixteenth century, and it saw assembled within its walls at different periods of his long administration, the most illustrious personages and distinguished officers of the Colony. The expeditions to the north-west—councils of war—conferences with the Indians and annual fairs, drew to Montreal, not only the Governor General, the Intendant and their respective suites, but crowds of the most remarkable personages of all classes. Sold in 1745 by the heirs De Ramezay to the East Indian Company, it was used for a time as a store-house for all sorts of merchandise, whilst in its vaults and cellars were piled the costly furs which the Indian hunters usually sold for trifling sums, far below their real value. Bought in 1750 by Mr. Grant,[4] the *château* afterwards passed into the hands of the government and became the official residence of the Governors of Montreal.

It was in this very building then, familiar to so many of our readers that Mr. De Vaudreuil held the grand *levée* at which all the rank and beauty of the city and its environs were expected to be present. What invested the event in question with double interest in young De Montarville's eyes, was the circumstance that Blanche De Villerai, who had just arrived in town with Mrs.

---

1 The Jacques Cartier Normal School opened in March 1857 with a mandate of training teachers for the Catholic schools of Montreal.
2 M. Hospice Verreau. [Leprohon's note] [Hospice-Anthelme Verreau (1828-1901) was a French-Canadian historian who, at the time *The Manor House of De Villerai* was published, was Principal of the Jacques Cartier Normal School.]
3 Claude de Ramezay (1659-1724).
4 William Grant (1744-1805), known also as William Grant of St. Roch.

Dumont, was to be presented, and make her *début* in the gay world of which she was so well calculated to be an ornament.

The important night came, the vice-regal residence was blazing with wax tapers, and though the casements were thickly encrusted with glittering frost, the heavy crimson curtains sweeping the ground within, imparted an air of cheerful warmth in striking contrast with the severity of the weather without. Animated—brilliant indeed, was the scene. Here gay cavaliers whispered and flattered whilst lovely ladies blushed and listened—there wily statesmen and distinguished soldiers discussed topics of engrossing interest often touching the very existence of the colony itself.

The French officers in their handsome uniforms seemed special favorites, at least with the younger ladies of the company, but whilst the greater number of them were waiting on and doing the agreeable to their fair friends, three or four young exquisites stood in a group near one of the doors, criticizing and commenting on the company in the most unsparing manner. Though some of the charming faces around them might have successfully competed in loveliness with the most renowned court beauties of Europe, these young gentlemen found nothing to admire, and the words "no style—no fashion,"—were disdainfully re-echoed from lip to lip, and invidious comparisons made between the Canadian *belles*, and some Countess A., or Duchess De B., whom the very particular young aristocrats in question had known and admired in France. Foremost among these latter in languid insolence and sublime self-conceit, was Gaston De Noraye, and as he took a last deliberate survey round the room, of course *lorgnette*[1] in hand, he coolly declared his intention of not dancing that night because he really saw no partner fit to dance with. The words had scarcely died on his lips when Blanche De Villerai, dressed with elegant simplicity but looking as graceful and stately as a young queen, entered the chamber.

"Ah! there is really beauty and style! who is she?" were the quick exclamations of the group of critics, but De Noraye without waiting to give them any information on the subject, instantly deserted the group, and in another moment he was at Blanche's side, eagerly soliciting her hand for the next dance. She replied with a cold self-possession which however, in no degree disconcerted the applicant, that it was already promised. "Would *Mademoiselle* favour him then for the following?"

---

[1] "A pair of eye-glasses held in the hand, usually by a long metal, ivory, or tortoise-shell handle" (*OED*).

The reply was in the affirmative, and as he turned away, De Montarville came up and he and Blanche were soon dancing together. Unanimous was the praise bestowed upon her by the party which De Noraye immediately rejoined, and the very pride of manner and look, the cold stateliness which many found Miss De Villerai's greatest drawback, was in their eyes her chief charm, united as it was to her extreme youth. Then her title of wealthy *seigneuresse*, and the proud ancestral claims of her family, invested her with additional charms, and De Montarville was unhesitatingly voted a most fortunate and enviable individual.

At once Miss De Villerai became the fashion, and the ardour and devotion of her numerous admirers, was only equalled by the calm indifference with which she received their homage.

Towards midnight, Gustave tired or wearied, was standing in the recess of one of the deep windows, his gaze absently resting on Blanche as she glided through the figures of the dance, when Colonel De Bougainville passed. He paused a moment beside the young lieutenant, and following the direction of the latter's looks, smilingly exclaimed,

"Watching your prize, Mr. De Montarville? You may well do so for she is a very fair one, methinks one of which many a young gallant would willingly rob you if they could." Gustave started and his face became crimson. Not of Blanche De Villerai was that perverse heart dreaming then—not of the glittering scene before him, but of a peasant girl in an humble village home, need we tell the reader who?

The gallant Colonel involuntarily smiled at the young man's confusion, of course misinterpreting the cause, and courteously bowing, passed on.

That entertainment was succeeded by others, and where ever Miss De Villerai went, she was courted and admired, but, neither the homage she received, generally so agreeable to the young and beautiful, nor the sparkling gaiety and novelty of the life on which she had entered, occupied or gratified that innocent yet proud young heart. It was ever with a feeling akin to weariness that she attired herself for the scenes of pleasure which others of her age usually seek with such joyous eagerness, and after the first few weeks, it was only in compliance with Mrs. Dumont's wishes that she participated in them at all. Sincerely happy was she then when the near approach of the penitential season of Lent, gave promise of a cessation from the winter's glittering dissipation, and of a speedy return to her loved country home.

She was sitting alone one afternoon in the drawing-room of the handsome roomy house they occupied in the east end of Notre Dame Street, then the most fashionable quarter of Montreal. Sadly she watched from the window, the leafless branches of the stately trees surrounding the ancient College of the Jesuits,[1] which latter building has long years since given place to our modern court-house, and ardently she longed at the moment for the quiet woods and almost unbroken solitude of De Villerai. Most disagreeably was her *rêverie* interrupted by the announcement of a visitor—the Viscount De Noraye. It was certainly an unpropitious moment for him to arrive, but never dreaming that so irresistible a cavalier as himself could be at any time unwelcome to any daughter of Eve, he entered the apartment where she was seated with a most provokingly complacent smile on his lip.

After a few moments of general conversation, he enquired with more earnestness than his usual flippancy of manner often permitted him to assume, "Was it really true that Miss De Villerai was thinking of returning to the country the following week."

"Yes, without doubt," was the indifferent reply.

"But, why should it be so?" he pressingly asked. "Why should Miss De Villerai deprive so soon her numerous friends of the sunshine of her presence?"

Blanche was so much accustomed to similar speeches that this platitude merely wearied her and she deigned no reply, but her look grew more serious, when the count after a somewhat extraordinary and high-flown preface expressive of his love and admiration for herself, concluded by asking her to share his title and estates in sunny France.

The young girl's brow became crimson and in a voice in which surprise and annoyance struggled for the mastery, she enquired, "If the Count was not aware that she was engaged to Mr. De Montarville?"

"Of course," was the unmoved reply, "but, still he dared to hope that that circumstance would influence in no manner the favorable answer he trusted to receive to his suit."

---

1 "A member of the 'Society of Jesus,' a Roman Catholic order founded by Ignatius Loyola in 1533, and sanctioned by Paul IV in 1540" (*OED*). In New France, the Jesuit colleges provided a classical education to boys. Leprohon refers here to the Jesuit College and Residence, which became Montreal's Court House in the mid-nineteenth century.

For a moment Blanche was silent through indignation, and then her delicate lip curling in scorn, she exclaimed, "Your simple mention of my engagement, Count De Noraye, is answer sufficient to your offer."

"But, *Mademoiselle*, if I mistake not, that engagement was entirely the act of your parents."

"Nevertheless, Count, till now we have held it sacred," was the frigid reply.

"And you actually refuse then to become Countess De Noraye?" enquired the young man, his countenance alternating between incredulity and irritation. "You will sacrifice the brilliant position I offer you, an honoured title which would bring you consideration even among the proud *noblesse* of the Court of France, wealth unbounded enough to satisfy the aspirations of a *millionaire's* heiress. If you think I exaggerate, speak to the Marquis De Vaudreuil, for he knows the De Norayes well, and he will tell you if the heir of their house is a *parti* to be refused for the fancied claim of an obscure Canadian Lieutenant. Take care, *Mademoiselle*, that even beautiful and courted as you are, regret may not yet be yours, if you persist in your unreasonable refusal."

The sublimity of the Count's self-conceit moved Blanche as much to mirth as anger, but still she could not help replying, "To be frank with you, Count, even if I were not the affianced wife of Mr. De Montarville, I would nevertheless decline the honour of becoming Countess De Noraye."

"So much the worse for yourself, *Mademoiselle*," was the easy reply. "I offered you a destiny such as this barbarous land of snow and savages could never have afforded you. You have declined it. I have but to say farewell, and wish you all the *humble* felicity which a union with Lieutenant Gustave De Montarville can confer."

Gracefully, carelessly the Count bowed himself out, and Blanche, scarcely knowing whether to feel vexed or amused, turned to the window to resume her former lonely pastime of watching the old trees swaying and bowing in the bleak March wind.

CHAPTER XIII.

Spring had set in, its first advent marked by melting icicles dropping from the roofs, by brown tracks and blotches staining the spotless purity of the winter snow, by the balmy soft winds playing so lovingly about all they met and whispering hopefully of coming sunshine and sweet spring flowers. In our stern clime in which during six long months we look on nothing but ice-bound rivers and bleak snow-covered hills and plains, the return of spring is an event which fills the coldest heart with pleasure, and forces the most enthusiastic lover of winter to acknowledge that it is time for his favorite season to give way to another. How heartily do we welcome the song of the *rossignol*,[1] even the hoarse unmusical cawing of the crow. How joyously do we notice the budding trees—the young shooting grass—the early violet. How eagerly we bend over the blue waters of lake or river, rippling in golden sunshine and how disdainfully we smile at the ice and snow still lingering here and there along the shores, knowing well that in a few additional days even this last vestige of conquered Winter will have vanished.

In her own pleasant country home, Blanche De Villerai solaced her loneliness by following all these changes, never wearying of watching that lovely Spring sky, of studying each change of the wakening earth.

Her parting with her betrothed on leaving for De Villerai had been calm and undemonstrative—her own gentle self-possession never varying for a moment. De Montarville, anxious, eager to repair the past, to fulfil the pledge he had given to Rose, shewed much more agitation and emotion than he had yet betrayed, and he was conscious of a secret feeling when he turned again into his quarters, after his farewell interview with Blanche, that the best thing that could possibly happen to him for both their sakes, during the coming campaign, would be the encountering of a stray bullet, which whilst putting an end to his life would also definitely terminate all his doubts and mental struggles. Active stirring occupation however, that best panacea for a restless unhappy mind or heart, was before him, for early in the summer, the Marquis of Vaudreuil received intelligence that a large body of

---

1 Nightingale.

English troops under the command of General Abercromby, was collecting at Albany with a view of making an attack on the important fortress of Carillon or as it was also styled, Ticonderoga. Immediately, therefore, a large body of troops including a detachment of Gustave's regiment, were collected, and on a lovely summer day, the expedition set out. Leading the van were the *batteaux*, containing stores, field pieces and ammunition, whilst the French soldiers and Canadian volunteers followed in the bark canoes which the Indians had taught the latter to guide with a dexterity rivalling that of the red men themselves.

What a solitary yet magnificent journey was that before them. With what intense, never wearying admiration did De Montarville and some of his companions gaze on the changing features of the lovely scenes through which they journeyed. That lonely silent river on whose mirror-like bosom they speeded on— the beautiful regions bounding its banks, with their bewildering depths of forest rich in the brilliant colouring of their summer foliage—the dark green pine-clad mountains towering to such lofty height above the spreading plains clothed in the velvet verdure of early June. Nor was the silence totally unbroken; the sweet song of the nightingale—the hoarse unmusical cry of the beautiful blue Jay—the monotonous noise of the bright hued wood-pecker, boring the trunk of some mighty lord of the forest whose destruction it was thus so perseveringly ensuring, all these sounds so strictly in unison with the scenes through which they passed, added a fresh charm to their wild and tedious journey. Nor were the very difficulties of the route which occasionally presented themselves in the shape of boiling rapids, dangerous or impassable breakers, obliging the troops to disembark and march on shore, unwelcome to these young adventuresome spirits. At length on the twentieth of June they arrived without accident at their destination.

On the 1st of July,[1] the Marquis of Montcalm sent forward Colonel De Bourlamaque with three French regiments, whilst he advanced with those of La Sarre, Languedoc and Roussillon as far as the falls where they encamped. The next day Colonel De Bourlamaque reconnoitred the mountains to the left of the camp and sent forward two companies to gain intelligence of the approach of the English army then at the farther end of Lake George. On the 6th of July, the advanced guard of the English was

---

1 William Smith, Esq. [Leprohon's note] [For an extract from Smith's account of the Battle of Fort Ticonderoga, see Appendix D3, p. 246.]

perceived and Bourlamaque retreated to Montcalm who had taken possession of the heights. Here, the chief engineer Pontlevoy had thrown up entrenchments and had formed a strong abbatis with felled timber. On the retreat of Bourlamaque, a French detachment lost their way, which the English under Lord Howe,[1] a young nobleman of most promising talents, encountered and routed with considerable loss, taking many prisoners. This trifling advantage was dearly bought with the death of Lord Howe who fell in the very beginning of the action. The state of Massachusetts with praise-worthy liberality erected a monument to his memory in Westminster Abbey.

On the 8th of July,[2] under the burning heat of a noon day sun General Abercromby with his gallant army of well drilled troops, advanced proudly confident of victory against the Fort of Carillon. General De Montcalm obliged to atone as much as possible for his numerical deficiency by the skilful disposition of his soldiers, entrusted the defence of the Fort itself to 300 chosen men, whilst the greater body of his army were spread out to defend the intrenchments. The gallant chevalier De Lévis who had only arrived that morning, was charged with the command of the right wing, Mr. De Bourlamaque of the left, whilst the centre division including De Montarville's regiment, the Royal Roussillon, was commanded by De Montcalm in person. At half-past twelve the advanced guard retreated within their lines, exchanging a brisk fire with the English infantry. General Abercromby[3] had divided his army into four columns in order that the enemy might be attacked on all points at the same moment. The grenadiers and picked men chosen to head the columns, received orders to advance against the intrenchments with fixed bayonets, and reserve their fire till they should have forced an entrance within them. At one o'clock the columns were in motion, and leaving the wood which had hitherto sheltered them they descended into the gorge fronting the intrenchments and advanced with the most admirable order and precision. The right column soon opened a vigorous fire on the French, whilst the left endeavoured to penetrate into that part of the works defended by Mr. De Lévis. The latter divining the intention of this detachment, composed of gallant highlanders and stalworth grenadiers, ordered the native Canadian troops forming his extreme right wing, to make a *sortie* and attack the foe in flank. The Canadians were divided into

---

1   George Augustus Howe, 3rd Viscount Howe (c. 1725-58).
2   Garneau's *Histoire du Canada*. [Leprohon's note]
3   General James Abercromby (1706-81).

four brigades, respectively commanded by M.M.[1] De St. Ours,[2] Raymond,[3] De Gaspé,[4] De Lanaudière,[5] and they were successful in obliging the attacking column to soon fall back to the right. For three long hours the English supported a charge with the utmost gallantry and under the most discouraging circumstances, but at length after prodigies of valor on both sides, Gen. Abercromby perceiving there was no hope of success, and anxious to prevent a total defeat, took measures for the retreat of the army, which retired unmolested to their former camp with a great loss of killed and wounded, including a large number of officers. Abercromby unwilling to stay in the neighbourhood of the French army, retired to his *batteaux*, and re-embarking his troops, returned to the camp at Lake George. Mr. De Bourlamaque was severely wounded but afterwards recovered. The conduct of Montcalm excited much praise. The disposition and arrangement he made, shewed his judgment and talents as an officer, and gained him the approbation of his sovereign and thanks of his country. But what of Gustave De Montarville whose name we have barely mentioned whilst enumerating the above events? Had he occupied a post of importance there is not the slightest doubt but that history would have handed down his name to us to be remembered and cherished, but, unfortunately, though a braver and more dauntless heart never beat in soldier's bosom, he was but an humble Lieutenant and his deeds of valour destined to remain in comparative obscurity. And yet dearly did he purchase his share in the day's glorious events, for when Abercromby's troops returned to make their last grand onslaught on the French lines, their murderous fire told terribly on their adversaries and among those severely wounded was Gustave De Montarville. A bullet from the unerring rifle of a tall English soldier shattered his arm, lodging itself in his shoulder, and faint from pain and loss of blood, he reeled after a few moments and fell to the ground. A few hardy men of his own company immediately raised him in their arms and carried him to the rear. On their way they encountered the Chevalier De Lévis who had just been exchanging a rapid word with De Montcalm, and as his eye fell on the death-like face of the young Lieutenant, an expression of deep regret passed over his features.

1　French *Messieurs*, or Misters.
2　Pierre Roch de Saint-Ours (1712-82).
3　I was unable to find birth and death dates for Lieutenant de Raymond.
4　Ignace-Philippe Aubert de Gaspé (1714-87).
5　Charles-François-Xavier Tarieu de La Naudière (1710-76).

"Not dead?" he hastily ejaculated.

"No, *Monsieur*," respectfully rejoined one of the men, "He has only fainted."

"*Tant mieux*! He will recover yet, and if he does," he murmured, as he rapidly passed on, "I shall take care that he will be fittingly remembered."

The following day when the definite retreat of General Abercromby was ascertained, the greatest satisfaction reigned throughout the French camp, but Gustave racked by pain, tossing on his restless, fever haunted couch, knew nothing of that general joy. De Lévis, mindful in the midst of the many engrossing subjects that occupied his time and thoughts, of the gallant youth whose bright handsome face and daring courage had so strangely interested him, found out De Montarville's quarters and hastened to them as soon as he could find a moment's leisure. On entering, he found the regimental surgeon standing by the patient's couch. "Well, Doctor, have you good hopes?" he rapidly enquired, earnestly scanning Gustave's flushed though sunken countenance. "Yes, Chavalier," was the respectful reply, "but the great degree of fever accompanying the wound, makes me less sanguine than I would otherwise be. In any case he will have no farther chance of winning laurels in this campaign, for his recovery will be slow and tedious." "Oh! if he recovers at all, it will be enough, for he is sufficiently young to be able to lose a year or two in inaction, and besides, I shall take good care that the gallantry which has cost him so dear, shall be reported in the proper quarters. Poor lad!" and he kindly smoothed back the heavy rich curls that clustered damp and neglected about De Montarville's temples. "There is one young heart I know of, that his loss would sadden if not break!"

"Ah! yes," rejoined the physician; "in the height of his delirium the name of Rose was ever on his lips."

"Rose!" re-echoed the Chevalier in evident surprise, for a naturally tenacious memory assured him that that was not Miss De Villerai's name. "Well, 'tis fortunate for him," he inwardly thought, "that during this sickness he is not tended by his LadyeLove. Surely the heiress of De Villerai is a fairer prize than any Rose that he can covet."

After courteously commending De Montarville to the Surgeon's particular care, he took his leave inwardly pondering on the strange perversity and fickleness of the human heart.

Skilful medical attendance and a naturally good constitution soon placed Gustave out of danger, but for many long weary months he remained feeble as a child, whilst his arm supported in a sling, gave little promise of becoming soon serviceable. Fate however was not entirely unpropitious, and his promotion to the rank of Captain some time after, served in some slight degree to compensate for the days of pain and weariness which had fallen to his lot. To follow up in detail the later successes or failures of the French arms, the limits of our tale will not allow, but we may briefly mention a few of the most striking vicissitudes that befell the colony. One of the most important results expected to arise from the late victory was the influence it would probably have in securing at least the neutrality if not the alliance of the powerful tribe of Indians called the Five Nations. Without delay then the Chevalier De Longueil was sent on this important mission,[1] having previously forwarded to them quantities of presents, thus ensuring his overtures a favourable reception. He was pretty successful for the Indians in their answer assured him of their attachment and friendly feelings.

Close upon the late victory, followed the taking of Fort Frontenac by the English under Col. Bradstreet[2] who after destroying it and many other buildings, recrossed the St. Lawrence on his return to Albany. De Montcalm however sent on a party, with the chief engineer Pontlevoy, and rebuilt the Fort and at the same time another reinforcement was pushed on under command of Capt. De Montigny to strengthen the garrison of Niagara and give assistance to M. De Lignières at Fort Duquesne, if assistance should be wanted there. To the reduction of Fort Frontenac succeeded that of Fort Duquesne, the name of which was changed to Pitt or Pittsburgh, by the conqueror, General Forbes, who after strengthening it with a powerful garrison returned to Philadelphia.[3]

The misery and distress that reigned throughout the Colony became finally so great that the Intendant issued orders that horses should be killed for the sustenance of the inhabitants and

---

1 Paul-Joseph Le Moyne de Longueil (Chevalier de Longueil; 1701-78). According to Andrew Rodger, in July 1758 de Longueil was sent "on a diplomatic mission to Cataraqui (Kingston, ON) and Chouaguen (Oswego; today Oswego, NY) to induce the Iroquois to support the French" (Le Moyne De Longueil, Paul-Joseph, *Dictionary of Canadian Biography Online*, accessed 2 May 2013).
2 John Bradstreet (1714-74).
3 Jean-Baptiste-Philippe Testard de Montigny (1724-86); François-Marie Le Marchand de Lignery (de Lignières, 1703-59); John Forbes (1707-59).

troops in the cities of Quebec and Montreal. An officer of note was also dispatched to the court of France that he might faithfully portray the terrible sufferings of the colonists, and urgently solicit the necessary relief, and though he started very late in the Autumn, despite of storms and tempest, he reached the shores of France in safety.

CHAPTER XIV.

The misery which was weighing so heavily on the inhabitants of the towns and cities was also filling with want and sadness many an humble country home, which a season or two previous had been the abode of comfort and plenty. Foremost among the sufferers, was Joseph Lauzon. He had at one time been ranked among the wealthiest farmers of the district, and it was supposed that his daughter Rose would have been able to bring another dower to her husband beside her rare beauty, but the entire failure of his crops for the last two or three years had greatly altered his circumstances. Towards the end of the winter poor Joseph was visited by a severe fit of illness from which he never rallied. After wearisome struggles with his daily increasing weakness and the disease which was slowly but surely sapping his life, he was obliged to abandon completely, the tillage of his farm. He had no sons to replace him, and labourers where the army had drawn off so great a portion of the rural population, were almost impossible to get, or were too exorbitantly high in their demands; so Lauzon's fields remained uncultivated, beyond a couple acres which some charitable neighbours ploughed and sowed for him. For the last two months the poor man had kept his bed, and he was now only waiting, as he expressed himself, for the final order from heaven to depart on his last long journey.

Soothing him in his hours of physical pain, cheering him in those of mental despondency, his daughter Rose, like some gentle angel was ever hovering about him, shedding a ray of happiness over that passage to the tomb which would have been indeed desolate without her ministering love.

Poverty and privation, so far from softening Mrs. Lauzon's tyrannical nature, had but rendered her more violent, more overbearing than ever, and Rose, the chief object of her malevolence, would long before have left for ever her wretched home had not love and pity for her helpless father kept her by his side. For him she patiently waited and suffered on. Well divining the strength of her filial love, Mrs. Lauzon most ungenerously profited by it, to almost daily taunt her unhappy step-daughter with her continuing to live on in their poverty stricken household to which she was an additional and unwelcome burden. This was unjust in the last degree, for Rose, an adept in all the mysteries of housekeeping and the management of dairy and poultry yard, was of priceless value in the establishment, a truth which Mrs. Lauzon, who the chief part of the time was completely engrossed by the care of her four troublesome ill-brought up children, often secretly acknowledged and experienced. The small sums of money, however, which Rose occasionally continued to make by the exercise of her needle, were always laid out in the purchase of some little dainty or delicacy likely to tempt the feeble appetite of her sick father.

It was a beautiful afternoon in October, that month when our forests stand forth in such unrivalled splendour and rich variety of tint, when the crimson and golden glories of the sky above seem reflected in the gorgeous foliage of the forest trees, that Rose Lauzon was returning at a rapid pace from the village, to which she had been on some errand. Keenly sensitive as was her refined imaginative nature to the beautiful, the loveliness of all around struck not on her sad heart that day. The gush of golden sunshine flooding the earth with light, the bright dyed woods skirting on one side the little path through which she passed, won not even a look from her. Those soft mournful eyes saw but the withered leaves strewing the damp dark earth at her feet. Hurrying on, she soon reached the cottage, and gently raised the latch. How the eyes of the sick man, who had been pining and watching for her return, brightened when she entered, and what a world of tender love, of mingled gratitude and parental pride, was expressed in the look he turned upon her as she softly approached and seated herself beside his bed. "See, dear Father," she exclaimed, taking out from a small basket she had carried on her arm, some bunches of fine garden grapes. "See what Madame Dubuc, our lawyer's kind wife gave me in return for the trifling sewing I found time to do for her this week. And this also," she added, placing a small silver coin beside the fruit. "You remember, dear father, saying some time ago that you felt assured grapes would relieve the parching thirst of which you complain so constantly,—eat some now, at once."

How happy Rose looked as she witnessed the eagerness with which he partook of the cooling pleasant fruit for which he had of late so much longed—what a sweet smile stole round that lovely mouth, to which smiles alas! were now such rare visitants, as he spoke of the good they had already done him, and wondered and conjectured at her good fortune in obtaining such a treat! But these pleasant moments were doomed to a speedy interruption, for with an abrupt click of the latch, announcing almost who the intruder was before hand, Mrs. Lauzon entered. "Oh! there you are at last," she exclaimed, angrily looking towards Rose. "Where have you been this last half hour? At the village indeed? And pray have you nothing else to do than amusing yourself running backwards and forwards to the village as you do? Are there not both churning and baking to be done—"

"I did both this morning," gently rejoined Rose. "Yes of course, you can be very smart when you have an object in view, but there are other things in the house to be done which are yet unattended to, and will likely remain so, if you continue as you are going on now. Grapes, indeed!" she resentfully added, her glance here falling on the basket and that part of its contents which were spread on the coverlet. "Grapes! and myself and children can scarcely get even dry bread to eat. Go out into the garden and see if you cannot pull up and store some of the vegetables and roots before a night's frost comes on us unexpectedly and kills them. As we have no grapes to depend on, we must look to the humbler resources left to us."

A quick sympathetic look passed between father and daughter, as the latter obedient to her stepmother's harshly expressed commands, left the chamber; and with her departure, the light her presence ever imparted to her parent's countenance faded away, showing fully and terribly the ravages of disease, and the foreshadowings of the stealthy approach of that undreaded visitant Death, which was soon to hush that weary heart to rest. Calmly, hopefully Lauzon looked forward to his end. His life had been honest and blameless, and now supported by the rights of his Church, encouraged by the frequent visits of the kind parish-priest, but few fears or regrets haunted his bed of sickness. The vexatious tyranny of his wife he considered more than compensated for by the unwearying watchful love of his gentle daughter, and his great confidence in the merciful care of Providence relieved his mind from the anxious fears which would otherwise have troubled it regarding that beloved daughter's future.

The golden month of October drew to a close, then came dreary, cheerless November, so aptly ushering in that saddest of days in the Catholic calendar, All Souls, or the commemoration of the dead.[1] Heavily had the morning dawned in clouds and rain, and the lightest heart would have borrowed a feeling of sadness from the sight of that dark lowering sky, the black, desolate fields and gardens, and the naked branches of the trees, to which a few sere yellow leaves here and there clung, mournful mementos of the faded brightness of departed summer.

Drearily sounded the tolling of the funeral bell which during the course of that lugubrious anniversary, is rung at short intervals, reminding the living of those that are gone before, those whom they are perhaps so soon to follow. Many hearts felt heavy that day in the village of DeVillerai; many eyes filled with tears as that solemn iron voice spoke forth from the belfry. Sons and daughters, mournfully recalled the loving gray-haired parents, whom they had perhaps within the last year committed to earth,—the widowed husband bethought him of the fair young bride who filled an early grave in the quiet church-yard,—the mother's heart yearned for the idolized child cut off in the bloom of youth, or the baby treasure that had passed in an hour from the warm clasp of her loving arms to its narrow bed of clay.

Faint but distinct, the sound of that requiem knell penetrated into the interior of Joseph Lauzon's cottage, and as he listened to it, his eyes half closed, his thin fingers twined together, no shade of sadness was visible on his face. Memory was busy with him then, and with a wistful longing he thought of the peaceful grave in the angle of the church-yard wall, where slept since many years his first wife, the fair, gentle mother of his well-loved Rose. Ah! what a welcome haven of rest would that grave be for his suffering, emaciated body—what a joyful meeting would be that of his spirit and hers in Heaven! The thought was bliss unspeakable, and in the happiness of it, he scarcely noted the strange feeling of torpor that was creeping slowly over him. A light footstep crossing the floor somewhat aroused his attention, and he murmured, "Rose," "Here, dear father," and she was instantly beside him, clasping his hand lovingly in hers. Her face was very pale and her red swollen eyes bore unmistakeable traces of recent tears.

"Where is your mother, *petite*?"

"At church, father, she will soon be home."

Mrs. Lauzon though sovereignly indifferent to practicing the dictates and principles of her religion, was yet, with strange

---

1 Held annually on 2 November, All Souls' Day is a Christian day of prayer for the dead.

though common inconsistency, most tenacious of the observance of many of its external rites and duties.

"And where are the children, dear?"

"At the next neighbour's, father. You know you kissed and blessed them this morning, and I have just left them there, so that their noise might not make your poor head ache."

"'Tis almost beyond that now, but come and sit beside me dear. I feel so tranquil, so free from pain."

Poor Rose obeyed but she dared not speak,—her voice would have betrayed her. Mr. Lapointe who had administered the last sacrament to her father the morning previous, and Doctor Deschamps, the physician, had both gently told her that the end of his earthly pilgrimage was close at hand. With sinking heart she had watched him since then, and a short time previous, when she noted that strange languor stealing over him, and saw the damp dew breaking out on his forehead, she hastened to take the children elsewhere, that her father's dying hours might not be troubled, nor their young hearts saddened by the mournful scene so soon to take place.

Little was said on either side, Rose at intervals reading aloud some prayers suitable to the circumstances, or wetting the poor lips whose parched dryness seemed always craving relief. An hour had quietly passed thus when Mrs. Lauzon thoroughly drenched and proportionately ill-tempered entered the house. A quick irritated look round the apartment followed by a sharp interrogation as to where were the children, was her first salutation.

In a whisper, Rose replied "that they were next door, at Ovide De Blois."

"And why next door?" she querulously enquired. "You know well they will be running in and out of the house there, and taking their deaths of cold. But, what do you care?" she continued, scornfully apostrophizing Rose, "I suppose if they were all dead, you would be more glad than sorry." "Woman, silence!" suddenly exclaimed the sick man, in a voice which though low and faint had yet the accent of authority. Mrs. Lauzon started and turned an astonished look upon her husband for the voice of command at least from him, was one with which she had never been familiar, but soon recovering herself, she rejoined, though with less acrimony than she usually displayed. "Surely, Lauzon, I may speak, if your daughter Rose ill-naturedly puts my poor children out of my own house, I may at least ask where they are. Go for the two youngest, immediately, girl, and do not venture on such a liberty again."

With an effort the invalid shook off for a moment the torpor enlacing him more closely every instant, and exclaimed in the same tone in which he had before spoken, "Rose shall not leave me while life lingers in my body, and you, Sophie, must go from me, or else, be quiet. If you have not allowed me to live, you must at least let me die in peace."

Mrs. Lauzon's face became perceptibly paler and she hurriedly exclaimed, "Nonsense, Joseph, you are only weak, and that alarms you,—try a spoonful of broth," but he merely shook his head and relapsed into his former dreamy silent state. The virago wife once convinced that her husband was actually passing from earth, overwhelmed him with unavailing attentions, arranging his pillows, moistening his lips and breaking forth at times into loud ejaculations of sorrow. Pushing aside Rose in whose grief-struck hopeless face she read the confirmation of her own sudden terrors, she peremptorily prevented the latter rendering any service to the dying man, insisting on doing everything herself.

Again that sinking spirit rallied for a moment, and murmuring, though so faintly that his words were almost inaudible, "Rose," he clasped his daughter's hand as the latter bent towards him, and turning his dim eyes on Mrs. Lauzon he whispered, "wife, let *her* with me to the end. Disturb her not."

Oh! restless perversity of the human heart! Even in the awful solemnity of that hour, the woman's heart swelled with feelings of anger and jealousy towards her step-daughter, but she did not dare again to oppose him; and when a few hours later the long-suffering, blameless spirit of Joseph Lauzon passed into eternal rest, it was on his daughter's arm that his dying head was pillowed.

To be continued.

CHAPTER XV.

It was the day of Joseph Lauzon's funeral. That morning his earthly remains had left his cottage home for a still narrower, lowlier abode. Seated beside his vacant bed, her forehead bowed down in utter abandonment of grief on the pillow on which his suffering weary head had so long lain, was his desolate-hearted daughter. Desolate was she now indeed, and in the bitterness of that hour she passionately asked of heaven that she might soon share his envied rest in the quiet church-yard. Not long was the luxury of quiet indulgence in her sorrow granted her. Soon the door of the bedroom opened and the new-made widow harshly enquired, "If she intended condescending to prepare the poor children their supper, or was she going to spend all the day in tears and idleness."

Brushing away the glittering drops from her eyes, the harrassed heart-broken girl rose to her feet and without a word, passed into the outer room. Her step-mother's gaze, however, had been rivetted for the last second on her person with a stare of intense astonishment, for Rose had on a black dress which though not perfectly new, was of a texture and make far superior to anything usually worn by persons of their rank in life.

With a jealousy of look and voice she could not control, Mrs. Lauzon begged, might she ask "where Rose had obtained so beautiful a dress."

"Dr. Deschamp's servant brought it to me this morning from his kind wife. She said she sent it in payment of some sewing I had done for her."

"Much sewing you did to earn that beautiful merino with its broad folds of crape, which I am sure had not been worn two months. Very fine, indeed, that you should be dressed like a lady, whilst I, your father's widow, have nothing but a cheap black and white calico to put on!"

Rose was too heart sick, too weary to attend to this speech which she had, at the most, barely comprehended, and in another moment she was going about her domestic avocations mechanically, but as skilfully as usual.

The following morning at her accustomed hour the gentle drudge of the household was up. Irreproachably did she fulfil all her onerous tasks that long weary day—patiently did she bear with the tyrannical caprices of her step-mother's ill-bred children, and then when with evening a momentary respite came, when she had hushed the youngest child to sleep, and arranged every thing in neat order in the cottage, she stole out to the church-yard to say a short prayer beside her father's grave.

Not long did she venture to absent herself, but her absence short as it was proved sufficient to arouse the domineering spirit of Mrs. Lauzon, already irritated by the present of the dress, to fiery wrath. On re-entering the house, the latter who was rocking in her arms a sturdy vigorous urchin of some three years old, the youngling of the flock, harshly exclaimed, "Where have you been, *Mademoiselle*? Answer me instantly!"

"In the church-yard," was the faltering reply.

"Church-yard, indeed," was the contemptuous rejoinder. "So you are again at your old game of playing the great lady! You have nothing then to do, but walk about the grave-yard and shew off your grand new mourning, leaving me to drudge at home, and the poor baby to scream his very life out!"

In justice to Rose, we must here mention that the baby thus compassionately alluded to, was in fact the identical lively young gentleman we have just described as reposing on his mother's lap, and whom the patient young nurse had hushed to sleep before leaving the house.

The girl made no reply, but with a look of hopeless weariness amounting almost to indifference, turned away to divest herself of her bonnet and shawl.

This new and unusual phase in her step-daughter's character, exasperated Mrs. Lauzon beyond all bounds, and imperiously stamping her foot, she exclaimed in her shrillest accents.

"Come back here instantly, insolent girl, and answer me."

Rose turned and stood there silently confronting her tyrant but she made no reply.

"How long is this to last?" questioned Mrs. Lauzon fiercely. "Do you think I'll keep you under my roof, eating my children's bread without your doing something to earn it? Do you think I am to play the drudge and you the mistress, the great lady?"

Still Rose did not speak but the deadly pallor of her cheek was slowly giving place to a deep feverish crimson.

"Who are you," continued the step-dame, "that you should give yourself such airs? A faded useless creature that no one would ever look at now for a wife. You've never had a single offer since your shameless advances to Miss De Villerai's young fop of a lover. Turned out of the manor house in disgrace—deserted by your former lovers—contemptuously avoided by the respectable young girls of the place, it befits you well indeed to assume the airs you do. Why do you stand staring at me there so insolently and so maliciously? Go to your work at once, if you have no better answer to give me." "Yes, Mrs. Lauzon," rejoined Rose in a firm voice, the very first accents of which caused her companion to start, so different were they from her usual low timid tones. "Yes, I have an answer and but one to make to all that you have just said to me—to all the injustice, the cruelty you have heaped upon me from the hour you entered beneath this roof, seven years ago, as my father's wife. It is this—that I go forth rejoicing from your house this very day, this very minute never to re-enter it—never to find myself again, even for an hour, beneath the same roof with yourself."

Had Rose suddenly presented a loaded revolver at Mrs. Lauzon's head that dauntless matron could not have looked more utterly confounded, stupefied, than she did. In the first years of her married life she had indeed done her best to drive Rose from the house; for with the paltry littleness peculiar to minds cast in the same stamp as her own, she was vindictively jealous of the deep confidence and affection subsisting between her husband and his eldest child. Since poverty and sickness however had come into their household, increasing the number of domestic tasks, whilst it precluded employing a hired assistant, Rose's presence had become as necessary as it had once been obnoxious, and if admirers and suitors had so suddenly fallen off from the village beauty, Mrs. Lauzon might have felicitated herself on the success of her own malicious inuendos and remarks in bringing about so desirable a result. Latterly she had hugged herself in the certainty that Rose, completely cast off by her former kind friends at the manor house, unsought of late in matrimony by any suitor however humble, and too proud to accept of menial service in any stranger family, would remain an eternal fixture in her household, the well-trained slave of her children and the patient butt of her own ill-temper. The sudden announcement then that she was about to lose thus unexpectedly and suddenly, the valuable assistant whom she inwardly felt even in that moment of intense passion she could never replace, for a moment almost bewildered her.

Recovering however by a great effort her outward composure, she mockingly rejoined "And, pray, will you also tell me where you will go to—what you will do? Recollect, girl, ere you forfeit a home that has sheltered you so many years, that there is none other open to receive you. The ill treatment of which you so loudly complain, you have borne, and may still easily bear for the sake of the respectable decent livelihood afforded you."

"And, do you think," questioned Rose, in a tone whose melancholy bitterness no words could do justice to, "Do you think, Mrs. Lauzon, I have sacrificed so many years of my young life, for the sake of the food and scanty clothing it has procured me here? Think you I would have borne with what I have borne, remained, aye! even for one short year with you, but for the sake of the poor heart-broken father whose happiness was dearer to me than my own. Oh! no, and now my weary duty fulfilled, I go forth on my way without one shadow of regret—nay, only thankful as you ought also to be, that the burden of my maintenance of which you have so often complained is removed from your household for ever."

Mrs. Lauzon was silent for a moment, almost speechless with rage and regret, and as she saw her step-daughter gather her shawl about her, she wrathfully exclaimed,

"But, you shall not go thus, ungrateful girl! My duty to your dead father bids me watch over you—save you from the misery or disgrace on which you would rush."

The excitement which for a time had so deeply flushed the young girl's cheek, had entirely died away, and her face was now pale, her manner listless, passionless as before.

"I know well, Mrs. Lauzon, and so also must you," she replied, "that wherever I may offer the services I have performed here, they will at least always obtain for me equal remuneration with what I have received from you. I have no fears on that head, and now, let me go without further discussion."

"What! Do I hear aright?" interrogated Mrs. Lauzon with scornful emphasis, "So the dainty Rose Lauzon with her pretty face and her great learning, she, the former companion, indeed rival of the *Seigneuresse* of De Villerai, is about to hire herself out as a common menial at so much a month! Well, that is indeed a fall for Pride, but, you have not told me where you are going," she persisted, as she noted that her step-daughter had just finished tying the strings of her bonnet. "Answer me, at least that." "Any where, any where, so that I may have peace," wearily sighed Rose, as with the one word "Good by," she passed out for ever from the threshold of that home, in which as she herself had said, so many years of her young life had been sacrificed. Not long did the desolate girl hesitate as to wither she would turn her steps. The one tried venerable friend to whom she had ever returned in her hours of trial—who alone was acquainted with the secret that had brought such sorrow to her youth, naturally recurred to her thoughts, and to the Presbytery she immediately bent her steps. Dispassionately, almost listlessly, as if she were speaking of some indifferent person instead of herself, she recounted the greater part of what had passed between her step-mother and herself.

Mr. Lapointe listened with sympathizing attention, and then when she had concluded, gently rejoined, "my dear child, I had expected, foreseen this, and think you are perfectly justifiable, now, that God has called your father from earth, in seeking some other home where you may be happier. The day after your father's death, I wrote to a wealthy and most benevolent widow lady in Montreal, with whom I have been for many years acquainted, mentioning the peculiar circumstances in which you are placed, and requesting that she might afford you a home, at least for a time, under her own roof. Your skill in needle-work which would render you useful in any household, and perfect acquaintance with reading and writing, will, I know, render you useful to her. Her answer, which I feel assured will be in the affirmative, for Madame De Rochon's charity is as active and speedy as it is boundless, will probably arrive to-morrow or the day following, and till then, my good sister Marie will give you a share of her room and make you comfortable."

Poor Rose overcome with gratitude and emotion, could scarcely falter forth her thanks; but Miss Marie most opportunely entered at the moment, and after a few words of cordial welcome, declared that the former had arrived just in time to help her with her Saturday's pie-making, a task on which they would enter as soon as their young visitor was ready. Meanwhile, whilst Rose and her kind hearted hostess were coring apples and shaping dainty tarts, in the neat and scrupulously clean kitchen, Mr. Lapointe sat quietly reading his breviary in the large, old-fashioned easy chair, which was drawn up a little distance from the sitting-room window, commanding a view of the narrow dahlia bordered walk leading up to the door of the Presbytery. Suddenly, however, the contented, complacent expression of the good pastor's face changed, as his eye fell upon a female figure advancing with masculine strides up the road, and casting every now and then a sharp scrutinizing glance towards the white curtained windows of the Presbytery.

"No wonder poor Rose was afraid of her," muttered the priest to himself, as he nervously closed his book and fidgetted in his chair. "I declare I feel quite timid, quite uneasy myself."

His courage, however, rose with the emergency, and when Mrs. Lauzon with a heightened colour on her cheeks, and a tremor in her voice, which was certainly not the effects of timidity or anxiety, bade him "good evening," his manner was full of calm quiet dignity.

"I have come, Mr. Le Curé," somewhat abruptly exclaimed the visitor, entering at once on the object of her mission, "I have come to speak to you about that ungrateful little hypocrite, my step-daughter Rose, and to let you see what I have to suffer at her hands," and with a volubility, an amount of emphasis and adjectives, which few of her sex could have rivalled, she entered upon an account of the parting interview between Rose and herself. Though the proportion of veracity in her tale, were as drops of truth to oceans of falsehood, Mr. Lapointe never interrupted her. Patiently he listened whilst she declaimed against Rose's ingratitude, duplicity and countless other bad qualities, till finally she was compelled by very breathlessness to pause.

Quietly then he exclaimed, "and so this refractory young girl has left you, it appears?"

"Yes sir, ungratefully, insolently left me."

"Then my good Mrs. Lauzon, allow me to congratulate you, for if she is only one half as bad as your late account would lead me to believe, it must be a perfect blessing for you thus to get rid of her."

Whether Mrs. Lauzon suspected that covert irony lurked beneath the good priest's apparently friendly words, or that the consolation which he sought to administer, irritated instead of soothing, she rejoined with an angry compression of her lips, which betokened an inward mental tempest, "that may be, sir, but bad as she is, 'tis still my duty to look after her, and see that no harm or shame befall her. May I then respectfully enquire do you know anything about where she is at present?"

"Certainly, my good woman, such solicitude if prompted by a worthy motive is most laudable. She is at the present moment an inmate of my own roof, and whilst she remains here, I will answer for the prudence and propriety of her conduct."

Mrs. Lauzon's sallow cheek paled, then flushed again, but with a mighty effort of self-command she calmly rejoined, "of course, then, Mr. Le Curé, you will enjoin her to return home with me at once, and endeavour by future submission to atone for her late wilfulness and disobedience. I am willing to overlook the past."

The Priest slowly took out his tortoise-shell snuff box, treated himself to a pinch and then with great deliberation rejoined, "no, my good Madame Lauzon, I will not."

"What, *monsieur!*" and Mrs. Lauzon's tones became shrill as the war blast of a trumpet. "Is it possible you will encourage her unnatural revolt against a just authority?—is it possible that you, who preach nearly every third or fourth Sunday from the pulpit, upon the sacredness of the commandment which tells us to 'honour father and mother,' will support thus a headstrong, undutiful girl of eighteen against a mother's lawful authority?"

Whether Mr. Lapointe felt that his feminine adversary had hit him somewhat hard here, or else that his patience was commencing to fail, he energetically rejoined:

"Yes, arbitrary woman, and you may also have heard me preach equally often on the sacred duties which parents owe to their children, on the sacred duties which the heavenly virtue of charity inculcates so loudly and unceasingly. Let me ask how have you fulfilled those duties? What motherly love or tenderness have you ever lavished on the patient young creature, who for so many years past, has been your patient uncomplaining drudge and who found in you not a mother but a stern, unrelenting mistress. She shall return to you no more unless of her own free-will, and if at times you miss her skilful active hand, her persevering, patient industry, remember that with you and you alone the fault rests."

"Very kind, very friendly of you, indeed, Mr. Le Curé," rejoined his fair companion, her ample chest heaving indignantly. "Of course, I am now only a poor helpless widow whom anybody may insult, abuse, trample upon; but no body would dare to treat me thus if poor Joseph were living."

"Much happier for him that he is not," inwardly thought the Curate; but Christian charity and prudence forebade the verbal enunciation of the sentiment, and in a calmer tone he exclaimed, "I have no hesitation in telling you, as it will effectually calm any scruples you may entertain regarding your duties towards your step-daughter, that your husband a few days before his death begged me to seek another home for her, assuring me he felt convinced she could never be happy where she was."

"The old dotard!" murmured the inconsolable widow, *sotto voce*, and feeling now that she was foiled at every point, she stiffly curtsied herself from the room, reminding the priest that he alone was responsible in future for the well-being, spiritual and temporal of her whilome charge, and would be equally accountable for whatever shame or disgrace the girl's pretty face and head-strong character might lead her into.

Mr. Lapointe with unruffled composure bade her good evening, and as the door closed upon her, he sank down serenely in his arm-chair, blandly rubbing his hands and smiling in pardonable triumph. It was indeed a victory on which he might lawfully pride himself. He had combatted, silenced, and defeated the virago of the village, and that without once forgetting the dignity due to his own sacred character and the courtesy owing to her sex.

CHAPTER XVI.

In the roomy though low ceiled drawing room of a comfortable stone house in the Place d'Armes,[1] on the site of which now rises a stately public building, an elderly lady dressed with nun-like simplicity was seated, occupying her busy fingers with fashioning articles of clothing whose coarse though comfortable texture betokened them destined for the poor. There was a singular mixture of wealth and plainness in the apartment. A simple drugget carpet covered the floor—dark chintz curtains shaded the windows—but oil paintings of exquisite beauty and priceless value decorated the walls. The subjects, however, were all religious as were also those of the few choice engravings suspended above the mantelpiece whose only other ornaments were an ivory crucifix of delicate workmanship, and a couple of faultless alabaster groups, the Holy Family and the Nativity. Many books were lying around, some of them richly bound; but any lover of "light reading" who might have taken them up in quest of amusement would have been utterly disappointed, for like the pictures, the topics treated of, were all serious and religious.

Madame De Rochon—our readers will probably have guessed it was that kind-hearted noble Christian woman—suddenly paused in her work and glanced towards the clock. "Nearly eleven," she exclaimed. "My little country friend will soon be here. Poor child! I must try and make her happy."

These few words, uttered as they were, in a kind soft voice, augured well for Rose's future, and when the latter soon after arrived and with nervous trembling timidity entered the presence of her new patronness, a kind encouraging sentence soon reassured her and quieted the beatings of her anxious little heart.

After some kind enquiries regarding Mr. Lapointe, Mrs. De Rochon rose, saying,—"Come with me now, *petite*, and I will shew you your room." The apartment was plain but very comfortable, and religious pictures, statuettes and books were scattered around with no sparing hand.

"This is your room Rose; you will always take your meals with myself, and your duties will be to accompany me occasionally in my visits to the poor, assist me in sewing for them, answer the letters and petitions I receive, I may say daily, and now and then to read aloud for me, for my eye-sight is beginning to fail. Will

---

1   The principal square in Montréal. [Leprohon's note]

you find your task too heavy, dear child?" and she caressingly patted the rich glossy hair of her young companion.

"How good God has been to me!" murmured the latter, pressing Mrs. De Rochon's hand to her lips. "In my most ambitious dreams I never dared to hope for such a position, such a home as this."

"But do you know, Rose, that I have been long expecting you. Months ago, when your poor father's illness first assumed a fatal character, my kind friend Mr. Lapointe wrote to me, recounting your story and praying me if I were wanting a young person to fill the place you have just entered on, to wait till you were free. He so deeply interested me in you that, notwithstanding my weak, failing eye-sight and many occupations, I have waited since then—unwilling to take another *protégée*, to whom I might attach myself and whom I might afterwards feel it an injustice to dismiss. You fulfilled your filial duty towards your poor father nobly, whilst a secret presentiment tells me that my own patience will be hereafter well rewarded—and now, I will give you to-day to install yourself and possessions in your new apartment. Here is the servant with your trunk, and in this *commode* you will find some simple materials of clothing which your own skilful fingers will make up for your wardrobe."

How the young girl's heart swelled with gratitude at this additional proof of the forethought and benevolence of her new friend—and with what pleasure she examined the web of spotless linen—soft new flannel, and the roll of fine mourning material destined for her holiday wear. Gloves, collars, aprons too, all were there, and though the simplicity which reigned throughout the house had also in great measure presided over the selection of her new outfit, the texture and quality of the materials themselves were irreproachable.

How consonant too with Rose's natural refinement of character was the exquisite neatness pervading the whole establishment—the scrupulous almost punctilious care with which the daily repasts were served. Spotless damask—glittering crystal—quaint old China, all worthy to receive the good things they were accustomed to contain, for Mrs. De Rochon though a rigid observer of the fasts prescribed by her church, never pushed her asceticism beyond that lawful point, and with the exception of the particular periods just mentioned, her table was one with which even few epicures could have been dissatisfied. In the evening, prayers (the reading aloud of which now devolved on Rose) were said in the sitting-room, and at these latter the servants of the household attended, always attired with the extreme simplicity but faultless neatness characterizing the toilet of their mistress.

Indeed the life on which our young country friend now entered was to her full of charm. A couple of leisure hours were always allowed her in the morning, and these with Mrs. De Rochon's advice she passed in the library, improving her mind from the stores of literature, ancient and modern, ranged on its well-filled shelves. No sentimental Miss fond of pathetic love verses would there have found much amusement—no young gentleman, admirer of the free bold immorality of writers of the Sue and Balzac school could have gleamed even a pamphlet to his taste, but the works of such men as Fenelon, Chateaubriand and Bourdaloue[1] who had turned their brilliant genius to the improvement of their kind and the glory of Him who gave it to them, were there in profusion, attesting well the judgement of the careful mind and heart that had presided over their selection.

A few days after her arrival, Rose was reading aloud to her benefactress in the cheerful sitting-room they usually occupied, when a sudden rustling of silks in the hall, followed by an affected feminine cough, betokened the advent of some lady visitor. A moment after a stylish elaborately attired young lady of some twenty summers glided into the apartment and sank on a sofa with a languid sigh as if the exertion of ascending the stairs was one almost beyond her strength.

"How are you, dear Pauline?" kindly enquired Mrs. De Rochon, suspending her knitting and affectionately smiling on the new comer.

"Pretty well, Aunt," faintly replied the latter, "but, really, if I did not love you as much as I do, I would give up completely visiting you here—your stairs are enough to kill me." Rose here glanced in covert wonder at the speaker, for in her tall well-rounded form and keen bright eye she read no outward tokens of the excessive delicacy which the words of the latter seemed to imply.

Mrs. De Rochon either accustomed to such exaggerated forms of speech, or else unwilling to wound the susceptibility of her

---

[1] The French writers Marie-Joseph (Eugène) Sue (1804-57); Honoré de Balzac (1799-1850); François de Salignac de La Mothe-Fénelon (1651-1715); François-René de Chateaubriand (1768-1848); and Louis Bourdaloue (1632-1704). Both Sue and Balzac were on the *Index Librorum Prohibitorum*, the List of Prohibited Books issued by the Roman Catholic Church.

visitor, exhibited neither surprise nor incredulity but merely enquired if Mr. De Nevers were well.

"Oh! Papa is quite well," was the languid reply, "except that he is suffering as usual from rheumatic gout—I cannot tell you how sick I am of the very name of that ailment, for Papa talks of nothing else from morning till night."

"Doubtless, because he suffers so much from it, my dear," rejoined Mrs. De Rochon gravely. "Believe me, the head-aches and languor of which you so frequently complain, are far from causing the same amount of suffering as your poor father's painful malady does."

"I do not believe that, Aunt," and Miss De Nevers untied her elegant bonnet and carelessly flung it on a side table near. "Men are so little accustomed to suffering that they always make a most absurd outcry about the slightest trifle."

"Well, we will not discuss the matter farther," rejoined the elder lady good-humouredly. "I only hope that you may never be enabled to judge from actual experience between the relative sufferings caused by the two; but, what have you been doing, Pauline, for the last week?"

"Going to *soirées* and balls—making conquests and breaking hearts."

"The hearts, dear niece, must have been of very brittle material indeed, to allow themselves to be shattered so easily."

"Why do you say that, Aunt," pouted the young lady. "I am sure there is Captain Frémont (I could name a dozen others besides him) who vowed when I refused him last summer that he would shoot or drown himself through despair."

"But he did not do so, child. He is living still as hale and hearty as ever. Ah! Pauline, the fortune you are destined to inherit, believe me, increases greatly the number and ardour of your admirers."

"Really, Aunt De Rochon," was the somewhat irritable reply, "you are more frank than complimentary this morning. Do you think that youth, good looks and lively fascinating manners, count for nothing with men?"

"Yes, my child, they have their weight, but money and fortune often count for still more, especially among the class of idle danglers, forgive me the word, by whom you are surrounded."

"Pray, what did Uncle De Rochon marry you for then? You were not wealthy."

"Certainly not, niece, neither did I possess good looks nor fascinating manners, so I will leave the problem to be solved by your own ingenuity. Let us turn, however, to some more interesting topic."

"Well, really, Aunt, that is difficult, for there are so few subjects in which we have anything in common," sighed the girl. "You care only for church-going, acts of charity and pious things in general—my tastes are entirely the other way, tending only to pleasure, fashion and gaiety. What interests me, cannot possibly interest you."

"And yet, Pauline," gravely rejoined her elder companion, "we were both put on the earth for the same purpose and tend towards the same end. We have both Death and Eternity before us."

"Oh, mercy! Aunt, if you begin moralizing thus, I must positively run off," and the frivolous girl affectedly placed her pretty fingers glistening with costly rings, over her ears. "Do you know that I always feel quite nervous and low-spirited after one of your sermons?"

"Well, you do not risk your equanimity often by listening to them," said Mrs. De Rochon, sadly smiling; "but tell me candidly, do you never meet, in the gay life you lead, with annoyances or disappointments which possess the power of depressing your spirits even as much as my dreaded sermons can possibly do?"

"Of course—plenty of them," was the prompt reply. "Now, at the present moment, I find myself, for at least the fiftieth time, irretrievably hopelessly in love."

"Pauline! Pauline!" exclaimed Mrs. De Rochon reprovingly, glancing at the same time towards Rose, who had taken up after the visitor's entrance a French-cambric collar she was hemming, and now sat bending over her work with an unusually flushed cheek, probably finding something in the random words of the giddy speaker which touched some secret chord in her own breast.

Pauline De Nevers tossed her head contemptuously, intimating thereby that the party thus mutely indicated was entirely out of the pale of her notice, and continued in the same strain as before.

"Yes, indeed, Aunt, I am telling you the candid truth. You know I never fall in love except in what I call hopeless cases, that is to say, those in which my affection is not likely to be returned. I am peculiarly unfortunate in this disposition, for as soon as any attachment that I may form, meets with the slightest response, that instant it melts into air. There was that handsome young

D'Albert, poor but a perfect Adonis. Well, you remember I had such an *engouement*[1] for him, that Papa almost forgot his eternal gout[2] in his anxiety lest it should end in a run-away match. The instant however that the unfortunate young man commenced love-making, bouquet sending, my affection changed to indifference, and finally when he proposed, I actually commenced to hate him."

"Well, let us hope, Pauline, that his present rival will cure you in like manner."

"No danger of that!" sighed the giddy girl, looking for the moment actually thoughtful, if not melancholy.

"He not only seems sovereignly indifferent to women, but the provoking creature will not even flirt with one. He is besides engaged to another."

"Then, that should be sufficient to prevent young ladies from seeking to flirt with, or even falling in love with him."

"Pshaw! dear Aunt, how little you know about such things! Why, that very circumstance is of itself enough to render the engaged individual all but irresistible, but he who reigns for the moment supreme in my affections, requires no such adventitious aid to increase his fascinations. Any woman would find Gustave De Montarville irresistible."

To the very roots of her hair did Rose's fair face crimson, as this name so secretly but devotedly cherished, fell thus unexpectedly upon her ear, but fortunately her head was bowed over her needle work and her confusion thus escaped the notice of her companions.

"Gustave De Montarville! Is not that the young Canadian belonging to the Roussillon regiment who behaved so gallantly at the siege of Carillon?"

"Yes, dear Aunt, he was wounded there, promoted afterwards, and you cannot imagine how charmingly interesting he looks with his arm in a sling, and that becoming invalid pallor on his clear dark cheek. I assure you I am not the only fair lady in love with him."

"I think you should all leave that to the young *demoiselle* to whom he is betrothed," said Mrs. De Rochon, smiling.

---

1 "Unreasoning fondness" (*OED*). Literally, obstruction in the throat.
2 "A specific constitutional disease occurring in paroxysms, usually hereditary and in male subjects; characterized by painful inflammation of the smaller joints" (*OED*).

"Oh! she is a perfect icicle—a marble statue—in short, a beautiful being without a heart. You surely must have heard of the proud cold Miss De Villerai!"

"I have heard of a Miss De Villerai, Pauline, but she was represented to me as a noble-minded, religious girl—one who added additional lustre to her gifts of birth and fortune by her many virtues. He who described her to me thus was one who ought to know her well—the parish-priest of De Villerai."

"Perhaps so," was the careless rejoinder. "Indeed, for ought I know, she may be a Lady Bountiful[1] in the way, but during all last winter which was her first season in society, she passed for being as haughty as she was handsome. I only wish you could hear De Noraye talk about her."

"Count De Noraye?" questioned Mrs. De Rochon with a meaning smile.

"Exactly, dear Aunt," and the young lady languidly adjusted her bracelet. "The very individual who last ruled this fickle heart of mine. His reign lasted just six weeks and three days. Though my love for him has entirely passed away, I have not quite done with him yet. He ranks first among my danglers."

"Then, he did not respond sufficiently to your preference, to turn your love into hate?"

"No, he never yet laid his title and fortune at my feet, though he often told me his heart was there. Should he actually come to the point, which he will probably do yet, there is no saying what answer I may make. It would not be a bad thing to be a Countess—not one with a paltry income of a few thousand francs, barely enough to keep one in gloves and ribbons, but the mistress of estates, forests and *châteaux*. To return, however, to what I was saying. You cannot imagine how De Noraye comments upon and criticizes Miss De Villerai, and he assured me, 'tis true he is very malicious, that the parties do not care at all for one another, giving that as the reason why the marriage is put off from season to season, despite all the efforts and representations of the lady's aunt, old Mrs. Dumont."

"Scandal—jealousy—Pauline, nothing more! They are both young enough to wait some time longer; but, Rose, you may go to the library now and read an hour there."

---

[1] A wealthy and generous woman. After Lady Bountiful, a character in *The Beaux' Stratagem* (1707), a five-act comedy by Irish-born British dramatist George Farquhar (1678-1707).

The latter promptly obeyed, and as the door closed upon her Mrs. De Rochon remonstratingly exclaimed,

"I must really protest, Pauline against your speaking in future, in so thoughtless and frivolous a strain, before that young girl. It may do her harm."

"Not at all, Aunt! In her position in society, there is of course, nothing of the sort. Why, I am certain she did not even comprehend what I was talking about—so different is life in our world and theirs! But, pray, tell me, where did you pick her up? She seems to me absurdly pretty for her station."

The elder lady could not refrain from smiling as she rejoined.

"But her being pretty need not interfere with the proper accomplishment of her duties, whilst it is as agreeable for me to have that fair bright young face occupying the chair opposite mine, as to have a plain, discontented or elderly countenance confronting me."

"Nay, you are mistaken, Aunt, and you will soon find that out. She will be always looking at her pretty face in the mirror, when she takes your sewing to her own room, and instead of applying herself to it, will be perpetually trying her hair in different fashions, or making bows and head-dresses for herself. Again, I repeat that you have done a most unwise thing in taking so young and pretty a girl into your service."

"Well, as I will be the chief sufferer, Pauline, you may spare me farther predictions on the subject. I will take due care that my *protégée* does not spend too much time at her looking glass, and you, on your part, will refrain from indulging before her in the strain of light frivolity with which you no doubt astonished her this morning."

"Then, when I come to see you, Aunt, let your *demoiselle de compagnie*[1] betake herself elsewhere, for I certainly will not trouble myself to fashion my conversation to suit her superlatively innocent ears."

"Well, Pauline, it shall be so, but are you going?"

"Oh! yes, dear Aunt," and she tied the strings of her bonnet as she spoke. "I have a world of business to do to-day. Two new dresses to purchase, a walking and a ball-dress, besides gloves, flowers and hosts of other things. Then I must call at my milliners, at the jewellers to have my ruby necklace repaired—"

"Tell me, Pauline," interrupted Mrs. De Rochon, gently laying her hand on the speaker's arm, "tell me, have you visited yet as

---

[1] A girl or unmarried female servant, usually hired for companionship.

you promised me you would, that poor family living in Campeau street?"

"Well, no, Aunt," rejoined the young lady looking somewhat confused. "I really intended doing so, but that meddlesome De Noraye frightened me out of it by telling me that there have been several authenticated cases of small-pox among the poor lately."

"De Noraye's advice, Pauline, will never lead you to Heaven. God forbid that you should often allow yourself to be guided by him!"

"Well, well, Aunt, do not look so doleful about it! Here, take this," and she placed a couple of gold pieces in her companion's hand. "Send them that. It will certainly do them as much good as a visit from myself."

"Yes, but it will not do you as much service, however, I thankfully accept it; and now, tell me, have you read much in that book I lent you last week?"

"One chapter, Aunt, but oh! it was so terribly dismal that I had to read ten chapters in a novel afterwards, to restore my nerves and spirits to their usual tone."

Poor Mrs. De Rochon! a spirit less patient and disciplined than hers was, would have long previously given up in sheer hopelessness the moral improvement of the silly unthinking being before her, but she merely rejoined in a gentle tone.

"Well, Pauline, return me my book, for I do not wish to afford you any pretext for reading out of those immoral senseless publications which will ultimately pervert everything that is good and noble in your nature."

"There, there, Aunt De Rochon, do not look so sad and woebegone. I will tell you what I will do this evening. I will read another chapter (oh! what an affliction that will be!) and abstain entirely from the antidote. *Au revoir!*" and lightly kissing Mrs. De Rochon's forehead, she passed down the stairs.

"Poor misguided child!" murmured the lady when she found herself alone. "At times, my hopes and courage almost fail me; but, still, I must not, will not relax my efforts. God may yet bless them!"

The deep interest taken by Mrs. De Rochon in her recent visitor, was easily explained by the fact that Pauline was the nearest living relative she possessed. The only child of a deceased sister, who had married a gentleman of rank and wealth in the colony, the little girl had been left motherless at the early age of four years. Vainly had Mrs. De Rochon, then a widow, petitioned the father to consign his infant daughter to her care. He had always refused, alleging that his sister-in-law was too strict in her religious ideas for his taste, and would bring up his child more fitted for a convent than adapted to preside over a gentleman's establishment. The result he attained has been seen. The girl grew up vain, selfish and frivolous—indifferent towards her father—living for, thinking only of self. Mrs. De Rochon, however, like some good angel, ever watched over her, enduring her empty talk, her frivolous impertinences, that she might have an opportunity of occasionally whispering some good word, some impressive though stern truth into her ear. Surely, surely, she did more for her Master's glory than if she had exiled from her hearth, the vain though perhaps not utterly irreclaimable child of the world.

[No. 9—Vol. I] [MONTREAL, WEDNESDAY, JANUARY 11, 1860]

CHAPTER XVII.

Quietly happy was Rose Lauzon's existence beneath Mrs. De Rochon's hospitable roof, and daily, hourly, did she gratefully compare the present calm tenour of her life, with the unremitting labour, the sunless wretchedness of her lot in her former home. Her gratitude and affection for her gentle benefactress were unbounded, whilst the latter felt the sentiment of simple benevolence she had at first experienced towards her young companion, deepening day by day into a feeling of almost motherly tenderness.

The only draw-back, if it were indeed worthy of the name to Rose's happiness, was the contemptuous indifference with which Miss De Nevers invariably treated her, ignoring her existence even by a bow, a nod, and resolutely resisting all her relative's attempts to induce her to show a little more kindness or consideration to the young orphan girl domesticated beneath her roof. Rose, however, had been brought up in too stern a school of suffering to attach undue importance to so trifling an annoyance, and though she sometimes sighed involuntarily when Miss De Nevers, rustling in silks and lace, brushed past her without vouchsafing her a look, even after she had been for months an inmate of Mrs. De Rochon's house, or abruptly informed her Aunt, on her entrance into the sitting-room that she wished to be alone with her, thus unceremoniously giving Rose to understand that she was *de trop*;[1] the latter never fretted or repined—good sense and christian humility prevented that.

One pleasant day in April, diversified by sunshine and shower, Rose was sitting near the window with her needle work, casting an amused look every now and then at the confusion and general scatter among the *belles* and *beaux* in the square below, caused by a fresh onset of the shower, when she was startled by hearing a loud tattoo[2] on the door knocker, (bells were rare in those days) followed by affected voices and laughter on the stairs.

"There, go into that room, you tiresome creature," exclaimed a voice, which she instantly recognized as Miss De Nevers. "No, you may not come with me." This was evidently said in reply to some appeal proffered in a masculine voice, the words of which Rose could not catch.

"I must go and arrange my bonnet and curls, both of which are in a shocking bad state. 'Tis all your fault! you persisted in saying that it would not rain, so go in there and do penance alone, till I come down."

The door opened, whilst Rose still fluttered and anxious, was hesitating what to do, and Count De Noraye entered the apartment.

On first perceiving Rose, he gracefully apologized, removing his cap with the high-bred ease and courtesy he could so well assume when he chose, when suddenly the expression of his face changed to one of intense astonishment, and in a tone of marked familiarity he exclaimed:

"Why, can it be possible! yes, surely *mademoiselle*, we have met before. May I take the liberty of enquiring your name?"

"Rose Lauzon," was the agitated, annoyed reply.

"Oh! I thought as much! Who, that ever looked upon the lovely features of the beauty of De Villerai, could forget them, even though *mademoiselle* has grown ten times more charming, since I first had the pleasure of meeting her beside the wicket gate of the manor house." The familiarity of his accents and the bold stare of admiration with which he regarded her, excited Rose, despite her natural gentleness, to positive anger, and she chillingly replied as she moved towards the door:

"That meeting was so disagreeable to me, Count, that I do not like to recall it."

---

1 "Too much, (one) too many, in the way" (*OED*).
2 "The action of beating, thumping, or rapping continuously upon something" (*OED*).

"Ah! 'tis an encouraging sign for me, fair lady, that you remember it at all, but I will take the liberty of doing now what I did then, namely detaining you till I obtain at least either one coy smile, or kind word from those lovely lips."

"You are not taking the proper way, Count, to obtain either," rejoined Rose with a heightened colour, caused as much by perplexity as annoyance, for with a rapid movement De Noraye had placed himself in front of the door over which he now stood sentinel, whilst he silently surveyed her in momentarily increasing admiration.

Never had Rose looked so lovely. The vivid carmine of her cheeks—the mingled vexation and insulted modesty, that caused her speaking dark eyes, now, to sparkle so angrily, then to droop so charmingly before the bold, eager gaze fixed upon her, imparted to her countenance a fascination which the critical *blasé* De Noraye found almost irresistible. Forgetting for the moment his usual languid lisp and drawl, he suddenly and energetically exclaimed, "*Ma foi!*[1] Rose Lauzon, you are wonderfully beautiful."

This honest compliment additionally irritated instead of soothing its fair object, and she quickly retorted:

"Thank you, Count De Noraye, but 'tis not the first time that you have insulted me! Will you let me leave the room?"

"Not till we understand each other. Do you mean to say *ma belle*, that telling a woman she is irresistibly handsome, is insulting her? Why, if you imagine so, you still know less of the world than I thought you did; but answer me in return *petite*, why are you so handsome that an anchorite[2] could not allow you to pass without complimenting you on your charms?"

"Any gentleman sir, would do so, when he saw that his flattery was painful or unwelcome."

"Why Rose, you are witty as well as beautiful. Child, child, you will drive me out of my senses if you go on thus, growing more charming every moment, but come, let us reasonably discuss the matter. Everything rests with my own magnanimity. There is no *preux chevalier* at hand, no blundering De Montarville to come now to the rescue."

At that name, the tell-tale blood rushed to Rose's temples, and the keen eye of the man of the world detected the emotion at

---

1   "My faith!"
2   "A person who has withdrawn or secluded himself from the world; usually one who has done so for religious reasons; a recluse, a hermit" (*OED*).

once. "Ah!" he coldly but mockingly exclaimed, "why did not *mademoiselle* tell me before that she had preferences—that the smiles demurely denied to one, are only reserved for another? Surely, De Montarville was born under a lucky star, for not only does he claim the wealthy *seigneuresse* of De Villerai as his own, but the smiles of its village beauty are also his. Oh! pass now, young lady, by all means, Gaston De Noraye cares not to reign in a divided heart," and with a low bow of affected deference, fully contradicted by the sneer on his handsome lip, the count moved aside, allowing Rose to make her escape.

This was barely effected in time, for almost simultaneously with the latter's disappearance, Miss De Nevers made her entrance into the room.

"Pray, with whom was Count De Noraye wiling his time in such friendly converse?" she asked with a curl of her lip.

"With one, whose beauty, wondrous as it is, sinks into insignificance when put into competition with that of Miss De Nevers," returned De Noraye, feeling for once in his life slightly embarrassed.

"Thank you, Count, for your intended compliment," replied the girl, drawing herself up with inexpressible haughtiness; but Mademoiselle De Nevers is not accustomed to hear comparisons instituted between herself and her aunt's *suivantes*,[1] even though they may result in some paltry compliment to herself."

"Ah! my charming Miss De Nevers," replied the young Frenchman, regaining without much effort his usual unruffled composure. "Man will always bow to beauty whether he meets it in the duchess or in her waiting maid—the queen or the peasant girl. Think you, if nature had unjustly ordained that you, instead of being the heiress of a proud old name, should have been born in little Rose's position, think you, I repeat, that I could have passed you by without a flattering look or word?"

The compliment was adroitly turned, and Pauline bit her lip to conceal the half smile stealing over her face, but determined not to let him off so easily, she rejoined:

"You were not long, indeed, in making yourself acquainted with your fair enslaver's name. Pray, is this the first time you have met?"

The question was asked at random.—Miss De Nevers never dreaming it would be answered in the affirmative; but to her sur-

---

1 "A confidential maid" (*OED*).

prise, De Noraye carelessly rejoined: "He believed he had indeed met the little girl previously, but he really could not recall where."

Here, indeed, was a discovery for Miss De Nevers to make! What! the shy, modest, blushing Rose, before whom her aunt had almost forbidden her to speak, lest her own reckless *badinage*[1] should startle or shock her immaculate innocence, she was acquainted with this gay and fashionable young nobleman, who knew her by name, and praised her beauty so patronizingly. It was certainly a fine occasion for triumphing over Mrs. De Rochon, who had so often upbraided her with her want of civility towards this same Rose, and in the satisfaction of that thought, her smiles and good humour completely returned.

Earlier than usual the following day, Pauline De Nevers, with a shade of unusual animation embellishing her customary languid elegance, sailed into Mrs. De Rochon's sitting-room, and finding that hapless lady alone, proceeded to communicate to her, with many a malicious inuendo and contemptuous remark the incident of the preceding day. The hostess was sceptical—incredulous—what value did she set on the word of such a man as Gaston De Noraye.

"Well, you will at least ask her, Aunt, if she ever met him before, and that at once, in my presence, unless indeed that you fear the reply may not be as satisfactory as you would wish." The latter remark decided Mrs. De Rochon immediately, and she rebukingly exclaimed. "Have patience and your uncharitable curiosity shall soon be gratified, Rose will be here in a moment." Needle work in hand, the latter soon after entered, but, on seeing Pauline, she hesitated, knowing well that the latter young lady rarely tolerated her presence. She was about returning, when her benefactress gently exclaimed "Be seated, Rose, my niece has no secrets to whisper in my ear this morning."

Rose obeyed and for a few minutes Pauline De Nevers silently but scrutinizingly surveyed her. Nothing escaped that keen glance and the more attentively she looked the more she wondered at the rare loveliness and grace of the young country girl. "'Tis not wonderful," was her inward comment, "that such beauty should nearly turn De Noraye's head;" and as the disagreeable reflection presented itself, she impatiently bit her own pretty lip.

---

[1] "Humorous, witty, or trifling discourse; banter; frivolous or light-hearted raillery" (*OED*).

"Will you please tell me," she suddenly asked with rather startling abruptness, "under what circumstances you made the acquaintance of the Count De Noraye?"

It was the first time in her life that the haughty Miss De Nevers had thus directly addressed Rose, and the latter, partly fluttered by that circumstance and by the unexpectedness of the question itself, coloured and stammered out, "at De Villerai, *Mademoiselle*."

"Indeed, and might I further ask under what peculiar circumstances, an acquaintance between persons in such different ranks of life was first formed?"

Before Rose's memory rose up at once the recollection of that meeting with De Noraye at the manor house gate when De Montarville had so generously freed her from the Count's insolent importunities, and the remembrance of that event which was deeply engraved on the secret tablets of her memory, dyed her cheek with sudden blushes.

"Well are you going to satisfy our curiosity, *Mademoiselle*," persisted the visitor, laying a scornful emphasis on the latter title.

The repugnance she felt towards recounting the meeting, increased the young girl's confusion, but, at length she rejoined in a low tone, "Miss De Nevers must excuse me if I decline doing so."

Pauline threw herself back in her chair, and eyed the speaker, with a mixture of insolence and mockery, which would have almost annihilated the latter had she encountered the look. Fortunately, however, her eyes were bent on her sewing, and Miss De Nevers was obliged to content herself with sarcastically exclaiming.

"So Mademoiselle declines satisfying us! Pray, what can there be of so secret or important a nature, in the first meeting between a poor country girl and a gentleman of Count De Noraye's standing in society? Ah! *bonne tante*[1] vanity and intrigue do not always dwell with silks and laces,—we as frequently find them concealed beneath the woolen serge and calico print of the peasant."

Mrs. De Rochon compassionating the intense distress exhibited in Rose's countenance, kindly exclaimed, "as Miss De Nevers is with me Rose, you can attend to any morning duties that may be awaiting you elsewhere."

"Now, Aunt," was Miss De Nevers' triumphant remark, when they found themselves alone, "what think you of that meek-faced

---

[1] "Good aunt," or "my good aunt."

little hypocrite? Is it not just as I thought—as I predicted? Oh I well knew that beauty like hers, in a waiting maid, could be productive of no good."

"She is no waiting maid, but my companion, Pauline, an humble one if you will; and as to her beauty—she is what providence made her. Really, niece, you are too suspicious—too severe!"

"And you, Aunt, are too weak and indulgent. Oh! I really have no patience with you! Did not that girl's blushes and embarrassment—her insolent refusal to answer the simple question I propounded, open your eyes to the reality?"

"I have yet to learn, child, that blushes are always the accompaniments of guilt. For my part, I as frequently find that they are tokens of innocence."

"So be it, Aunt, cherish your own opinions as firmly as you like, till some fresh and more striking proof of duplicity in your precious favorite oblige you to acknowledge at length the truth of my representations, and the blindness of your own weak incredulity."

"My good niece, Pauline, you are really growing rather warm in the discussion, but I will excuse you, charitably hoping that your earnestness is entirely prompted by interest in myself, and not by prejudice or personal dislike towards Rose Lauzon; but, let us waive the subject for the present, and turn to some more agreeable topic. How is your poor father this morning?"

"Do you call that turning to a more agreeable topic?" irritably questioned the young lady. "'Tis just about the most unwelcome one on which you could have touched. Papa, with a degree of selfishness and obstinate egotism, which I could scarcely believe it possible for a parent to possess, persists in refusing me permission to give a grand ball or dinner, I do not care which, before the officers of the Roussillon regiment leave for Quebec."

"But that is not answering my question, Pauline, as to how your father really is."

"Oh! of course suffering from his old complaint rheumatism, but when is it ever otherwise! That is no valid excuse for refusing my reasonable request. He might sit in his easy chair, well wrapped up in flannel."

"Pauline! Pauline!" gravely interrupted her companion. "You can never have experienced such a thing as real pain, or you would not speak thus. How could your poor father, racked by physical suffering, remain quietly for hours in the midst of noisy mirth and revelry?"

"There, there, Aunt, that is enough! I really believe you are all leagued against me of late, but, indeed, you need not take Papa's part so warmly, for he said only the other day, that the manner in which you lavished your wealth on nominal charities, encouraging actually, all the while idleness, and imposture, was absurd and ill-judged in the highest degree. But, I feel so out of sorts and temper, I must bid you good morning at once."

"Not in anger, I hope, Pauline!"

"No, who could be angry with you? You are too patient to afford the most irascible a chance, but I will come to see you again to-morrow, only keep that dreadful little hypocrite out of the room while I am with you."

Mrs. De Rochon accustomed since Pauline's childhood to such interviews, calmly resumed her previous occupation. She was joined by Rose, as soon as the latter had ascertained the departure of Mademoiselle De Nevers, and after a few moments silence the elder lady quietly said:

"Have you any objections, Rose, to give me the information, you perhaps justly refused to my niece's arbitrary questioning?"

The girl coloured, but immediately, though with some slight hesitation of manner, recounted the meeting with De Noraye near the manor house, and De Montarville's timely and generous intervention.

"Just as I thought, dear child, you are perfectly blameless in the matter, so we will dismiss the event and the actors entirely from our minds. Pray read me now a chapter from our 'lecture book'[1]—it will be an agreeable diversion to our thoughts."

CHAPTER XVIII.[2]

Towards four o'clock in the afternoon of a warm sunny day, a young officer, dressed in the uniform of the Roussillon regiment, was sauntering up Notre Dame Street with a slow step and languid gait which might have indicated equally either affectation, *ennui*,[3] or ill health. He seemed a personage of some impor-

---

1 A "livre de lectures" (book of readings), perhaps a reader for use in schools.
2 *The Family Herald* identifies this chapter, along with the previous, as Chapter XVII, an error. Beginning with this, Chapter XVIII, all chapters follow the correct numerical sequencing.
3 Boredom.

tance, at least with the fair sex, to judge by the number of sweet smiles and flattering bows lavished on him by the ladies he encountered, but surely a greater stoic, or one more indifferent to female charms the chivalrous regiment of Roussillon usually famed for being

"So gallant in love
And so dauntless in war,"[1]

did not count among its ranks.

Vainly did the young budding beauties with whom Gustave De Montarville, for he it was, had perhaps danced an evening previous, raise their soft dark eyes in passing to his, as if mutely inviting him to turn and tender his escort;—vainly did the practised flirt, simper and nod, and the dashing, dauntless Miss De Nevers, colour up to the temples and smile so irresistibly upon him, when the young soldier carelessly touched his cap in recognition of her blushing bow. For that day at least, he was proof against all.

Within the last year Gustave had greatly changed, but still, though considerably thinner from the wearing effects of long illness, his countenance and whole bearing had wonderfully gained in manly beauty and grace, excusing certainly, if not justifying the degree of admiration he excited among his fair friends.

He had obtained permission from the army surgeon, a few days previously, after repeated requests on his part, to join his regiment at Quebec, and he now looked forward with restless impatience to that long desired event. His engagement with Blanche De Villerai still subsisted, but she had put off their marriage for another additional year, an arrangement in which he had tacitly, silently acquiesced. Mrs. Dumont had fretted and scolded on the occasion, but Blanche had remained inflexible alike to reproaches or entreaties.

Whatever were De Montarville's thoughts as he strolled that warm afternoon along the rough pavement of Notre Dame Street, they must certainly have been very wearisome, to have judged from the expression of his features. Suddenly, however, his cheek flushed, his eye brightened, and his whole countenance as if by magic, underwent a most extraordinary change. But what wonderful or unexpected event had caused all this?

---

1 From the heroic ballad "Lochinvar" by Sir Walter Scott: "So faithful in love, and so dauntless in war, / There never was knight like the young Lochinvar" (lines 5-6).

His gaze had suddenly and accidentally fallen on a slight female figure, draped in black, hurrying quickly but lightly past the spot where he stood. The object of his attention was closely veiled, but through the thick folds of the black net, he had recognized the faultless features of Rose Lauzon.

His first impulse was to spring towards and address her, but suddenly remembering her firmness and decision in what she deemed the path of duty, he determined on not presenting himself to her notice till he should have ascertained, if possible, her place of abode. Quietly, therefore, though at a considerable distance, he followed her, till at length she stopped before the door of Mrs. De Rochon's mansion.

The latter lady, he merely knew by rumour, as belonging to one of the oldest families of the province, one who had rendered herself remarkable by her generous, active benevolence, and supposing that Rose had merely entered there on some message, he resolved to await her coming forth. Whilst doing so, he inwardly revolved the probable reasons that had brought the latter to Montreal, and blessed, again and again, the fortunate chance that had obtained him an opportunity of meeting the being, who despite all obstacles, still reigned supreme in his wayward heart. Finding after a half hour that Rose still lingered, he was just on the point of crossing the road to the house, when the door opened, and an elderly lady, simply dressed, whom he justly divined to be Mrs. De Rochon, descended the steps. This decided him on remaining where he was for some time farther, and he waited until the lady crossed the street and disappeared within the portal of the parish church.[1] He then hastened up the steps and plied the knocker for admittance.

"Is Miss Lauzon here?" he somewhat hesitatingly asked of the servant who answered his summons.

"Yes, sir, she is upstairs," and the round black eyes of the speaker wonderingly scrutinized the fashionable exterior of the epauletted gallant, who enquired about her mistress's humble *demoiselle de compagnie*.

"I wish to see her for a moment," hurriedly exclaimed De Montarville, feeling as he spoke, that he would have forfeited

---

1 The edifice in question, a simple construction of rough stone, was situated in the Place D'Armes, opposite the site now occupied by the magnificent French Cathedral, and was pulled down in 1830, but the belfry or tower of it remained standing till 1843, when it also was removed, thus giving size and symmetry to the square. [Leprohon's note]

then every hope of promotion or glory, rather than the prospect of seeing her he enquired for.

"I shall tell her, *Monsieur*," replied the woman, still in the same state of blank amazement, and she slowly led the way to the drawing room, "what name shall I say?"

"Only tell Miss Lauzon that there is a person here who wishes to see her."

How long the moments seemed to De Montarville. What if Rose should suspect from the domestic's description who the visitor was, and refuse to see him, or perhaps await the return of her protectress ere venturing into the drawing room. These unpleasant doubts were soon set at rest, for the door of the apartment softly opened, and Rose in all her freshness and beauty,— Rose as he had often seen her in his dreams, not attired in the garb of a *paysanne*, but in a dress more consonant with her own delicate form and exquisite beauty stood before him.

Paler than marble became her cheek as her glance fell upon her visitor, and trembling with agitation, she sank upon the nearest seat, faltering forth his name.

"Yes, Rose, 'tis I.—I, who have asked for, sought you for months, till I had almost given up all hopes of ever meeting you again."

"And, why, should you wish it to be otherwise?" she asked, in a low agitated tone. "What is—what can Rose Lauzon ever be to you, Captain De Montarville?"

"Ah! you are Rose Lauzon, still!" he rapidly rejoined. "Thank God! at least, for that!"

"Did I not tell you," was the somewhat reproachfully uttered answer, "that I would never change that name?"

"Oh! yes, Rose," he impetuously exclaimed, seizing her small hand and pressing it closely within his own. "You shall change it for mine, for that of De Montarville. I tell you, child, that it is in vain to will it otherwise! I have done my best to forget you—I have sought in active, stirring occupation, in idle pleasure, to banish your image from that heart wherein you refuse so obstinately to reign, and, now, that you are again before me, I feel that you are more firmly throned there than ever."

"And your betrothed—your promises to Miss De Villerai?"

"I tell you, as I told you before, that Blanche De Villerai loves me not. Had she done so, would she have postponed our marriage for another year, which was to have taken place on my promotion?"

"And, if she did so, Mr. De Montarville, whose was the fault?

She must have perceived some coldness, some change in yourself—heard some idle talk, oh! how my cheek burns whilst I mention it, about your passing fancy for an inferior, the creature of her former bounty. Think you, a noble young lady like Miss De Villerai, who could choose a mate among the highest in the land, would force herself on a cold or unwilling bridegroom?"

"'Tis no use Rose, 'tis no use!" he groaned. "I feel the truth of all you say—I feel respect, esteem for Miss De Villerai, but I love only you, you alone. Ah! the very firmness with which one, usually so gentle as yourself, resists all my pleading—the noble generosity, with which every thought of self, every idea of worldly advancement is forgotten in your devotion to another, but adds new links to the chain that binds me to you. And you have to struggle too, against the same subtle power to which I have long since yielded, for you love me, Rose! Start not thus—strive not to look so coldly upon me, for, I tell you, that if you laid that gentle head down upon my breast and whispered the sweet truth in my ear, I could not feel more convinced of it than I do now."

The girl listened to him with cheek varying from the deepest crimson to deadliest pallor, and when he had concluded, she murmured. "Be it so, but know, that the greater the affection I may entertain for yourself, the farther will you be from the consummation of your present wishes. A career, brilliant and glorious as that now opening before you, shall never be marred by the weak selfishness of a lowly-born village girl.

"Think of the consequences Mr. De Montarville, of the *mésalliance*[1] on which you would rush. Think how friends would rebuke and shun you—how enemies would sneer and triumph—how the world would mock and laugh! Think of the noble powerful families, connected closely with your betrothed, whom you would outrage also, in outraging her.—And, Blanche De Villerai herself, that fair and noble young lady who would be a fit bride for a prince, she to be contemned, cast aside for such as I!—never, never, and, now, Captain De Montarville, we must part—I have already delayed here too long. What would Mrs. De Rochon say or think were she to return and find me here?"

"One question, Rose, answer me one question, and, then, I will leave you in peace. Are you really living here, and in what capacity?"

---

[1] "A union between two people that is thought to be unsuitable or inappropriate; *esp.* a marriage with a person of a lower social position" (*OED*).

"Humble companion to the kindest, the best of women."

"Ah! how could she be otherwise to you, my gentle one!" and he looked tenderly, earnestly upon her. "And, yet, I forget, your infamous step-mother! Oh, how I loathe, how I hate that woman! Give me another moment, Rose, and I will recount the last interview I had with her. Ordered by the physician to the country, whenever my wound permitted of the journey, I accepted Mrs. Dumont's pressing, unceasing invitations to the manor house, and went to De Villerai. Whilst there, I made some indirect enquiries about yourself, but, to no purpose. I merely learned that your father had died, and that your step-mother's cruelty had compelled you shortly afterwards, to leave the house. You had gone, the people I enquired of, knew not whither, but they added that *Monsieur* Le Curé could certainly inform me. I felt pretty confident of the manner in which the good priest would probably receive my request for information regarding you; but the dreadful state of uncertainty in which I was, regarding your real fate, not knowing but that you might be exposed to poverty's worst trials and temptations, nearly drove me wild, and I fearlessly presented myself at the Presbytery. Mr. Lapointe, though perhaps a little cold at first, was perfectly courteous, but he declined giving me the slightest clue to your whereabouts, merely assuring me solemnly that you were entirely out of the reach of want or even of unkindness. For a few days this assurance somewhat satisfied me, but soon the old longing to know where you were, or to be candid with you, Rose, to see you once more, came back upon me stronger than ever, and, on the eve of my departure from De Villerai, I went to your step-mother's residence, resolving to flatter or frighten her into giving me the information I coveted. Oh! Rose, what an interview I had, and what an insight I obtained into all that you had suffered—suffering, alas, which I fear my own thoughtlessness, in great measure brought upon you. You Rose, that had refused to become my loved and honoured wife spoken of—accused—but, I will not insult your innocent ears by repeating any of the calumnies of that vile woman. Suffice it to say, I returned to Montreal, wearied and dispirited, hopeless of finding any clue to the discovery of your abode, till to-day when I so fortunately and unexpectedly met and followed you. But, you look uneasy—restless; you are wearied of me. Well, I will soon be gone, and, this will probably be our last meeting for a long time. In two days I rejoin my regiment in Quebec, where we will perhaps soon have active work. You need not turn so fearfully pale, Rose. Rejoining one's regiment does not necessarily imply incurring either peril or danger."

"But, you are still an invalid," she faltered.

"Ah! Rose, if I were one-half as sound in heart as I am in body, few stronger and gayer soldiers would fight under King Louis' banners; but, I must say farewell. I know not whether we should bless or regret the day we first met, but, surely, we have brought only sorrow and grief to each other. Tell me, this, Rose, only this. Would you, if the power were yours, blot that day from your life and memory?"

Eagerly he bent over her, looking closely down into that sweet, crimsoning face, and then when she softly whispered "No" he pressed her to him, passionately exclaiming; "Thanks, thanks, even for that! Ah! come what will, to me, it has been the dearest, the brightest, of my existence!"

Another agitated farewell word—a shower of kisses on her hands, her brow, her soft, shining hair, and he was gone—gone, leaving a blank in that young heart, which even the sense of duty fulfilled, the enthusiasm of gratitude and self-sacrifice, never afterwards sufficed to fill.

Mrs. De Rochon on her re-entrance half an hour afterwards, missing Rose from the sitting-room, sought her in her own apartment. She found her lying on a sofa, her face deadly pale, whilst her eyes were red and swollen from excessive weeping.

"Are you ill, *petite*?" she kindly enquired, laying her own cool hands on the burning fingers, clasped, different to their usual wont, idly together.

"Come, tell me is it mental or bodily pain, Rose?"

The latter replied only by a low sob, and Mrs. De Rochon surveyed her with a sorrowful anxious look. "My dear child," she at length exclaimed, taking her companion's hand in hers. "I do not wish to force you into giving me your confidence, but, may I ask the name of the gay handsome officer, whom Marie says called here some time since to see you?"

"Gustave De Montarville," faltered Rose and as she spoke, the thought of all the suspicions and surmises which that name would probably excite in Mrs. De Rochon's mind, dyed her palid cheek with crimson.

Despite Mrs. De Rochon's theory regarding blushes being proofs of innocence, a theory propounded by herself a few weeks previous to Pauline De Nevers, we are bound to confess that on this present occasion she seemed almost as incredulous as her niece herself, with respect to the doctrine in question, for in a tone of cold surprise she repeated.

"Captain De Montarville, the affianced lover of Miss De Villerai?"

An affirmative sob was the only reply.

"Rose! Rose!" she gravely exclaimed. "I do not like this. What had Captain De Montarville to tell you of sufficient importance to authorise your remaining in converse with him for nearly an hour, and to leave you on his departure, overcome with emotion—deluged in tears? Surely, surely, child, Pauline De Nevers cannot be right in her suspicions! you are not the intriguing flirt—the artful hypocrite, she would lead me to believe. And yet what am I to think? With regard to De Noraye, I did not even give the matter a second thought, for I knew that he had probably by accident or design intruded himself into your presence; but Captain De Montarville in calling here to-day, asked for you by name and you received him. I reiterate the question my niece put to you about Count De Noraye—where did you meet Gustave De Montarville? In De Villerai, say you. Oh! Rose, Rose, if you would not be misjudged—if you would set my anxious troubled mind at rest, tell me what had that gay man of the world to say to you to-day that agitated you so terribly?—what is the extent of your acquaintance with him?"

Again did that same sharp pang shoot through Rose's breast as on that former, bitter occasion, when Blanche De Villerai herself, had so entreatingly implored her to speak and prove her innocence. Why, why, must she, blameless in action as well as thought, ever appear guilty to those whose good opinion and affection she prized most. Yet what could she say? Even for Blanche's sake, and for his, the more fondly, dearly loved than ever, she must be silent.

"You will not, or, is it, that you dare not speak, Rose?" was Mrs. De Rochon's question, uttered in a graver tone than she had yet employed.

"Oh! my kind, my noble benefactress!" suddenly ejaculated the weeping girl, clasping Mrs. De Rochon's hand in hers, and imploringly looking in her face, "I know that appearances are against me—I know there is much to excite blame and suspicion, but, oh! believe me, I am ignorant of even the shadow of wrong. Willingly would I tell you all—lay open my heart to you, but alas! the secrets of another are in my possession, and them I must hold sacred."

Mrs. De Rochon was silent for a moment. The excuse, if indeed it at all deserved the name, was most unsatisfactory, but the pleading was so eloquent, so touching, and the lady's own heart was so good and gentle, that she finally exclaimed,

"Be it as you wish, Rose. I will question you no more on the past, and overlook the occurrences of to-day, only exacting from you in return, a solemn promise, that you will neither meet nor see this fascinating captain De Montarville again."

"Willingly do I give the promise," was the eager reply, "and, if ever I depart from it, kind friend, I will not murmur, even if you banish me from under this happy roof, where the most peaceful days of my life have been passed."

"Poor child!" sighed Mrs. De Rochon, and again her hand stole caressingly as was its wont, amid the glossy silken tresses of her young companion. "That rare beauty with which a merciful providence has, for its own wise purposes endowed you, seems as yet to have brought you little happiness, but much, oh! much, peril and danger. 'Tis it that brings such men as De Noraye and De Montarville around you—men, who to-morrow, if the smoothness of your skin, or the brightness of your eyes by chance left you, would not stop to cast you a passing glance. Shun them, my child, shun them! They would cull the flower but to trample on and despoil it—seize the gem but to break and destroy."

Rose listened in submissive silence. Much as it pained her to hear the chivalrous De Montarville put on the same level with such a man as Gaston De Noraye, she dared not for his own sake, speak in his behalf, and when her companion kindly bade her lie down till tea-time, she gratefully but silently accepted the permission.

It was with a troubled countenance that the worthy mistress of the mansion seated herself at her afternoon knitting, and once she paused and laying it down, thoughtfully exclaimed, "Yes, I suppose that young De Montarville loves her in his way, loves her for the moment—for her own wondrous beauty. Her best defence then against his dangerous homage, is my watchful protection—the shelter of my roof, and if she loves him, why, still greater need has she of my care and guidance. Ah! to send her from me, might be to send her to him!"

And thus this good womanly Samaritan[1] thought and reasoned. If her judgment was at all deficient in worldly wisdom, surely, it was at least rich in christian charity.

---

1   See Luke 10.33; a kind and helpful person.

CHAPTER XIX.

The day following the interview we have just recorded between Rose and Captain De Montarville, a party of officers were standing in a group at the corner of the Place D'Armes, gaily interchanging smiles and jests, and freely criticizing the passers by, especially the members of the fair sex.

"Well," exclaimed one of the number, a slight, boyish looking young man, dressed with most fastidious elegance, "so to-morrow, we bid good-bye to this pleasant little Montreal, with its narrow, dirty streets and pretty women, to embark for the fortress city, Quebec. Let us hope, that as its streets are still narrower and dirtier, its women in the same ratio of increase, are still fairer and handsomer than their Montreal rivals."

"For my part," lisped the Count De Noraye, "I am quite charmed to get away, for really, I find myself surrounded by such a net-work of flirtation entanglements, that if the present excuse for departure did not present itself, I should really have no alternative save that of shooting myself, or breaking a dozen of female hearts."

A merry peal of laughter went round the group at this sally, whilst a tall, stalwart looking officer, in the dashing uniform of the Chasseur regiment, rejoined,

"Oh! provided you endowed them previously with your title and estates in Normandy, I think you might put a bullet through your brain, without at all endangering the hearts in question."

"Is that really your opinion, De Cournoyer?" rejoined the Count listlessly. "Well, I do not wonder at it, for doubtless your own personal experience in the hardness of female hearts, has had great weight in influencing your decision; but, remember, my dear fellow, though ladies may not often die of despair for a massive six-foot Hercules like yourself, they are more susceptible when an Apollo or Endymion is in the case."[1]

Again another laugh burst from the group, whilst De Cournoyer good-humouredly replied, "I suppose you are right,

---

[1] Figures in ancient Greek mythology. Hercules: son of Zeus, famed for his exceptional strength and courage. Apollo: presiding deity of higher expressions of civilization, such as the arts, philosophy, and law.
Endymion: a beautiful young shepherd loved by the moon goddess Selene.

for I think my *forte* lies more in breaking men's heads than women's hearts."

"Ho! De Noraye, hit again!" exclaimed the boyish looking Lieutenant Duperri.

Whatever reply the Count meditated, and that it was one of supreme impertinence was easy divined by the sarcastic curve of his haughty lip it was prevented by the slight sensation caused among the party by the approach of Miss De Nevers, who came floating towards them, over the rough irregular pavement, with the grace of a swan gliding on its favorite element.

"Ah! there comes one of your broken hearts, De Noraye," exclaimed Major Decoste, a rival lady-killer as he twisted a portentous moustache black as a raven's wing. "Considering the dilapidated state of so vital an organ, she looks remarkably well."

"Perhaps you are reversing the case, Decoste," remarked another. "Instead of De Noraye's having broken the dashing Pauline's heart, she may all the while be slowly breaking his. I have really found him looking somewhat pale and drooping for the last few days."

"Remorse, *mon cher*, remorse," drawled the Count, "for having made so many conquests, and not having left even half a one for a poor unfortunate like yourself."

"Hush! here she comes," ejaculated Major Decoste. "*Diantre!*[1] she is splendidly exquisitely dressed."

"And carries herself like a duchess!" chimed in young Duplessis.

"Yes, but who could tolerate such a pair of bold, *stand-and-deliver*[2] eyes, as she has got?" enquired a third. "Why, she could look down our whole regiment!"

"Yes, you are all such a set of timid, modest young gentlemen," sneered De Noraye. "The regiment of La Salle is we all know so famous in the service for its excessive bashfulness; but who is going to join the fair De Nevers? She expects some of us, of course, to turn out, and offer our escort."

"Why not go yourself, oh! irresistible Count?" asked his nearest neighbour.

"Because, it is not my turn to mount guard. She had me on fatigue duty all yesterday afternoon, and I feel quite done up to-day. A whole afternoon passed in making love and paying compliments, is very trying to the system. Ah! Here she is. Present arms—salute!"

---

1 "Devil!"
2 "A command to come to a halt, e.g., as a sentry's challenge" (*OED*).

As Pauline passed the group, all hats were simultaneously removed and she was greeted by bows of the most chivalrous gallantry. Two of the party immediately joined her—the fascinating Decoste, who was a fortune-hunter as well as lady-killer, and young Duplessis, whose blushing face and embarrassed air proved him to be at least sincere in his protestations of devotion; and thus escorted, the fair Pauline went on her way rejoicing.

For some time longer the little knot of idlers kept up the same strain of *badinage*, when Captain De Cournoyer animatedly exclaimed, "Talk of lovely faces!—there goes the prettiest I have ever yet seen in my life!"

All eyes were instantly turned in the direction towards which the speaker was looking, and a simultaneous murmur of admiration arose as Rose Lauzon hurried past, crossing at an angle into the street, to avoid coming in closer proximity with the gay group monopolizing the corner of the pavement. One rapid half glance she involuntarily hazarded towards them, as she thus turned partly out of her direction, and De Noraye, who was on the watch for an opportunity, instantly doffed his foraging cap with an elaborate, over-wrought courtesy, which savoured far more of mockery than respect.

"What! you know her, De Noraye?—What a lovely creature!—Who is she?" were the eager exclamations that resounded on all sides. "Tell us, man, if you can!"[1]

"One at a time, gentlemen, if you please!" he rejoined with his cold cynical smile. "Yes, I do know her and she is certainly a lovely creature. Her name is Rose.—Her other appellation, I shall with your permission, reserve."

De Noraye's smile and sneer seemed to convey a covert meaning which his words did not fully express, but his companions were well acquainted with his inveterate love of boasting, and the tall, Chasseur Captain, bluntly replied,

"Well, if you do know her, De Noraye, she does not seem to care much about knowing you, for she never even noticed your magnificent bow."

"But, did you not see how she blushed, *mon cher*?"

"Oh! her blushes were for ourselves as well as for you. I'll bet a *Louis d'or* to a *centime*, that any modest young girl obliged to

---

[1] In the *JCF* edition, Sorfleet transcribes this line as "Tell us more, if you can!" (112). The French version translates the passage as "Parlez donc, si vous pouvez" (278).

pass near such a bold disreputable looking set as we are, will blush up to her very eyes."

"Really, De Cournoyer, you are complimentary to your friends in general," rejoined De Noraye, who felt far more irritated than he chose to shew, by the doubts and incredulity of his companions, and Rose's manifest contempt.

"Well, then, sceptics that ye all are, if ye must have day and date to convince ye of the truth of what I say, I may as well acknowledge that I first met that little Rose bud of beauty, whose real name is Rose Lauzon, in the small village of De Villerai, some twenty months ago. I met her again last week, and shall do so the next—or, whenever I choose."

A prolonged whistle from one of the party—a discomfited regretful shake of the head from De Cournoyer, who had been quite "taken" with Rose's modest, fresh young beauty, followed this significant announcement, when suddenly a voice exclaimed close to the Count's ear.

"De Noraye, you are a liar and a slanderer!" Furiously the Count bounded rather than turned towards the quarter whence the insulting words had proceeded and standing there, pale with a passion, terrible as that raging at the moment within his own breast, was Gustave De Montarville.

"Was it you who dared address those words to me?" questioned De Noraye, almost beside himself with rage.

"Yes," was the clear distinct answer, "and, I again repeat them. Gaston De Noraye, you are a liar and a slanderer!"

The Count who had now lost all self-control, raised his clenched hand to strike the speaker, but Captain De Cournoyer elevated his stalwart arm in time to intercept the blow, ere it fell.

"In France, Gaston," he quietly said, "we always answered such words, not with blows, but with bullets or steel. They are the only means gentlemen can use. Be patient, man! you can have pistols and satisfaction, to-morrow morning, as early as you like."

This reflection somewhat calmed De Noraye's wrath for he was an excellent marksman, and the prospect of a sure and deadly revenge thus offered him, enabled him to quickly regain the cynical composure he so rarely lost.

"Thank you for the suggestion De Cournoyer," he calmly rejoined. "It will be a sort of *coup d'appétit*[1] before breakfast, and

---

1 The "customary *coup d'appétit*—that is, brandy for the men and mild cordials for the women—was the signal that supper was served" (74). From Philippe Aubert de Gaspé, *Les Anciens Canadiens* (tr. Jane Brierley).

promote digestion, which this horrid climate we are doomed for a time to endure, sadly deranges. To conclude, however, gentlemen, the subject so inopportunely interrupted," and he glanced round the circle, his eyes sparkling with malice, "I have only to add that whatever little claims I may possess on Rose Lauzon's regard, those of Captain De Montarville are at least prior to, if not greater than mine. She has been a powerful rival, long since, to the heiress of De Villerai, in his affections!"

Poor Gustave! his honest manly indignation was scarcely a match for the cunning, crafty composure of his subtle adversary, but, for the sake of Rose's good name, he forced himself to be calm, and in an earnest tone he exclaimed:

"I know you will all believe me, when, I assure you, on the word of a soldier, and of a man of honour, of one, at least, who has never *lied*," here he glanced disdainfully towards De Noraye, who was smilingly adjusting his watch guard, "that the young girl Rose Lauzon, is as irreproachable in conduct, as worthy of respect in every way as the high-minded Blanche De Villerai herself."

There was that in the clear manly tones of the speaker, in his truthful open countenance that conveyed perfect conviction to the minds of his hearers, and, with the exception of De Noraye, they all warmly replied, "We believe you, De Montarville, we believe you."

The Count feeling that the tide of general sympathy was turning against him, looked towards a member of the party, and drawled forth, "You are really all getting so melodramatic and tiresome, that I must be off, *au revoir*, my friends," and, so saying, the elegant exquisite strolled listlessly down the street.

"This is really a most disagreeable and unfortunate affair," exclaimed Captain De Cournoyer. "Just on the eve of rejoining our friends in Quebec, and to add the climax to the matter two officers in the same regiment. Is there no possible way, De Montarville, of compromising the affair?"

"None, whatever, unless indeed, that De Noraye, will openly retract and apologize for the slanders he has uttered to-day, against one whose only fault in his eyes, has been her repulsing with disdain the insulting attentions he would have forced upon her."

"That, he will never do, then," ejaculated Ensign Delaunais, with emphasis. "De Noraye is as brave as he is wrong-headed and vain, and that is saying a great deal. Besides, he is too good a shot! Whoever heard of a crack marksman like him, apologizing?"

"Too bad!" exclaimed De Cournoyer, laying his hand heavily on De Montarville's shoulder, "too bad that this brave life which escaped so narrowly at Carillon, should be risked again in so miserable a broil. You, too, who for so many months have been condemned to an invalid's wearisome inaction!"

"What will your betrothed say, Gustave, when she comes to hear of this affair?" enquired another. "Your name and that of so notorious a fellow as De Noraye mixed up in a quarrel about a pretty girl. The tale can scarcely prove very agreeable to her ears."

De Montarville slightly coloured, but he calmly replied. "Miss De Villerai is too noble-hearted a woman to feel either pique or irritation from such a cause. She is as good as she is beautiful."

"Well," exclaimed the other, disguising a slight yawn. "If that lovely little girl that you are going to exchange shots about, was also a *seigneuresse* and an heiress, I would prefer her, even to the queen-like Blanche herself: but, come, let us take a turn down the street,—I am positively sick of standing at this corner."

CHAPTER XX

Mrs. De Rochon was sewing in her sitting-room, and standing at a table near, cutting out some articles of coarse but comfortable clothing, intended for some of the claimants of the latter lady's bounty, was Rose Lauzon. She looked both ill and pale, and her little fingers moved about their task with a listlessness most unusual to them.

Poor Rose! her sacrifice had been nobly, generously made, but the remembrance of it was beginning to eat like some corroding sorrow into her heart. Her love for De Montarville had been doubled—trebled within the last few hours by the deep devotion he had displayed towards herself, and even whilst endeavouring to strengthen still farther her resolution of seeing him no more, the pang inflicted by that simple thought, surpassed in bitterness the sharpest sorrow her life had ever yet known.

The sound of a carriage stopping at the hall-door broke in upon the silence that reigned throughout the room, and Mrs. De Rochon exclaimed, "Who can this be, at so late an hour? 'Tis nearly tea-time."

"Perhaps Miss De Nevers," suggested Rose.

"Yes, it must be Pauline."

A moment afterwards the door was ceremoniously thrown open, and to Rose's mingled wonder and consternation, Pauline, accompanied by her former benefactress, Mrs. Dumont entered. She dropped that latter a timid courtesy but the lady took no notice of her whatever, beyond regarding her with a passing glance of stony severity.

"Aunt De Rochon—Mrs. Dumont"—exclaimed Pauline performing the ceremony of introduction. The two ladies exchanged courteous words telling how they had met many years ago—had preserved each a pleasant recollection of that meeting, though the seclusion both had observed since their respective widowhoods had prevented the continuation of an intercourse which would doubtless have proved most agreeable to both parties. Mrs. De Rochon, however, though too well-bred to shew it, was in reality greatly surprised by this unexpected visit, and sat patiently waiting the explanation of the cause by which it had been prompted. She had not long to wait, for Pauline with a heightened colour and cruel smile, soon exclaimed,

"Your residence, or rather one of its inmates is becoming quite notorious, Aunt De Rochon. We shall soon have travelling artists taking wood-cuts of the edifice, and the curious, flocking from all parts of the city to take a look at it."

"How so, Pauline?" was the somewhat uneasy query.

"Why, all Montreal is talking about nothing else this morning but your *protégée* Miss Rose Lauzon, and the duel that has just been fought on her account, between two of His Majesty's officers."

Mrs. De Rochon's only reply was a look of wondering astonishment, whilst Rose a prey to sudden fears and thoughts the most conflicting and confusing, felt as if her limbs could scarcely support her weight.

"Yes, Aunt, this morning in the presence of witnesses and principals, a duel was fought between the Count De Noraye and Captain De Montarville, in which one of the parties was wounded."

Rose turned deadly pale and sank on her seat, unable to control her emotion or conceal her fear, and utterly unmindful in her terrible anxiety regarding Gustave, of the cruel eyes fixed so coldly upon her, for both Pauline and Mrs. Dumont were scrutinizing every change of her pallid face.

"Ah! if I had known that my intelligence would have affected *Miss* Lauzon so deeply, I would have been more guarded in communicating it," continued the malicious heiress of De Nevers. "Pray, take a glass of water, *Mademoiselle*," and she mockingly pushed over a crystal *caraffe* which stood on the table near Rose.

"What do you mean, Rose Lauzon, by daring to exhibit such emotion?" asked Mrs. Dumont in great wrath. "Pray, what is Captain De Montarville to you, that you should presume to shew more agitation regarding his safety, than his betrothed wife, Miss De Villerai, herself?"

"For heaven's sake, Pauline, be more explicit?" exclaimed Mrs. De Rochon. "What does all this mean?"

"It simply means, Aunt, that your fair *protégée*'s charms and flirtations have been the cause of a duel between two gentlemen of high birth and position. Did I not warn you of the probable result when I first saw that pretty but deceitful face installed in your sitting-room?" "This is terrible!" murmured Mrs. De Rochon, "you said that one of the parties was wounded. Seriously so?"

"No, though his Quixotic[1] foolhardiness well deserved it. The ball merely grazed De Montarville's shoulder, drawing a little blood, whilst his adversary escaped entirely unhurt. But it might have been otherwise—one or both might have been mortally wounded. Ridiculous, to think of the lives of a Count De Noraye, or a Gustave De Montarville being risked for such as *her*!" and the speaker cast a glance towards her humble rival, in whose withering scorn there lurked no small proportion of vindictive jealousy.

"Rose, can you not speak and disprove the charges brought against you?" exclaimed Mrs. De Rochon, her countenance and voice both exhibiting perplexity and distress.

"What can I say?" questioned Rose. "I know nothing whatever of the event of which Miss De Nevers has been speaking. I know not even of what she accuses me!"

"I will tell you, then, girl, what you have done," interrupted Mrs. Dumont, severely. "In return for the protection and kindness myself and niece lavished on you from your childhood—in return for the superior education we conferred on you—the kindness with which we made the manor house of De Villerai your second home, you artfully, dishonourably alienated, or rather endeavoured to alienate from my niece Blanche, the affections of her betrothed husband—he to whom she had been affianced

---

[1] "Of an action, attribute, idea, etc.: characteristic of or appropriate to Don Quixote; demonstrating or motivated by exaggerated notions of chivalry and romanticism; naively idealistic; unrealistic, impracticable" (*OED*). From the Spanish novel *Don Quixote* (2 vols., 1605 and 1615) by Miguel de Cervantes.

from her cradle. But for you, the dearest wish of my old age would ere this have been accomplished, and Blanche would have been to-day the beloved wife of Captain De Montarville. Stop! I know you would insolently answer that 'tis Miss De Villerai herself who has put off the marriage. Why? Because, thanks to your cunning intrigues, your dishonourable artifices, you introduced coldness and disunion between them; and my niece, noble in heart as well as birth, would not stoop to wed a man who permitted even for an hour the semblance of a rival to reign in his affections. However, months had elapsed since the period of the first *esclandre*[1] you caused in De Villerai;—insensibly they were drawing nearer again to each other. De Montarville had grown once more devoted, and Blanche forgiving, when a second time you must appear on the scene to work even more mischief than you have yet done. Girl, you do well to preserve silence, for what answer have you to give?"

Patient Rose! had she but chosen to speak, how utterly could she have confounded her persecutors; but the true womanly instinct of self-sacrifice which she possessed in so eminent a degree, kept her silent.

Miss De Nevers was leaning carelessly back in her chair, tossing in her fingers the *casserole* of perfumes attached to her wrist by a slender golden chain; but the animation of her eyes and complexion, plainly evinced her keen enjoyment of the scene.

Mrs. De Rochon, utterly confounded by all these unexpected revelations, had risen from her seat, and now stood looking from Mrs. Dumont to her *protégée*, unwilling to condemn the latter, and yet fearing to excuse her. As her eye rested on the fair gentle girl, she had learned within so short a time to love so well, she could find no traces of guilt or hypocrisy in that sweet childish face, and she hesitatingly replied:

"But, my dear Mrs. Dumont, are you quite certain that Rose is so much to blame? God has given her great beauty, and may not this have attracted Captain De Montarville as it has done Count De Noraye, whom she ignominiously repulsed the other day in this very house?"

"Repulsed!" sneered Miss De Nevers. "Yes, that is her story; but he, doubtless could tell a different one."

"Pauline, be silent!" exclaimed Mrs. De Rochon, sternly.

---

1 "Unpleasant notoriety; an occurrence which gives rise to it; a disturbance, scene" (*OED*).

"My dear madam," enquired Mrs. Dumont, in a voice in which politeness and anger struggled for the mastery, "are you really serious in your last remark? Do you think for one moment that any man, however eccentric his tastes and ideas might be, would turn from the beautiful Blanche De Villerai, who had been the most admired young lady in every ballroom or *reunion*[1] in which she has yet appeared, to play the lover to an insignificant little girl, unless she had previously drawn him to her by the most artful snares and coquetry. No, that idea is ridiculous; and apparently she is still pursuing her old course. As she did to my niece, so she is endeavouring to do to yours; for report says that Count De Noraye, Rose's latest conquest, once ranked among Miss De Nevers' most favoured and devoted lovers."

"Oh! I am able to take care of my own lovers," exclaimed the fair Pauline, with a contemptuous toss of her head. "Impossible that I should dread a rival in one like *her*!"

"And yet, young lady," retorted Mrs. Dumont, who seemed to think that this remark reflected indirectly on her own niece, "I do not think the two valiant and inconstant gentlemen we have just been talking about, would be perhaps as ready to risk their lives in a duel for you to-morrow, as they have been to do for her to-day."

"Arguing on such a point is simply absurd," was Miss De Nevers' cold supercilious reply. "'Tis not as a wife they seek my aunt's *suivante*—."

"Rose, you had better go to your room," hastily interrupted Mrs. De Rochon. "When these ladies shall have left, I can discuss the subject with you alone."

"And now, Mrs. Dumont," she continued, turning abruptly from her niece, "now, that we are alone, will you kindly relate to me all the particulars you may have heard regarding this unfortunate event?"

"My knowledge of the affair is very limited. I merely know that a number of officers were standing together at the corner of Notre Dame Street, when the young girl, Rose Lauzon, passed them. Thereupon, Count De Noraye made some depreciating or mocking remark regarding her moral character, and that hot-headed boy De Montarville, who happened to be at his elbow, turned furiously on the speaker, branding him as liar and slanderer. Such words between men are never forgiven. So they met, and risked their lives this morning in a cause most unworthy,

---

1 A social gathering.

indeed, of their prowess. It remains but to enquire now, my dear Mrs. De Rochon, how you intend acting with regard to the author of all this mischief?"

The lady thus addressed, looking both distressed and puzzled, the interlocutor continued, though in a louder, sterner key:

"To be plainer with you, madam, you surely do not intend sanctioning the shameless conduct of that artful girl, by affording her longer the shelter of your honoured name and roof?"

"But, what would you have me do?" pleaded the kind-hearted hostess. "She has no family, no friends to receive her—no home to return to."

"Send her back to her step-mother," replied Mrs. Dumont harshly. "She will be out of the way of temptation there."

"Pardon me—'tis there that temptation might most successfully seek her; besides, I question much if she would even consent to go back there."

"Oh! probably not," said Pauline with a sarcastic laugh. "She would prefer remaining in Montreal, where she could find admirers in plenty, and create a sensation by having gentlemen fight duels in her cause. Really, Aunt, you will soon acquire considerable celebrity through her, though a celebrity somewhat different to the kind you have heretofore enjoyed. Instead of paupers—distressed orphans besieging your doors, you will have dashing officers, elegant cavaliers, soliciting admittance, and permission to gaze on the wonderful beauty you have drawn from her sylvan seclusion to create a sensation in our good city."

"Pauline, your *persiflage*[1] only pains, it does not irritate me. Pray cease it!"

"But, you have not answered Mrs. Dumont's question," persisted the haughty girl, fixing her determined gaze on her relative. "After all that she has told you—after all that has taken place this morning, are you still bent on giving Rose Lauzon a place in your house, and at your table? Think you, that if you do so, I will again enter beneath your roof to breathe the same air with one so vile as she must be?"

"Listen to me Pauline, and you also, Mrs. Dumont. When, after serious reflection, I took Rose beneath my protection, I became responsible to God for her destiny, as far as I could control it. Even, then, if she were as unworthy, as culpable as you would have me believe, 't would be my duty to endeavour to

---

[1] "Light raillery or mockery; bantering talk; a frivolous or mildly contemptuous manner of treating any subject" (*OED*).

reclaim her—how much more sacredly then am I bound to protect her if she is really innocent, and sought after—followed against her will by these gay, heartless men of the world. Pauline, would you, a virtuous, well brought up young girl—you, Mrs. Dumont, who unites the experience of age to knowledge of life, would you have me thrust forth from my doors, that young inexperienced child with her dangerous gift of beauty, to become at once the victim of the slanderer—the aim of the libertine?[1] Ah! no! Such, surely, is not my duty, and even at the risk of offending where I would willingly please, I must declare my firm intention of still protecting—still guarding the motherless girl I have taken under my charge."

Mrs. Dumont was touched despite herself by the affecting simplicity of this appeal, and though her parting address was stately and ceremonious, something inwardly whispered that when the first emotions of anger should have subsided, she would feel grateful that Mrs. De Rochon had allowed herself to be guided alone by the dictates of her own gentle heart. Not so Pauline. She was made of sterner material, and besides had thoughts and feelings concealed in the depths of her own breast, such as tormented not the peaceful soul of Mrs. Dumont.

"So, Aunt," she coldly exclaimed as she rose to take leave, "you have decided between myself and your *protégée*—your dead sister's only child, and that artful pauper, thrust on your charity by chance! Well, I only hope that you may never have cause to regret your choice."

"But, Pauline, my child!" tenderly exclaimed Mrs. De Rochon; "you are as dear—you will be as dear to me as you have ever been. Surely, I can continue to love you without abandoning her."

"You cannot, Aunt, you cannot!" was the imperious reply; "so, I leave your house to-day, to return to it only, when that vile girl, who seems to have bewitched you, shall have left, or been turned from it."

"So be it, Pauline," was the sad reply. "The decision is yours—not mine. You have a father, home, wealth, social position, to protect you, and can easily do without me. She has none of all these and consequently needs me most."

---

1 "A person (typically a man) who is not restrained by morality, esp. with regard to sexual relations; a person of dissolute or promiscuous habits" (*OED*).

Rigid and unbending, the haughty girl slightly inclined her head and swept from the room in the wake of Mrs. Dumont, leaving their late hostess with a heavy anxious heart.

"May God direct me in the right path!" she murmured. "Surely, I have done my duty and yet I feel most unhappy. Oh! if my poor sister had but lived to watch over her thoughtless child, how many unhappy hours would have been spared me! And, Rose! Can she really be the ungrateful, artful being Mrs. Dumont described? Can that fair child-like brow—those clear truthful eyes, really mask such deep hypocrisy and guile? Alas! Mrs. Dumont's tale seemed plausible enough, and was sadly corroborated by Rose's silence and confusion. Whatever her degree of culpability, though, Pauline's angry denunciations of her, were surely unkind and unchristianly in the extreme—unjust too, for if Rose really strove to win De Montarville from his betrothed, it was only doing what she herself and half of her young friends have been striving to do for the last six months: but, I must speak now with Rose herself!"

Summoning Marie, she bade her send Miss Lauzon to her immediately. Soon the latter came with wearied listless step and dejected look.

"Rose," said Mrs. De Rochon, kindly but gravely, "Now, that I am alone, what have you to tell; or say to me?"

"Nothing, only, that I must go from you at once," was the mournful reply. "Free you from the annoyance and mental anxieties my unhappy presence has already introduced beneath your peaceful roof."

"And where would you go to, child? What would you do?"

"Perhaps your kind influence might procure me some humble situation as nursery governess, but, alas!" she bitterly added, "Who would take me now? My very name would be sufficient to bar all doors upon me. No, that avenue is closed, but I might procure needlework, or some honest employment, however menial."

"It would never do, poor child! Such a step would expose you to trials and temptations of which you have not now a suspicion. No—you will remain with me still, and whatever your past conduct may have been, let your future life be free from even the shadow of blame. And, now, is there anything you would ask me," she continued seeing that her companion essayed once or twice to speak. "Do not fear Rose! Be candid with me!"

Thus encouraged, the latter timidly enquired if the ladies had given any farther explanation regarding the event for which they had blamed herself so bitterly, an event of which she as yet knew positively nothing.

"All I know, Rose, is that De Noraye like a coward, calumniated you—De Montarville took your part. Hasty words passed between them and the result was this morning's meeting: but let us return to our usual duties, child. We have sadly wasted the last hour," and Mrs. De Rochon departed on some household mission happy that the disagreeable discussions of the day were at an end.

"Perilled his life for me!" murmured Rose. "Oh! De Montarville, was there ever a love ennobling, devoted as thine!" and with this new trait of her lover's generous affection to dwell upon, Rose mechanically pursued her task, heart and thought wrapped up in sweet though painful reverie.

Dangerous indeed for her peace of mind were the events of the last few days, and the struggle between duty and inclination, which in the beginning had been merely nominal, now became active, and painful. Often did the voice of temptation whisper that the terrible sacrifice she was making, was more than she was called on to offer—that De Montarville loving her as he did, would be happier with one like herself, who would study, anticipate his slightest wish, than wedded to the stately Miss De Villerai, who seemed to set such small store on his love, to prize it so little. Then, hurriedly, blushingly she would banish the selfish thought, condemning herself the while for having indulged it even for a moment—severely asking herself would she repay De Montarville's generous love by marring his future career—by permitting him to commit a folly, which terrible thought! he might afterwards repent for a life time.

Often too did she anxiously wonder what Blanche had thought or said when the intelligence of the duel between her betrothed and Count De Noraye, had reached her. On that point however there was no cause for uneasiness, for that very evening Gustave had written a simple straight forward letter to Miss De Villerai, recapitulating word for word the altercation which had passed between De Noraye and himself, as well as the falsehoods of the latter which had given rise to it, and concluding by saying he knew well that she was too true—too noble-hearted a woman to blame him for what he had done. He was right in his supposition and when Blanche folded up the letter after its perusal, though a slight sigh escaped her, no expression of irritation or annoyance overshadowed her countenance.

CHAPTER XXI.

After the taking of Louisburg by the English, the latter turned their thoughts to the reduction of Quebec, the stronghold of Canada. A body of ten thousand men was placed under the command of General Wolfe, a gallant young Officer who had already distinguished himself in a brilliant manner at the siege of Louisburg.[1]

Vessels from Europe confirmed the public rumours that an English squadron was already *en route* for the shores of Canada and on the 23rd of May, they were seen off Bic,[2] steering up the river. This however, was merely the vanguard commanded by Admiral Durell which had been sent on from Louisburg to intercept the supplies from France. A large squadron under the command of Admiral Saunders had sailed from England in the month of February with orders to transport General Wolfe and his army then at Louisburg to Quebec. They sailed up the St. Lawrence and arrived at the Island of Orleans on the 25th of June,[3] without having met with the slightest accident, notwithstanding the many perils and difficulties with which the navigation of the stream was usually attended. This good fortune was owing to the treachery of the commander of a French frigate, Denis De Vitre,[4] taken prisoner by the English during the war, and who piloted them safely to Quebec, his native birth place, for which act of treachery he was repaid by a commission in the English service.

Admiral Saunders ordered an examination to be made of the harbor and port of Quebec, and Captain Cook,[5] who afterwards

---

1 James Wolfe (1727-59), the famed commander of the British forces that took Quebec in September 1759, who was killed at the Battle of the Plains of Abraham. The Battle of Louisbourg (June-July 1758), one of the key battles in the North American theatre of the Seven Years' War.

2 Located in what is now the Province of Quebec, on the south shore of the St. Lawrence River (today's municipality of Rimouski).

3 Vice-Admiral Philip Durrell (1707-66); Vice-Admiral Charles Saunders (1715-75); Island of Orléans, located approximately five kilometres east of Quebec City.

4 Denys de Vitré (1724-75).

5 James Cook (1728-79), English explorer and navigator.

immortalized himself by his famous voyages and discoveries, was employed upon this service. 'Tis worthy of note that two of the earliest navigators who sailed round the globe, Captain Cook and Colonel De Bougainville, were then beneath the walls of Quebec. Soon after the landing of the troops on the Island of Orleans, De Montcalm taking advantage of a dark stormy night, prepared seven fire-ships and sent them down at midnight amongst the English transports grouped together off the Island. Partly owing to their having been set on fire too soon, and partly to the coolness and dexterity of the English Admiral and seamen, they were towed ashore by the latter, where they harmlessly burned down to the water's edge. A month afterwards another attempt of the same nature was made but with as little success.

De Montcalm had posted a body of men with several pieces of cannon at Pointe Lévi,[1] but, these troops were soon compelled to retire, and the post taken possession of by the English, under the command of General Moncton. Fifteen hundred French troops were then despatched across the river to attack and destroy the works but they retreated in the utmost confusion, without effecting anything.[2] On the same night the batteries at Pointe Lévi opened their fire upon Quebec, and the lower town was soon a heap of ruins. Amongst the many fine buildings destroyed was the Cathedral, with all its valuable paintings and ornaments. The cannon on the ramparts were useless, for owing to the width of the river which is here more than a mile across, they could not reach the English batteries, doubly protected by the trees and shrubs surrounding them.

Having destroyed the city, General Wolfe turned his arms against the surrounding country. All the parishes from Montmorenci, to Cape Tourmente on the left bank of the St. Lawrence, were ravaged and destroyed. Those of Malbaie, St. Paul, and the island of Orleans, also all those situated on the right bank, from Berthier to River du Loup below Quebec, including the parishes of Pointe Lévi, Saint Nicholas and St. Croix, shared the same fate. According to a journal of the expedition published in the New York Mercury in 1759, upwards of 1400 fine farm houses were burned and destroyed about this time, so that to

---

1 Alternate spelling, Pointe-Lévy: the main camp for the British army during the siege of Quebec, summer 1759, located on the south shore of the St. Lawrence River, across from Quebec City.
2 See Garneau's Histoire du Canada. [Leprohon's note]

quote the narrator still farther "it was computed that more than half a century would be required to repair the damages."[1]

In the month of July, Wolfe made a desperate attack on the French lines at Montmorenci but was repulsed with the loss of 500 men, including a number of gallant officers. He then endeavoured to communicate with General Amherst[2] by Lake Champlain, but without success. These reverses preying on the mind of the gallant young soldier, developed the germs of a severe illness which brought him almost to the gates of the tomb. Fortunately, however, for the glory of the cause for which he fought he recovered, and as soon as he was able to attend to duty, wrote a long dispatch to the Home Government, describing the many difficulties and unexpected obstacles he had met with, and the intense disappointment he experienced at the futility of his own efforts.[3] The letter, breathing in every line the gallantry of heart, and devotion to king and country animating the breast of the writer, was well received in England, and excited more sympathy for his grief than annoyance at the reverses which had attended his arms.

Wolfe then held a council with his Lieutenant-Generals Moncton, Townshend and Murray,[4] three young men of talents and courage as illustrious as their birth, and their advice was that a sufficient force should be left at Pointe Lévi, whilst the main army should pass up the river, endeavour to take the heights of Abraham by surprise and thus force the French to leave the situation they occupied. To have assaulted the Lower Town, would have been an enterprise fraught with danger, for though the ships of war might have silenced the batteries of the latter, the upper works could not have been affected and would consequently have kept up a galling fire on the assailants. De Montcalm in the meantime stationed troops from Quebec to Jacques Cartier, to protect the left bank of the St. Lawrence.

---

1 For relevant extracts from Colonel Malcolm Fraser's journal entries, published in the *Mercury* (New York), see Appendix D1, p. 239.
2 Jeffrey Amherst (1717-97), an English-born officer in the British Army. Montreal was surrendered to Amherst on 8 September 1760.
3 For Wolfe's letter, see Appendix E1, p. 253.
4 Robert Moncton (alt. Monckton, 1726-82), an army officer and colonial administrator in British North America; Brigadier General George Townshend, First Marquis Townshend (1724-1807); and General James Murray (1721-94), an army officer who became the military governor of Quebec in 1760.

The latest intelligence received from Lake Champlain and Ontario proved anything but satisfactory to the French commander. Mr. De Bourlamaque had been obliged to retreat towards Isle aux Noix, blowing up Forts Carillon and Frederick before abandoning them for General Amherst while a force of 12,000 men was advancing against him. Fort Niagara had been taken by the English General Prideaux[1] and the French obliged to retire to La Présentation, below Lake Ontario.

General Wolfe having received information from two French deserters, that on the night of the 12th, an escort of provisions was to pass by water to Quebec, the land *route* from Trois-Rivières being too tedious and laborious, resolved to profit by the circumstance. The deserters had communicated the pass-word which the boats were to give to the sentinels placed on the river's bank, and to add the climax to the impending danger, De Montcalm had recalled the evening previous, without notifying the Governor,[2] the battalion which he had sent to the heights of Quebec, two days before. On the 13th of September then, at one o'clock in the morning, the darkness of course being still intense, a body of troops embarked in flat bottomed boats and floated noiselessly down with the tide, to Foulon. Officers acquainted with the French language had been chosen to reply to the *Qui vives*[3] of the sentries on shore and when challenged by the latter, replied: "No noise, it is the supplies." In the darkness they were allowed to pass and Admiral Holmes followed at a quarter of a mile's distance with the rest of the troops. By daybreak the English army was drawn up in battle array on the plains of Abraham.

When General De Montcalm at six in the morning received this unexpected intelligence, he almost refused to believe it, but he immediately proceeded to the spot, taking 4,500 men with him and leaving the rest in camp. On coming in sight of the foe, he at once resolved on hazarding a battle, and at 9 o'clock, (September 13th) advanced against them, his troops keeping up a spirited but irregular fire.

---

1 Brigadier-General John Prideaux (1718-59), killed during the taking of Fort Niagara.
2 Governor Vaudreuil.
3 "Chiefly in France or in French-speaking contexts: a cry of 'qui vive,' typically used as a challenge by a sentry. Cf. *who goes there?* ... Now rare" (*OED*).

General Wolfe always fearlessly exposing himself wherever the attack was fiercest, was soon wounded in the wrist, but notwithstanding the accident, continued to charge the foe, at the head of his Grenadiers with their fixed bayonets. He had advanced but a few steps farther when another ball pierced his breast, and he fell, just as the French (a portion of whom were unarmed with bayonets) gave way. Wolfe was carried to the rear and one of his staff on perceiving the flight of the enemy, exclaimed: "They run—they run;" "Who run?" questioned the dying soldier, his death struck features lighting up with sudden animation. "The French," was the reply. "What, already! then I die happy!" and the youthful hero soon after breathed his last.[1]

General Montcalm who had already received two severe wounds, did his best to rally his troops, now flying on all sides, and to regulate their retreat, but a musket ball struck him and he fell from his horse mortally wounded. The following morning he died in the Château St. Louis, Quebec,[2] having previously received the sacred rites of religion, with the calm faith and humble tranquillity of a Christian hero. He was buried in the Chapel of the Ursuline nuns in a hollow formed in the wall by the passage of a bomb shell. 'Tis said that when his principal wound was dressed, he enquired of his medical attendants if it were mortal and if so, how long could he survive. The reply was, "not more than a dozen of hours—perhaps less." "So much the better, then," he calmly rejoined; "I shall not live to see the surrender of Quebec."

Brigadiers Senesergues and St. Ours,[3] also mortally wounded in the same fatal engagement, fell into the hands of the victors and died shortly after. That very night the French army, under the command of M. De Vaudreuil, commenced its retreat

---

1 See relevant entries on the Battle of the Plains of Abraham and the fall of Quebec, by Fraser and Garneau, in Appendices D1 and D5, pp. 239 and 251.
2 The Château St. Louis was the residence of the French and British colonial governments in Quebec. Its architectural remains lie beneath what is today the Dufferin Terrace in Quebec City, in close proximity to the Château Frontenac.
3 Étienne-Guillaume de Senesergues (alt. Senezergues, 1709-59), who was treated by British surgeons but died the day after the battle, on September 14; François-Xavier de Saint Ours (1717-59) who, according to J.R. Turnbull, "was killed on the battlefield" (*Dictionary of Canadian Biography Online*) and not, as Leprohon suggests, in the hands of the British.

towards Pointe-aux-Trembles and Jacques Cartier, where they awaited the arrival of the intrepid Chevalier De Lévis. It had been the intention of the latter to attack the English within their lines and he had already commenced his march towards Lorette, when he learned at Cap Rouge that Quebec had capitulated. Though the terms of surrender were most favorable, he was bitterly incensed and expressed his indignation in the most unmeasured terms. The evil, however, admitted now of no remedy, so he proceeded without delay to Jacques Cartier River, on the right bank of which he commanded a fort to be erected, and left six hundred men there under the command of Major Dumas.

Such was the result of the first battle of the plains of Abraham, a battle which decided the fate of a country almost as large as the half of Europe.

CHAPTER XXII.

Death is ever silently, quietly busy, and amongst the many his invincible power had stricken down within the few preceding months was Mrs. Dumont. She had been attended in the closing hours of life's final scene, by Rose's old friend, the parish priest of De Villerai; and as she had evinced in the beginning of her illness the greatest bitterness towards her former *protégée*, declaring that but for her duplicity and ingratitude, she would have had the happiness of leaving Blanche a loved and cherished wife instead of an isolated orphan, the clergyman took upon himself to reveal enough of Rose's secret to enable the old lady to die in a perfectly Christian spirit, leaving not only her love and dying blessing to the object of her late anger, but a more substantial proof of her renewed regard in the form of a handsome legacy. After Mrs. Dumont's demise, Blanche took an elderly maiden lady, a distant relative of her own, to reside with her; and Miss De St. Omer willingly exchanged the genteel, though pinched poverty in which she had previously lived, for the comforts of the manor house, and the gentle though quiet companionship of its young mistress.

After some time, however, as the state of public matters daily became worse, and the hopes and courage of the colonists decreased, Blanche was induced by the representations of her friends to leave her loved home in De Villerai, which they averred was too lonely a spot for two defenceless women, and take up her abode with Miss De St. Omer in Montreal. Here Blanche led a most retired existence, mourning for Mrs. Dumont, as if she had been by consanguinity what she had indeed been by kindness and affection, a mother; and finding occupation for many an hour that would otherwise have hung heavily upon her hands, in accompanying the excellent Miss De St. Omer in many of the missions of charity in which that worthy lady was constantly engaged.

On one of these benevolent expeditions both ladies set out one pleasant afternoon, bending their courset towards an obscure street in the St. Mary's,[1] or Quebec suburbs, as they are as frequently called. The object of their visit was a poor woman whose husband, a Canadian volunteer, had been killed on duty a few weeks previous, and who now found herself left to struggle through the world with a large family of young and helpless children. The house in which the widow lived, was divided into three or four different tenements, occupied by as many families. In passing out, after leaving joy and gladness behind them, Blanche heard on the second landing the sobbing accents of a woman's voice raised in passionate grief; and as the door through which the sounds came was partly unclosed, she pushed it gently open and entered.

A woman dressed in the threadbare habiliments of poverty was bending over a low pallet on the floor, on which a human form was stretched, either in the repose of sleep or of death, and murmuring mingled prayers and wild lamentations.

"You seem very unhappy!" kindly exclaimed Miss De St. Omer, laying her hand gently on the female's arm.

"Unhappy!" repeated the woman with a look of anguish. "See—there lies my only child! my sole earthly comfort and solace!—Seven days ago, he was full of life and strength, and to-day—." She paused abruptly and drew down the worn sheet, exhibiting the corpse of a lad of fifteen, whose ghastly countenance was one fearful mass of disfiguring scars and blotches.

"Heavens! What is that?" questioned Blanche turning deadly pale as her eye fell on the terrible spectacle.

"Small-pox," answered the bereaved mother, utterly unmindful in her own deep misery, of the risks or fears of others.

Miss De St. Omer with a face white as the sheet covering the dead, pushed Blanche before her to the door, and throwing down

---

1 "Bending their courset" is probably a typographical error for "bending their course"; the Sainte-Marie neighbourhood, formerly a working-class area of Montreal.

some silver coin on the floor, hurried her companion from the house, as rapidly as she could.[1] Arrived at home she busied herself in concocting draughts and potions which by dint of earnest entreaty, she coaxed Blanche into swallowing, besides obliging the latter to submit to many precautionary measures some of which no doubt would call up a smile to the lips of the reader at the present day. All that evening she was in a state of feverish anxiety, asking Blanche every second minute how she felt, and deploring again and again the unfortunate chance which had led to such a perilous encounter. Her young companion by her advice retired early to bed, and Miss De St. Omer either imagined, or actually perceived that her look and voice were unusually languid.

Early the following morning whilst the *Angelus*[2] was yet pealing through the still air, she was in Miss De Villerai's room. "How do you feel, dear Blanche?" was the anxious query.

Alas! courageously as she strove to disguise it, Blanche both looked and felt very ill.

A physician was immediately sent for. He came, questioned and examined. Miss De St. Omer's fears were all verified and the heiress of De Villerai was really stricken down by that terrible enemy of the young and lovely—the small-pox.

The attack was of a most virulent nature, and medical skill and care seemed doomed at times to yield to the fearful adversary they strove to master. Poor Miss De St. Omer was unremitting in her attentions, and night and day she was watching by the sick couch, fearing to trust that precious life for even one moment to the care of hirelings, however devoted they might be. The third evening of Blanche's illness, the servant entered the apartment to say "that two ladies were waiting in the drawing-room to see her."

"Did I not tell you," she rejoined, turning angrily on the messenger, "that whilst Miss Blanche was so ill, I could not see any person?"

"Yes, Miss, but the ladies, at least the eldest one would not be denied. She said she must see you and sent her name. Mrs. De Rochon."

---

1 The reader will please remember that vaccination was somewhat uncommon at this period, and the small-pox consequently much dreaded by rich and poor. [Leprohon's note]
2 The Angelus bell, rung to incite Roman Catholics to perform a series of devotional exercises.

Miss De St. Omer felt too much respect for the virtues of the benevolent woman who bore that application so well known to the indigent and suffering, to hesitate farther, and bidding the woman remain by the side of her young mistress who was lying in a sort of lethargic slumber, strictly enjoining her if the latter even moved, to call her up, she hurried down stairs.

A few rapid questions and answers passed between Miss De St. Omer and her eldest visitor, after which the latter turning to her companion, who was Rose Lauzon, exclaimed, "Here is a former *protégée* of Miss De Villerai's—one whom that good young lady nobly befriended, and who desires now to prove her gratitude by sharing with you the cares and attentions you so unremittingly lavish on your sick charge. Do not refuse!" she added, seeing that Miss De St. Omer hesitated. "You will greatly pain my young friend, and at the same time mortify myself, who can bear ample testimony to her skill and fidelity as an accomplished nurse."

Miss De St. Omer merely knowing Rose as a gentle quiet young girl in whom Mrs. De Rochon placed the greatest confidence, no longer demurred, and half an hour after the lady's carriage had driven from the door, Rose, in a simple morning dress was installed beside Blanche's bed, her gaze mournfully dwelling on the sad changes which were already marring the pure pale beauty of that lovely face.

Miss De St. Omer's first care was to explain to her new assistant every possible precaution or solace which their patient might require, making her also acquainted with the names of the various remedies and the exact periods at which they should be administered. This done, a long silence followed during which the elder lady's gaze remained steadily, thoughtfully fixed upon the beautiful features of her unconscious companion. Suddenly she abruptly asked if the latter had ever had the small-pox. The reply was in the negative.

"Then dear child, you should not have run the risk of coming here. That young face is too fair and handsome to expose it so rashly to disfigurement."

"Ah! *mademoiselle*, that consideration would never induce me to forfeit the priceless opportunity thus afforded me of showing in some slight degree my gratitude for all Miss De Villerai's former benefits to myself."

"'Tis not every heart which is as grateful as your own, Rose," replied Miss De St. Omer, "and I begin to think I have not only found an efficient nurse who will greatly aid me in my anxious task, but a true-hearted companion with whom I can warmly sympathize, even though, dear child, you are as young and pretty, as I am old and plain."

Eloquently did Rose by word and look express the gratitude she felt for the kindness of her companion, and the latter every hour felt more and more thankful for the efficient timely assistance thus sent her in her task.

With what a light noiseless tread did Rose glide about—how skilfully, yet how gently she adjusted the pillows or raised the sick girl's head: and then the inimitable broths and jellies she prepared—the cool refreshing drinks, so grateful to the parched lips of sickness, that she invented. Often did Miss De St. Omer declare in perfect simplicity of heart, that she felt assured that Rose's real vocation in life was that of being a nun in the Hotel-Dieu Hospital, so admirably did she seem qualified for waiting on, and taking care of the sick.

Some days after her arrival she was taking her usual post near Blanche's pillow, when on glancing towards the patient, she encountered the clear earnest gaze of the latter fixed steadily upon her.

"Is that really Rose Lauzon?" at length enquired the sick girl.

"Yes, dear Miss De Villerai," was the faltering reply, for Rose remembering the circumstances under which she and the young *seigneuresse* had last parted, felt both anxious and uncertain regarding the manner in which the latter might welcome her.

"And what brought you here, Rose?" was the quiet interrogation.

"Gratitude and affection, my dear young lady. I came to nurse you during your illness."

"Illness!—yes, I have been very ill, and I still feel strangely weak. I remember it all now. That terrible corpse—and then the awful suffering, the long dark blank that followed. Am I much altered?"

"Very little *mademoiselle*, considering how dangerously ill you have been."

"Well, I will not think of that to-day," and she checked a deep sigh. "I must not murmur if God has seen fit to withdraw some of the gifts he had previously bestowed.—But when did you come here Rose?"

"The day following that on which you fell sick. Mrs. De Rochon knowing how much I owed you, willingly listened to my request, praying permission to be allowed to offer my services to attend on you, and even came with me to insure their being accepted."

"And you have never had the small-pox?" questioned Miss De Villerai, in an earnest, softened tone.

"Pray do not think of that, dear Miss Blanche,—I do not fear infection in the least, so there is no danger for me whatever."

"That reason, Rose, does not diminish in the slightest degree the generosity of your devotion, but have you no fears, child, that your young face might become as loathsome—as disfigured, as 'tis now fresh and beautiful?"

"Ah! *mademoiselle*," and the speaker's eyes filled with tears, "the little beauty you have been pleased to notice, has never brought me much happiness. Little indeed, would I regret its loss."

"Well Rose, be that as it may, you have fearlessly exposed both it and your life for my sake. I will yet, I hope, if God restores me to health, be able to repay you in some degree for it,—in the meantime, as one proof of gratitude, I will never question you directly or indirectly on the past, never even recur to it. If, of your own accord, you decide at some future time on giving me an explanation, I shall willingly listen to it, but never ask, never exact one."

Rose caught the hand of the speaker which had grown so thin and fragile, and pressed it again and again to her lips. "Thanks, thanks, dear, generous Miss Blanche! this is more, far more than I dared to expect. Yes, it will be as it used to be long ago, in the dear old manor house, when I was so happy and light-hearted, despite my step-mother, and my other childish troubles."

Blanche looked earnestly at her companion; for although the cheeks were still rounded and bright, the eyes still liquid and softly brilliant, there were unmistakeable traces of mental pain round the little mouth, an expression of subdued, quiet sorrow now habitual there, and Blanche sighed as she exclaimed,

"I fear, Rose, that years and acquaintance with the world, have brought neither of us much happiness; but still, the joy or grief of earth is but a dream, from which death is the awakening. A day or two ago, how near was I to the end of my career—but you begin to look restless, as if you feared I was talking too much, so lips, if not thought will be quiet for a time."

Blanche's recovery was slow but satisfactory, and Rose's companionship so much more interesting and cheering, than that of the well-meaning but prosaic Miss De St. Omer, tended far more than strengthening portions to restore her to health. Miss De St. Omer, now freed from her late overwhelming anxieties regarding her charge, found herself at liberty to resume in a great measure, her usual missions and visits of charity.

Letters from Captain De Montarville, who was still of course with his regiment, frequently arrived to break the monotony of the sick room, but whenever Blanche received any of these missives, she usually sighed after their perusal, and put them away to lie undisturbed in her writing desk, never to be drawn forth again for a second perusal. And yet the letters in question were kind and affectionate, and from the period that Gustave became acquainted with the severe illness of his betrothed they were tender and devoted.

When Miss De Villerai was convalescent enough to walk about her chamber, she quietly approached a mirror, and surveyed in its truthful surface the sad changes wrought in her personal appearance, by a few weeks' illness, but no exclamations, no murmurs of regret escaped her. She merely turned to the sympathising Rose, and calmly asked "if the physician had said whether the marks of her malady would permanently remain."

Rose hesitatingly replied, that "Dr. Tourville had assured them that the most striking traces of it would after a time, entirely disappear."

"Do not falter so, dear Rose, in telling me the truth," was the calm-toned reply, "even if I have lost forever, the slight portion of beauty I may once have possessed, might I not say as truthfully as yourself, 'what happiness has it ever brought me?' No, if health still remains, I will not grieve for the rest."

[No. 12—Vol. I]   [MONTREAL, WEDNESDAY, FEBRUARY 1, 1860]

CHAPTER XXIII

Ample occupation was given to the thoughts and conversation of Blanche and her companion by the changing fate attending the French arms, and whilst anxiously following the course of public events, often did they both secretly tremble for the life of the gallant De Montarville, whose letters betrayed how keenly his ardent patriot heart felt for his unhappy country. Between the two girls, however, his name was rarely mentioned, and though the faint pink-glow on Rose's cheek deepened to a feverish flush whenever a letter directed in the well-known hand writing was presented to Miss De Villerai, the latter, mindful of her promise, made no comment on the circumstance whatever.

Blanche, either divining and pitying the intense anxiety that never dared to seek relief in words, or else listening merely to the dictates of simple courtesy, generally read aloud some slight detail Gustave wrote concerning the war, and then closed the letter, exclaiming; "he is well." What a relief did this announcement ever prove to Rose, continually tortured as she was by fears for the life and safety of one whose existence she now felt too keenly, was dearer to her, far—far more than her own, and how deeply grateful did she feel to Blanche, who so generously overlooking all petty feelings of jealousy, gave her the information she so eagerly longed to hear. About this time the hopes and courage of the colonists were considerably raised by the brilliant success which had crowned General De Lévis' bravery at the second battle fought on the ever memorable plains of Abraham, (August 28, 1760) the result of which was that the English were obliged to shut themselves up in Quebec, to which the French laid siege, whilst awaiting the succours they had so earnestly demanded from France.[1] These came not, but instead, the following spring, an English fleet anchored in the St. Lawrence, and De Lévis had no alternative left, but that of raising the siege and retreating to Montreal, which he did unmolested. From that hour the French cause was hopelessly and irreparably lost.

Three powerful armies were now directing their march towards Montreal, one from Quebec under General Murray—another from Lake Champlain, commanded by General Haviland, and a third (the largest and most formidable) from Oswego, under General Amherst.[2] Though the descent of the rapids was an enterprise fraught with much danger, the latter general determined on choosing that way, so as to leave no other mode of escape to the French, who had spoken of retreating, if necessary from Montreal to Detroit, and from Detroit to Louisiana. In the Cedar Rapids, he lost 64 barges and 88 men, but at length reached the village of Lachine, nine miles above Montreal. He disembarked there and marched without delay towards the town itself, around which the other two armies were encamped, await-

---

1   Also known as the Battle of Sainte-Foy (28 April 1760, not 28 August, as Leprohon indicates above), a victory for the French side. For its part, France failed to send reinforcements. Montreal eventually capitulated and Britain established military rule in the colony, pending the ratification of the Treaty of Paris.
2   James Murray (1721/22-94); William Haviland (1718-84); Jeffery Amherst (1717-97).

ing his arrival, so that it was now environed by an armed host of more than 17,000 men, furnished with powerful artillery.

Montreal, built on the southern side of the island of the same name, between Mount Royal and the blue St. Lawrence, was then enclosed by a simple wall from two to three feet thick, constructed with the view of defending the town from the incursions of the Indians and was of course merely serviceable against arrows and musketry. This wall, surrounded by a ditch, was defended by six pieces of cannon. A battery composed of another half dozen of guns, rendered almost unserviceable from rust, crowned a little eminence situated in the interior of the city.[1] Such were the fortifications protecting the residue of the French army, reduced to about 3,000 men, including the inhabitants still remaining under arms, besides 500 soldiers defending St. Helen's island opposite. The city itself barely contained provisions for an additional fortnight, and ammunition sufficient for one more engagement.

That night, Governor De Vaudreuil called a council of war, and it was unanimously decided that a capitulation which should protect both the interests of the people and the honour of the troops, was preferable to a fruitless and unavailing defence. In the morning, Colonel De Bougainville was sent to propose a month's armistice to the assailants, but the proposal was instantly rejected. He then returned to offer the capitulation of which we have just spoken, and General Amherst granted almost every thing that was asked, except the perpetual neutrality of the Canadians and the honours of war to the troops. The last mentioned refusal wounded deeply the brave and sensitive De Lévis, and he eagerly insisted on being allowed to retire to St. Helen's island to fight there to the last extremity,[2] but the Governor ordered him to lay down his arms.

The capitulation was signed on the 8th of September, and by this celebrated act, Canada passed definitely under the power of the British crown. The nunneries and religious communities with some exceptions, were preserved in their privileges, possessions and constitutions, the *seigneurs* also were allowed to preserve their feudal rights, and the free exercise of their religion was guaranteed to the Canadian people.[3]

---

1 The old Citadel (Dalhousie Square). No vestige of it now remains. [Leprohon's note]
2 St. Helen's Island, in the St. Lawrence River, lies to the south-east of Montreal.
3 For more on the terms of capitulation contained in the Treaty of Paris, see Appendix E2, p. 257.

It was evening. Blanche was sitting alone in the drawing-room, finding the twilight gloom more congenial to the mood and thoughts of the moment than the glare of lamp or taper, when a quick peal on the hall-door knocker solicited admittance. A moment after a servant entered to announce Captain De Montarville. Rapidly, suffocatingly Blanche's heart beat, but disguising all outward tokens of emotion, she calmly rejoined, "Show him in."

"Shall I bring lights, *Mademoiselle*?"

"No, not for some time yet. 'Tis not dark enough," and thankful that this long anticipated meeting between herself and her betrothed would take place in the favorable shade of twilight, she sank back in her chair and endeavoured to prepare herself as best she might, for the coming interview.

A rapid springing step on the stairs, a sudden opening and shutting of the sitting-room door, and almost before she had time to rise from her seat to welcome him, she was clasped to De Montarville's heart. Never before had he ventured on such a liberty—Never had he evinced such affectionate ardour, but Blanche in her own noble nature found the key to this, and justly supposed that the warmth he evinced was prompted more by sympathy and compassion for her late illness and suffering, than by love.

Gently she disengaged herself from his embrace and murmured some kindly word of welcome.

"Yes, Blanche," he exclaimed in a tone of deep emotion: "You, once, jestingly told me that I might claim you as my bride, when the war should be at an end. That time has arrived, though, alas! under different circumstances to what we both then fondly anticipated, and now, if you will allow it, I will claim, dearest, the speedy fulfillment of your promise."

"At an end!" she quickly rejoined, without heeding his last words. "Do you mean to say that no hope, no chance remains?"

"None, none," was the sorrowful rejoinder. "Montreal has capitulated, and at this moment the standard of England waves above our heads."

"Alas!" she murmured, covering her face with her hands. "Have all the tears that have been wept? the blood that has been shed, come only to this? Could not the struggle have been at least protracted—continued?"

"It might, indeed, Blanche, though of course, unavailingly in the end. They say that it was to ensure favorable terms of capitulation that M. De Vaudreuil yielded so soon. 'Tis the only alleviation of our deep sorrow and humiliation that the conditions of surrender are honourable in the highest degree, protecting not only the individual rights and property of our countrymen, but also respecting in every manner, our time honoured ancient faith. True, I and hosts of others, concurring in the sentiments of the gallant general De Lévis, would have preferred resisting till the last possible hour, but our rulers have willed it otherwise. Already Governor De Vaudreuil, General De Lévis, the civil and military officers of the administration, together with the French troops and all those who are unwilling to live beneath a foreign yoke however merciful, are preparing to embark for the shores of France. Thither I go, and thither you will not refuse to accompany me, for I know your patriot heart throb as proudly as my own, against the thought of foreign bondage. Listen to me then, I implore you, Blanche, and grant me, without delay, a husband's title to cherish and protect you!—You do not speak, your hand lies cold and pulseless in mine. Give me one slight pressure from those little fingers to whisper hope and consent."

"You shall have your answer, Gustave, ere you leave me this evening. A half hour is not too much to allow for a girl's timid scruples and hesitation."

"Certainly not, dearest, and you are only too indulgent to listen to my imperative demand so kindly. But, speak to me, now about yourself. You have been very very ill—illness too, brought on by your own noble charity and devotion to suffering and poverty."

"Yes, but, I had an admirable nurse and it is in great part owing to her tender care that I have been restored to health so soon."

"Oh! yes, Miss De St. Omer is an excellent woman, and I must see and thank her this evening ere I leave."

"Miss De St. Omer has also been very kind, but the nurse to whom I owe most, is certainly Rose Lauzon. A day or two after I fell ill, she came to me unasked, unsolicited; but, how your hand trembles, De Montarville, and how hot it has suddenly grown. Are you ill?"

"Not at all. Pray continue," was his hurried, indistinct reply.

"Well, she has been with me ever since, lavishing night and day the most devoted care upon me till I have learned to love her as a sister—learned to love her so well that I think I could scarcely ever consent to be again separated from her. I must make you promise to grant me a favour, Gustave. You know I do not ask them often."

"Could I refuse you!" was the gentle, low-toned reply.

"Well, it is, that if I should promise to ratify immediately the solemn engagement of our childhood—should consent to accompany you to France as your wife, you will in return promise that Rose Lauzon shall accompany us—that our home for the future, shall also be hers?"

"Never Blanche!" he replied in a stifled tone, springing to his feet, as he spoke. "Never. Make what friendly arrangements you like with regard to her—settle if you will, your Seigniory of De Villerai, all that you possess, upon her, but she must seek another home than ours."

"Yet, 'tis precisely a home she wants, Gustave. She is so lonely—so unprotected, and withal, so young and lovely. Come—you will, you must say yes, especially as I will make it the condition of my yielding to your own lately preferred prayer."

"Blanche, you are too good, too reasonable to do that," he rejoined in a tone almost harsh from suppressed emotion. "I cannot give you my reason—I cannot yet allow your pure gaze to read into the depths of my heart, but, I know you will no longer insist when I tell you that it cannot, that it must not be so."

"Well, I see, I must begin my wifely duty of yielding even before marriage," she replied, faintly smiling, "but I must order in lights. Fanchette is forgetting us."

She left the room with the graceful ease of old, though, her step, probably from recent illness, was less buoyant than it had once been, and as the door closed upon her, De Montarville sighed heavily, and murmured to himself, "Surely she is all that man could wish for, and yet—this wayward, ungrateful heart is not content!"

Soon after a servant entered bearing two silver candelabra, each massive branch garnished with waxen tapers, which she set down on the table, close to the chair which Gustave had just resumed. In another moment the young mistress of the mansion herself entered, and walking up to where her betrothed sat, she stood confronting him, full in the brilliant glare of the lighted tapers.

"I will fulfil to-night, Gustave," she said in a clear, almost solemn tone, "my promise of giving a final decisive answer to that all-important question which so nearly concerns our future happiness: but, first, look at me—steadily—well. Mark the changes that a terrible disease has made in colour and feature, the seams it has left in a once fair face, and tell me candidly and honourably, do you still wish me to be your wife?"

"Blanche, dear Blanche," he hurriedly but tenderly rejoined, as he drew her towards him. "Think you that anything like that could change me? Oh! do not judge me so unfairly, so unkindly, but, believe my solemn assurance that you are dearer to me now, than you were a year ago, in the proud flush of beauty and of health."

"I believe you, Gustave," she replied resting her clasped hands on his shoulder with an affectionate freedom she had never yet displayed in the long course of their engagement. "I believe you;" and her eyes met his with a clear unfaltering gaze, whose expression, however, he could not fathom. "Aye! and I honour you for your truth, though it was only what I might have expected from you but, listen, now, to my answer. We will be friend and counsellor, sister and brother, what you like to each other, but never man and wife. Gustave, I have read more deeply than you think into your own generous heart—I have understood its struggles, its sufferings, its noble devotedness. I have fathomed, too, the secrets of another heart, than which a nobler never beat in woman's breast; one who loves you as no woman ever yet has done—better, a thousand times better than I have ever loved, or ever could learn to love you; and who, despite her inferiority to yourself in point of wealth and station, can alone, I feel convinced, render you happy. She is the wife, Gustave, I would give you. Need I say, I speak of Rose Lauzon?!"

"Blanche, do I hear you aright?" he faltered, his cheek flushing and paling in his mighty efforts to restrain all external evidence of the flood of emotion which swept so suddenly on his soul. "I know not what to say—this announcement so sudden and unexpected—"

"For me 'tis neither one nor the other," she gently replied. "From the time my late severe illness attacked me, I have been quietly making up my already wavering mind to the present step, and every additional hour has but confirmed me in the wisdom of my decision. No prayers, no representations of yours could ever induce me to change it, so let us regard it as a thing that is settled beyond recall. Tell me now, Gustave, even as you would a sister, for I wish henceforth to hold that dear relationship towards you, do you not love Rose Lauzon?"

Deeply even as a woman might have coloured, De Montarville's face flushed as he rejoined in a low tone: "Yes."

"And how long back does your affection for her date?"

"Almost since I first met her," was the impetuous reply. "Yes, Blanche, I will lay bare my heart to your gaze, tell you all, and though I know you may condemn, blame, aye! despise my weakness, you will at least mercifully pardon it."

And there as she sat opposite to him, he told her all, concealing nothing, not even his own wild pleadings to Rose to become his wife, nor the noble firmness with which the latter, for Blanche's sake, had ever resisted his prayers.

"True-hearted Rose!" murmured Miss De Villerai, whilst a soft smile played round her lips. "How cruelly she has been misjudged, and yet I never could bring myself to believe that she was so culpable as she appeared. Oh! Gustave, you have indeed won a precious prize in the love of that noble womanly heart, nor are you undeserving of her. You have nothing to reproach yourself with, and even if you had, the generosity and firm principle you have just displayed in your present interview with myself, would have more than atoned for all. You will not refuse now," and she softly smiled as she spoke, "to take Rose Lauzon with you to France—to let your future home be also hers?"

Again De Montarville's brow flushed with a tide of mingled emotions; but suddenly his look and voice became grave, and he earnestly exclaimed:

"And you, Blanche, what will you do? Will you not come with us, to be our dear, our cherished sister and friend?"

"No, no," and she gently shook her head. "Even though I might do so in a sisterly capacity, with more safety than pretty Rose could have done. I will remain in Canada, my home, my birth-place, and even though I will henceforth be under a foreign rule, I am a woman and can easily bow my neck to it."

"But, Blanche, you will marry, will you not?" he earnestly asked. "Ah! you would be happier; and how many manly hearts would love and worship you, if you would but allow them. The changes in your beauty, which you have spoken of to-night, exist more in your imagination than in reality, and—."

"Peace, brother mine," she gently interrupted. "I know well that the lands and seigniory of De Villerai will never want admiration, nor their mistress suitors whilst she calls them hers; consequently whenever I wish to change my single state, I suppose I can accomplish the step without much difficulty; but I hope, Gustave, you do not share the vulgar error, that an unmarried woman must necessarily be unhappy. Think you that in the exercise of charity and benevolence, the intercourse of friendship and congenial society, the resources of intellect both in herself and the companions she may select, she cannot find sufficient to occupy her time and heart? Certainly: and one unalterable resolution of mine I will communicate to you, which is, that though I may eventually marry, if I chance to meet one of your sex whom I may learn to love and respect, I certainly will never marry simply to please them, and to escape the dreaded appellation of an old maid. But I will send Rose to you now, claiming as my reward for having been the instrument of smoothing the course of your 'true love,' the privilege of first announcing the happiness in store for her."

Gently, tenderly, as an elder sister, a mother would have done, Blanche, bearing ever in mind the noble truth and gratitude the young girl had so long secretly preserved towards herself, communicated to her all that had passed in her late interview with De Montarville; and as Rose wept tears of gratitude and happiness upon her bosom, she whispered in her ear what pride and pleasure she herself would find in preparing her marriage outfit, and that few brides would go to their husbands with a richer *trousseau*[1] than Rose Lauzon should do to hers.

Shall we recount the meeting between Rose and her impassioned lover? Shall we tell how ardently he vowed, promised, and protested, and how she wept, smiled, and listened, doubting all the while if she were not under the influence of some ecstatic dream, from which she would soon waken to find herself from the contrast more lonely and wretched than ever? We had better, however, resist the temptation. Our reader, if matter-of-fact and practical, would turn over the page with a contemptuous "pshaw!" whilst, if sentimental and romantic, would probably imagine the scene far better than we could recount it.

CHAPTER XXIV.

Mrs. De Rochon was sitting in her favorite room, the one in which she and Rose had passed so many quietly happy hours, and her thoughts were now sadly dwelling on the last great public event, the capitulation of her native city; then wandering to Rose, whilst she indulged in conjectures and wishes that Miss De Villerai might soon permit her *protégée* to return again to the large old house, so quiet—so lonely in her absence. Her reverie was interrupted by the entrance of Pauline De Nevers, who seemed

---

[1] "A bride's outfit of clothes, house-linen, etc." (*OED*).

in very good spirits and ran over as usual, a string of frivolous sentences, till suddenly noting how dull and silent her relative seemed, she exclaimed.

"Pray, what is the matter, Aunt? You seem so much depressed and cast down, this morning?"

"Well, Pauline, I have not your happy elasticity of spirits, and cannot immediately forget that the country of my birth has but just passed under the power of a conqueror, stranger alike to our tongue and faith."

"Yes, but you know that the treaty they are all talking about, completely protects both, so what can we expect more? I am a woman and hate the very sound of anything pertaining to politics, besides, I have so much else to think of just now. Most of the French officers will be returning to their native land, and the event will bring many matrimonial entanglements to a crisis. My maid saw De Noraye, De Montarville, Major Decoste and young Duplessis passing our house this morning, so, of course, some of them will come to see me this afternoon, and I have the loveliest dress, *demi toilette*,[1] to wear, that you can imagine. The certainty that I could not come to see you at a later hour, brought me here so early. Say, Aunt De Rochon, am I not a pattern niece since that dreadful little hypocrite Rose, left you?"

"You have indeed been very attentive, Pauline, as far, I suppose, as lay in your power, but still the ten minutes visits you occasionally pay me, do not entirely fill up my leisure time."

"True, but then you have sewing for the poor and all that kind of thing to amuse you. I am sure I hope you will never take her back again, for from the instant she returns here, I again discontinue my visits."

"Well, 'tis time enough to talk about that when she does come. She is still with Miss De Villerai who seems in no hurry to part with her."

"What an idiot that De Villerai girl must be!" exclaimed Pauline, with a contemptuous flash of her black eye. "To think of her receiving that creature again after her having been actually the cause of a duel between De Noraye and her own *fiancé!*"

"But you forget that Rose has been nursing Miss De Villerai through a terrible disease which caused even paid hirelings to shrink from her in terror."

---

1 By contrast to full dress, which was required for formal dinner parties, the "demi toilette" was acceptable dress for unceremonious events.

"All an artful trick of the little *parvenue's*[1] to get reinstated in Miss De Villerai's favour, and thus obtain an opportunity of occasionally meeting De Montarville. Fool, fool, that Blanche is, not to see through her! But, they tell me, Aunt, that her sickness has completely destroyed her beauty. Is that true?"

"In part. I believe she will be considerably marked, though the delicacy and perfect regularity of her features will preserve her still from the appellation of plain."

"Oh! dear Aunt, don't believe it. The traces of small-pox are always frightfully disfiguring."

There was an animation, a nervous excitement in Miss De Nevers' manner as she spoke, communicating both light to her eye and colour to her cheek, which Mrs. De Rochon at first could not understand, but the secret was solved for her, when her niece a moment afterwards, added, "You'll see, Aunt, that the changes in her beauty will effectually cool De Montarville's already lukewarm love, and then—he will be free!"

"And what of that, Pauline?"

"Why, others will have a chance of winning him," she pettishly rejoined. "Surely, your strict morality will find nothing to carp at in that?"

"Well, from what I have heard of Captain De Montarville," resumed Mrs. De Rochon, "I would be tempted to judge him very differently; but, supposing, for argument's sake, that he were base enough to desert the being to whom he has been solemnly affianced for so long a time, and that, merely because passing illness had perhaps slightly marred her beauty, leaving heart and mind as fair and loveable as ever, surely, he would find no wellborn girl base enough to accept him."

"Oh! how absurdly you talk, Aunt," she rejoined in her sharpest tones. "I tell you that half a dozen of the prettiest girls in Montreal would throw themselves at his feet, if they received the faintest encouragement."

"And, you Pauline—what would you do?"

"Like the others, Aunt. Become Mrs. De Montarville tomorrow, if I could."

"But what of De Noraye, Decoste and the rest of the cavaliers with whom you have danced, walked and flirted for the last twelve months?"

---

1 "A person from a humble background who has rapidly gained wealth or an influential social position; a nouveau riche; an upstart, a social climber" (*OED*).

"Oh! I hate them all now. I am sick of the horrid creatures! De Noraye, I would marry; because it would be a pleasant thing to be a Countess, though, I know well, I never could learn to tolerate, much less like him. De Montarville I would take to-morrow, even if he were penniless, and settle half my own fortune upon him."

"Pauline, Pauline, you are chasing dreams and shadows, my poor child!" replied Mrs. De Rochon with a heavy sigh. "Never will your wayward worldly heart find peace or content till it turns to the one only source of happiness."

"Listen, Aunt, I hear voices in the hall," interrupted Pauline, anxious to change the moralizing strain into which the conversation was verging. "There are visitors coming up stairs."

A moment afterwards, Miss De Villerai accompanied by Rose, entered.

Miss De Nevers never bestowed even a second glance upon the latter, but the young *seigneuresse* herself she received with great apparent cordiality, scanning anxiously though covertly all the while, the alterations that had passed over the stately beauty she had once so bitterly envied. Mrs. De Rochon welcomed both visitors affectionately, and expressed her delighted surprise at seeing Blanche abroad so soon.

"Yes, 'tis the first time I have been permitted to leave the house since my late illness, but, I am recovering fast and will soon be as well as ever."

[No. 13—Vol. I] [MONTREAL, WEDNESDAY, FEBRUARY 8, 1860]

CHAPTER XXIV.—*Continued.*

"Oh! Miss De Villerai," smilingly exclaimed Pauline, who was bent on finding out the exact state of affairs between Blanche and her lover, "I doubt not but that you have already seen a powerful physician this morning. One whose single visit would doubtless tend more to your restoration than all Dr. Tourville's prescriptions and potions. I mean of course Captain De Montarville."

"I saw him last night," rejoined Blanche in her stateliest tone.

Miss De Nevers' countenance slightly fell. Such *empressement*[1] in Gustave augured ill for her own secret hopes and wishes, but

---

1 "Animated display of cordiality" (*OED*).

then it might have been curiosity that prompted the speediness of his visit. "And how was the gallant hero?" she resumed, in a light careless tone.

"Well enough in health but somewhat depressed in spirits, as every true Canadian must be at the present hour."

"Oh! yes," and Pauline's look and voice instantly became sentimental. "'Tis really shocking to think that those dreadful English with their barbarous dialect and uncouth style of dress will be lording it over us now; but then, many of our number fortunately possess the power or the chance of leaving our conquered country. The gallant officers who have fought so unavailingly in her service, and the happy women they may choose not only as the companions of their voyage to France, but as the sharers of their life's journey. You, Miss De Villerai, will be among the favored few, for pardon the freedom of an old acquaintance, are you not soon to be married to Captain De Montarville?"

"Since you ask the question in such plain terms, Miss De Nevers, I will be equally explicit in my answer, 'No, I am not on the point of marriage with the gentleman you mention.'"

"But at some distant period," persisted the determined questioner.

"Neither now, nor never," was the cold calm reply.

Pauline was a good dissembler—one well trained not only in the worldly science of disguising her actual thoughts and sentiments, but also of often simulating those she did not feel, but for once she failed to mark in time the triumphant gleam that flashed from her eyes as she heard this joyful assurance. Miss De Villerai caught that look, instantly repressed as it was, but she made no remark and turning to Mrs. De Rochon, rejoined in answer to her look of troubled commiseration,

"'Tis my own wish, kind friend, that it should be so, and a far happier destiny awaits him than what would probably have been his as Blanche De Villerai's husband."

"Ah! that destiny!—'tis I, who will make, who will share it," inwardly thought the exulting Pauline.

"But when will my little Rose return to me?" enquired Mrs. De Rochon, anxious to change the subject which she feared was painful at least to one of her visitors.

"'Tis chiefly about that, that we came to see you to-day, dear friend," replied Blanche smiling, "and I fear if you have become only one half as much attached to Rose as I have done, the news we bring you will scarcely be as welcome as it ought to be."

"What, you are going to take her from me—to keep her with yourself?" questioned Mrs. De Rochon, in a grieved sad tone. "Well, I half expected it, and as you knew and befriended her long before I did, you have of course prior claims on her affection and gratitude."

"Ah! dear Mrs. De Rochon," exclaimed Rose seizing the former's hand and pressing it again and again to her lips, "whatever may be the changes time or fortune may bring to me—in whatever clime or rank my future destiny may be cast, never, never, will I forget all I owe to you, you who bore with, believed in, protected me, when the world, appearances and my own silence, were all against me."

Miss De Nevers, perceiving that her ample robe had come slightly in contact with Rose's garments as the latter bent down to kiss Mrs. De Rochon's hand, haughtily gathered the folds of her rich silk around her, as if there were contamination in that touch, and regarded her Aunt's whilom *protégée* with a look whose scornful disdain incensed Blanche still more than the triumphant glance she herself had lately called forth. But sure and justifiable revenge was in her power, and she resolved to take it without delay.

Turning to Mrs. De Rochon, she exclaimed with a smile of peculiar meaning, "Indeed, 'tis not with myself, either, that the little ingrate intends choosing her home but impatient probably of the foreign rule to which Miss De Nevers has just so touchingly alluded, she has decided on granting Captain De Montarville's prayer and accompanying him to France, as his cherished well loved wife."

Miss De Nevers sprang to her feet, her cheek pale as death, but almost immediately resuming her seat, she exclaimed,

"You are more facetious than truthful, this morning, Miss De Villerai."

"I do not think my worst enemies can tax me with having ever uttered a deliberate falsehood," coldly rejoined the heiress. "Yes, dear Mrs. De Rochon, the news will probably prove as welcome to you as it appears to be distasteful to others, but, you may believe my solemn assurance that before a fortnight, our dear Rose will have changed her maiden name for that of De Montarville, and will have probably embarked for France with the most loving and adoring of husbands."

The intelligence was nigh too much for Pauline and with some scornful passionate exclamation she swept from the room, almost suffocated by the angry, jealous feelings surging within her. Mrs.

De Rochon fondly embraced and felicitated the gentle bride elect, and then, when her two visitors, after communicating all particulars, took leave, she hastened to seek Pauline, anxious to console her under what she well knew would prove a terrible disappointment to her wayward, undisciplined nature.

She found her standing before the mirror in the dressing-room, quietly adjusting the rich ties of her bonnet, but the ashy pallor of her cheek and lips—the lurid light of her eyes, were in singular contrast with that forced calm.

"Are you going so soon, Pauline?"

"Yes," and the speaker smiled—a strange bitter smile. "I know there are some devoted cavaliers awaiting me at home and I must return to them for I would not they should prove as faithless as Blanche De Villerai's volatile lover has done. Oh!" she added with a hysterical laugh; "it passes all belief. Had he wedded Blanche herself, or any other, his own equal in point of birth and station, it might have been borne; but, that wretched little upstart—!"

Pityingly Mrs. De Rochon drew her niece towards her, and affectionately embraced her, but the latter after suffering, not returning her caress, hurried away.

On entering her own luxurious home, she was immediately informed by her maid that Count De Noraye was awaiting her in the drawing room. Smoothing her troubled brow, she glided into her perfumed gilded saloon, all smiles and suavity, determined since she could not wed for love, she would for interest. But, alas! five minutes in the company of the elegant fop with whom she had so long flirted, convinced her that all hopes in that quarter were fully as futile as those she had indulged in with regard to De Montarville.

Listlessly the Parisian dandy spoke of the termination of the war, declaring that but for the species of disgrace reflected upon the arms of France, he was almost indifferent with regard to the manner in which it had ended. Victory or defeat were almost the same to him, provided they brought the welcome opportunity of escape from a country which was scarcely fit for civilized people to dwell in.

This was too much for Miss De Nevers' patience, and she replied in the same strain of easy insolence, "that she shared in his sentiments of satisfaction with regard to the definite conclusion of the struggle, for one immediate good effect accruing from the conquest, would be that it would rid the country of the host of French adventurers and paupers who had been beggaring it so long, and who would now be replaced by those splendid dashing officers who were, report said, every one of them at least six feet high, and handsome gallant men besides." "Indeed," she added with a smiling serenity which exasperated the vain De Noraye beyond all bounds, and amply revenged the annoyance he had previously inflicted on herself: "Indeed, 'tis no wonder, my dear Count, *entre nous*,[1] that such a powerful race of heroes should have defeated such puny adversaries as you Gallic gentlemen must have proved to be."

Count De Noraye dared not trust himself to answer, but seizing his hat, honoured his fair hostess with a ceremonious chilling bow and made his exit, anathematizing Canadian women as much as he had often previously done the men, and the country itself.

Pauline had scarcely recovered from the effects of this second agitating and vexatious interview, when Major Decoste, the irresistible lady-killer was announced. He entered—all homage, tenderness and devotion, deploring the failure of Canada's hopes of freedom and pitying his own evil destiny in being compelled to leave so soon the country he had learned to love far—far beyond his own sunny climate of Provence.

What a contrast did not this interview present to the two preceding! What a welcome balm to the girl's wounded vanity, writhing under the two bitter mortifications it had just experienced, was the polished flattery, the lover-like devotion of the wily fortune hunter! Time and mood were both propitious and when the elegant major turned from Miss De Nevers' mansion, he was her accepted lover, destined within the short space of a couple of weeks to become her husband, even though in her secret heart there lurked not for him one spark of love or esteem. We may give a word or two more to Pauline and then dismiss her from the scene for ever.

She married Major Decoste despite the representations and entreaties of her father and aunt, accompanied him to France, and discovered ere she had been his wife one brief month that she had wedded a tyrant and a spendthrift. Fearful was the struggle at first between them, for Pauline's nature was violent and imperious in the extreme, but she had to deal with a heartless and unscrupulous master, and after a long and unavailing resistance kept up with fearful suffering to herself, she had to succumb. Her fortune, which the death of her father a few months after her marriage, put the Major in full possession of, was spent lavishly

---

1 "Between ourselves."

and soon absorbed in every idle excess of folly. The gambling table, the race-course, all had their share; and then when they were reduced to penury, degraded from the high social position they had once held, compelled to associate with the vile and debased, he died, leaving her a destitute, heart-broken woman, faded in face and form, broken down in health and spirits.

The earnest prayers, however, which the benevolent Mrs. De Rochon had daily offered up for her erring relative were at length heard, and on her becoming accidentally acquainted with the death of Major Decoste, she instituted at once the most active measures to find out Pauline's place of abode, and then sent her ample means to return to Canada, accompanied by letters full of the tenderest affection, offering her the future shelter of her home and protection. Willingly, gratefully, the desolate and now penitent woman grasped at the fortunate chance thus offered her, and she returned heart-sick and world-weary to that peaceful shelter, returned to share her aunt's labours of charity and benevolence— to soothe the declining days of the kind-hearted relative who loved her and rejoiced over her return, as much as ever the forgiving father had done over that of the prodigal son.[1]

CHAPTER XXV.

And now our tale is drawing rapidly to an end, but before closing it, we will look in for a few moments into the cottage of the Widow Lauzon, as she was familiarly called in the village of De Villerai. It was about five in the afternoon. September's golden sunset was flooding the earth but vainly its cheering beams poured in through the windows of the cottage; they brought neither joy nor gladness to the hearts of its inmates. What a sad change was there, since we last paused beneath that roof. The exquisite neatness, the air of cheerful comfort that had once characterized it, had long since given place to an air of the most squalid and hopeless poverty. Not that the Widow Lauzon was deficient in cleanliness or order—no, the latter attributes were

---

[1] A reference to the Parable of the Prodigal Son, which appears in the Gospel of Luke (15.11-32), and tells the story of a younger son who, having wasted his inheritance, returns home to his older brother and father, the latter celebrating his return. The word "prodigal" means "[e]xtravagant" or "recklessly wasteful of one's property or means" (*OED*).

among the few good qualities she possessed—but how purchase panes to replace the windows broken by accident, how find ways and means to provide for the slightest repairs about their cottage home, when there was scarcely money enough to purchase the bare necessaries of life.

As we have already said, it was about five in the afternoon. The four little Lauzons, dressed in garments, resembling from the number and variety of the pieces employed in mending them, coarse patch-work, were seated around a table, corroborating in their pinched sunken features and large hungry eyes, the utter penury that the appearance of every thing around, seemed to indicate. Little however, was there on that table to satisfy the cravings of hunger or appetite. Four small morsels of dry black bread, and a little tin mug containing spring water, were all the board afforded.

Seated on the door-step, dressed in habiliments as wretched as those covering the children, was the Widow Lauzon herself, her face furrowed and marked by the traces of care, and privation, her coarse black hair once kept so smooth and shining, now dull and lustreless, and thickly mixed with gray. The children were greedily devouring rather than eating their wretched meal, when suddenly the elder brother, who had despatched his in two or three moments, snatched the younger child's portion out of his hand, and commenced swallowing it with the same ravenous haste with which he had previously disposed of his own. The loud lamentations uttered by the young unfortunate thus despoiled of his meal, brought the mother to the rescue, and she imperiously commanded the elder boy to restore his plunder, but he sullenly refused, alleging that as it was he who did all the work, who had gathered in the bush the wood for the fire, he would not consent to be starved to death, adding that he would soon run away to seek a better and more comfortable home.

"How can you talk so unfeelingly, Jacques," rejoined the miserable woman, "when you know well that I have not tasted food myself to-day. 'Tis my breakfast and dinner that you are now dividing among you;" and unable to struggle longer against her misery, she sank on a rough bench and covering her face with her hands, sobbed aloud. Suddenly the latch of the dwelling was raised, and the parish priest, our old acquaintance Mr. Lapointe entered. His arrival was the signal for a joyous tumult among the children, who knew from long experience that the good man never sought their dwelling with empty pockets, and after he had distributed among them a dozen of the light dainty cakes his sister Mrs. Messier always provided for the Presbytery table, he turned to the unhappy looking mother, kindly exclaiming,

"Well, Widow, how goes it with you!"

"Worse and worse," was the gloomy reply. "But for your kind visits and the help you each time bring me, I would curse my miserable lot and lie down and die."

"And what would become of the little ones then, Widow? They still want your care."

"'Tis because I can do nothing for them, that I would like to escape for ever out of their view and hearing. Ah! Mr. Le Curé, you do not know what it is to hear the children you have given birth to, crying day after day for bread, and to have none to offer them."

The priest's eyes filled with tears as he rejoined, "It must indeed be a grievous trial, but still the Lord chasteneth us for His own wise purposes, and 'tis often when we are on the point of yielding to despair—often when the cup of our misery seems full to overflowing that relief and help are at hand. So it has been with you, Widow Lauzon, for look, see what Providence has sent you, just when your prospects were gloomiest, your courage at its lowest ebb," and he held up as he spoke, a well filled purse, through the dark green meshes[1] of which gleamed both silver and gold.

The woman with a half laugh half cry sprang towards him, hesitating, however, before taking it, as if she feared some mockery or mistake.

"Take it fearlessly," exclaimed the priest. "It was sent to me for you, and forget not to humbly thank God to-night, for so mercifully coming to your relief when faith and hope were almost giving way."

Like one in a dream she received the gift, timidly opening the clasps and drawing forth a small silver coin as if still doubting her right to even touch the treasure. On receiving, however, an encouraging nod and smile from her pastor, she put the piece of money she had abstracted, into Jacques' hand, and bade him proceed at once to the village and purchase some articles of food, an announcement which instantly filled the children with exuberant delight.

"And, now, Mr. Le Curé," exclaimed the widow with a look of smiling complacency such as her care-worn features had not

---

[1] The word "green," in the phrase "dark green meshes," is partially obscured in the copy text, while appearing in square brackets in Sorfleet's *JCF* edition (147).

worn for many long months, "Will you not tell what generous benefactor has thus come so unexpectedly to our relief? Kind and charitable as you have ever been to us since the day poverty first came into our household, I know it cannot be yourself, for this purse" and she gently patted the gleaming net-work as she spoke, "contains more money than the Presbytery has perhaps ever done at a time. Who then is the giver?"

"You shall know all in good time, Widow, so have patience. Let us talk about other subjects a little. Have you never heard anything about your step-daughter since she left you?"

An angry look fitted over the woman's face as she rejoined, "Mr. Lapointe, you are surely amusing yourself at my expense. You know well that since the ungrateful creature left me so unexpectedly, I have never seen or heard anything of her beyond receiving your own occasional assurance that she was well and comfortable, more than we have ever been since," she muttered to herself. "Oh! I had almost forgotten," she resumed with a vindictive smile, "I received a visit (you remember, *Monsieur*, I told you about it) from that gay young poppinjay of an officer, Miss De Villerai's lover, but I gave him a welcome warmer than he had probably expected."

The priest smiled, a thing he rarely did at any of Widow Lauzon's little exhibitions of malice, and for a moment she felt slightly abashed, but the theme was one on which she loved to dilate, and profiting by the tacit encouragement thus given her, she continued,

"Yes, when he came here with his flattering promises and smooth speeches, offering I know not what rewards if I would only tell him where I thought she had gone, I boldly answered, that I was an honest woman and this a respectable house, so it was not the place to come to look for such as her. Not for fifty gold pieces, like the one he had put into little Jacques' hand, and which the dear child cunningly ran up and hid in the garret when he saw *Monsieur* getting into a passion, not for fifty of the like, I repeat, would I have told him where she was."

"Your firmness seems meritorious in the highest degree," rejoined Mr. Lapointe with a slight twinkle in his keen grey eye, "especially when we lose sight of the fact that you yourself had no more idea at the time of where she really was, than the young gentleman who so audaciously endeavoured to bribe you into telling him of her whereabouts."

"It would have been all the same thing even had I known it;" rejoined Madame Lauzon, her face crimsoning. "I knew Rose

Lauzon's character too well to expose her to almost certain ruin by placing her in the way of that bold insolent Captain De Montarville."

"Well, your efforts were useless, worthy Mrs. Lauzon," replied the priest, who, dearly loved a quiet joke at times. "Your efforts, I say were useless, for she is with him now. They are staying at the grandest hotel in Quebec, preparatory to their embarking together for France, next week."

A gleam of exultant satisfaction, alas! that we should be obliged to record it! flashed across Mrs. Lauzon's face as she triumphantly exclaimed;

"Did I not tell you so, Mr. Le Curé?—Did I not prophecy again and again how it would all end?"

"I never remember you doing so correctly, Widow."

"Mr. Lapointe!" and his companion rose to her feet in the intensity of her excitement, gesticulating in a most energetic manner. "How can you say such a thing? Do you not remember my often telling you in this very room and in the Presbytery parlour, that Rose Lauzon's pretty face and silly upstart vanity would yet bring her to sorrow, if not shame? Did I not tell you what Captain De Montarville was after her for and how weak and empty-headed she was?"

"I perfectly remember your telling me all that, good woman," replied the priest as he helped himself to a pinch of snuff, "but, I really cannot recall your ever prophecying that little Rose would one day become Madame Gustave De Montarville."

Mrs. Lauzon recoiled with a bound equal to that which Pauline De Nevers had given when the same announcement had first fallen upon her ear, and she stood silently, steadfastly staring upon the speaker. It was now the hour of the latter's triumph, and a little pardonable malice lurked in the quiet demure smile playing round his lips, and the merry tattoo his forefinger played on the lid of his snuff-box.

Yes, she comprehended, believed it all. The mingled satisfaction and triumph beaming in the countenance of the priest boded only good for his former favorite, and she repeated in a bewildered manner, "Rose Lauzon married to Captain De Montarville!"

"Yes, and Miss De Villerai herself was bride's-maid; but, I must be going Widow," and he rose briskly to his feet. "I must be going and leave you to enjoy and digest at leisure, the good intelligence I have just communicated to you. I have only to say, now, that the purse you have received to-night, is from Rose—hem! I mean Madame De Montarville, and to announce to you that whilst she lives, you will receive twice a year a similar sum, for she does not wish that the widow or children of the father she loved so dearly, should ever know want. She might perhaps have come to see you, but Captain De Montarville, who seems to retain no very pleasant recollection of his previous visits here, would not hear of such a thing. The generous bride, did not forget our little church either, and when you next step down to the Presbytery, I will shew you a silver lamp, and some solid silver candlesticks, the equal of which the Parish church of Montreal itself does not contain. Good day, Mrs. Lauzon, good day," and the worthy man smilingly departed, leaving the widow in a sort of waking stupor. From the latter state she was only aroused by the entrance of little Jacques, laden with various articles of wholesome food, the arrival of which was of course greeted by the other children with a most jubilant tumult of delight.

CONCLUSION.

It was a calm and pleasant Autumn day—the golden hazy atmosphere of the Indian summer communicating an indescribable charm to earth and air, to sea and sky. With white sails outspread to catch the favoring breeze, a French vessel was leaving the harbour of Quebec. Most precious was the living freight she carried, for on board were many of those whose illustrious names have been handed down by history to become household words in our homes.[1] Amongst these were the chivalrous De Lévis, Colonel De Bourlamaque and others of equal fame and dauntless courage. Sad and regretful were the looks directed towards Cape Diamond, on the majestic heights of which waved the proud standard of England, replacing the old *Fleur De Lys*[2] which had floated there so long.

---

1 According to special articles of the treaty, convenient suitable vessels, victualled at the expense of his Britannic Majesty, were furnished to convey to France the Marquis De Vaudreuil, Mr. De Rigaud, Mr. De Longueil, Mr. Bigot, the Intendant, with their respective suites, as also all the officers, soldiers and seamen, with their wives and children. [Leprohon's note] [For details about terms of capitulation, see "Article IV, Treaty of Paris" in Appendix E2, p. 257.]

2 Or *fleur de lis*: a stylized lily associated with French royalty. It appeared on the flag of New France, and is featured today on the flag of the Province of Quebec.

Some turned away with quick impatient sigh and paced the deck with rapid steps, whilst others looked lovingly, lingeringly on the magnificent country they were leaving, the grave of so many gallant hearts, of so many lofty hopes and aspirations. Others, there were too, who sorrowed perhaps less for Canada's downfall, than for their separation from some fair being, who had become dearer to them during their sojourn amid its snows, than aught they had left in the native land to which they were returning.

At the extreme end of the vessel a female figure was seated, and bending over her with a devoted tenderness which scarcely permitted him to give a second glance to the familiar shores he was perhaps leaving for ever, was a manly soldier form. It was De Montarville and his bride, and the reader will judge him leniently, if we candidly acknowledged that in the joy of calling the gentle Rose his own, every other feeling of regret or sadness was for the time completely lost. And Rose! what did she think—what feel? There were times when she trembled at the intensity of her own happiness, fearing it was too perfect to last—too perfect for earth: but she had also passed a long noviciate in the school of suffering and sorrow, and it was perhaps but the recompense of the patience and courage which she had ever unfalteringly displayed in the days of trial.

Happy indeed was their subsequent career and in the land of their adoption they acquired friends as devoted as any they had left behind in their own. Vainly some malicious tongues whispered abroad, the lowliness of Rose's origin, striving thus to keep the fair young bride outside the charmed, impenetrable circle, calling itself "good society." The effort was futile. Whatever Rose might once have been, she was now Madame De Montarville, the owner of a time-honoured irreproachable name, and that, coupled with her own matchless grace and exquisite beauty, made her a welcome guest in the *salons* of the most exclusive.

Some sorrows they had—who has not? Three noble boys, the pride of their father's manhood, the joy of their gentle mother's youth, were successively taken from their hearts and home, and laid beneath the flower-gemmed turf of Père La Chaise,[1] but others came and were spared to them, and whatever were the trials that subsequently swept over their household, they found in the deep fond love uniting their hearts, solace and balm for all.

---

1 Presumably Père La Chaise (Lachaise) cemetery in Paris, France. As the cemetery did not open until 1804, however, this reference is anachronistic.

Much as De Montarville caressed, worshipped, idolized his wife, there was ever mingled with her own absorbing affection for him, a species of reverence, of deep boundless gratitude which made his slightest word a law to her; she never forgot, though he never once remembered that she was the humble peasant girl, whom his generous love had raised to so proud a destiny.

And Blanche De Villerai, calmly happy also was her lot, though the golden circlet of marriage never glittered on her finger. Admired, courted in society—worshipped by the poor whose friend and benefactress she pre-eminently was—honoured for her rare mental gifts by men of the highest intellect as well as social position, her life was one of those rare careers of exemption from care, which fall, alas! so rarely to the lot of earth's children. When the close of that pure blameless life came, truly might it have been said her "end was peace."

Of her large fortune, a considerable portion was left in charitable bequests and annuities, but the Seigneury and Manor House of De Villerai were bequeathed to the children of Rose and Gustave De Montarville.

Though these latter never returned to Canada, some of their immediate descendants did, and the manorial home of De Villerai was inhabited by successors worthy of the noble-hearted Blanche herself. Long years have passed since then. Time which marks its footprints so legibly in our towns and cities, leaves also some traces of his passage in our quiet country homes, and the old manor house has probably before this been pulled down, but some of the collateral descendants of the De Montarvilles, yet reside on the quiet banks of the Richelieu, perpetuating in their irreproachable and christian lives, the noble qualities and virtues of their early ancestors.

THE END.

Appendix A: Contemporary Reception of Leprohon's Works

1. From Susanna Moodie, "Editor's Table," *Victoria Magazine* 1 (June 1848): 240

[The editorial is comprised largely of Moodie's book review of *Tupper's Proverbial Philosophy*,[1] although it concludes with a review of the recent instalment of the Canadian periodical *The Literary Garland* (May 1848), containing the serialized novel, *Ida Beresford; or, The Child of Fashion*, one of Leprohon's earliest works of fiction, published over a decade before *The Manor House*, when she was 19 years old.]

THE LITERARY GARLAND, FOR MAY.—This excellent periodical, of which the Colony may justly feel proud, has well, since the commencement of the year, sustained its well earned reputation. The tales and poems which have graced its pages are of a very superior class, and possess great interest and originality. Foremost of these, we would particularize, "Ida Beresford:" [*sic*] a story written with great power and vigor. The character of Ida, is very finely and effectively cast, and with all her faults, there is thrown around her, the fascination of a noble frank independence [*sic*], which genius alone could imagine, and call into existence. The writer is still very young—One of the gifted, upon whom fancy smiled in her cradle, and genius marked her for his own. As a Canadian born, we augur for her a bright wreath of fame. Let her keep truth and nature ever in view, and scorn not the slightest teaching of the "Divine Mother," and she may become the pride and ornament of a great and rising country.... [I]ndependently of the interest we feel in the success of the Garland, we reccommend [*sic*] it heartily to our Correspondents. All who could afford to patronize it should do so, for the honor of Canada.

2. From George P. Ure, "Prospectus of *The Family Herald*," *The Family Herald* (16 November 1859)

This morning Wednesday, the 16th of November, 1859, we publish the first number of *The Family Herald*, a Weekly Journal [*sic*], devoted to

---

1 *Tupper's Proverbial Philosophy: A Book of Thoughts and Arguments, Originally Treated. Also, A Thousand Lines, and Other Poems* (1848) by Martin Farquhar Tupper (1810-89).

Literature, Art, Science, Horticulture, Agriculture, and General Intelligence, and free from political or other party bias.

The object of the proprietors is the establishment of a Journal that shall address itself to the family circles of all classes in Canada; furnishing acceptable reading for all, without the alloy which is too often apparent in political journalism, or in the cheap periodicals which are imported from the United States and the parent land.

The periodical press is admitted to be the great instructor of the time. Circulating everywhere, it does much towards moulding the character of youth, and contributes not a little to the enlightenment and amusement of society. That its functions are often abused is a fact which serves to exemplify its power, and to afford a motive to the securing of its proper exercise. "Yellow-covered literature"[1] and newspapers, that rely upon "sensation" romances as their chief feature, are influences too potent for mischief to be overlooked. They are encountered everywhere. Pictorial art adds to their attractiveness, whilst their cheapness wins for them admittance to the humblest home. The circulation which this class of papers has obtained in Canada is enormous, and without an exception, they are imported. Not one is of domestic production; not one is "racy of the soil" on which we live, or in any particular adapted to the development of qualities which, as Canadians, we desire to cultivate. With political journals in our midst characterized by great ability and commendable enterprise,—with denominational papers of the highest respectability,—we are nevertheless destitute of that species of journalism which aims at the cultivation of taste, the diffusion of information, and the encouragement of innocent amusement, on ground common to people of all shades of political and christian opinion.

THE FAMILY HERALD is intended to supply the omission....

3. From George P. Ure, "Our First Number," *The Family Herald* (16 November 1859)

OUR FIRST NUMBER

The tale which opens our first number is written by a Lady, who has before this day delighted many circles in Canada as well as in the States, by her graceful pen. The Manor House of Villerai [sic], was not written as a serial tale, and the opening chapters may seem devoid of that dramatic interest, which they would doubtless have possessed had

---

1 Cheap sensational novels or literary magazines, formerly bound in yellow (or boldly coloured) paper.

it been designed for the columns of a periodical. But the power of the author is strikingly manifested as the persons and incidents of the tale are developed. Learning that the work was about completed for publication as a volume, we considered ourselves fortunate in having secured it for the *Family Herald* through the intercession of a mutual friend.

4. From Henry J. Morgan, "Mrs. Leprohon," *Sketches of Celebrated Canadians* (1862)

MRS. LEPROHON

We feel much satisfaction in being enabled to give a notice of one of the few native born Canadian ladies who have devoted themselves to the advancement of our native literature.

Mrs. Leprohon, better known to the public and most of our Canadian readers by her maiden name of Miss Rosanna Elenor [sic] Mullins, the accomplished and talented authoress, was born at Montreal, and received her education in that city.

At the early age of fourteen,[1] she evinced a strong inclination for writing; and from that time became a steady contributor, both of prose and verse, to the celebrated *Literary Garland*, published by John Lovell, of Montreal.[2] Under the initials of "R.E.M.," she became speedily known; and her pieces were invariably admired and received the encomiums of all. Every one was surprised to see in one so young, talents of so high an order, capable of producing compositions of such grace and beauty. Among the many tales contributed by her to the *Garland*, none were so well received or so popular as "*Ida Beresford*," (since translated and published in French), "*Florence Fitz Hardinge*" [sic], and "*Eva Huntingdon*," tales of fiction and pathos of so high a character, that they may, without exaggeration, be ranked among those of the same class, by the best English or American contributors to the periodical press. She afterwards became enrolled on the staff of some of the American journals and magazines.[3]

---

1 Leprohon was popularly thought to have been born in 1832, making her 14 years old when she published her first poem in *The Literary Garland*. André Deneau has since confirmed that Leprohon was born in 1829 (see Deneau 3).
2 *The Literary Garland and British North American Magazine* (Montreal, 1838-51).
3 *The Pilot* [Boston], in which Leprohon published *Eveleen O'Donnell* from 29 January to 26 February 1859, that is, a few months prior to the serial publication of *The Manor House of De Villerai* in *The Family Herald*.

In 1860, Mrs. Leprohon became connected with the *Family Herald* by the same publisher, and whilst engaged on that paper, wrote her celebrated tale of the "*Manor House of De Villerai*," wherein she made it her object to describe faithfully the manners and customs of the peasantry or *habitants*, as they are called, of Lower Canada. It was also written to illustrate that period of our history embracing the cession of Canada to England.[1] In all that she purposed, the authoress was eminently successful, and so popular was this work, that it was translated into French, and published in book form.[2] This work has, according to general opinion, been considered as the very best written on Canada, and adds another laurel to Mrs. Leprohon's well earned fame.

5. From Edmond Lareau, *Histoire de la littérature canadienne* (1874) [My translation][3]

Few writers have contributed as much [as Mrs. Leprohon has] to giving our literature a national shape. All her stories are taken from real life and are based on purely local subjects. Her novels are essentially Canadian; they reflect our society such as it existed either before or after the Conquest. In reading them, one inhales the scent of nationality, of patriotism; they are suffused with a local scent that recalls the genuine land; one feels "chez soi," *at home*, as the English say. The geographical descriptions, the historical details, the painting of manners, the personality of the characters, the setting, taken as a whole and in their details, remind me of Canada with its great natural beauty, its exceptional climate, its snow, its frost, its July sun, its great lakes, its beautiful rivers, its entertainments, the trends and tastes of its inhabitants.

By clothing her works in these local colours, Mrs. Leprohon has ensured that they would be destined to live longer than pure adventure tales foreign to Canada and its population. She has carved a distinguished place for herself in our national literature. Her opinions and judgements are not offensive to the French-Canadian nationality, and in all respects she knows how to do justice to our countrymen. This is not a negligible quality.

---

1 The Seven Years' War (1756-63), culminating in the Fall of New France (1759-60) and ending with the Treaty of Paris (1763).
2 *The Manor House of De Villerai* was translated into French by Leprohon's nephew by marriage, Joseph-Édouard Lefebvre de Bellefeuille. It was serialized in the French-Canadian newspaper, *L'Ordre*, then published in book form in 1861, bearing the title *Le manoir de Villerai*.
3 This extract can be found on pp. 306-07.

From a purely literary point-of-view, her works are distinguished by their purity of style and pleasant smoothness of ideas and expression[.] ... *Antoinette de Mirecourt*, by far Mrs. Leprohon's best work, is the natural continuation of *The Manor House of De Villerai*; the scenes of the latter refer to the Seven Years' War which preceded the Cession [of New France from France]; the former refers to the period that immediately followed the Conquest.

6. From Anon., "The Late Mrs. Leprohon," *Canadian Illustrated News* (4 October 1879)

Our friends will find, on another page, enrolled in our Canadian Portrait Gallery, the likeness of the late Mrs. Leprohon, who departed this life, in Montreal, on Saturday, the 20th inst. She was born in 1832,[1] her maiden name being Mullins, and it was over the initials R.E.M. that she published her first contributions to Canadian literature in that pioneer magazine, the *Literary Garland*,[2] which Mr. John Lovell conducted many years ago. In 1851, she was married to Dr. Leprohon, the well-known physician of that name, who also holds with distinction the office of Spanish Vice-Consul for this district.[3] Her literary activity did not cease with that event, however, as is too frequently the case, but ripened and expanded until she added a new lustre to her husband's name. She contributed many poems to various magazines and periodicals, but finally fixed her vocation and secured her reputation by the production of family and domestic novels. Her first important work of this character was "Ida Beresford," which was followed, at regular intervals, by "Florence FitzHarding" [sic], "Eva Huntingdon," "Clarence Fitz-Clarence," and "Eveline [sic] O'Donnell," the latter a prize novel, we believe, contributed to the *Boston Pilot*. These works spread her fame throughout the United States and especially among the Irish people, and earned for her the flattering title of the Canadian Mrs. Sadlier.[4] The designation was not only complimentary

---

1 See p. 211, note 1.
2 See p. 211, note 2.
3 In the *Dictionary of Canadian Biography*, Monique Leclerc-Larochelle observes that, in 1872, Jean-Lukin Leprohon "was named vice-consul of Spain in Montreal, a position that, although more honorary than lucrative, bore witness to the esteem in which he was held. In 1881 the Spanish government awarded him the Order of Charles III in recognition of his services" (n. pag.).
4 Mary Anne Sadlier (née Madden, 1820-1903), a prolific Irish-Catholic writer born in Co. Cavan, Ireland, who emigrated to Montreal in 1844, marrying publisher James Sadlier two years later, moving for a time to New York, and returning to Montreal as a widow.

but just, inasmuch as there is great similitude in the talents of these two gifted ladies, who were, besides, bound to each other by ties of friendship and neighbourhood, as Mrs. Sadlier was half a Canadian through the old publishing house here, as well as through her connection with the family of the late lamented D'Arcy McGee.[1] But Mrs. Leprohon did not rest satisfied with her Irish-American repute. She aimed to portray certain phases of Canadian life and leave lasting tokens of her ability in quasi-historical romances. This ambition led to the composition of "The Manor House of de Villerai" and "Antoinette de Mirecourt," which can safely be pronounced her best works. Not only were they well received in their original English garb, but were immediately translated into French by M. Genand, then a prominent journalist, and now of the Ottawa Civil Service, as "Ida Beresford" was, we believe, previously translated by M. D. Lef. DeBellefeuille [sic], a prominent lawyer of this city.[2] It is remarkable how far a sterling work of fiction will travel, and Mrs. Leprohon's books have had that fate. A few years ago, on his arrival in Canada,[3] the present writer, when travelling through some of the French parishes in the Richelieu peninsula, stopped at a hospitable farm-house to pass the night. There were pretty girls there who contributed much to his enjoyment, but what interested him most was the conversation of the old mother, who, sitting at the edge of a table and hard at work at her knitting-needles, regaled him with the pathetic story of "Antoinette de Mirecourt," which she had just finished reading. Her graphic rehearsal was wonderful and she told him that she had been equally pleased with the "Manoir de Vellerai" [sic]. Based upon such simple and unconscious criticism as this, it is certain that these two works are sure to live in Canadian literature. Mrs. Leprohon excelled in the delineation of female characters, and displayed much skill in the difficult art of construction. She evidently wrote with ease, but there are no traces of haste in her manner, while her style is always correct and perspicuous. Her work was a substantial one and it is to be hoped that means will be found to publish all her productions in a collected form, which will

---

1 Thomas D'Arcy McGee (1825-68), journalist, poet, orator, and a Father of Canadian Confederation.
2 The author is mistaken when he refers to *The Manor House of De Villerai* as having been translated by J.A. Genand. *The Manor House* was translated into French by Leprohon's nephew by marriage, Joseph-Édouard Lefebvre de Bellefeuille, who also translated *Ida Beresford* (tr. 1859-60). Genand translated *Antoinette de Mirecourt* (1864) and *Armand Durand* (1868).
3 Although anonymous, this obituary was likely penned by the novelist and editor, John T. Lesperance (1835-91). Born in St. Louis, Missouri, Lesperance moved to Montreal in the mid-1860s.

be the easier as we understand that she was engaged, during her latter years, in the revision and collocation of them.[1] During the past decade or so, owing to feeble health and the cares of a growing family, Mrs. Leprohon did not publish so freely, and it is with pleasure that we record that, in this space, most of her contributions appeared in the CANADIAN ILLUSTRATED NEWS, in the success of which she always took a kindly interest. For several years in succession, she would send in, with her compliments, a short story for the Christmas and holiday season. Her domestic virtues and amiable social qualities endeared her to a wide circle of friends, who mourn her untimely loss and will cherish her remembrance, while her name will live in Canadian history as one who furnished a large measure to our literary annals.

---

1 This claim remains unverified.

Appendix B: Commentary on Canadian Literature and Nationality in the Confederation Period

1. From Thomas D'Arcy McGee, "The Mental Outfit of the New Dominion," *Gazette* (Montreal) (5 November 1867)

[It is difficult to overestimate Thomas D'Arcy McGee's importance to the political, cultural, and literary life of Canada in the Confederation period. He was a prominent journalist, editor, poet, and politician who is often remembered today for his support of Confederation and his outstanding skills as an orator. Like Leprohon, McGee was a member of Montreal's Irish-Catholic community. By contrast to Leprohon, who was born in Canada, McGee was born in Ireland, immigrating to the United States in 1842 and to Canada in 1857. Prior to moving to Canada, McGee was an Irish nationalist who supported the Fenians, a group advocating Irish separation from Britain, and a proponent of the annexation of Canada to the United States. After moving to Canada, however, McGee's political views became more moderate: he became a supporter of the federation of British North America and denounced the Irish-American Fenians. Having moved to Montreal at the invitation of the local Irish community, McGee published the newspaper *The New Era* (1857-58), which he used as a springboard to enter Canadian politics. In 1858, he was elected to the Legislative Assembly of the Province of Canada for the riding of Montreal West. On 7 April 1868, after a late session in the House of Commons, McGee was assassinated in front of his boarding house in Ottawa, Ontario. James Patrick Whelan, a suspected Fenian sympathizer, was hanged for the crime in 1869, although his guilt remains in doubt even today. McGee was buried in Montreal's Notre-Dame-des-Neiges cemetery, where Leprohon was also buried in 1879. A vocal and eloquent advocate of Canadian Confederation, McGee also held strong views about the role that literature and print culture played in shaping the national character. His views about literary nation-building are captured in his well-known speech, "The Mental Outfit of the New Dominion," delivered in Montreal on 4 November 1867 and printed in the Montreal *Gazette* the following day.]

All political observers are, I believe, now agreed that all the forces of a nation may be classed under the three heads, of moral, mental, and physical force.[1] It needs no argument to prove, that in this reading and writing age; "the age of the press" as it has been called, power must be wherever true intelligence is, and where most intelligence, most power.... Regarding the New Dominion as an incipient new Nation, it seems to me, that our mental self-reliance is an essential condition of our political independence; I do not mean a state of public mind, puffed up on small things; an exaggerated opinion of ourselves and a barbarian depreciation of foreigners; a controversial state of mind; or a merely imitative apish civilization. I mean a mental condition, thoughtful and true; national in its preferences, but catholic in its sympathies; gravitating inward, not outward; ready to learn from every other people on one sole condition, that the lesson when learned, has been worth acquiring. In short, we should desire to see, Gentlemen, our new national character distinguished by a manly modesty as much by mental independence; by the conscientious exercise of the critical faculties, as well as by the zeal of the inquirer....

Our reading supplies are, as you know, drawn chiefly from two sources; first, books, which are imported from the United States, England, and France—a foreign supply likely long to continue foreign. The second source is our newspaper literature, chiefly supplied, as we have seen, from among ourselves, but largely supplemented by American and English journals....

This newspaper literature forms by much the largest part of all our reading. There are in the four United Provinces[2] about one hundred and thirty journals, of which thirty at least are published daily. Of the total number of habitual readers it is not possible to form a close estimate, but they are probably represented by one-half of the male adults of the population—say 400,000 souls. However ephemeral the form of the literature read by so many may be, the effect must be lasting; and men of one newspaper, especially, are pretty much what their favourite editors make them. The responsibility of the editor is, therefore, in the precise proportion to the number and confidence of his readers. If they are 500, or 5,000, or 50,000, so is the moral responsibility multiplied upon him. He stands to hundreds or thousands, in a relation as intimate as that of the physician to his patient, or the lawyer to his client; and only in a degree less sacred, than that of the pastor to his people. He is their harbinger of light, their counsellor, their director; it is for him to build up the gaps in their educational training; to cut away the prejudices; to enlarge the sympathies; to make of his readers

---

1 The occasion of McGee's address is his speech to the members of the Literary Club, Montreal, 4 November 1867.
2 Today's Ontario, Quebec, New Brunswick, and Nova Scotia.

men, honest and brave, lovers of truth and lovers of justice. Modern society does not afford educated men any position, short of the pulpit and the altar, more honorable, more powerful for good or evil, and more heavily responsible to society. The editorial character as we now know it, is not above a century old; that length of time ago, correspondents addressed the publisher or printer, but never the editor. Original views on events and affairs were in those days usually given to the press in pamphlet form—of which subdivision in literature England alone has produced enough to fill many libraries. This pamphlet literature is now for the most part a dead letter; as ephemeral as old newspapers; unless when falling into the hands of men like Swift, Addison, Johnson and Burke,[1] the publication of a day in dealing with great principles and great characters, rose to the dignity and authority of a classic. There is no insuperable obstacle in the case, to prevent our newspaper writing undergoing a similar improvement. The best English and American journals are now written in a style not inferior in finish to the best books, and though ours is the limited patronage of a Province, it is not unreasonable that in our principal cities we should look for a high-toned, thoughtful, and scholarly newspaper style of writing....

As to the other branch of supply, I believe our booksellers have nothing to complain of. The sale of books is on the increase, though not at all so largely as the sale of newspapers. Our books are mainly English, or American reprints of English originals. In point of price the editions are not so far apart as they were on the other side of the Civil War.[2] As to the classes of books most in request, I have been informed by one of our members well informed on the matter, that the sales may be divided somewhat in these proportions; religious books, 18 per cent; poetical works, 10 per cent; books on historical, scientific and literary subjects, 28 per cent; and works of fiction 44 per cent. My obliging informant, (Mr. Samuel Dawson)[3] adds in relation to the comparative money value of the several classes of books most in demand, that the historical, literary and scientific works would represent about 45 per cent, the works of fiction 22, the poetical 15, and the religious 18 per cent of the whole. We thus have this striking result, that whereas the works of fiction are in volume, nearly one-half of all the reading

---

1 Jonathan Swift (1667-1745), Anglo-Irish writer and satirist; Joseph Addison (1672-1719), English politician, writer, and co-founder of the short-lived but influential daily paper, *The Spectator* (1711-12); Samuel Johnson (1709-84), influential English writer, literary critic, and lexicographer; and Edmund Burke (1729-97), Anglo-Irish writer, politician, and political philosopher.
2 The American Civil War (1861-65).
3 Publisher Samuel Edward Dawson (1833-1916).

done among us, in cost they come to less than one-fourth what is expended for other and better books. An accurate analysis of these books would be a valuable index to what it much concerns us to know, whether *Thomas A. Kempis* is still the book most read next to the Bible.[1] How many of Shakspeare [sic], and how many of Tupper[2] [note] go the hundred; whether the *Pilgrim's Progress* is bought chiefly as a child's book, and whether Keble's "Christian Year" sells as well or better than Don Juan?[3] "The demand for novels," says my informant, "is not nearly so great as it was," and this he traces to the growing preference for newspapers and periodicals, continuing serial stories and romances in chapters. On the general subject of reading fictitious works, I hold by a middle opinion. I hold that a bad novel is a bad thing, and a good one a good thing. That we have many bad novels, ushered from the press every day is a lamentable fact; books just as vile and flagitious in spirit as any of Mrs. Behns [sic] abominations of a former century.[4] The very facility with which these books are got together by their authors, might itself be taken as evidence of their worthlessness, for what mortal genius ever threw off works of thought or of art worthy of the name with such steam-engine rapidity? It is true Lopez de Vega could compose a comedy at a sitting, and Lafontaine, after writing 150 sentimental stories, was obliged to restrain himself to two days' writing in the week, otherwise he would have drowned out his publisher.[5] But you know what has been said of "easy writing" generally. For my own part, though no enemy to a good novel, I feel that I would fail of my duty if I did not raise a warning voice against the promiscuous and exclusive reading of sensational and sensual books, many of them written by women, who are the disgrace of their sex, and read with avidity by those who want only the opportunity equally to disgrace it. We must battle bad books with good books. As our young people in this material age will hunger and thirst for romantic relations, there is no better corrective for an excess of imaginative reading than the actual lives and books of travel of such men as Hodson, Burton, Speke, Kane, Du Chaillu, Hue, and Livingstone.[6] These

---

1 Thomas à Kempis (c. 1380-1471), author of *The Imitation of Christ* (c. 1418-27).
2 Martin Farquhar Tupper (1810-89), author of *Proverbial Philosophy* (1838).
3 *The Pilgrim's Progress* (1678) by John Bunyan; *The Christian Year* (1827) by John Keble; *Don Juan* (1819-24) by Lord Byron.
4 Aphra Behn (1640-89), author of *Oroonoko* (1688), among many other works.
5 Félix Arturo Lope de Vega y Carpio (1562-1635), Spanish playwright and poet; Jean de La Fontaine (1621-95), renowned French poet most famous for his *Fables*.
6 William Stephen Raikes Hodson (1821-58); Sir Richard Burton (1821-90); John Hanning Speke (1827-64); Elisha Kent Kane (1820-57); Paul du Chaillu (1831-1903); and David Livingstone (1813-73).

books lead us through strange scenes, among strange people, are full of genuine romance, proving the aphorism, "truth is strange—stranger than fiction."[1] But these are books which enlarge our sympathies, and do not pervert them; which excite our curiosity, and satisfy it, but not at the expense of morals; which give certainty and population to the geographical and historical dreams of our youthful days; which build up the gaps and spaces in our knowledge with new truths, certain to harmonize speedily with all old truth,—instead of filling our memories with vain, or perplexing, or atrocious images, as the common run of novelists are every day doing. Then, there is always as a corrective to diseased imaginations the Book of books itself—the Bible. I do not speak of its perusal as a religious duty incumbent on all Christians; it is not my place to inculcate religious duties; but I speak of it here as a family book mainly; and I say that it is well for our new Dominion that within the reach of every one, who has learned to read, lies this one book, the rarest and most unequalled as to matter, the cheapest of books as to cost, the most readable as to arrangement....

As to other correctives, I do not advocate a domestic spy system on our young people; but if one knew that a young friend or relative was acquiring a diseased appetite for opium-eating, would we not interfere in some way? And this danger to the mind is not less poisonous than that other drug to the body. "The woman that hesitates,"[2] says the proverb, "is lost;" as truly might it be said, "the woman who hides her book is lost." And in this respect, though Society allows a looser latitude to men, it is doubtful if Reason does; it is very doubtful that any mind, male or female, ever wholly recovers from the influence on character, of even one bad book, fascinatingly written....

From all these sources—our numerous reading class—our colleges—our learned professions—we ought to be able to give a good account of the mental outfit of the new Dominion. Well, then, for one of those expected to say what he thinks in these matters, I must give it as my opinion that we have as yet but few possessions in [sic] this sort that we can call strictly our own. We have not produced in our Colonial era any thinker of the reputation of Jonathan Edwards or Benjamin Franklin;[3] nor any native poet of the rank of Garsilaso [sic] de la Vega—the Spanish American.[4] The only sustained poems we have of

---

1   From Lord Byron's *Don Juan* (1823): "'Tis strange—but true; for truth is always strange, / Stranger than fiction" (XIV, stanza 101).
2   From Joseph Addison's *Cato* (1713): "The woman that deliberates is lost" (iv, i).
3   Jonathan Edwards (1703-58), American theologian; Benjamin Franklin (1706-90), American polymath and Founding Father.
4   Garcilaso de la Vega (1539-1616), a historian and writer from the Spanish Viceroyalty of Peru, a Spanish colonial administrative district, governed from Lima, comprising most of Spanish-ruled South America.

which the scenes are laid within the Dominion are both by Americans. Longfellow's "Evangeline," and Mr. Street's "Frontenac"—the latter much less read than it deserves.[1] One original humorist we have had, hardly of the highest order, however, in the late Judge Haliburton; one historian of an undoubtedly high order, in the late Mr. Garneau; one geologist, Sir William Logan;[2] but, as yet, no poet, no orator, no critic, of either American or European reputation.... Still we are not entirely destitute of resident writers. Dr. Dawson has given the world a work on his favourite science, which has established his name as an authority; Dr. Daniel Wilson's speculations and researches on Pre-historic Man have received the approval of high names; Mr. Alpheus Todd has given us a masterly original treatise on Parliamentary Government, which will be read and quoted wherever there is constitutional government in the world; Mr. Fennings Taylor has given us an excellent series of sketches, on contemporary Canadians;[3] Heavysege, Sangster and McLachlin [sic] are not without honour among poets.[4] An amiable friend of mine, Mr. J. LeMoine, of Quebec, has given to the world many *Maple Leaves* worthy of all praise—the only thoroughly Canadian book, in point of subject, which has appeared of late days, and for which, I am ashamed to say, the author has not received that encouragement his labours deserve.[5] If he were not an enthusiast he might well have become a misanthrope, as to native literature, at least. Another most deserving man in a different walk—a younger man, but a man of untired industry and very laudable ambition—Mr. Henry J. Morgan, now of Ottawa, announces a new book of reference, the *Bibliotheca canadensis* [sic],[6] which I trust will repay him for the enormous labour of such a compilation. These are, it is true, but streaks on the horizon, yet even as we watch others may arise; but be they more or

---

1 Henry Wadsworth Longfellow (1807-82) and Alfred Billings Street (1811-81).
2 Thomas Chandler Haliburton (1796-1865); François-Xavier Garneau (1809-66); Sir William Edmond Logan (1798-1875). See the extract from Garneau's *Histoire du Canada* in Appendix D5, p. 251.
3 John William Dawson (1820-99), the noted geologist; Sir Daniel Wilson (1816-92), author of *Prehistoric Man* (1862); Alpheus Todd (1821-84), author of the two-volume *On Parliamentary Government in England* (1867-69); and John Fennings Taylor (1817-82), author of the three-volume *Portraits of British Americans* (1865-68).
4 Charles Heavysege (1816-76); Charles Sangster (1822-93); and Alexander McLachlan (1817-96).
5 Sir James MacPherson Le Moine (1825-1912), author of the series *Maple Leaves* (1863-1906).
6 Henry James Morgan (1842-1913), author of *Sketches of Celebrated Canadians* (1862; see Appendix A4, p. 211) and *Bibliotheca Canadensis* (1867), among others.

less, I trust every such book will be received by our public less censoriously than is sometimes the case; that if a native book should lack the finish of a foreign one, as a novice may well be less expert than an old hand, yet if the book be honestly designed, and conscientiously worked up, the author shall be encouraged, not only for his own sake, but for the sake of the better things which we look forward to with hopefulness. I make this plea on behalf of those who venture upon authorship among us, because I believe the existence of a recognized literary class will bye and bye be felt as a state and social necessity. The books that are made elsewhere, even in England, are not always the best fitted for us; they do not always run on the same mental guage [sic], nor connect with our trains of thought; they do not take us up at the bye stages of cultivation at which we have arrived, and where we are emptied forth as on a barren, pathless, habitationless heath. They are books of another state of society, bearing traces of controversies, or directed against errors or evils, which for us hardly exist, except in the pages of these exotic books....

If English made [sic] books do not mortice closely with our Colonial deficiencies, still less do American national books. I speak not here of such literary universalists as Irving, Emerson, and Longfellow;[1] but of such American nationalists as Hawthorne, Bancroft, Brownson, Draper, and their latter prose writers generally.[2] Within the last few years, especially since the era of the civil war, there has been a craving desire to assert the mental independence of America as against England; to infuse an American philosophy of life, and philosophy of government, into every American writing and work of art. Mr. Bancroft's oration on the death of Mr. Lincoln was an example of this new spirit; and Dr. Draper's "Civil Policy of America" affords another illustration. It is a natural ambition for them to endeavour to Americanize their literature more and more; all nations have felt the same ambition, earlier or later; ... As long as justice, and courtesy, and magnanimity are not sacrificed to an intolerant [sic] nationalism, the growth of new literary States must be to the increase of the universal literary republic. But when nationalism stunts the growth, and embitters the generous spirit which alone can produce generous and enduring fruits of literature, then it becomes a curse, rather than a gain to the people, among whom it may find favor; and to every other people who may have relations with such a bigoted, one-side nationality.

---

1 Washington Irving (1783-1859); Ralph Waldo Emerson (1803-82); and Henry Wadsworth Longfellow (1807-82).
2 Nathaniel Hawthorne (1804-64); George Bancroft (1800-81); Orestes Augustus Brownson (1803-76); and John William Draper (1811-82).

It is quite clear to me, that if we are to succeed with our new-Dominion [sic], it can never be by accepting a ready-made-easy literature, which assumes Bostonian culture to be the worship of the future, and the American democratic system to be the manifestly destined form of government for all the civilized world, new as well as old....

It is usual to say of ourselves, Gentlemen, that we are entering on a new era. It may be so, or it may be only the mirage of an era painted on an exhalation of self-opinion. Such eras, however, have come for other civilized States, why not for us also?... How far we, who are to represent British ethics and British culture in America—we, whose new Constitution solemnly proclaims "the well understood principles of the British Constitution;" how far we are to make this probable next era our own—either by adhesion or resistance—is what, Gentlemen, we must all determine for ourselves, and so far forth, for the Dominion.

I shall venture in concluding this merely preliminary paper, to address myself directly to the educated young men of Canada, as it now exists. I invite them, as a true friend, not to shrink from confronting the great problems presented by America to the world, whether in morals or in government. I propose to them that they should hold their own, on their own soil, sacrificing nothing of their originality; but rejecting nothing, nor yet accepting anything, merely because it comes out of an older, or richer, or greater country.... North America is emerging; and why not our one-third of the North rise to an equal, even if an opposing altitude, with the land conterminous? Why not? I see no reason, why not? What we need are the three levers—moral power, mental power, and physical power....

I venture humbly to suggest that we need more active conscientiousness in our choice of books and periodicals, for ourselves and for our young people; that the reading acquirement which moves, and embraces and modifies, every faculty of our immortal souls, is too fearful an agent to be employed capriciously, or wantonly, much less wickedly, to the peril of interests which will not be covered up forever, by the Sexton's last shovel of church-yard clay....

I am well convinced that there do exist, in the ample memories, the northern energy, and the quick apprehensiveness of our young men, resources all unwrought, of inestimable value to society. I would beseech of that most important class, therefore, to use their time; to exercise their powers of mind as well as body; to acquire the mental drill and discipline, which will enable them to bear the arms of a civilized state in time of peace, with honor, and advantage. If they will pardon me the liberty I take, I venture to address them an apostrophe of a poet of another country, slightly altered to suit the case of Canada:

"Oh brave young men, our hope, our pride, our promise,
    On you our hearts are set,—
In manliness, in kindliness, in justice,
    To make *Canada* a nation yet!"[1]

2. From John T. Lesperance, "The Literary Standing of the Dominion," *Canadian Illustrated News* (24 February 1877)

The Literary Standing of the Dominion[2]

Different men have different ways of testing the progress of a country. My test is the progress of its literature. The deduction is easily made. Where there is an active commerce, there is a free circulation of money; where money is plentiful, a surplus is devoted to education. Education creates a demand for books and the different forms of reading, and to meet this demand publishers eagerly come forward, backed by a host of writers in the divers walks of letters. In a financial crisis the book-trade is the first to suffer. In an era of financial prosperity literature always flourishes.

    Tried by this standard, there can be no question that Canada is progressing. Twenty years ago, as I am informed, elementary schools were scanty; colleges and academies were few, and making only faint beginnings; special courses were unknown, and the people had little to read beyond newspapers and political pamphlets. Now, all this is changed. The common school system is established everywhere with results that obtain even European commendation; there are colleges and universities mounted on a fair footing; a spirit of inquiry pervades all classes and the consequence is that Canada is fast laying the foundation of a literature of her own. This is a matter for congratulation. Science, letters and the arts are the triple crown of a people. Dr. Johnson has said that "the chief glory of a nation lies in its authors."[3]

---

1 McGee's adaptation, for his purposes, of Sir Samuel Ferguson's "Lament for Thomas Davis," whose final stanza reads as follows: "Oh, brave young men, my love, my pride, my promise, / 'Tis on you my hopes are set, / In manliness, in kindliness, in justice, / To make Erin a nation yet."
2 Paper read at the regular meeting of the Kuklos Club of Montreal, Saturday, February 17th. [Original note]
3 Samuel Johnson (1709-84). In the preface to *A Dictionary of the English Language* (1755), Johnson writes: "The chief glory of every people arises from its authors" (12).

I

In reviewing the links of this literary progress, I begin with the French language. The distinction is due to its priority of age in Canada, as well as to the exceptional obstacles it has had to contend with. Indeed, considering the position of the Franco-Canadian population, which has been nothing less than a political and social struggle for upwards of a hundred years, it is a marvel that they have preserved the French language in anything like its native purity. Yet the feat has been accomplished....

Within the past few years, Franco-Canadian writers have boldly attempted every branch of composition, and in each, several names have acquired lasting reputation.

Garneau's History of Canada is a work of high aim, solid, learned, and written in that severe style which recalls the manner of Guizot, Barante, and DeGerlache.[1] There may be different opinions about its impartiality, but its literary excellence is beyond cavil.... Other writers have taken up the lighter scraps of Canadian history, such as local traditions, antiquarian curiosities, monographs of distinguished men. Particularly successful among these are M. DeGaspé, author of *Les Anciens Canadiens*, and M. J.M. LeMoine, a gentleman equally at home in the English language, and whose *Maple Leaves* are quite commendable for their sketchiness [sic].[2]

No country, from its peculiarities, presents a fairer field for fiction than does Lower Canada, and its writers have not been slow to improve their opportunity. Several of these novels are sure to live. M. Chauveau's *Charles Guérin* is a description of social manners; M. Gérin-Lajoie's *Jean Rivard* is a gossipy account of pioneer life in the Townships; M. DeBoucherville's *Une de Perdue Deux de Trouvées* draws some of its materials from the rebellion of 1837-38, and contains an elaborate narrative of the battle of St. Denis. M. Bourassa's *Jacques et Marie* is a brilliant episode of the expulsion of French families from Nova Scotia by the British, another "Evangeline" hardly less touching than the story of Longfellow. M. Marmette, a young writer of Quebec, has lately put forth two historical novels, illustrative of the more ancient days of the Province. One is *François de Bienville*; the other,

---

1 François-Xavier Garneau (1809-66); François Guizot (1787-1874); Amable-Guillaume-Prosper Brugière, Baron de Barante (1782-1866); Étienne Constantin, Baron de Gerlache (1785-1871). For extracts from Garneau's *Histoire du Canada* (tr. Andrew Bell), see Appendices D4 and D5.
2 Philippe Aubert de Gaspé (1786-1871); Sir James MacPherson Le Moine (1825-1912).

L'Intendant Bigot. And, as I write, there is announced still another romance from the pen of M. Legendre, a young author of the Pontmartin school, who is remarkable for the purity and finish of his style....[1]

There is nothing like a good periodical to waken up young writers. In a new country, more especially where there must necessarily be plenty of latent talent, all it wants is half a chance to produce itself. This opportunity has often been afforded French-Canadian authors. Formerly it was *Les Soirées Canadiennes*; now it is *La Revue Canadienne*.[2] The latter is a monthly magazine published at Montreal, and already advanced in its thirteenth year. It has formed a galaxy of fine writers in history, philosophy, criticism, and the lighter works of the imagination....

The French population of Canada may be set down, in round numbers, at a million. Of this number, taking the usual average of ten per cent., not more than 100,000 can be said to be educated, and of the latter—according to another estimate—only a fourth, or 25,000, form what is called the reading public. Now, in view of these figures, the literary activity of French-Canadians is a very noticeable fact; and, perhaps, when we come to compare it with the literary movement of other nationalities, we shall be forced to own that the former have proudly and successfully held their own against all rivals. A good word, then, for the French-Canadian literature.

II

We all remember how long it took American writers to attain the honour of literary citizenship in England. It required no less than the genius of Irving to break down the barrier of exclusion.[3] American national literature may be said to date from *The Sketch Book*, and now the popular authors of the United States are as much read in Britain as they are at home.

Canadian literature had precisely the same obstacle to meet, or rather its task was still more difficult, for it had to fight its way into the

---

1 Pierre-Joseph-Olivier Chauveau (1820-90); Antoine Gérin-Lajoie (1824-82); Georges Boucher de Boucherville (1814-94); Napoléon Bourassa (1827-1916); Joseph Marmette (1844-95); and Napoléon Legendre (1841-1907).
2 *Les Soirées canadiennes* (Quebec City, 1861-65); and *La Revue canadienne* (Montreal, 1864-1922).
3 The *British Critic* complained in 1818 that "[t]he Americans have no national literature, and no learned men" (vols. 9-10, p. 497). Often seen as the Father of American Literature, Washington Irving (1783-1859) published *The Sketch Book of Geoffrey Crayon, Gent.* one year later, in 1819.

neighbouring Republic as well as into the mother country. But it, too, has succeeded in partially accomplishing the double triumph. And, singularly enough, it owes the recognition to its poets....

For some reason that I cannot determine, Canadian works of fiction have been neither numerous nor of the highest class, though I will not be surprised if the next important publication announced to the country proves to be a splendid novel.

The series of Madame Leprohon is chiefly devoted to the delineation of social manners at or before the time of the Conquest. Of these *The Manor House of De Villerai* appears to me the best. That work, with *Antoinette De Mirecourt* and *Ada Dunmore*, certainly place the authoress at the head of Canadian novelists.

Mrs. Moodie has more individuality. Apart from their literary merit, her *Roughing it in the Bush* and *Life in the Clearings* have a force of realism about them which accounts for their reputation both in England and the United States. Mrs. Noel's best works are *The Secret of Stanley Hall* and *The Merchant's Secret*.[1]

In the domain of history, I find a multiplicity of pamphlets, short notices, and partial narratives, but critical research of any extent seems to have been left to the transactions of the Historical Societies. I am not surprised at this, being aware that the pursuit of history requires much time, involves considerable expenditure for the purposes of investigation, and, in these days of superficial reading, is less patronized by the public than it ought to be. There is, however, a good translation of Garneau's History by Bell; and Christie's History of Lower Canada is the only one which we have in English that is at all based on official documents and *pièces justificatives*. Croil, Canniff, Coffin may be consulted with advantage, but the history of Canada from the British stand-point has yet to be written....[2]

III

These signs of progress in both the English and French languages are very satisfactory, but if Canada aims to have a literature of her own—at least, to a certain extent—something more is required. She must be self-sufficing in the way of publishing facilities, and as to "specialities"

---

1 Susanna Moodie (née Strickland; 1803-85), author of *Roughing It In the Bush* (1852) and *Life in the Clearings Versus the Bush* (1853), among others; Mrs. J.V. Noel (née Ellen Kyle; 1815-73), novelist and short story writer.

2 See Appendix D4, p. 247, and D5, p. 251 for extracts from Andrew Bell's translation of Garneau's *Histoire du Canada*; Robert Christie (1787-1856); James Croil (1821-1916); William Canniff (1830-1910); and William Foster Coffin (1808-78).

in both science and letters, these must be edited here and not imported from England or the United States....

The copyright law of 1868, though by no means perfect in all its provisions, has provided great benefit to the country, and publishers have taken advantage of it to inaugurate a series of home publications.[1] The Canadian houses have already taken a start in the matter, and their reprints of popular works of both English and American writers prove, perhaps better than nothing else, how much Canadians have learned to rely upon themselves. The time is not far distant when there will be Canadian editions of most standard authors, as well printed and sold at least as cheap as those imported from abroad.

It was long believed that literary weeklies and pictorial papers could not be produced in Canada. But several have lately sprung into existence and are flourishing. Ontario and Quebec have each a weekly of the kind, made up of light reading of every description, and while both appear equal to American papers of the same standard, their moral tone is healthier, and they really deserve the appellation of "family" papers. With regard to an illustrated paper, the Dominion can point to its own,[2] now nearly in the eighth year of its existence, as not inferior to the best pictorials of London, Paris, Berlin, or New York. Nay, to Canada belongs the honour of having first brought out the process of reproducing pictures directly from photographs, without the intermediary of wood engraving.[3] This new method is destined with time to operate important changes in the pictorial art, the chief of which will be to place the copies of the finest pictures within reach of the most modest purse.

From weekly publications the natural transition is to monthly ones. It is a long step to take, but the country has taken it.[4] Nothing strikes me as better illustrating the progress about which I write, than the fact that the Canadian people are prepared for and demand

---

1 George L. Parker writes that, in contrast to "[t]he British copyright acts of 1709 and 1842[,]" in which British and colonial writers effectively "assigned their 'copyright' to publishers in return for either an outright payment or a split of the profits[,]" the first dominion act (An Act Respecting Copyright, 1868) "protected" writers "locally" (148). Unfortunately, the 1868 law only granted protection in Canada, and further negotiations between the Canadian and British governments was needed in order to arrive at the more "compromis[ing]" Copyright Act of 1875 (Parker 152).
2 The *Canadian Illustrated News* (Montreal, 1869-83), published by George-Édouard Desbarats (1838-93).
3 Leggotype, a "photoelectrotyping process" (Galarneau 89) co-invented by William Augustus Leggo (1830-1915) and Desbarats. Early examples of photographs published using Leggotype can be found in the *Canadian Illustrated News* and its sister paper, *L'Opinion publique* (Montreal, 1870-83).
4 *The New Dominion Monthly* (Montreal, 1867-79).

monthly magazines of their own. It is only yesterday that a gentleman who had witnessed the inauguration of Confederation in 1867, and who has since been away, asked me how the "new nation" had been getting on in his absence. For my answer, I pointed to the first number of a monthly periodical which had just been laid on my table. "I am satisfied," said my friend, "five years ago such a publication would have been impossible." ...

This brief sketch would not be complete without a word respecting the newspapers of the Dominion. They are not only a special department of literature in themselves, but they are the means of fostering and propagating a taste for literature among the masses. The number of Canadian newspapers, including, for reference, those of the colonies not yet united to the Dominion, reaches the handsome total of 510.... These papers present a fair average of ability and enterprise, and as to dignity of tone, they are not below the standard of the foreign press. They are not however so remunerative as they ought to be, owing to want of common understanding as to business management. Ontario has its Press Association, but that is not enough. There should be a Dominion Press Association to regulate the rates of advertisements, the vital question of pre-payment, a uniform system of telegraphic reports, and other equally important matters.

Canada has now only to continue the good work which she has begun. If she is destined—as there is reason for believing—to become a great and prosperous nation, it rests with her to take a distinct place in the world of letters.

3. From Edmond Lareau, *Histoire de la littérature canadienne* (1874) [My translation][1]

[While its negative commentary on the state of French-Canadian novel-writing presents a marked contrast to Lesperance's positive comments, above (pp. 225-26), about the state of French-Canadian literature compared to that of English Canada, the following extract is of particular interest for Lareau's identification of the historical novel as the genre best suited to the sympathies of French-Canadian writers—a statement that bears witness to the Romantic nationalism that underpins Lareau's entire analysis. Together with his observation that French-Canadian literature's greatest source of originality lies with French-Canadian history and legends, along with Lareau's advice to prose-writers to read Garneau's *Histoire du Canada*, this extract touches on key reasons why Leprohon's novels of Quebec,

---

1 This extract can be found on pp. 274-78.

including *The Manor House*, might have been so positively received by French-Canadian readers.]

The novel, in Canada, has a special character, for it is essentially national. It has contributed a great deal to the originality of our national literature, as much as our literature has any.

We would be searching in vain if we were trying to find, in the narratives of our prose writers, any intrigues of the boudoir, any accumulation of feelings—each as improbable as the next—any patterns that are resolved only to resume again with new complications, any superfluity of feelings, characters and types largely absent from society, or any of those attentions that effeminate or those little nothings that often serve little purpose other than to distort judgements among men and feelings among women. Our novelists have rejected all of that, and have borrowed nothing, in this respect, from transatlantic writers.

Rarely does the setting take place other than in America and almost always in Canada.

Here, a vast subject matter lends itself to numerous uses, while offering itself naturally to the imaginations of our prose writers. Here, we have all that we need to supply themes for honest novels. Have we not our past, our history, fertile in beautiful devotion, in traits of heroism, in touching anecdotes? Have we not our forests with their poetic aspects, the Indian peoples with their bizarre mythology, their original values and the struggles they waged against civilized man? Have we not our legends, the adventures of our *coureurs des bois*[1] [sic] and of our *voyageurs*[2] from *yonder*! There is a legendary and fantastic world, a drama of palpitating interest in the great act of the colonization of America....

We have generally understood that Canadian narratives could further interest the Canadian reader. Our prose writers, with few exceptions, have remained content to explore the fertile field of our history. Maybe we have even transformed this quality into an error by not broadening the scope of our narratives. Our novelists have not yet made great efforts of the imagination. Our novels, or if you prefer our sketches of manners, are of a primitive character, bringing them closer to history or the chronicle. There is something like a too-great simplicity in the narration of events. The plot is too uncomplicated and

---

1 "A woodsman, hunter, trader, etc., of French or French-Indian origin, in Canada and the northern and western United States" (*OED*).
2 "In Canada, a man employed by the fur companies in carrying goods to and from the trading posts on the lakes and rivers; a Canadian boatman" (*OED*).

the book often lacks interest. We seem to have no knowledge of the secrets of this difficult art which combines flexibility of style with exact portraiture of manners, variety of scene with simplicity of narrative, rendering of character with descriptions of the beauties of nature. But these flaws will certainly be corrected....

Our legends comprise the most original part of our literature; they are, in a way, the clearest and best part of our literary glory. Every people has its legends, the people of the South as much as those of the North. Our own resemble the adventurous feats of the Normans and Bretons; sometimes they possess those magical and fantastic features that characterize the vast and vaporous South of France. The accomplishments of our forefathers, their superstitions, their long wars against many enemies, their missions in wild lands,—all these subjects lend themselves to bright and varied representations.

I advise anyone who wants to spend his time and talent writing fiction to read Garneau's *Histoire du Canada*.[1] He will find that nearly every page contains the subject matter for a fine novel. The historical novel alone is called upon to live in Canada. It is at least the one that should continue to appeal to the sympathies of our writers.

---

1 For extracts, see Appendices D4 and D5, p. 247 and p. 251.

Appendix C: Literary Precedents

1. From Samuel Richardson, "Preface by the Editor," *Pamela; or, Virtue Rewarded* (1740)

[The following extract from Samuel Richardson's preface to the epistolary novel, *Pamela*, illuminates Leprohon's debt to eighteenth-century English fiction, in particular to novels of sensibility that famously intervened in contemporary debates about the social value of virtue. There are many points of comparison between *Pamela* and *The Manor House of De Villerai*, including the plot, which revolves around a courtship, and the storyline, which hinges on a servant who avoids seduction, is rewarded by marriage, and wins over skeptics.]

IF to *Divert* and *Entertain*, and at the same time to *Instruct*, and *Improve* the Minds of the *YOUTH* of *both Sexes*:

IF to inculcate *Religion* and *Morality* in so easy and agreeable a manner, as shall render them equally *delightful* and *profitable* to the *younger Class* of Readers, as well as worthy of the Attention of Persons of *maturer* Years and Understandings:

IF to set forth in the most exemplary Lights, the *Parental*, the *Filial*, and the *Social* Duties, and that from *low* to *high* Life:

IF to paint *VICE* in its proper Colours, to make it *deservedly Odious*; and to set *VIRTUE*[1] in its own amiable Light, to make it *truly Lovely*:

IF to draw Characters *justly*, and to support them *equally*:

IF to raise a Distress from *natural* Causes, and to excite Compassion from *proper* Motives:

IF to teach the Man of *Fortune* how to use it; the Man of *Passion* how to *subdue* it; and the Man of *Intrigue*, how, gracefully, and with Honour to himself, to *reclaim*:

IF to give *practical* Examples, worthy to be followed in the most *critical* and *affecting* Cases, by the modest *Virgin*, the chaste *Bride*, and the obliging *Wife*:

IF to effect all these good Ends, in so probable, so natural, so *lively* a manner, as shall engage the Passions of every sensible Reader, and strongly interest them in the edifying Story:

---

1 Denoting sexuality chastity, adherence to standards of moral conduct, and "abstention on moral grounds from ... vice" (*OED*), "virtue" was one of the most important, and frequently discussed, values in eighteenth-century Britain.

AND all without raising a *single Idea* throughout the Whole, that shall shock the exactest Purity, even in those tender Instances where the exactest Purity would be most apprehensive:

IF these (embellished with a great Variety of entertaining Incidents) be laudable or worthy Recommendations of any Work, the Editor of the following Letters,[1] which have their Foundation in *Truth* and *Nature*, ventures to assert, that all these desirable Ends are obtained in these Sheets: And as he is therefore confident of the favourable Reception which he boldly bespeaks for this little Work; he thinks any *further Preface* or *Apology* for it, unnecessary[.] ...

The Editor

2. From Sir Walter Scott, "A Postscript, Which Should Have Been a Preface," Chapter XXIV of *Waverley; or, 'Tis Sixty Years Since* (1814)

[Sir Walter Scott's *Waverley* was one of the most influential novels of the nineteenth century and a model for literary nation-builders throughout Europe and the Americas. The following extract from the "Postface" represents an important account of Scott's views about the clash of cultures in processes of nation-formation in modernity. In emphasizing the seismic socio-historical and cultural changes that Britain underwent in a few short decades in the eighteenth century, the "Postface" sheds light on Scott's complex views of Scotland's place in Britain while also illuminating important points of comparison with Leprohon's treatment of the French Canadians in eighteenth-century New France.]

There is no European nation which, within the course of half a century, or little more, has undergone so complete a change as this kingdom of Scotland. The effects of the insurrection of 1745,[2]—the destruction of the patriarchal power of the Highland chiefs,—the abolition of the heritable jurisdictions of the Lowland nobility and barons,—the total eradication of the Jacobite party, which, averse to

---

1 *Pamela* is an epistolary novel. The author, Richardson, presents himself as the "editor" of the letters.
2 The Battle of Culloden (September 1745) between Scottish Jacobites, supporters of the House of Stuart, and British Unionists, supporters of the House of Hanover, stemmed from discontent arising from the legislated Union of Scotland with England in 1707. The aftermath of the battle, which the Jacobites lost, included the legislated stripping of power from Scottish Highland chiefs.

intermingle with the English, or adopt their customs, long continued to pride themselves upon maintaining ancient Scottish manners and customs, commenced this innovation. The gradual influx of wealth, and extension of commerce, have since united to render the present people of Scotland a class of beings as different from their grandfathers, as the existing English are from those of Queen Elizabeth's time.... But the change, though steadily and rapidly progressive, has, nevertheless, been gradual; and, like those who drift down the stream of a deep and smooth river, we are not aware of the progress we have made until we fix our eye on the now-distant point from which we have been drifted. Such of the present generation as can recollect the last twenty or twenty-five years of the eighteenth century, will be fully sensible of the truth of this statement; especially if their acquaintance and connexions lay among those who, in my younger time, were facetiously called, "folks of the old leaven," who still cherished a lingering, though hopeless attachment, to the house of Stuart. This race has now almost entirely vanished from the land, and with it, doubtless, much absurd political prejudice; but also many living examples of singular and disinterested attachment to the principles of loyalty which they received from their fathers, and of old Scottish faith, hospitality, worth, and honour.

It was my accidental lot, though not born a Highlander, (which may be an apology for much bad Gaelic) to reside, during my childhood and youth, among persons of the above description; and now, for the purpose of preserving some idea of the ancient manners of which I have witnessed the almost total extinction, I have embodied in imaginary scenes, and ascribed to fictitious characters, a part of the incidents which I then received from those who were actors in them. Indeed, the most romantic parts of this narrative are precisely those which have a foundation in fact....

It has been my object to describe these persons, not by a caricatured and exaggerated use of the national dialect, but by their habits, manners, and feelings; so as, in some distant degree, to emulate the admirable Irish portraits drawn by Miss Edgeworth,[1] so different from the "dear joys" who so long, with the most perfect family resemblance to each other, occupied the drama and the novel....

I would willingly persuade myself, that the preceding work will not be found altogether uninteresting. To elder persons it will recall scenes and characters familiar to their youth; and to the rising generation the tale may present some idea of the manners of their forefathers....

---

1 Maria Edgeworth (1767-1849), prolific Anglo-Irish writer and author of *Castle Rackrent* (1800), among other works.

3. From John Richardson, "Introductory," Chapter 1 of *Wacousta; or, The Prophecy: A Tale of the Canadas* (1832)

[Although *Wacousta* is set on the border of today's state of Michigan and province of Ontario, Richardson opens his novel with an introductory chapter that summarizes recent history, including an evaluation of the outcome of the Seven Years' War and its impact on intercultural relations between the British, the French-Canadians, and Native North Americans, from Lower Canada (Quebec) to Upper Canada (Ontario). Of particular relevance in this context are the narrator's expressed prejudices toward the French-Canadians, against which *The Manor House of De Villerai* mounts an implicit defence.]

As we are about to introduce our readers to scenes with which the European is little familiarised, some few cursory remarks, illustrative of the general features of the country into which we have shifted our labours, may not be deemed misplaced at the opening of this volume.

Without entering into minute geographical detail, it may be necessary merely to point out the outline of such portions of the vast continent of America as still acknowledge allegiance to the English crown, in order that the reader, understanding the localities, may enter with deeper interest into the incidents of a tale connected with a ground hitherto untouched by the wand of the modern novelist.

All who have ever taken the trouble to inform themselves of the features of a country so little interesting to the majority of Englishmen in their individual character must be aware,—and for the information of those who are not, we state,—that that portion of the northern continent of America which is known as the United States is divided from the Canadas by a continuous chain of lakes and rivers, commencing at the ocean into which they empty themselves, and extending in a north-western direction to the remotest parts of these wild regions, which have never yet been pressed by other footsteps than those of the native hunters of the soil. First we have the magnificent St. Lawrence, fed from the lesser and tributary streams, rolling her sweet and silver waters into the foggy seas of the Newfoundland....

Such being the general features of the country even at the present day, it will readily be comprehended how much more wild and desolate was the character they exhibited as far back as the middle of the last century, about which period our story commences. At that epoch, it will be borne in mind, what we have described as being the United States were then the British colonies of America dependent on the mother-country; while the Canadas, on the contrary, were, or had very recently been, under the dominion of France, from whom they had been wrested after a long struggle, greatly advanced in favour of

England by the glorious battle fought on the plains of Abraham, near Quebec, and celebrated for the defeat of Montcalm and the death of Wolfe.

The several attempts made to repossess themselves of the strong hold [sic] of Quebec having, in every instance, been met by discomfiture and disappointment, the French, in despair, relinquished the contest, and, by treaty, ceded their claims to the Canadas,—an event that was hastened by the capitulation of the garrison of Montreal, commanded by the Marquis de Vaudreuil, to the victorious arms of General Amherst. Still, though conquered as a people, many of the leading men in the country, actuated by that jealousy for which they were remarkable, contrived to oppose obstacles to the quiet possession of a conquest by those whom they seemed to look upon as their hereditary enemies; and in furtherance of this object, paid agents, men of artful and intriguing character, were dispersed among the numerous tribes of savages, with a view of exciting them to acts of hostility against their conquerors. The long and uninterrupted possession, by the French, of those countries immediately bordering on the hunting grounds and haunts of the natives, with whom they carried on an extensive traffic in furs, had established a communionship [sic] of interest between themselves and those savage and warlike people, which failed not to turn to account the vindictive views of the former. The whole of the province of Upper Canada at that time possessed but a scanty population, protected in its most flourishing and defensive points by stockade forts; the chief object of which was to secure the garrisons, consisting each of a few companies, from any sudden surprise on the part of the natives, who, although apparently inclining to acknowledge the change of neighbours, and professing amity, were, it was well known, too much in the interest of their old friends the French, and even the French Canadians themselves, not to be regarded with the most cautious distrust....

When at a later period the Canadas were ceded to us by France, those parts of the opposite frontier which we have just described became also tributary to the English crown, and were, by the peculiar difficulties that existed to communication with the more central and populous districts, rendered especially favourable to the exercise of hostile intrigue by the numerous active French emissaries every where dispersed among the Indian tribes. During the first few years of the conquest, the inhabitants of Canada, who were all either European French, or immediate descendants of that nation, were, as might naturally be expected, more than restive under their new governors, and many of the most impatient spirits of the country sought every opportunity of sowing the seeds of distrust and jealousy in the hearts of the natives. By these people it was artfully suggested to the Indians, that their new oppressors were of the race of those who had driven them from the sea, and were progressively advancing on their territories until scarce a hunting ground or a village would be left to them. They described them, moreover, as being the hereditary enemies of their great father, the King of France, with whose governors they had buried the hatchet for ever, and smoked the calumet of perpetual peace. Fired by these wily suggestions, the high and jealous spirit of the Indian chiefs took the alarm, and they beheld with impatience the "Red Coat" ... usurping, as they deemed it, those possessions which had so recently acknowledged the supremacy of the pale flag of their ancient ally. The cause of the Indians, and that of the Canadians, became, in some degree, identified as one, and each felt it was the interest, and it may be said the natural instinct, of both, to hold communionship of purpose, and to indulge the same jealousies and fears. Such was the state of things in 1763, the period at which our story commences,—an epoch fruitful in designs of hostility and treachery on the part of the Indians, who, too crafty and too politic to manifest their feelings by overt acts declaratory of the hatred carefully instilled into their breasts, sought every opportunity to compass the destruction of the English, wherever they were most vulnerable to the effects of stratagem....

While giving, for the information of the many, what, we trust, will not be considered a too compendious outline of the Canadas, and the events connected with them, we are led to remark, that, powerful as was the feeling of hostility cherished by the French Canadians towards the English when the yoke of early conquest yet hung heavily on them, this feeling eventually died away under the mild influence of a government that preserved to them the exercise of all their customary privileges, and abolished all invidious distinctions between the descendants of France and those of the mother-country. So universally, too, has this system of conciliation been pursued, we believe we may with safety aver, of all the numerous colonies that have succumbed to the genius and power of England, there are none whose inhabitants entertain stronger feelings of attachment and loyalty to her than those of Canada; and whatever may be the transient differences,—differences growing entirely out of circumstances and interests of a local character, and in no way tending to impeach the acknowledged fidelity of the mass of French Canadians,—whatever, we repeat, may be the ephemeral differences that occasionally spring up between the governors of those provinces and individual members of the Houses of Assembly, they must, in no way, be construed into a general feeling of disaffection towards the English crown.

In proportion also as the Canadians have felt and acknowledged the beneficent effects arising from a change of rulers, so have the Indian tribes been gradually weaned from their first fierce principle of hostility, until they have subsequently become as much distinguished by their attachment to, as they were three quarters of a century ago remarkable for their untameable aversion for, every thing that bore the English name, or assumed the English character.

Appendix D: Historical Sources

1. From Colonel Malcolm Fraser, *Extract from a Manuscript Journal, Relating to the Siege of Quebec in 1759* (1759; rpt. 1866)[1]

[This entry contains Fraser's references to the orders to burn French-Canadian houses, to which Leprohon refers in *The Manor House of De Villerai*. It also contains Fraser's description of the Battle of the Plains of Abraham on 13 September 1759. Fraser includes a transcription of Wolfe's last orders, written on board the *Sutherland* on 12 September 1759. These orders were written on the same ship as the letter by Wolfe dated 9 September 1759, which follows in Appendix E1 (p. 253).]

Friday, 17th August.—Crossed from the Isle of Orleans to St. Joachim. Before we landed we observed some men walking along the fences, as if they intended to oppose us; and on our march up to the Church of St. Joachim, we were fired on by some party's [sic] of the Enemy from behind the houses and fences, but upon our advancing they betook themselves to the woods, from whence they continued popping at us, till towards evening, when they thought proper to retire, and we kept possession of the Priest's house, which we set about fortifying in the best manner we could....

Thursday, 23rd.—We were reinforced by a party of about one hundred and forty Light Infantry, and a Company of Rangers, under the command of Captain Montgomery of Kennedy's or forty-third Regiment,[2] who likewise took the command of our detachment, and we all marched to attack the village to the west of St. Joachim, which was occupied by a party of the enemy to the number of about two hundred, as we supposed, Canadians and Indians, when we came pretty near the village, they fired on us from the houses pretty smartly; we were ordered to lie behind the fences till the Rangers, who were detached to attack the Enemy from the woods, began firing on their left flank, when we advanced briskly without great order; and the

---

1 Entries from Fraser's journal were published in the New York *Mercury*, no. 385, 31 December 1759, p. 4. Over a century later, they were assembled and published under the auspices of the Literary and Historical Society of Quebec. In *The Manor House*, Leprohon refers to the *Mercury* entries.
2 The leader of the forlorn hope who fell at Pres De Ville [sic] 31st. December 1775. [Original note. Richard Montgomery (1738-75), the Irish-born Major-General of the Continental Army during the American Revolution, led the attack on Quebec and was killed in action on 31 December 1775.]

French abandoned the houses and endeavoured to get into the woods, our men pursuing close at their heels. There were several of the enemy killed, and wounded, and a few prisoners taken, all of whom the barbarous Captain Montgomery, who command [sic] us, ordered to be buchered [sic] in a most inhuman and cruel manner; particularly two, who I sent prisoners by a sergeant, after giving them quarter, and engaging that they should not be killed, were one shot, and the other knocked down with a Tomahawk (a little hatchet) and both scalped in my absence, by the rascally sergeant neglecting to acquaint Montgomery that I wanted them saved, as he, Montgomery, pretended when I questioned him about it; but even, that was no excuse for such an unparalleled piece of barbarity. However, as the affair could not be remedied, I was obliged to let it drop. After this skirmish we set about burning the houses with great success, setting all in flames till we came to the church of St. Anne's, where we put up for this night, and were joined by Captain Ross, with about one hundred and twenty men of his company.

Friday, 24th August. Began to march and burn as yesterday, till we came to Ange Gardien where our detachment and Captain Ross, who had been posted for some days at Chateau [sic] Richer, joined Colonel Murray with the three companies of Grenadiers of the 22nd, 40th and 45th Regiments, where we are posted in four houses which we have fortified so as to be able, we hope, to stand any attack which we can expect with small arms....

Wednesday, 29th August.—Captain Ross, with the Subalterns and about one hundred men went out reconnoitring, returned about eleven o'clock with a Canadian, whom they took prisoner. He says he came from Quebec three days ago, but knows nothing.

Thursday, 30th August.—Remain at Chateau Richer fortifying ourselves in the house and Church in the best manner we can.

Friday, 31st August.—Received orders to burn the houses at Chateau Richer, but not the Church, and return to Montmorency tomorrow morning.

Saturday, 1st September.—Our Detachment marched from Chateau Richer to Montmorency, where we, [sic] were cantoned in some houses and barns, having been joined on our march by Colonel Murray, with the three Companies of grenadiers from Louisburg at Ange Gardien. We burnt all the houses &c. between that and the Camp....

Wednesday, 5th September.—I hear the 28th, 47th, 35th. and 58th. Regiments, with the whole of the Light Infantry; have marched on the south shore, above the town, and embarked on board the ships above the town; the 15th. 43rd. and a detachment of six hundred of our regiment are ordered to follow them to-morrow.

Thursday, 6th September.—The 15th, 43rd, and a Detachment of six hundred of our Regiment marched about five or six miles above Point Levy, when we crossed the river ... and embarked on board the ships above the town. We are much crowded: the ship I am in, [sic] has about six hundred on board, being only about two hundred and fifty tons.

Friday, 7th September.—The army above the town being about four thousand strong, continue on board the ships, most of the men above deck, tho' it is very rainy weather.

Saturday, 8th September.—Remain as formerly on ship board; very bad weather.

Sunday, 9th September.—About fifteen hundred men were ordered on shore, on the south side of the river. We hear we are to land soon on the north side. We see a number of the French intrenched [sic] there, on a beach, where they have got some floating batteries....

Wednesday, 12th September.—We were busied in cleaning our arms and distributing ammunition to our men. This day our brave General [Wolfe] gave his last written orders in the following words:

"ON BOARD THE SUTHERLAND,
"12th September, 1759.

"The Enemy's force is now divided; great scarcity of provisions in their Camp, and universal discontent among the Canadians. The second Officer in command (Levi) is gone to Montreal or St. John's, which gives reason to think that General Amherst is advancing into the Colony. A vigorous blow struck by the Army at this juncture may determine the fall of Canada. Our troops below are in readiness to join us. All the Light Artillery and tools are, [sic] embarked at the Point of Levy, and the Troops will land where the French seem least to expect them.

"The first body that gets on shore is to march directly to the Enemy, and drive them from any little post they may occupy. The Officers must be careful that the succeeding bodies do not, by any mistake, fire upon those that go on before them.

"The Battalions must form upon the upper ground with expedition, and be ready to charge whatever presents itself.

"When the Artillery and Troops are landed, a Corps will be left to secure the landing place, while the rest march on and endeavour to bring the French and Canadians to a battle.

"The Officers and men will remember, what their Country expects from them, and what a determined body of soldiers inured to war are capable of doing against five weak French Battalions, mingled with a disorderly Peasantry.

"The Soldiers must be attentive and obedient to their officers, and resolute in the execution of their duty.

[Fraser resumes his entry.] About 9 o'clock, the night of the 12th. we went into the Boats as ordered. Rendezvoused abreast of the Sutherland; fell down with the tide about 12 o'clock, and a little before four in the morning, were fired on by a French four gun Battery, about two miles above the Town. Pushed towards the shore at day break on.

Thursday, 13th September 1759. The Light Infantry under the command of Colonel Howe, immediately landed and mounted the hill. We were fired on in the Boats by the Enemy who killed and wounded a few. In a short time, the whole Army was landed at a place called "Le Foulon," (now Wolfe's Cove) about a mile and a half above the Town of Quebec, and immediately followed the Light Infantry up the hill. There was [sic] a few tents and a Picket of the French on the top of the hill whom the Light Infantry engaged, and took some of their Officers and men prisoners. The main body of our Army soon got to the upper ground after climbing a hill or rather a precipice, of about three hundred yards, very steep and covered with wood and brush. We had several skirmishes with the Canadians and Savages, till about ten o'clock, when the army was formed in line of battle, having the great River, St. Lawrence on the right with the precipice which we mounted in the morning; on the left, a few houses, and at some distance the low ground and wood above the General Hospital with the River St. Charles; in front, the Town of Quebec, about a mile distant; in the rear, a wood occupied by the Light Infantry, (who had by this time taken possession of the French four gun Battery) and the third Battalion of the Royal Americans. In the space between which last and the main body, the 48th. Regiment was drawn up as a body of reserve. The Army was ordered to march on slowly in line of battle, and halt several times, till about half an hour after ten, when the French began to appear in great numbers on the rising ground between us and the Town, and having advanced several parties to skirmish with us; we did the like. They then got two Iron field pieces to play against our line. Before eleven o'clock, we got one brass field piece up the Hill, which being placed in the proper interval began to play very smartly on the Enemy while forming on the little eminence. Their advanced parties continued to annoy us and wounded a great many men. About this time, we observed the Enemy formed, having a bush of short brush wood on their right, which straitened [sic] them in room, and obliged them to form in columns. About eleven o'clock, the French Army advanced in columns till they had got past the bush of wood into the plain, when they endeavoured to form in line of Battle, but being much galled by our Artillery, which consisted of only one field piece, very well served, we observed them in some confusion. However they advanced at a brisk pace till within about thirty or forty years of our front, when they gave us their first fire, which did little execution. We returned it, and continued firing very hot for about six, or (as some say) eight minutes, when the fire slackening, and the smoke of the powder vanishing, we observed the main body of the Enemy retreating in great confusion towards the Town, and the rest towards the River St. Charles. Our Regiment were then ordered by Brigadier General Murray to draw their swords and pursue them; which I dare say increased their panic but saved many of their lives, whereas if the artillery had been allowed to play, and the army advanced regularly there would have been many more of the Enemy killed and wounded, as we never came up with the main body. In advancing, we passed over a great many dead and wounded, (french [sic] regulars mostly) lying in the front of our Regiment, who,—I mean the Highlanders,—to do them justice, behaved extremely well all day, as did the whole of the army. After pursuing the French to the very gates[1] of the Town, our Regiment was ordered to form fronting the Town, on the ground whereon the French formed first. At this time, the rest of the Army came up in good order. General Murray having then put himself at the head of our Regiment, ordered them to face to the left and march thro' the bush of wood, towards the General Hospital, when they got a great gun or two to play upon us from the Town, which however did no damage, but we had a few men killed and Officers wounded by some skulking fellows, with small arms, from the bushes and behind the houses in the suburbs of St. Louis and St. John's. After marching a short way through the brush, Brigadier Murray thought proper to order us to return again to the high road leading from Porte St. Louis, to the heights of Abraham, where the battle was fought, and after marching till we got clear of the bushes, we were ordered to turn to the right, and go along the edge of them towards the bank, at the descent between us and the General Hospital, under which we understood there was a body of the Enemy who, no sooner saw us, than they began firing on us from the bushes and from the bank; we soon dispossessed them from the bushes, and from thence kept firing for about a quarter of an hour on those under cover of the bank; but as they exceeded us greatly in numbers, they killed and wounded a great many of our men, and killed two Officers, which obliged us to retire a little, and form again, when the 58th. Regiment with the 2nd. Battalion of Royal Amer-

---

1 Few of them entered the town the great bulk making towards the bridge of boats, near the General Hospital and regained the camp at Beauport. [Original note.]

icans having come up to our assistance, all three making about five hundred men, advanced against the Enemy and drove them first down to the great meadow between the Hospital and town and afterwards over the River St. Charles. It was at this time and while in the bushes that our Regiment suffered most: Lieutenant Roderick, Mr. Neill of Bana, and Alexander McDonell, and John McDonell, and John McPherson, volunteer, with many of our men, were killed before we were reinforced; and Captain Thomas Ross having gone down with about one hundred men of the 3rd. Regiment to the meadow, after the Enemy, when they were out of reach, ordered me up to desire those on the height would wait till he would come up and join them, which I did, but before Mr. Ross could get up, he unfortunately was mortally wounded in the body, by a cannon ball from the hulks, in the mouth of the River St. Charles, of which he died in great torment, but with great resolution, in about two hours thereafter.

In the afternoon, Mons. Bougainville with the French Grenadiers and some Canadians, to the number of two thousand who had been detached to oppose our landing at Cape Rouge, appeared between our rear and the village St. Foy, formed in a line as if he intended to attack us; but the 48th Regiment with the Light Infantry and 3rd Battalion Royal Americans being ordered against him, with some field pieces, they fired a few cannon shot at him when he thought proper to retire.

Thus ended the battle of Quebec, the first regular engagement that we was [sic] fought in North America, which has made the king of Great Britain master of the capital of Canada, and it is hoped ere long will be the means of subjecting the whole country to the British Dominion; and if so, this has been a greater acquisition to the British Empire than all that England has acquired by Conquest since it was a nation, if I may except the conquest of Ireland, in the reign of Henry the 2nd....

We had only about five hundred men of our Army killed and wounded, but we suffered an irreparable loss in the death of our commander the brave Major General James Wolfe, who was killed in the beginning of the general action; we had the good fortune not to hear of it till all was over.

The French were supposed to have about one thousand men killed and wounded, of whom five hundred killed during the whole day, and amongst these Monsieur le Lieutenant Général Montcalm, the commander in chief of the French Army in Canada, one Brigadier General, one Colonel and several other Officers.

2. From William Smith, "Preface," *History of Canada; From Its Discovery to the Peace of 1763* ([1815] 1826)

[The appearance of Smith's *History* in 1826 coincided with the increasing political influence of the nationalist *Parti patriote* led by the prominent French-Canadian politician and orator, Louis-Joseph Papineau. Smith's assertion, in the extract below, that benevolent British rule had brought about wealth and prosperity in Canada was at once widely held and hotly debated. The French-Canadian historian, François-Xavier Garneau, takes it up in his own *History of Canada* (see Appendix D4).]

CANADA of late years, has been an object of such enquiry, that a knowledge of the early settlement of the Colony is eagerly desired by all. While it was under the dominion of France, several histories were published, but none have given a narrative of events subsequent to the period when Charlevoix finished his History.[1] The present work will embrace the occurrences down to the period when he ended, and also, those events that took place between that period and the Peace of one thousand seven hundred and sixty-three....[2]

WHEN I began this Narrative ... I intended it only for my private use: I well knew the detail of the occurrences of an inconsiderable Colony, so long struggling in its birth, could afford but little amusement to Gentlemen of Taste, and under this impression, I had relinquished all idea of publishing it. The solicitations of my Friends at length prevailed, and I consented to put this Narrative to the Press, in the hope, that it might be serviceable to the Public, by giving, as it does, a true and faithful account of a Colony daily augmenting in Wealth, Prosperity and Happiness: now fortunately placed under the dominion of Great Britain, and with a Constitution framed after her own—a Constitution which has long been the envy and admiration of the World;[3] and by its happy combinations in establishing and assigning to its various branches, rights, peculiar to each, but necessary to the preservation of all, has been found in the harmony and co-operation of all its powers, to give the best practical effect to its principles,

---

1 Pierre-François-Xavier de Charlevoix (1682-1761), a French Jesuit historian, whose authorship of the first detailed history of New France, the three-volume *Histoire et description générale de la Nouvelle France* (1744), earned him the designation of New France's first historian.
2 The Treaty of Paris (1763), which put an end to the Seven Years' War and ceded New France to Britain.
3 The Constitutional Act (1791) gave Canada its first parliamentary constitution.

and to lead directly to that system of efficient Government, best adapted to the spirit and happiness of a Free People....

3. From William Smith, ["The Battle of Fort Ticonderoga,"] *History of Canada; From Its Discovery to the Peace of 1763* ([1815] 1826)

[The extract below recounts the Battle of Fort Ticonderoga (Smith 263-64), known by the French as Fort Carillon, a pivotal battle in the Seven Years' War to which Leprohon devotes Chapter XIII of *The Manor House*.]

Early in the summer of this year, the Marquis de Vaudreuil received certain intelligence, that a large body of English troops, under the command of General Abercrombie, was collected on Ticonderoga.[1] To secure that important Fortress, was an object too important to be neglected, and having collected a considerable body of troops, they were sent on to Ticonderoga, where they arrived on the twentieth of June. The Marquis de Montcalm, on the first of July, sent forward Mr. de Bourlamaque, with the regiments de la Reine, Guienne and Bearn, while he advanced with those of La Sarre, Royal Roussillon, Languedoc and the second battalion of Berry, as far as the Falls, where he encamped.[2] The second battalion of Berry and several companies of Canadians, were left as a garrison for that Fort. The next day, Mr. de Bourlamaque, reconnoitered the mountains to the left of the camp, and formed two companies of volunteers, under the command of Captains de Bernard and Duprât, of the regiments of Bearn and de La Sarre, who were sent forward to gain intelligence of the approach of the English army, then at the further end of Lake George. On the fifth of July, a signal was made by one of these parties, that the English army was embarked, and on its way down the Lake. The English army, [*sic*] consisted of seven thousand regulars and ten thousand provincials. They embarked on Lake George, on the fourth of July, and with the necessary Artillery disembarked next day and formed in three

---

1 Pierre de Rigaud de Vaudreuil de Cavagnial, Marquis de Vaudreuil (1698-1778), the last Governor General of New France (1755-60); General James Abercrombie (1706-81), commander of the British forces during the failed attack on the French at Fort Ticonderoga.
2 François-Charles de Bourlamaque (1716-64), officer of the French army and commander during the successful defence of Fort Ticonderoga (Fort Carillon) against the British in 1758; La Reine, Guienne, Bearn, La Sarre, Royal Roussillon, Languedoc, and Berry were all regiments of the French Colonial Forces, predominantly infantry units.

columns. As soon as this intelligence was made known, Mr. de Bourlamaque detached Captain de Trépezé, with three hundred men, to watch their motions, and to prevent their landing.

On the sixth, the advanced guard of the English was perceived, and on their approach to the carrying place, Boulamaque [sic] retreated to Montcalm, who had taken possession of the heights, and where the chief engineer de Pont Le Roy [sic], had thrown up entrenchments and had formed a strong abbatis [sic] with felled timber. On the retreat of Bourlamaque, who had been hard pressed by the English, a French detachment lost their way, which the English under Lord Howe encountered, when the French were routed with considerable loss, several men were killed and one hundred and forty-eight taken prisoners, including five officers. This petty advantage was dearly bought with the loss of Lord Howe, who fell in the beginning of the action, unspeakably regretted as a young nobleman of the most promising talents.[1]

4. From François-Xavier Garneau, "Preliminary Discourse," *History of Canada, From the Time of Its Discovery Till the Union Year (1840-1)*, Volume 1 (1845; tr. 1860)

[In plot, theme, and characterization, *The Manor House* variously upholds or deploys important arguments about French-Canadian culture, history, and nationality that Garneau influentially mounts in his groundbreaking *History of Canada*. The following extract contains many of Garneau's key arguments: that the roots of present-day misunderstandings between the French- and the English-Canadians lie in colonial-period conflicts; that the historical, institutional, and cultural foundations of modern French-Canadian nationhood need to be better understood by English-Canadians; that the French-Canadians have demonstrated ongoing resilience in the face of successive political and cultural obstacles to their survival; and that the French-Canadians' historical attachment to France is not incompatible with their proven loyalty to the British crown. In its defence of the French-Canadian point-of-view, the extract from Garneau presents a remarkable contrast to the extract from Smith's *History* in Appendix D2.]

When we contemplate the history of Canada as a whole, from the time of Champlain[2] till our own day, we first remark its two great divi-

---

1 The Province of Massachusetts, erected a monument to his memory, in Westminster Abbey [Smith's note. Smith refers to the death of Brigadier General Lord Howe (1725-58) at Ticonderoga.]
2 Samuel de Champlain (1570-1635), explorer, cartographer, and governor of New France.

sions,—the period of French supremacy, and that of British domination. The annals of the former are replete with the incidents of wars against the savages and the people of the conterminous British colonies, since become the United States; the other portion is signalised by parliamentary antagonism of the colonists to all infractions of their nationality and designs against their religion. The difference of the arms defensively used during these two periods, shows the Canadian nation under two very distinct aspects; but it is the second epoch which, naturally enough, may most interest the existing generation. There is something at once noble and touching in the spectacle of a people defending the nationality of their ancestors; that sacred heritage which no race, how degraded soever [sic], has ever yet repudiated. Never did cause of a loftier character or more holy nature inspire a heart rightly placed, or better merit the sympathies of all generous minds....

From the circumstance that Canada has had to undergo many evil vicissitudes, and not through her own fault but arising out of her colonial dependence, what progress she did make was effected amidst obstacles and social shocks; obstructions which have been aggravated, in the present day, by the antagonism of two races confronted with each other; as also by the hates, the prejudices, the ignorance, and the errors of governments,—sometimes, too, through the faults of the governed. The authors of the Union of the two Canadian provinces, projected in 1822 and realised in 1840,[1] have adduced in favour of that measure divers specious reasons to cover, as with a veil, its manifest injustice. Great Britain, prone to regard the French Canadians only as turbulent colonials, as ill-disposed aliens, feigns to mistake for indubitable insurrectionary symptoms ... their inquietude and their firm attachment to menaced institutions and habitudes.

Britain's general conduct, however, proves too well that while she believes not what is advanced against them, no regard for treaties nor official acts, drawn up for the protection of her Canadian subjects, has prevented her agents from violating concessions, which ought to have been all the more carefully respected for being regarded as forming an

---

1 Garneau has in mind, first, the proposed Union of Lower and Upper Canada in 1822 (also known as the Union Bill of 1822), authored by Lord Bathurst, Secretary of the Colonial Office, and Robert John Wilmot-Horton, his undersecretary; and second, the legislative Union of Lower and Upper Canada in 1840, the end-result of a recommendation contained in the *Report on the Affairs of British North America* (1839), authored by Lord Durham. For an extract from the Durham Report, see Appendix E3, p. 257.

aegis to protect the weak against the oppression of the strong. But whatever may betide, the perdition of a people is not so easily effected as its enemies may imagine.

While we are far from believing that our nationality is secured against all further risks, like many more we have had our illusions on this subject. Still, the existence of the Canadians as a distinct people, is not more doubtful than it was a century ago. At that time, we were a population of 60,000; we now exceed a million souls....

All things concur to prove, that the French settled in America retain ... characteristics of their ancestors, near and remote; that they possess a strong yet undefinable buoyancy of mind, peculiar to themselves, which, invulnerable as mind itself, eludes political guile, as spirit is unassailable by the sword. The type of the race remains, even when all seems to forebode its extinction. Is the nucleus of a French community found amid alien races? it [sic] grows apace, but always in isolation from others with whom it is possible to live, but never to incorporate. Germans, Dutch, Swedes, who came in groups into the United States, and lived apart for a while, have insensibly been fused in the general mass of population, and left no trace of their origin.[1] On the contrary, two sections of the Gallic race, one at each extremity of this continent,[2] not only maintain their footing in two countries so wide apart, of contrasted climate and under diverse political constitutions; but, as if by instinct, concur in repelling all infractions of their nationality.... In fine, that cohesive force, peculiar to their moral temperament, develops itself in proportion to the efforts made to overcome it.

The eminent statesmen who guided the destiny of Great Britain after the acquisition of Canada in 1763, well comprehended that the position of its people, relatively to the neighbouring Colonists of English origin, would be confirmatory of their fidelity to the British crown; and their expectations, wisely conceived, were not disappointed.

Nevertheless, left to ponder on their position, after the prolonged and sanguinary struggles they had erewhile to sustain, and in which they had shown so much devotedness to France, the Canadians regarded the future with inquietude. Abandoned by the most opulent and intelligent of their compatriots, who, in quitting the country, carried with them that experience which would have been so useful

---

[1] The ready amalgamation of these races with the Anglo-Saxons of America, was chiefly due to the common Protestantism of all four.—B. [Andrew Bell's note. Garneau supplies no note in the French-language original.]

[2] Quebec and Louisiana.

had they remained;[1] so few in number, and put helplessly, for a season, at the discretion of the populous British Provinces near by, whose overbearingness they had resisted for a century and a half with so much spirit, they yet did not mistrust their fortune. They advertised the new Government of their wants, and reclaimed the rights guaranteed to them by treaties; they represented, with admirable tact, that the discrepancies existing between them and their neighbours over the lines, the diversity of races and interests, would attach them rather to the British monarchy, than induce them to make common cause with democratic denizens of the English plantations. They had divined, in fact, the [American] Revolution soon to ensue....

The Government of Great Britain, influenced by such considerations as the foregoing, left undisturbed the Canadian language, laws, and religion, at a crisis when it would have been comparatively easy to compass the abolition of all three; for at that time the British possessed a moiety of North America. They had soon cause for rejoicing at their wise forbearance. Two years had scarcely elapsed after the promulgation of the law of 1774 when all the Anglo-American colonies were up in arms against the mother country;[2] and during the content ensuing, the people of the former wasted a considerable part of their resources in vain attempts to wrench from her that Canada which they had helped to conquer for her special glorification![3]

The Canadians, called upon to defend their institutions and laws, guaranteed to them by that same law of 1774, which the Congress of the insurrectionary provinces had so injudiciously denounced, just before, as "unjust, unconstitutional, very dangerous, and subversive of American rights,"—the Canadians, we say, promptly ranged themselves under the banner of their new Protectress, who now profited, more than she had ventured to hope for, by the effects of the wise because liberal policy of her general Government. That policy was sanctioned and extended on two memorable occasions afterwards: namely, in 1791, when the British Parliament accorded a representa-

---

1 After the Fall of New France, many members of French Canada's nobility left the colony for France. This exodus was the result of Article IV of the Treaty of Paris (1763), in which Britain granted open emigration, for a period of 18 months, to French-speaking inhabitants who refused to swear allegiance to the British crown. *The Manor House of De Villerai* reflects these real-historical events. For Article IV, see Appendix E2, p. 257.
2 The Quebec Act (1774) and the American Revolutionary War (1775-83).
3 The Invasion of Canada (1775) during the American Revolutionary War by the Continental Army, whose objective was to gain control of Quebec while convincing the French-Canadians to join the Thirteen Colonies.

tive Constitution to the Provinces; and again, in 1828, when the Imperial Parliament enacted, that Canadians of French origin should never be disturbed in the enjoyment of their laws, their religion, or those privileges which had been already assured to them.[1]

If this polity, which twice became the means of saving Canada to Great Britain, was virtually repudiated by the Union Act, it is not improbable that it will be found expedient to revert to it; for the time that has elapsed since 1840, has manifested that Canada has become anything rather than *anglified*; and nothing indicates that the future will differ from the present or past in this respect. A return to that policy may become inevitable, if only through the continued expansion of the colonies still remaining to Britain on this continent; and by the prospects of a new revolution, similar to that which paved the way to independence for the United States. Were it otherwise, we should opine that the people of Great Britain, coinciding in sentiment with some of their statesmen, ... ought to be left to herself; the British nation not caring to expend its resources in keeping much longer an uneasy foothold on the nearer parts of the North American continent.

5. From François-Xavier Garneau, ["The Fall of Quebec,"] *History of Canada*, Volume 2 (1846; tr. 1860)

[The extract below recounts the fall of Quebec (Garneau 24-25) to which Leprohon refers in *The Manor House* and which is described in detail by Colonel Malcolm Fraser, above. As the final paragraphs of the extract make clear, Garneau's translator permitted himself to comment on, even dispute, Garneau's version of events.]

After destroying the city, General Wolfe fell upon the country parishes. He burnt all the dwellings, and cut all the fruit-trees, from Montmorenci Falls to Cape Torment (30 miles below Quebec), on the left bank of the St. Lawrence. He did the same at Malbaie (90 miles), and the bay of St. Paul (60); also throughout the Isle d'Orléans, which is 20 miles long. The parishes on the right bank of the flood, from Berthier (24 miles) to the Rivière du Loup (80 miles), a range of twenty-three leagues, were ravaged and burnt in their turn; as well as those of Pointe-Lévy, St. Nicholas, Sainte-Croix (33), &c. ... As the season advanced, this war of brigands extended itself; for Wolfe indulged in it to avenge himself for the checks he received, as well as to terrify the inhabitants. A detachment of 300 men, under Captain Montgomery, having been sent to St. Joachim, where some of the

---

1 The Constitutional Act (1791) and the Report of the Special Committee of the House of Commons on the Civil Government of Canada (1828).

people stood on their defence, committed there the greatest cruelties. The prisoners taken were coolly and most barbarously slaughtered.[1] M. de Portneuf, curate of the place, who stuck by his parishioners, in view of ministering to their spiritual needs, was attacked and hewn to pieces with sabres. From the Beauport camp were seen, simultaneously, the flames rising from Beaupré, and from the Isle d'Orléans, also from sundry parts on the right bank of the flood.

These devastations, in which more than 1,400 houses were consumed in the rural districts,[2] did not tend to bring the war to a nearer conclusion; for still the French stirred not one foot.

---

[1] "There were several of the army killed and wounded, and a few prisoners taken, all of whom the barbarous Captain Montgomery, who commanded us, ordered to be butchered in a most inhuman and cruel manner." Manuscript Journal relating to the Operations before Quebec in 1759, kept by Colonel Malcolm Frazer [sic], Lieutenant of the 78th or Frazer's Highlanders. (The captain here slandered was the gallant and humane General Richard Montgomery, who afterwards fell in an heroic attempt, as an American leader, to take Quebec by a midnight assault.—B.) [Andrew Bell's note. The English-language quotation from Colonel Fraser appears in the original English in Garneau (318).]

[2] "We burned and destroyed upwards of 1,400 fine farm-houses, for we, during the siege, were masters of a great part of their country; so that 'tis thought it will take them many a century to recover damage." Journal of the Expedition up the river St. Lawrence, &c., published in the [sic] New York Mercury of 31st December, 1759. Nevertheless a contemporary writer, speaking of the conduct of M. de Contades and Marshal Richelieu in Germany, as contrasted with Wolfe's in Canada, adds; "But, said the late General Wolfe, Britons breathe higher sentiments of humanity, and listen to the merciful dictates of the christian religion; which was verified in the brave soldiers whom he led on to conquest, by their shewing more of the true christian spirit than the subjects of His Most Christian Majesty can pretend to."—[Mark the *naïveté* of all this, mockingly adds M. Garneau.—B.] [Bell's original note. The two English-language quotations also appear in English in Garneau's text. Garneau's original comment on "naïveté," to which Bell refers in his note, reads: "Il est impossible de pousser la naïveté plus loin" (Garneau 318).]

Appendix E: Historical Documents

1. From General James Wolfe, "Major-General Wolfe to the Earl of Holdernesse.[1] On Board the Sutherland, at Anchor off Cape Rouge, September 9, 1759" ([1759] 1838)

[Of particular interest is the original, lengthy, editorial note that appears attached to the published version of this letter (see note 2 below, and Select Bibliography, p. 286), containing pertinent historical information about the reception in England of Wolfe's efforts on the Plains of Abraham, while also corroborating Leprohon's observation about the sympathy with which Wolfe's letters were received by the English public (see *Manor House*, 200). The bulk of the note's content derives from Horace Walpole (1717-97), the third and final volume of the *Memoirs of the Reign of King George the Second* (esp. 217-22). Please note that the author of the footnote provides a page reference to a different edition of Walpole than the one contained in the Select Bibliography here (p. 286).]

Major-General Wolfe to the Earl of Holdernesse.
On board the Sutherland, at anchor off Cape Rouge, September 9, 1759.

My Lord,
If the Marquis de Montcalm had shut himself up in the town of Quebec, it would have been long since in our possession, because the defences are inconsiderable and our artillery very formidable;[2] but he

---

1 Robert D'Arcy, fourth Earl of Holdernesse (1718-78), Secretary of State for the Northern Department at the time this letter was written and thus Secretary during the administration of William Pitt, first earl of Chatham (1708-78), Britain's political leader during the Seven Years' War.

2 This painfully interesting letter was written on the 9th of September; only *four* days before the death of Wolfe. It reached England on the 14th of October; and three days after, in the midst of gloom and despair, an express arrived that Quebec was taken. The following is Horace Walpole's animated description of this memorable event:—"The incidents of dramatic fiction could not be conducted with more address to lead an audience from despondency to sudden exultation, than accident prepared to excite the passions of a whole people. They despaired—they triumphed—and they wept,—for Wolfe had fallen in the hour of victory! Joy, grief, curiosity, astonishment, were painted on every countenance: the more they inquired, the higher their admiration rose. Not an incident but was heroic and affecting! Wolfe, between (*continued*)

has a numerous body of armed men (I cannot call it an army)[1] and the strongest country, perhaps, in the world to rest the defence of the town and colony upon. The ten battalions, and the grenadiers of Louisbourg, are a chosen body of troops, and able to fight the united force of Canada upon even terms. Our field artillery, brought into use, would terrify the militia and the savages; and our battalions are in every respect superior to those commanded by the Marquis, who acts

> persuasion of the impracticability, unwillingness to leave any attempt untried that could be proposed, and worn out with anxiety of mind and body, had determined to make one last effort above the town. He embarked his forces at one in the morning of the 13th, and passed the French sentinels in silence that were posted along the shore. The current carried them beyond the destined spot. They found themselves at the foot of a precipice, esteemed so impracticable, that only a slight guard of a hundred and fifty men defended it. Had there been a path, the night was too dark to discover it. The troops, whom nothing could discourage, pulled themselves and one another up by stumps and boughs of trees. The guard, hearing a rustling, fired down the precipice at random, as our men did up into the air; but, terrified by the strangeness of the attempt, the French picquet fled,—all but the captain, who, though wounded, would not accept quarter, but fired at one of our officers at the head of five hundred men. Daybreak discovered our forces in possession of the eminence. Montcalm could not credit it, when reported to him—but it was too late to doubt, when nothing but a battle could save the town. Even then, he held our attempt so desperate, that, being shown the position of the English, he said, 'Oui, je les vois où ils ne doivent pas être' [Yes, I see them where they shouldn't be]. Forced to quit his entrenchments, he said, 'S'il faut donc combattre, je vais les écraser!' [Then if we must fight, I will crush them!] He prepared for engagement, after lining the bushes with detachments of Indians. Our men, according to orders, received their fire with a patience and tranquillity equal to the resolution they had exerted in clambering the precipice; but when they gave it, it took place with such terrible slaughter of the enemy, that half an hour decided the day. The French fled precipitately; and Montcalm, endeavouring to rally them, was killed on the spot.
>
> "The fall of Wolfe was noble indeed. He received a wound in the head, but covered it from his soldiers with his handkerchief. A second ball struck him in the belly: that too he dissembled. A third hitting him in the breast, he sunk under the anguish, and was carried behind the ranks. Yet, fast as life ebbed out, his whole anxiety centred on the fortune of the day. He begged to be borne nearer to the action; but his sight being dimned [sic] by the approach of death, he entreated to be told what they who supported him saw: he was answered, that the enemy gave ground. He eagerly repeated the question; heard the enemy was totally routed; cried, 'I am satisfied!'—and expired!— *Memoirs*, vol. ii. p. 385. [Original note]

1 Along with the French regulars, Montcalm's army was comprised of colonial militia, including French-Canadians and Natives.

a circumspect, prudent part, and entirely defensive; except, in one extraordinary instance, he sent sixteen hundred men over the river to attack our batteries upon the Point of Levy, defended by four battalions. Bad intelligence, no doubt, of our strength, induced him to this measure: however, the detachment judged better than their general, and retired. They dispute the water with the boats of the fleet, by the means of floating batteries, suited to the nature of the river, and innumerable battoes.[1] They have a great artillery upon the ramparts towards the sea, and so placed that shipping cannot affect it.

I meant to attack the left of their entrenchments, favoured by our artillery, the 31st July. A multitude of traverses prevented, in some measure, its effect, which was nevertheless very considerable: accidents hindered the attack, and the enemy's care to strengthen that post has made it since too hazardous. The town is totally demolished, and the country in a great measure ruined; particularly the lower [sic] Canada. Our fleet blocks up the river, both above and below the town, but can give no manner of assistance in an attack upon the Canadian army. We have continual skirmishes; old people, seventy years of age, and boys of fifteen, fire at our detachments, and kill or wound our men from the edges of the woods. Every man able to bear arms, both above and below Quebec, is in the camp of Beauport. The old men, women, and children are retired into the woods. The Canadians are extremely dissatisfied; but, curbed by the force of this government, and terrified by the savages that are posted round about them they are obliged to keep together, to work and to man the entrenchments. Upwards of twenty sail of ships got in before our squadron, and brought succours of all sorts; which were exceedingly wanted in the colony. The sailors of these ships help to work the guns, and others conduct the floating batteries; their ships are lightened and carried up the river out of our reach, at least out of the reach of the men of war. These ships serve a double purpose: they are magazines for their provisions, and at the same time cut off all communication between General Amherst's army and the corps under my command; so that we are not able to make any detachment to attack Montreal, or favour the junction, or, by attacking the fort of Chambly, or Bourlemaqui's [sic] corps behind,[2] open the general's way into Canada; all which might have been easily done with ten floating batteries carrying each a gun, and twenty flat-bottomed boats, if there had been no ships in the river. Our poor soldiery have worked without ceasing and without murmuring; and as

---

1 Flat-bottomed rowboats (adapted from the French, *bateaux*, "boats").
2 Fort Chambly, built by the French in 1711, located on the Richelieu River; François-Charles de Bourlamaque (1716-64), promoted from Colonel to Brigadier-General in 1759.

often as the enemy have attempted upon us, they have been repulsed by the valour of the men. A woody country so well known to the enemy, and an enemy so vigilant and hardy as the Indians and Canadians are, make entrenchments everywhere necessary; and by this precaution we have saved a number of lives, for scarce a night passes that they are not close in upon our posts, watching an opportunity to surprise and murder. There is very little quarter given on either side.

We have seven hours, and sometimes (above the town, after rain) near eight hours of the most violent ebb tide that can be imagined, which loses us an infinite deal of time, in every operation on the water; and the stream is so strong, particularly here, that the ships often drag their anchors by the mere force of the current. The bottom is a bed of rock; so that a ship, unless it hooks a ragged rock, holds by the weight only of the anchor. Doubtless, if the equinoctial gale has any force, a number of ships must necessarily run ashore and be lost.

The day after the troops landed upon the Isle of Orleans,[1] a violent storm had nigh ruined the expedition altogether. Numbers of boats were lost; all the whale boats and most of the cutters were stove; some flat-bottomed boats destroyed, and others damaged. We never had half as many of the latter as are necessary for this extraordinary and very important service. The enemy is able to fight us upon the water, whenever we are out of the reach of the cannon of the fleet.

The extreme heat of the weather in August, and a good deal of fatigue, threw me into a fever; but that the business might go on, I begged the generals to consider amongst themselves what was fittest to be done. Their sentiments were unanimous, that (as the easterly winds begin to blow, and ships can pass the town in the night with provisions, artillery, &c.) we should endeavour, by conveying a considerable corps into the upper river, to draw them from their inaccessible situation, and bring them to an action. I agreed to the proposal; and we are now here, with about three thousand six hundred men, waiting an opportunity to attack them, when and wherever they can best be got at. The weather has been extremely unfavourable for a day or two, so that we have been inactive. I am so far recovered as to do business; but my constitution is entirely ruined, without the consolation of having done any considerable service to the state; or without any prospect of it. I have the honour to be, with great respect, my Lord,

Your Lordship's most obedient
and most humble servant,
Jam. Wolfe.

---

[1] The Island of Orleans, located in the St. Lawrence River, to the east of Quebec City.

2. Article IV, Treaty of Paris (1763)

[Signed on 10 February 1763 by France, Britain, and Spain, the Treaty of Paris put an end to the Seven Years' War (1756-63), and New France officially became a British possession, although it remained under military occupation and martial law until 1764. The terms outlined in the Treaty, with particular respect to the permission granted the "French inhabitants" to emigrate within an eighteen-month period, make their way into the conclusion of *The Manor House of De Villerai*.]

[Article] IV. His most Christian Majesty [the King of France] ... cedes and guaranties [*sic*] to his said Britannick Majesty, in full right, Canada, with all its dependencies, as well as the island of Cape Breton, and all the other islands and coasts in the gulph [*sic*] and river of St. Lawrence[.] ... His Britannick Majesty, on his side, agrees to grant the liberty of the Catholick [*sic*] religion to the inhabitants of Canada: he will, in consequence, give the most precise and most effectual orders, that his new Roman Catholic subjects may profess the worship of their religion according to the rites of the Romish church, as far as the laws of Great Britain permit. His Britannick Majesty farther agrees, that the French inhabitants, or others who had been subjects of the Most Christian King in Canada, may retire with all safety and freedom wherever they shall think proper, and may sell their estates, provided it be to the subjects of his Britannick Majesty, and bring away their effects as well as their persons, without being restrained in their emigration, under any pretence whatsoever, except that of debts or of criminal prosecutions: The term limited for this emigration shall be fixed to the space of eighteen months, to be computed from the day of the exchange of the ratification of the present treaty.

3. From John George Lambton, First Earl of Durham, *Report on the Affairs of British North America, from the Earl of Durham, Her Majesty's High Commissioner* (1839)

[The *Report on the Affairs of British North America* (1839) is a pivotal document in Canadian history. Not only did it result in the Union of Lower and Upper Canada (1840-41), a precursor to Canadian Confederation (1867), but its notoriously negative perspective of the French-Canadians has had the paradoxical effect of serving as a catalyst for the development of Quebecois culture and identity, its ramifications being felt as late as the Quiet Revolution (1960-66), if not later. The Whig politician, John George Lambton, First Earl of

Durham (1792-1840), was appointed Governor General and sent to the two Canadian provinces in 1838 to investigate the causes of recent uprisings. Durham expected to find that matters of government or economics lay at the roots of the uprisings. Instead, he became convinced that Canada's progress was inhibited by profound intercultural differences between the French and the English Canadians.[1]]

In a despatch which I addressed to your Majesty's Principal Secretary of State for the Colonies, on the 9th of August last, I detailed with great minuteness the impressions which had been produced on my mind by the state of things which existed in Lower Canada. I acknowledge that the experience derived from my residence in the Province had completely changed my view of the relative influence of the causes which had been assigned for the existing disorders.... From the peculiar circumstances in which I was placed, I was enabled to make such effectual observations as convinced me that there had existed in the Constitution of the Province, in the balance of political powers, in the spirit and practice of administration in every department of the Government, defects that were quite sufficient to account for a great degree of mismanagement and dissatisfaction. The same observation had also impressed on me the conviction that, for the peculiar and disastrous dissensions of this Province, there existed a far deeper and far more efficient cause—a cause which penetrated beneath its political institutions into its social state—a cause which no reform of constitution or laws that should leave the elements of society unaltered could remove, but which must be removed ere any success could be expected in any attempt to remedy the many evils of this unhappy Province. I expected to find a contest between a government and a people: I found two nations warring in the bosom of a single state: I found a struggle, not of principles, but of races; and I perceived that it would be idle to attempt any amelioration of laws or institutions, until we could first succeed in terminating the deadly animosity that now separates the inhabitants of Lower Canada into the hostile divisions of French and English.

It would be vain for me to expect that any description I can give will impress on your Majesty such a view of the animosity of these races, as my personal experience in Lower Canada has forced on me. Our happy immunity from any feelings of national hostility, renders it difficult for us to comprehend the intensity of the hatred which the difference of language, of laws and of manners, creates between those who inhabit the same village, and are citizens of the same state. We are

---

1 From J.W. Southgate edition (1839) pp. 7-12, 16, 26, 128, 135, 138-39.

ready to believe that the real motive of the quarrel is something else, and that the difference of race has slightly and occasionally aggravated dissensions, which we attribute to some more usual cause. Experience of a state of society, so unhappily divided as that of Lower Canada, leads to an exactly contrary opinion. The national feud forces itself on the very senses, irresistibly and palpably, as the origin or the essence of every dispute which divides the community; we discover that dissensions, which appear to have another origin, are but forms of this constant and all-pervading quarrel; and that every contest is one of French and English in the outset, or becomes so ere it has run its course....

It is scarcely possible to conceive descendants of any of the great European nations more unlike each other in character and temperament, more totally separated from each other by language, laws, and modes of life, or placed in circumstances more calculated to produce mutual misunderstanding, jealousy and hatred. To conceive the incompatibility of the two races in Canada, it is not enough that we should picture to ourselves a community composed of equal proportions of French and English. We must bear in mind what kind of French and English they are that are brought in contact, and in what proportions they meet.

The institutions of France, during the period of the colonization of Canada were, perhaps, more than those of any other European nation calculated to repress the intelligence and freedom of the great mass of the people. These institutions followed the Canadian colonist across the Atlantic. The same central, ill-organized, unimproving and repressive despotism, extended over him. Not merely was he allowed no voice in the government of his Province, or the choice of his rulers, but he was not even permitted to associate with his neighbours for the regulation of those municipal affairs, which the central authority neglected under the pretext of managing. He obtained his land on a tenure singularly calculated to promote his immediate comfort, and to check his desire to better his condition: he was placed at once in a life of constant and unvarying labour, of great material comfort, and feudal dependence. The ecclesiastical authority to which he had been accustomed established its institutions around him, and the priest continued to exercise over him his ancient influence. No general provision was made for education; and, as its necessity was not appreciated, the colonist made no attempt to repair the negligence of his government. It need not surprise us that, under such circumstances, a race of men habituated to the incessant labour of a rude and unskilled agriculture, and habitually fond of social enjoyments, congregated together in rural communities, occupying portions of the wholly unappropriated soil, sufficient to provide each family with material comforts, far beyond their ancient means, or almost their conceptions; that they made little advance beyond the first progress in comfort, which the bounty of the soil absolutely forced upon them; that under the same institutions they remained the same uninstructed, inactive, unprogressive people.... They remain an old and stationary society, in a new and progressive world. In all essentials they are still French; but French in every respect dissimilar to those of France in the present day. They resemble rather the French of the provinces under the old *regime*....

As they are taught apart, so are their studies different. The literature with which each is the most conversant, is that of the peculiar language of each; and all the ideas which men derive from books, come to each of them from perfectly different sources. The difference of language in this respect produces effects quite apart from those which it has on the mere intercourse of the two races. Those who have reflected on the powerful influence of language on thought, will perceive in how different a manner people who speak in different languages are apt to think; and those who are familiar with the literature of France, know that the same opinion will be expressed by an English and French writer of the present day, not merely in different words, but in a style so different as to mark utterly different habits of thought. This difference is very striking in Lower Canada: it exists, not merely in the books of most influence and repute, which are, of course, those of the great writers of France and England, and by which the minds of the respective races are formed, but it is observable in the writings which now issue from the colonial press. The articles in the newspapers of each race, are written in a style as widely different as those of France and England at present—and the arguments which convince the one, are calculated to appear utterly unintelligible to the other....

Circumstances having thrown the English into the ranks of the government, and the folly of their opponents having placed them, on the other hand, in a state of permanent collision with it, the former possess the advantage of having the force of government and the authority of the laws on their side in the present stage of the contest. Their exertions during the recent troubles have contributed to maintain the supremacy of the law and the continuance of the connection with Great Britain; but it would in my opinion be dangerous to rely on the continuance of such a state of feeling as now prevails among them[.] ... They do not hesitate to say that they will not tolerate much longer the being made the sport of parties at home, and that if the mother country forget what is due to the loyal and enterprising men of her own race, they must protect themselves. In the significant language of one of their own ablest advocates, they assert that, "Lower Canada must be English, at the expense, if necessary, of not being British."

A plan by which it is proposed to ensure the tranquil government of Lower Canada, must include in itself the means of putting an end to the agitation of national disputes in the legislature, by settling, at once and for ever, the national character of the Province. I entertain no doubts as to the national character which must be given to Lower Canada; it must be that of the British Empire; that of the majority of the population of British America; that of the great race which must, in the lapse of no long period of time, be predominant over the whole North American Continent. Without effecting the change so rapidly or so roughly as to shock the feelings and trample on the welfare of the existing generation, it must henceforth be the first and steady purpose of the British Government to establish an English population, with English laws and language, in this Province, and to trust its government to none but a decidedly English Legislature....

The only power that can be effectual at once in coercing the present disaffection, and hereafter obliterating the nationality of the French Canadians, is that of a numerical majority of a loyal and English population; ...

Two kinds of union have been proposed,—federal and legislative. By the first, the separate legislature of each Province would be preserved in its present form, and retain almost all its present attributes of internal legislation; the federal legislature exercising no power, save in those matters of general concern, which may have been expressly ceded to it by the constituent Provinces. A legislative union would imply a complete incorporation of the Provinces included in it under one legislature, exercising universal and sole legislative authority over all of them, in exactly the same manner as the Parliament legislates alone for the whole of the British Isles....

If the population of Upper Canada is rightly estimated at 400,000, the English inhabitants of Lower Canada at 150,000, and the French at 450,000, the union of the two Provinces would not only give a clear English majority, but one which would be increased every year by the influence of English emigration; and I have little doubt that the French, when once placed, by the legitimate course of events and the working of natural causes, in a minority, would abandon their vain hopes of nationality. I do not mean that they would immediately give up their present animosities, or instantly renounce the hope of attaining their end by violent means. But the experience of the two Unions in the British Isles[1] may teach us how effectually the strong arm of a popular legislature would compel the obedience of the refractory population; and the hopelessness of success would gradually subdue the

---

1 The Union of England and Scotland to form Britain (1707) and the Union of Britain and Ireland (1800-01).

existing animosities, and incline the French Canadian population to acquiesce in their new state of political existence.

4. From *Parliamentary Debates on the Subject of the Confederation of the British North American Provinces* (1865)

[Common threads running throughout the debates include representation by population, the Durham Report, the American Civil War, the benefits of British connection and of constitutional monarchy (versus republicanism). Of particular interest are the rhetorical means to which the politicians resorted to variously dispute or justify the capacity of constitutional monarchy to accommodate "different races and religions," as George-Étienne Cartier puts it in his speech, below. Extracts selected for inclusion encapsulate a variety of perspectives on Confederation, from Francophone and Anglophone to Irish-Catholic and Protestant French-Canadian. Note that the debates begin in the third person, eventually switching to first-person transcription.]

a. Hon. George-Étienne Cartier, Attorney General East (Montreal East)[1]

From Legislative Assembly, 7 February 1865[2]

At present the question was: Was Confederation of the British North American Provinces necessary in order to increase our strength and power and secure to us the continuance of the benefits of British connection? He had no doubt that the measure was necessary for those objects. It would be observed that the English speaking opponents of the scheme, in Lower Canada, pretended a fear of this element being absorbed by the French Canadian; while the opponents, composed of the latter origins—of men who might be called the old Papineau Tail[3]—whose sole idea was annexation to the United States—said they were afraid of the extinction of French Canadian nationality in the great Confederation....

---

1 Sir George-Étienne Cartier (1814-73), co-premier with Sir John A. Macdonald of the United Province of Canada (1857-62) and a Father of Confederation.
2 See *Parliamentary* 56-62.
3 Louis-Joseph Papineau (1786-1871), leader of the Patriote party and member of the committee that wrote the Ninety-Two Resolutions, a long series of demands for political reform passed by Lower Canada's Legislative Assembly on 21 February 1834. Their rejection in the form of British Colonial Secretary Lord Russell's ten resolutions (the "Russell Resolutions") resulted in part in the Lower-Canadian uprisings of 1837-38.

Some parties—through the press and by other modes—pretended that it was impossible to carry out Federation, on account of the differences of races and religions. Those who took this view of the question were in error. It was just the reverse. It was precisely on account of the variety of races, local interests, &c., that the Federation system ought to be resorted to, and would be found to work well. (Hear, hear.) We were in the habit of seeing in some public journals, and hearing from some public men, that it was a great misfortune indeed there should be a difference of races in this colony—that there should be the distinction of French Canadian from British Canadian. Now, he (Hon. Mr. CARTIER) desired on this point to vindicate the rights, the merits, the usefulness, so to speak, of those belonging to the French Canadian race. (Hear, hear.) In order to bring these merits and this usefulness more prominently before his hearers, it would be only necessary to allude to the efforts made by them to sustain British power on this continent, and to point out their adherence to British supremacy in trying times. We were all conversant with the history of the circumstances which had brought about the difficulties between England and her former American colonies in 1775.[1] Lower Canada,—or rather he should say, the Province of Quebec, for the colony was not then known by the name of Canada, but was called the Province of Quebec,—contained the most dense population of any British colony in North America at that time. The accession of Lower Canada was of course an object of envy to the other American colonies, and strenuous efforts were made by those who had resolved to overthrow British power on this continent to induce Canada to ally herself to their cause. As early as 1775,[2] the French Canadians were solemnly addressed in a proclamation by General WASHINGTON, who called upon them to abandon the flag of their new masters, inasmuch as they could not expect anything from those who differed from them in language, in religion, in race, and in sympathies. But what was the conduct of the French Canadian people under these circumstances—what was the attitude of the clergy and the seigniors? ... A few years only had elapsed at that time since the transfer of the country and its population from the Crown of France to the Crown of Great Britain; but even within that brief interval of time, they were enabled to appreciate the advantages of their new position, notwithstanding the fact that they were still struggling and complaining. The people, as well as the clergy and aristocracy, had understood that it was better for them to remain under the English and Protestant Crown of England, rather than to become republicans. (Hear, hear.) They were

---

1 The American Revolutionary War (1775-83).
2 The Battle of Quebec (September-December 1775), part of the American invasion of Canada during the Revolutionary War.

proof against the insidious offers of GEORGE WASHINGTON;[1] and not only so, but when the Americans came as invaders, they fought against the armed forces of ARNOLD, MONTGOMERY and others.[2] (Cheers.) Attempts were made to excite hostility to Federation on the ground that, under the regime of a local legislature, the English Protestant minority would not be fairly dealt with. He thought the way in which the French Canadians had stood by [the] British connection, when there were but few British in the province, was a proof that they would not attempt to deal unjustly now by the British minority, when their numbers were so much greater.... Had [the French-Canadians] yielded to the appeals of WASHINGTON ... it is probable that there would not have been now a vestige of British power on this continent. But, with the disappearance of British power, they too would have disappeared as French Canadians. (Hear, hear.) These historical facts taught that there should be a mutual feeling of gratitude from the French Canadians towards the British, and from the British towards the French Canadians, for our present position, that Canada is still a British colony.... The question for us to ask ourselves was this: Shall we be content to remain separate—shall we be content to maintain a mere provincial existence, when, by combining together, we could become a great nation? It had never yet been the good fortune of any group of communities to secure national greatness with such facility.... It was lamented by some that we had this diversity of races, and hopes were expressed that this distinctive feature would cease. The idea of unity of races was utopian—it was impossible. Distinctions of this kind would always exist.... He viewed the diversity of races in British North America in this way: we were of different races, not for the purpose of warring against each other, but in order to compete and emulate for the general welfare. (Cheers.) We could not do away with the distinctions of race. We could not legislate for the disappearance of the French Canadians from American soil, but British and French Canadians alike could appreciate and understand their position relative to each other.... Of course, the difficulty, it would be said, would be to deal fairly by the minority. In Upper Canada the Catholics would find themselves in a minority; in Lower Canada the Protestants would be in a minority, while the Lower Provinces were divided.[3] Under such circumstances, would any one pretend that either the local or general governments

---

1 George Washington (1732-99), the first President of the United States and a leader of the Continental Army during the American Revolution.
2 Colonel Benedict Arnold (1741-1801) and Brigadier General Richard Montgomery (1738-75).
3 The "Lower Provinces" include today's New Brunswick, Nova Scotia, Prince Edward Island, and Newfoundland.

would sanction any injustice. What would be the consequence, even supposing any such thing were attempted by any one of the local governments? It would be censured everywhere. Whether it came from Upper Canada or from Lower Canada, any attempt to deprive the minority of their rights would be at once thwarted.... He would now conclude his remarks by asking honorable gentlemen to consider well this scheme. It was his hope, his cherished hope, that it would be adopted by the House. The time was opportune, as his honorable colleague (Attn. Gen. MACDONALD)[1] had so ably stated last evening; the opportunity might never offer itself again in such a facile and propitious manner. We knew we had, in all our proceedings, the approbation of the Imperial Government. So if these resolutions were adopted by Canada, as he had no doubt they would, and by the other Colonial Legislatures, the Imperial Government would be called upon to pass a measure which would have for its effect to give a strong central or general government and local governments, which would at once secure and guard the persons, the properties and the civil and religious rights belonging to the population of each section. (Loud cheers.)

b. Hon. Thomas D'Arcy McGee, Minister of Agriculture (Montreal West)[2]

From Legislative Assembly, 9 February 1865[3]

Mr. SPEAKER, before I draw to a close the little remainder of what I have to say—and I am sorry to have detained the House so long—(cries of "No, no")—I beg to offer a few observations *apropos* of my own position as an English-speaking member for Lower Canada. I venture, in the first place, to observe that there seems to be a good deal of exaggeration on the subject of race, occasionally introduced, both on the one side and the other, in this section of the country.... [T]his theory of race is sometimes carried to an anti-christian and unphilosophical excess. Whose words are those—"GOD hath made of one blood all the nations that dwell on the face of the earth?"[4] Is not that

---

1 Sir John A. Macdonald (1815-91), the first Prime Minister of Canada who also occupied the position of Attorney General (Canada West) from 1864 to 1867.
2 Thomas D'Arcy McGee (1825-68), journalist, poet, and a Father of Confederation.
3 See *Parliamentary* 143-46.
4 Acts 17:26: "And hath made of one blood all nations of men for to dwell on all the face of the earth" (King James Version).

the true theory of race? For my part, I am not afraid of the French Canadian majority in the future Local Government doing injustice, except accidentally; not because I am of the same religion as themselves; for origin and language are barriers stronger to divide men in this world than is religion to unite them. Neither do I believe that my Protestant compatriots need have any such fear. The French Canadians have never been an intolerant people; it is not in their temper, unless they had been persecuted, perhaps, and then it might have been as it has been with other races of all religions....

We have here no traditions and ancient venerable institutions; here, there are no aristocratic elements hallowed by time or bright deeds; here, every man is the first settler of the land, or removed from the first settler one or two generations at the farthest; here, we have no architectural monuments calling up old associations; here, we have none of those old popular legends and stories which in other countries have exercised a powerful share in the government; here, every man is the son of his own works.... This is a new land—a land of pretension because it is new; because classes and systems have not had that time to grow here naturally. We have no aristocracy but of virtue and talent, which is the only true aristocracy, and is the old and true meaning of the term. (Hear, hear) There is a class of men rising in these colonies, superior in many respects to others with whom they might be compared. What I should like to see is—that fair representatives of the Canadian and Acadian aristocracy,[1] should be sent to the foot of the Throne with that scheme, to obtain for it the royal sanction—a scheme not suggested by others, or imposed upon us, but one the work of ourselves, the creation of our own intellect and of our own free, unbiassed [sic] and untrammelled will. I should like to see our best men go there, and endeavor to have this measure carried through the Imperial Parliament—going into Her Majesty's presence, and by their manner, if not actually by their speech, saying—"During Your Majesty's reign we have had Responsible Government conceded to us; we have administered it for nearly a quarter of a century, during which we have under it doubled our population and more than quadrupled our trade. The small colonies which your ancestors could scarcely see on the map have grown into great communities. A great danger has arisen in our near neighborhood. Over our homes a cloud hangs, dark and heavy. We do not know when it may burst. With our own strength we are not able to combat against the storm, what we can do, we will do cheerfully and loyally. But we want time to grow—we

---

1 By "Canadian," McGee means the French-Canadians inhabiting today's province of Quebec; by "Acadian," he means the French-speaking Acadians of Atlantic Canada (New Brunswick, Nova Scotia, Prince Edward Island and, to a lesser extent, Newfoundland).

want more people to fill our country, more industrious families of men to develope [*sic*] our resources—we want more land tilled—more men established through our wastes and wildernesses. We of the British North American Provinces want to be joined together, that if danger comes, we can support each other in the day of trial. We come to Your Majesty, who have given us liberty, to give us unity, that we may preserve and perpetuate our freedom; and whatsoever Charter, in the wisdom of Your Majesty and of Your Parliament, you give us, we shall loyally obey and fulfil it as long as it is the pleasure of Your Majesty and Your Successors to maintain the connection between Great Britain and these Colonies." (The hon. gentleman then sat down amid prolonged cheers.)

c. Hon. L. Letellier de St. Just (Grandville)[1]

From Legislative Assembly, 14 February 1865[2]

It is stated that the federal union provides a means of forming a great people, and of raising us to a position in which we may take a place among the nations of the globe. But if into that people, by the Constitution itself, the seeds of discord are introduced, will any one believe that it would not be better to live apart, as at the present time, than to live together with disunion in our midst? ... I have heard it said that the Protestants of Lower Canada ought to be satisfied with their prospects for the future, because we have always acted with liberality towards them. But that is no guarantee for them, for we would not content ourselves with a mere promise to act liberally, if we considered that our interest or our institutions were threatened by a majority differing in race and religion from ourselves; and in any case that is not the way to ensure the peace of the country.... When we make a Constitution, we must in the first place settle the political and religious questions which divide the populations for whom the Constitution is devised; because it is a well known fact, that it is religious differences which have caused the greatest troubles and the greatest difficulties which have agitated the people in days gone by. We must learn to prevent them for the future.... We are told to vote Confederation first, and that the details will be arranged at a subsequent period; that a measure will then be brought down to regulate the sectional or sectarian difficulties. I am quite willing to admit that such a measure will be presented; but, should not the majority choose to adopt it, we

---

1 Luc Letellier de Saint-Just (1820–81), notary, politician, and member of the Liberal party, opposed to the project of Confederation, although he rallied to it after 1867.
2 See *Parliamentary* 187–88.

should then be compelled to remain with the seeds of trouble and dissension, which the House will not have succeeded in eradicating, implanted among us.... I must say that if I am in the House when the vote is called on this measure, I shall have to record my name against it, and in so doing I shall be acting conscientiously. I shall do so because I think it a duty incumbent on me, however painful it may be for me to vote contrary to the views of the Government in this respect, and contrary to a large majority of this House. And while I would concede to every hon. gentleman who may differ from me the same freedom of judgment that I claim for myself—while I would look with all charity on the course thought proper to be taken by my fellow members, I feel persuaded that they will not begrudge me the right of discharging my duty in accordance with the dictates of my conscience, and what I believe to be for the good of my constituents.

d. Hon. H.G. Joly (Lotbinière)[1]

From Legislative Assembly, 20 February 1865[2]

What is our position? In what respects is it more favorable than that of other confederations? Let us begin with Lower Canada; its population is composed of about three-fourths French-Canadians [sic], and of one-fourth English-Canadians. It is impossible, even for the blindest admirers of the scheme of Confederation, to shut out from their view this great difference of nationality, which is certainly fated to play an important part in the destinies of the future Confederation. When Lord DURHAM wrote his celebrated report in 1839,[3] he said, when speaking of the English-Canadians of Lower Canada:—"The English population will never submit to the authority of a parliament in which the French have a majority, or even the semblance of a majority." A little further on, he added:—"In the significant language of one of their most eminent men, they assert that Lower Canada must become English, even if to effect that object it should be necessary that the province should cease to belong to England." Whatever errors Lord DURHAM may have fallen into in judging the French-Canadians, he certainly cannot be reproached with having shewn too great severity towards the English-Canadians. He merely depicted their sentiments,

---

1 Sir Henri-Gustave Joly de Lotbinière (1829-1908), lawyer, politician, and French-speaking Protestant; as a member of the Liberal party, he was opposed to Confederation, although he came to terms with it afterwards.
2 See *Parliamentary* 350-62.
3 For an extract from the Durham Report, see Appendix E3, p. 257.

as they manifested themselves in his day. Since then, things have undergone a change. And last autumn, at Sherbrooke, the Honorable Minister of Finance presented to us a very different picture,[1] when he said:—"For five and twenty years harmony has reigned in Lower Canada, and the English and French populations have entered into a compact to labor together to promote the common interests of the country." This picture is a true one at the present time, as was also that drawn by Lord DURHAM in his day; things have changed! In the Parliament of the United Canadas, the English are in a majority; they have not to deal with a French majority. But, if circumstances have altered, men have not; place them in the same position in which they were previous to 1839, and again you will perceive in them the same sentiments as were depicted by Lord DURHAM. The seed lies hid in the soil, it does not shew itself on the surface; but a few drops of rain are all that is necessary to cause it to spring up....

I asked of myself, with all seriousness, what ... are the aspirations of the French Canadians? I have always imagined, indeed I still imagine, that they all centre in one point, the maintenance of their nationality as a shield destined for the protection of the institutions they hold most dear. For a whole century this has ever been the aim of the French Canadians; in the long years of adversity they have never for a moment lost sight of it; surmounting all obstacles, they have advanced step by step towards its attainment, and what progress have they not made? What is their position to-day? They number nearly a million ... [and] [a] people numbering a million does not vanish easily, especially when they are the owners of the soil.... The French-Canadians hold a distinguished position in the commerce of the country; they have founded banks and savings banks; on the St. Lawrence between Quebec and Montreal, they own one of the finest lines of steamboats in America; ... we have foundries and manufactories, and our shipbuilders have obtained a European renown. We have a literature peculiarly our own; we have authors, of whom we are justly proud; to them we entrust our language and our history; they are the pillars of our nationality. Nothing denotes our existence as a people so much as our literature; education has penetrated everywhere; we have several excellent colleges, and an [sic] university in which all the sciences may be studied under excellent professors. Our young men learn in the military schools how to defend their country. We possess all the elements of a nationality. But a few months ago, we were steadily advancing towards prosperity, satisfied with the present and confident in the

---

1 Hon. Alexander Tilloch Galt (1817-93), Minister of Finance from 1858-66; also, following Confederation, Minister of Finance from 1 July to 7 November 1867.

future of the French-Canadian people. Suddenly discouragement, which had never overcome us in our adversity, takes possession of us; our aspirations are now only empty dreams; the labors of a century must be wasted; we must give up our nationality, adopt a new one, greater and nobler, we are told, than our own, but then it will no longer be our own. And why? Because it is our inevitable fate, against which it is of no use to struggle. But have we not already struggled against destiny when we were more feeble than we are now, and have we not triumphed? Let us not give to the world the sad spectacle of a people voluntarily resigning its nationality. Nor do we intend to do so. In conclusion, I object to the proposed Confederation, first, as a Canadian, without reference to origin, and secondly, as a French Canadian. From either point of view, I look upon the measure as a fatal error; and, as a French Canadian, I once more appeal to my fellow-countrymen, reminding them of the precious inheritance confided to their keeping—an inheritance sanctified by the blood of their fathers, and which it is their duty to hand down to their children as unimpaired as they received it. (Cheers.)

e. Mr. C.B. de Niverville (Three Rivers)[1]

From Legislative Assembly, 10 March 1865[2]

Mr. SPEAKER, as the junior member of this honorable House, it was proper that I should be the last to speak on the question which now engages our attention.... I hold it to be my duty, and I do not hesitate to give my vote in favor of the principle and the project of Confederation. Certain apprehensions have arisen in the public mind relative to the project in question; these fears, I need not say, have been excited by the opponents of the measure, who make themselves hoarse with crying that French-Canadian nationality would be swallowed up by Confederation, and that in twenty-five or thirty years' time there would not be a single French Canadian left in Lower Canada. Well, Mr. SPEAKER, I appeal, to prove the falsehood of these declarations, to the men who in 1840—the time of the union of the two provinces—labored with so much zeal and energy to guard the natural depository of our social and religious rights from danger—I appeal, to prove it, to those men who applied all their energy, their abilities, and their patri-

---

[1] Louis-Charles (Charles) Boucher de Niverville (1825-69), lawyer, politician, member of the Conservative party, and supporter of Confederation. Rosanna Mullins Leprohon was related by marriage to the De Niverville family.

[2] See *Parliamentary* 947-49.

otism to prevent the union; to those men who, endowed with a singleness of mind at least equal to that which animates the opponents of Confederation, procured numerous petitions to be signed against the union of Upper and Lower Canada; to those men, in short, who predicted that in ten years' time there would not be a single French Canadian left—these men I summon to the bar of public opinion, and I ask them—"Gentlemen, did you predict truly? What has become of that French-Canadian nationality which was to be swallowed up by the union? Has it disappeared, as you said it would? See and judge for yourselves."

Appendix F: Contemporary Maps and Illustrations

1. **From Reuben Gold Thwaites, "Eastern North America (1740),"** *France in America, 1497-1763,* **Vol. 7 (New York and London: Harper & Brothers, 1905), 106**

[This map helps to shed light on the massive amount of land that France and Britain disputed in the North American theatre of the Seven Years' War. Following France's loss on the Plains of Abraham (see *Manor House*, Chapter XXI), the capitulation of Montreal (see Chapter XXIII), the transfer of New France to Britain (see Chapters XXIII and XXIV), and the ratification of the Treaty of Paris (1763), Britain effectively came to possess all of mainland North America east of the Mississippi River.]

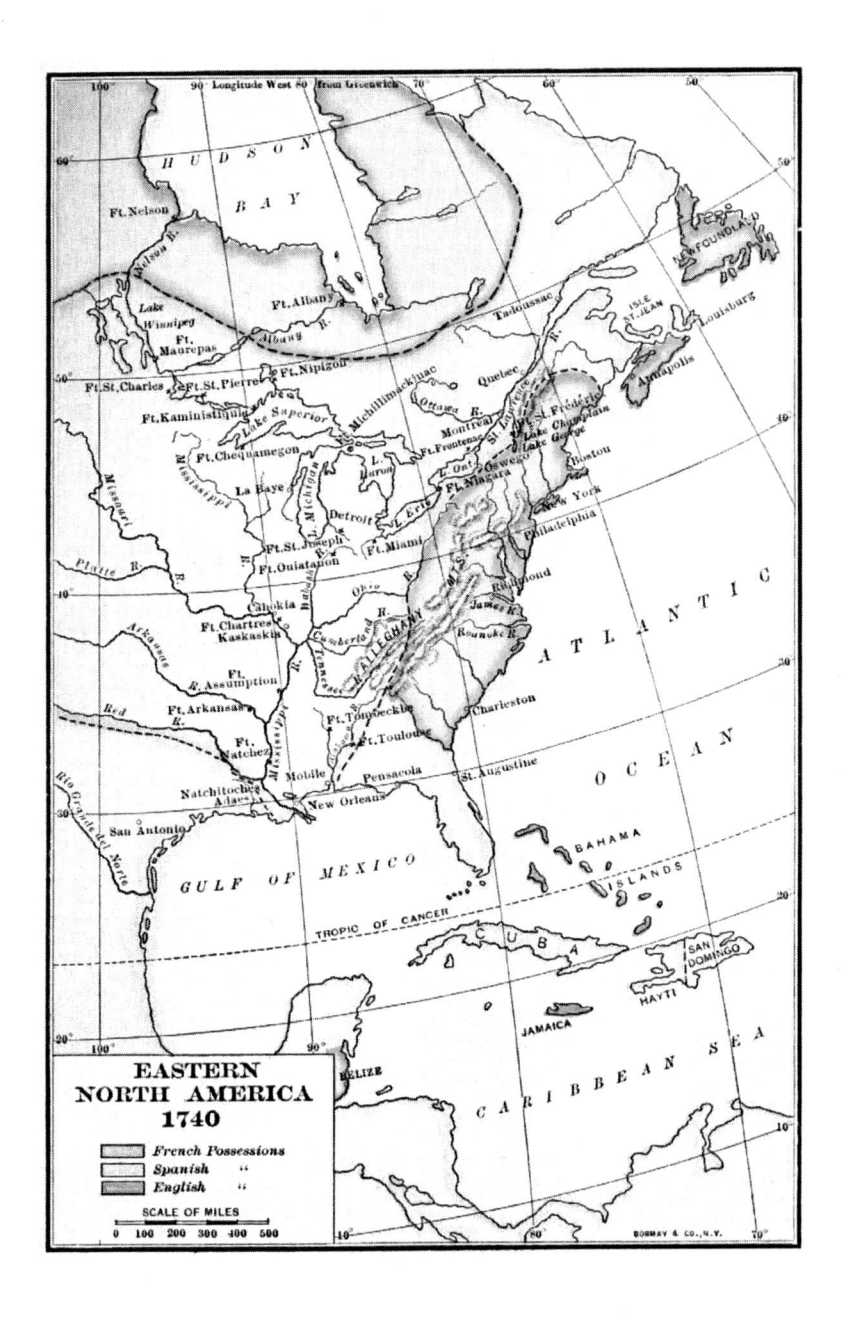

THE MANOR HOUSE OF DE VILLERAI 273

2. **John Henry Walker, "Engraving. Winter Attack on Fort William Henry, 1757" (Courtesy of the McCord Museum, Montreal)**

[Walker's (1831-99) famous engraving depicts the French campaign against Fort William Henry from January to March 1757. (See also Chapter V of *The Manor House*).]

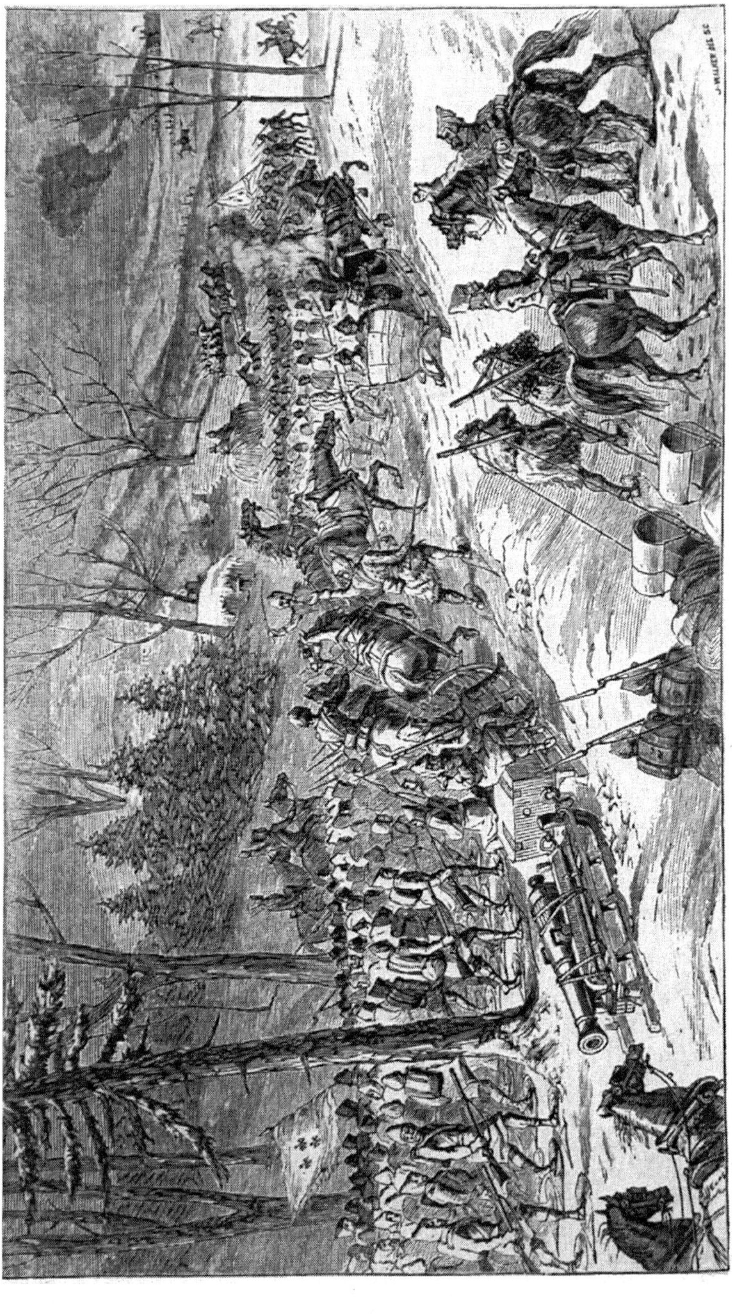

3. Anon., "A View of the Taking of Quebec September 13th 1759" (Courtesy of the McCord Museum, Montreal)

[This well-known illustration depicts the taking of Quebec that followed the famous Battle of the Plains of Abraham on 13 September 1759 (see *Manor House*, Chapter XXI).]

A View of the Taking of QUEBEC September 13, 1759.
Vüe de la Prise de QUEBEC le 13 Septembre 1759.

Select Bibliography

Primary Sources

Rosanna Eleanor Mullins

Mullins, Rosanna Eleanor. "Alice Sydenham's First Ball." *The Literary Garland*, NS 7 (Jan.-Dec. 1849): 1-14. Rpt. *Nineteenth-Century Canadian Stories*. Ed. David Arnason. Toronto: Macmillan, 1976. 96-127. Rpt. *Pioneering Women: Short Stories by Canadian Women, Beginnings to 1880*. Ed. Lorraine McMullen and Sandra Campbell. Ottawa: U of Ottawa P, 1993. 155-88.
——. "Clarence Fitz-Clarence." *The Literary Garland*, NS 9 (Jan.-May 1851).
——. "Eva Huntingdon." *The Literary Garland*, NS 8 (Jan.-Dec. 1850).
——. "Florence; or, Wit and Wisdom." *The Literary Garland*, NS 7 (Feb.-Dec. 1849).
——. "Ida Beresford; or, The Child of Fashion." *The Literary Garland*, NS 6 (Jan.-Sept. 1848).
——. "The Stepmother." *The Literary Garland*, NS 5 (Feb.-June 1847).

Rosanna Eleanor Leprohon

Leprohon, Rosanna Eleanor. "Ada Dunmore; or, A Memorable Christmas Eve: An Autobiography." *Canadian Illustrated News*, I, 25 Dec. 1869-12 Feb. 1870.
——. *Antoinette de Mirecourt; or, Secret Marrying and Secret Sorrowing*. Montreal: Lovell, 1864. Rpt. Toronto: U of Toronto P, 1973. Rpt. New Canadian Library. Toronto: McClelland & Stewart, 1973. Rpt. Carleton UP, 1989. Rpt. New Canadian Library, 2000 and 2010.
——. *Armand Durand; or, A Promise Fulfilled*. Montreal: Lovell, 1868. Rpt. Tecumseh, 1994.
——, trans. *Cantate en l'honneur de Son Altesse Royale Le Prince de Galles*. By Édouard Sempé. Montreal: Louis Perrault, 1860.
——. "Clive Weston's Wedding Anniversary." *The Canadian Monthly and National Review* 2 (Aug.-Sept. 1872). Rpt. *The Evolution of Canadian Literature in English: Beginnings to 1867*. Ed. Mary Jane Edwards. Toronto: Holt, Rinehart and Winston, 1973. 266-301.

———. "The Dead Witness; or, Lillian's Peril." *The Hearthstone*, 3 Aug.-5 Oct. 1872.

———. "Eveleen O'Donnell." *The Pilot* [Boston], 24 Jan.-26 Feb. 1859.

———. "The Manor House of De Villerai." *The Family Herald* [Montreal], 16 Nov. 1859-8 Feb. 1860.

———. *The Manor House of de Villerai: A Tale of Canada under the French Dominion*. Edited with an Introduction by Dr. John R. Sorfleet. *Journal of Canadian Fiction* 34 (1985).

———. "My Visit to Fairview Villa." *Canadian Illustrated News*, 14 May-28 May 1870. Rpt. *Literature in Canada*, Vol. I. Ed. Douglas Daymond and Leslie Monkman. Toronto: Gage, 1978. 200-20. Rpt. *Pioneering Women: Short Stories by Canadian Women, Beginnings to 1880*. Ed. Lorraine McMullen and Sandra Campbell. Ottawa: U of Ottawa P, 1993. 189-215. Rpt. *Early Canadian Short Stories: Short Stories in English before World War I: A Critical Edition*. Ed. Misao Dean. Ottawa: Tecumseh, 2000. 25-50.

———. *The Poetical Works of Mrs. Leprohon (Miss R.E. Mullins)*. Montreal: Lovell, 1881. Rpt. Toronto: U of Toronto P, 1973.

———. "A School-Girl Friendship." *Canadian Illustrated News*, 25 Aug.-15 Sept. 1877.

———. "Who Stole the Diamonds?" *Canadian Illustrated News*, 2 Jan.-9 Jan. 1875.

French Translations of Leprohon's Novels

Béchard, Auguste, trans. *Ada Dunmore ou Une veille de Noël remarquable. Autobiographie. Le Pionnier de Sherbrooke*, 18 Apr.-21 Nov. 1873.

Genand, Joseph-Auguste, trans. *Antoinette de Mirecourt ou Mariage secret et chagrins cachés*. Montreal: Beauchemin & Valois, 1865.

———, trans. *Armand Durand ou la Promesse accomplie*. Montreal: J.B. Rolland & fils, 1869.

Lefebvre de Bellefeuille, Joseph-Édouard, trans. *Ida Beresford ou la Jeune Fille du grand monde. L'Ordre*. 27 Sept. 1859-21 Feb. 1860.

———, trans. *Le manoir de Villerai. Roman historique touchant le Canada sous la domination française. L'Ordre*. 14 Nov. 1860-3 April 1861. Montreal: De Plinguet, 1861.

Secondary Sources on Leprohon

Anon., "The Late Mrs. Leprohon," *Canadian Illustrated News*, 4 October 1879. 211. Bibliothèque et Archives nationales du Québec. 27 May 2014.

Brady, Elizabeth. "Towards a Happier History: Women and Domination." In *Domination*. Ed. Alkis Kontos. Toronto: U of Toronto P, 1975. 17-31.

Cabajsky, Andrea. "Lost and Found: *The Dead Witness* (1872), Rosanna Mullins Leprohon's Final Novel." *Canadian Literature* 217 (Summer 2013): 196-202.

Champagne, Guy. "Cantate en l'honneur de Son Altesse Royale Le Prince de Galles, par Édouard Sempé." *Dictionnaire des oeuvres littéraires du Québec*. Vol. I. Ed. Maurice Lemire. Montreal: Fides, 1978.

Cuder-Domínguez, Pilar. "Negotations of Gender and Nationhood in Early Canadian Literature." *International Journal of Canadian Studies* 18 (Fall 1998): 115-31.

D.J. "Madame Leprohon." *L'Opinion publique*, 2 Oct. 1879. 469-70. *Bibliothèque et Archives nationales du Québec*. 27 May 2014.

De Bellefeuille, Joseph-Édouard Lefebvre. "*Antoinette de Mirecourt*." *La Revue canadienne* 1.7 (July 1864): 442-44. *Early Canadiana Online*. 27 May 2014.

Deneau, Henri. (Brother Adrian). "The Life and Works of Mrs. Leprohon, née R.E. Mullins." MA Thesis. U de Montréal. 1948.

Edwards, Mary Jane. "Essentially Canadian." *Canadian Literature* 52 (Spring 1972): 8-23.

——. "Rosanna Eleanor Leprohon." *Canadian Writers before 1890*. Ed. W.H. New. Detroit: Thomson Gale, 1990. 206-08.

Gadpaille, Michelle. "If the Dress Fits: Female Stereotyping in Rosanna Leprohon's 'Alice Sydenham's First Ball.'" *Canadian Literature* 146 (Autumn 1995): 68-83.

Gerson, Carole. "Three Writers of Victorian Canada and Their Works." In Robert Lecker, Jack David, and Ellen Quigley, eds. *Canadian Writers and Their Works*. Fiction Series. Vol. 1. Toronto: ECW, 1983. 195-256.

——. "Rosanna Leprohon (1829-79)." *ECW's Biographical Guide to Canadian Novelists*. Ed. Robert Lecker, Jack David, and Ellen Quigley. Toronto: ECW, 1993. 39-41.

Hart, Julia Catherine Beckwith. *St. Ursula's Convent, or, The Nun of Canada: Containing Scenes from Real Life*. 1824. Ed. Douglas G. Lochhead. Ottawa: Carleton UP, 1991.

Hughes, Kenneth. "Le Vrai Visage du [sic] *Antoinette de Mirecourt* et *Kamouraska*." *Sphinx: A Magazine of Literature and Society* 2.3 (1977): 33-39.

Klinck, Carl F. Introduction. *Antoinette de Mirecourt; or, Secret Marrying and Secret Sorrowing*. By Rosanna Leprohon. New Canadian Library No. 89. Toronto: McClelland & Stewart, 1973. 5-12.

McMullen, Lorraine and Elizabeth Waterston. "Rosanna Mullins

Leprohon: At Home in Many Worlds." *Silenced Sextet: Six Nineteenth-Century Canadian Women Novelists.* Ed. Carrie MacMillan, Lorraine McMullen, and Elizabeth Waterston. Montreal: McGill-Queen's UP, 1992. 14-51.

Moodie, Susanna. "Editor's Table." *The Victoria Magazine* I (June 1848). Rpt. The University of British Columbia Library. Edited with an Introduction by William H. New. 238-40.

Morgan, Henry J. "Leprohon, Mrs. Rosanna Eleanor." *Bibliotheca Canadensis; or, A Manual of Canadian Literature.* Ottawa: Desbarats, 1867. 224. The Internet Archive. 27 May 2014.

Murphy, Carl. "The Marriage Metaphor in Nineteenth-Century English Canadian Fiction." *Studies in Canadian Literature* 13.1 (1988): 1-19.

O'Donnell, Kathleen M. "The Heroine of *The Manor House of De Villerai.*" *Studies in Canadian Literature* 10.1-2 (1985): 162-69.

"The Old Thing." Rev. of *Antoinette de Mirecourt. The Saturday Reader* 1.1 (9 Sept. 1865): 4. Early Canadiana Online. 27 May 2014.

"The Poetical Works of Mrs. Leprohon." Rev. of *The Poetical Works of Mrs. Leprohon. Rose-Belford's Canadian Monthly* 8.3 (Mar. 1882): 324-25. Early Canadiana Online. 27 May 2014.

Shohet, Linda. "Love and Marriage—Canada 1760." *Journal of Canadian Fiction* 2.3 (Summer 1973): 101-03.

Sorfleet, John Robert. Introduction to *The Manor House of De Villerai, A Tale of Canada Under the French Dominion* by Mrs. J.L. Leprohon. Edited with an Introduction by Dr. John R. Sorfleet. *Journal of Canadian Fiction* 34 (1985): 3-12.

Stockdale, John C. "Mullins, Rosanna Eleanora (Leprohon)." *Dictionary of Canadian Biography* X (1972): 536-38.

——. "Ada Dunmore," "Antoinette de Mirecourt," "Armand Durand," "Ida Beresford," and "Le Manoir de Villerai." *Dictionnaire des oeuvres littéraires du Québec* I (1978). Montreal: Fides, 1978.

Ure, George P. "Our First Number," *The Family Herald,* 1.1 Wednesday, November 16, 1859, 4. Microform. MIC A988.

Willmott, Glenn. "Canadian Ressentiment." *New Literary History: A Journal of Theory and Interpretation* 32.1 (Winter 2001): 133-56.

Other Primary and Secondary Works Cited in A Note on the Text, Introduction, and Appendices

Altick, Richard D. *The English Common Reader: A Social History of the Mass Reading Public, 1800-1900.* Chicago: U of Chicago P, 1957.

Arnason, David, ed. *Nineteenth-Century Canadian Stories*. Toronto: Macmillan, 1976.

Aubert de Gaspé, Philippe. *Canadians of Old*. Tr. Jane Brierley. Translation of *Les Anciens Canadiens*. 1863. Montreal: Véhicule, 1996.

Baker, Ray Palmer. *A History of English-Canadian Literature to the Confederation: Its Relation to the Literature of Great Britain and the United States*. Cambridge, MA: Harvard UP; London: Humphrey Milford and Oxford UP, 1920.

Bosher, J.F. and J.C. Dubé. "Bigot, François (d. 1778)." *Dictionary of Canadian Biography*. Vol. 4. University of Toronto / Université Laval, 2003-. 31 May 2014.

Boucher de Boucherville, Georges. *Une de perdue, deux de trouvées, 1864-65*. Montreal: Eusèbe Sénécal, 1874. *The Internet Archive*. 27 May 2014.

Canada. Census Dept. *Census of the Canadas*. 1860-61. Vol. 1. Quebec: S.B. Foote, 1863. *The Internet Archive*. 31 May 2014.

Daymond, Douglas and Leslie Monkman, eds. *Literature in Canada, Vol. I*. Toronto: Gage, 1978.

Dean, Misao, ed. *Early Canadian Short Stories: Short Stories in English before World War I: A Critical Edition*. Ottawa: Tecumseh, 2000.

———. *Practising Femity: Domestic Realism and the Performance of Gender in Early Canadian Fiction*. Toronto: U of Toronto P, 1998.

Desrosiers, Joseph. "Pierre Corneille" in *La Revue canadienne* 5.3 (Feb.-Mar. 1885). *Early Canadian Online*. 27 May 2014.

———. "Le roman au foyer chrétien." *Le Canada français* 1.2 (April 1888): 208-27. *Early Canadian Online*. 27 May 2014.

Dostaler, Yves. *Les infortunes du roman dans le Québec du XIXe siècle*. Montreal: Hurtubise HMH, 1977.

Doutre, Joseph. *Les Fiancés de 1812*. 1844. Montreal: Réédition-Québec, 1969.

Durham, Lord. *Report on the Affairs of British North America, from the Earl of Durham, Her Majesty's High Commissioner*. London: J.W. Southgate, 1839. *The Internet Archive*. 27 May 2014.

Edwards, Mary Jane, ed. *The Evolution of Canadian Literature in English: Beginnings to 1867*. Toronto: Holt, Rinehart and Winston, 1973.

Fraser, Col. Malcolm. *Extract from a Manuscript Journal, Relating to the Siege of Quebec in 1759, Kept By Colonel Malcolm Fraser, Then Lieutenant of the 78th (Fraser's Highlanders,) and serving in that Campaign*. Quebec: Literary and Historical Society, 1866. 13-24. *The Internet Archive*. 27 May 2014.

Frye, Northrop. "Conclusion to a *Literary History of Canada*." *The*

Bush Garden: Essays on the Canadian Imagination. Toronto: Anansi, 1971. 213-51.

Fuller, Margaret. *Woman in the Nineteenth Century.* 1845. Ed. Donna Dickenson. Oxford: Oxford UP, 1994.

Galarneau, Claude. "Case Study: The Desbarats Dynasty in Quebec and Ontario." *History of the Book in Canada. Volume 2. 1840-1918.* Ed. Yvan Lamonde, Patricia Lockhart Fleming, and Fiona A. Black. Toronto: U of Toronto P, 2005. 87-89.

Garneau, François-Xavier, "Preliminary Discourse." *History of Canada, from the Time of Its Discovery Till the Union Year (1840-1).* Vol. 1. Tr. Andrew Bell. Translation of *Histoire du Canada depuis sa découverte jusqu'à nos jours.* 1845-48. Montreal: Lovell, 1860. xi-xxii. *Google Books.* 31 May 2014.

Gerson, Carole. *A Purer Taste: The Writing and Reading of Fiction in English in Nineteenth-Century Canada.* Toronto: U of Toronto P, 1989.

———. *Canadian Women in Print, 1750-1918.* Waterloo, ON: Wilfrid Laurier UP, 2010.

Gilbert, Sandra M. and Susan Gubar. *The Madwoman in the Attic: The Woman Writer and the Nineteenth-Century Literary Imagination.* 1979. New Haven: Yale UP, 2000.

Hook, Andrew. Introduction. *Waverley; or, 'Tis Sixty Years Since 1814.* By Sir Walter Scott. Ed. Andrew Hook. London: Penguin, 1972. 9-27.

Houston, William, ed. "Treaty of Paris, 1763." *Documents Illustrative of the Canadian Constitution,* Toronto: Carswell, 1891. 61-65. *The Internet Archive.* 23 December 2013.

Huyghue, Douglas. *Argimou: A Legend of the Micmac.* 1847. Ed. Gwendolyn Davies. Maritimes Literature Reprint Series. Sackville, NB: Ralph Pickard Bell Library, 1977.

Johnson, Samuel. *A Dictionary of the English Language: in which the Words are Deduced from their Originals, and Illustrated in their Different Significations by Examples from the Best Writers. To which are Prefixed, a History of the Language, and English Grammar. In Two Vols.* 1755. Vol. I. 6th ed. London: Printed for G. and J. Offor, 1822. *The Internet Archive.* 31 May 2014.

Kirby, William. *Le Chien d'or/The Golden Dog: A Legend of Quebec.* 1877. Ed. Mary Jane Edwards. Montreal: McGill-Queen's UP, 2012.

Klinck, Carl F. and Sandra Djwa. *Giving Canada a Literary History: A Memoir.* By Carl F. Klinck. Edited with an introduction by Sandra Djwa. Ottawa: Carleton UP for the U of Western Ontario, 1991.

Lareau, Edmond. *Histoire de la littérature canadienne.* Montreal: Lovell, 1874. *The Internet Archive.* 31 May 2014.

Leclerc-Larochelle, Monique. "Jean-Lukin Leprohon." *Dictionary of Canadian Biography*. 23 December 2013.

Le Moine, James MacPherson. *Maple Leaves: A Budget of Legendary, Historical, Critical, and Sporting Intelligence*. 7 ser. Quebec: Hunter, Rose. 1863-1906.

Lesperance, John Talon. "The Literary Standing of the Dominion." *The Canadian Illustrated News* 15.8 (24 February 1877): 118-19. *Bibliothèque et Archives nationales du Québec*. 24 May 2014.

Logan, J.D. and Donald G. French. *Highways of Canadian Literature: A Synoptic Introduction to the Literary History of Canada (English) from 1760 to 1924*. Toronto: McClelland & Stewart, 1924.

Marquis, T.G. *English Canadian Literature*. Toronto, Glasgow: Brook and Co., 1913. 543.

McGee, Thomas D'Arcy. "The Mental Outfit of the New Dominion." *Gazette* (Montreal), 5 November 1867. Montreal: s.n., 1867. 1-7. *The Internet Archive*. 31 May 2014.

McMullen, John Mercier. *History of Canada from its First Discovery to the Present Time*. Brockville, ON: J. M'Mullen, 1855. *Google Books*. 31 May 2014.

McMullen, Lorraine and Sandra Campbell, eds. *Pioneering Women: Short Stories by Canadian Women: Beginnings to 1880*. Ottawa: U of Ottawa P, 1993.

Morgan, Henry J. "Leprohon, Mrs." In *Sketches of Celebrated Canadians, and persons connected with Canada, from the earliest period in the history of the province down to the present time*. Quebec: Hunter, Rose; London: Trubner, 1862. 746-47. *The Internet Archive*. 31 May 2014.

Naves, Elaine Kalman. *The Writers of Montreal*. Montreal: Véhicule, 1993.

Parker, George L. "English-Canadian Publishers and the Struggle for Copyright." *History of the Book in Canada: Volume 2: 1840-1918*. Ed. Fiona Black, Patricia Lockhart Fleming, and Yvan Lamonde. Toronto: U of Toronto P, 2005. 148-59.

Parkman, Francis. *France and England in North America*. 7 vols. Boston: Little, Brown. 1865-92.

Parliamentary Debates on the Subject of the Confederation of the British North American Provinces, 3rd Session, 8th Provincial Parliament of Canada. Printed by Order of the Legislature. Quebec: Hunter, Rose, 1865. *Google Books*. 31 May 2014.

Rhodenizer, V.B. *A Handbook of Canadian Literature*. Ottawa: Graphic, 1930.

Richardson, John. "Introductory." Chapter 1 of *Wacousta; or, The Prophecy: A Tale of the Canadas*. Vol. 1. London: T. Cadell; and Edinburgh: W. Blackwood, 1832. 1-24. *The Internet Archive*. 27 May 2014.

Richardson, Samuel. "Preface by the Editor." *Pamela; or, Virtue Rewarded. In a SERIES of FAMILIAR LETTERS FROM A Beautiful Young Damsel, To her PARENTS. Now first Published In order to cultivate the Principles of VIRTUE and RELIGION in the Minds of the YOUTH of BOTH SEXES. A Narrative which has its Foundation in TRUTH and NATURE; and at the same time that it agreeably entertains, by a Variety of curious and affecting INCIDENTS, is intirely* [sic] *divested of all those Images, which, in too many Pieces calculated for Amusement only, tend to* inflame *the Minds they should* instruct. 1740. Vol. 1. 3rd ed. London: C. Rivington and J. Osborn, 1741. iii-vi. *The Internet Archive.* 23 December 2013.

Scott, Sir Walter. "A Postscript, which should have been a Preface." Chapter XXIV of *Waverley; Or, 'Tis Sixty Years Since.* In Three Volumes. Vol. 3. Edinburgh: Constable; and London: Longman, Hurst, Rees, Orme, and Brown, 1814. 364-71. *The Internet Archive.* 23 December 2013.

Smith, William. Preface. *History of Canada; From Its Discovery to the Peace of 1763.* Quebec: John Neilson, [1815] 1826. i-iii. *Google Books.* 27 May 2014.

Ure, George P. "Prospectus of *The Family Herald.*" *The Family Herald,* 1.1, Wednesday, November 16, 1859, p. 4. Microform. MIC A988.

Ville de Montréal. *Les membres des conseils municipaux de 1833 à 1899. Texte préparé par la division des archives.* "Democracy in Montreal from 1830 to the present." *Ville de Montréal.* 3 December 2013.

Voltaire. *Candide, or Optimism.* 1759. Trans. Theo Cuffe. Introduction by Michael Wood. London: Penguin, 2005.

Walpole, Horace. *Memoirs of the Reign of King George the Second.* Ed. Lord Holland. 3 vols. London: H. Colburn, 1846-47. *The Internet Archive.* 27 May 2014.

Wolfe, General James. "Major-General Wolfe to the Earl of Holdernesse. On board the Sutherland, at anchor off Cape Rouge, September 9, 1759." *Correspondence of William Pitt, Earl of Chatham. Edited by the executors of his son, John, Earl of Chatham, and published from the original manuscripts in their possession.* Vol. 1. London: John Murray, 1838. 425-30. *The Internet Archive.* 31 May 2014.

Woodcock, George. "Introduction." *Canadian Writers and Their Works: Fiction Series.* Vol. 1. Ed. Robert Lecker, Jack David, and Ellen Quigley. Toronto: ECW, 1983. 7-22.

from the publisher

A name never says it all, but the word "broadview" expresses a good deal of the philosophy behind our company. We are open to a broad range of academic approaches and political viewpoints. We pay attention to the broad impact book publishing and book printing has in the wider world; we began using recycled stock more than a decade ago, and for some years now we have used 100% recycled paper for most titles. As a Canadian-based company we naturally publish a number of titles with a Canadian emphasis, but our publishing program overall is internationally oriented and broad-ranging. Our individual titles often appeal to a broad readership too; many are of interest as much to general readers as to academics and students.

Founded in 1985, Broadview remains a fully independent company owned by its shareholders—not an imprint or subsidiary of a larger multinational.

If you would like to find out more about Broadview and about the books we publish, please visit us at **www.broadviewpress.com**. And if you'd like to place an order through the site, we'd like to show our appreciation by extending a special discount to you: by entering the code below you will receive a 20% discount on purchases made through the Broadview website.

Discount code: **broadview20%**

Thank you for choosing Broadview.

Please note: this offer applies only to sales of bound books within the United States or Canada.

The interior of this book is printed on 100% recycled paper.